KingI

Part III – Bannockburn

Michael Alexander McCarthy

Rogue Maille Publishing

Also by Michael Alexander McCarthy

The First War of Scottish Independence Series

KingMaker – Army of God

KingMaker – Traitor

KingMaker – Bannockburn

KingMaker – Death of Kings

Dedication

Georgia and Katie – when my journey is done, know that I travelled through a better, lighter and more joyful world when you walked at my side.

Scots Wha Hae

Scots, wha hae wi' Wallace bled,
Scots, wham Bruce has aften led;
Welcome to your gory bed,
Or to victory!

Now's the day, and now's the hour;
See the front o' battle lour;
See approach proud Edward's power—
Chains and slavery!

Wha will be a traitor knave?
Wha can fill a coward's grave!
Wha sae base as be a slave?
Let him turn and flee!

Wha for Scotland's king and law
Freedom's sword will strongly draw,
Freeman stand, or freeman fa',
Let him on wi me!

By oppression's woes and pains!
By your sons in servile chains!
We will drain our dearest veins,
But they shall be free!

Lay the proud usurpers low!
Tyrants fall in every foe!
Liberty's in every blow!—
Let us do or dee!

Written by Robert Burns in 1793 in the form of a speech given by
King Robert the Bruce before the Battle of Bannockburn in 1314.

Deaf Forever

March or croak, flame and smoke,
Burn forever in eternal pain,
Charge and fall, bugle call,
Bone splinter in the driving rain
Horses scream, Viking dream,
Drowned heroes in a lake of blood
Armoured fist, severed wrist,
Broken spears in a sea of mud.

Sword and shield, bone and steel,
Rictus grin,
Deaf forever to the battle's din.

Kilmister, Campbell, Burston & Gill.

1

Walter Langton, Bishop of Coventry and
Lichfield, Lord High Treasurer and Minister to
the King, paused at the door of the chamber and
took a moment to observe the figure sleeping by
the roaring fire. With a woollen blanket wrapped
tightly around his knees and his halo of thinning
white hair, Edward Plantagenet was the very
picture of a benevolent, old grandfather enjoying
a well-deserved rest after a lifetime of trouble
and toil. In peaceful repose, his gaunt and lined
face showed no sign of the energy, ambition,
cruelty and rage which so often animated it
during his waking hours. No stranger who
happened upon this cosy, fire-side tableau would
guess that this gently snuffling, fire-reddened
sexagenarian was King Edward I of England,
Lord of Ireland, Conqueror of Wales, Hammer of
the Scots, Duke of Aquitaine and Duke of
Gascony. Langton smiled wryly at the realisation
that it gladdened his heart to see his King
enjoying such comfortable rest after so many
long years of hardship. The Scots' stubborn
resistance to English rule had necessitated a
decade of bitter campaigning and the rigours of
that struggle and the miserable climate of that

1

wretched country had taken a terrible toll on the King's health. Langton decided that he would leave the King to snooze while he could and that he would not trouble him with his present business. He had scarcely turned for the door when the King awakened with a loud snort and called to him.

'Walter? Is that you, Walter?' King Edward stretched his long arms above his head and yawned.

'It is I, my Lord.' Langton replied, as he strode towards the fire. 'I thought to let you rest.'

'I dreamed that I was back in Scotland. You remember that damp, sodden hill close to Edinburgh?'

'I do, my Lord. How could I forget it?' Langton met the King's gaze and shook his head at the memory.

'It seemed that all was lost to me and then you came. You brought me word which turned disaster into triumph on the bloody field at Falkirk.' Edward gazed into the flames for a moment and nodded with satisfaction. 'I take it that you come to me with similar glad tidings this day. How fares the kingdom?'

'All is well, my Lord.' Langton replied with a smile.

'The magnates?'

'Just the usual petty complaints, my Lord. All are happy in the King's peace and seek only to have you intervene in their little squabbles and disagreements. Now that they are free of demands for men and silver for campaigning in Scotland, they are content.'

'Wales?'

'All is calm in Wales.'

'Ireland?'

'The Irish nobles are similarly content.'

Edward narrowed his eyes as if preparing himself for unwelcome news. 'And what of my northern kingdom?'

Langton smiled broadly as he replied. 'All is well in Scotland, my Lord. The Scottish magnates are broken and now rule their land in your name. Comyn and Bruce distrust one another so much that all of their energies are devoted to ensuring that the other does not usurp them in your favour.'

'Good!' Edward replied with satisfaction. 'Now that we have peace, you must be awash with silver, my Lord Treasurer.'

Langton beamed with delight and good humour. 'The Treasury is indeed in rude health. Taxes and duties flow in steadily and we make good progress in reducing our not inconsiderable debts. The Pope has also kept to his word and silver from the crusading tax pours in from the English clergy.'

Edward laughed heartily and wagged his finger in mock admonishment. 'I know well that you disapprove of my taking the cross, but I vowed to go to Jerusalem long ago and have fixed my whole heart upon it now that I am no longer hindered by war. There is more to life than hoarding silver, Walter. I must think of my legacy. No other English king has achieved more than I. I have retained my French possessions against all of the odds, recovered Wales for the

3

English throne and added the crown of Scotland to that of England. What glory it would be to add the recovery of Jerusalem and the Holy Sepulchre for Christendom to that legacy.'

'Glory indeed, my Lord. I think not of the hoarding of silver, but of your health, my King. I, more than anyone, have seen how much you have suffered in pulling this united kingdom together through the sheer strength of your will. I want nothing more than to see you take rest and comfort enough to recover your strength.' Langton paused and looked directly into King Edward's eyes. 'I would say that you deserve the reward of taking some time to revel in a victory that was so hard won.'

'Be not mistaken, Walter. I revel in my victory over the Scots each and every day. I give thanks for it at every shrine I pass. I cannot describe the sense of power it gives me to know that I have brought a whole kingdom to its knees and forced an unconquered race to bow to my authority. It may have taken a decade longer than I had hoped, but the crushing of the Scots was all the sweeter for their stubborn and dogged resistance. It rejuvenates me to know that I have snuffed out the flame of rebellion and left no Scot alive who would dare defy me.'

John Edward pulled his cloak tightly around his shoulders in a vain effort to stop the bitingly frigid wind from freezing him to the bone. In the glen below, the English wagons were making slow progress along the snow-covered track. He shivered involuntarily and curled and uncurled his toes inside his boots in a bid to restore the circulation to his numbed extremities. His brother Scott stood at his side and watched impassively as the three heavily laden wagons and their escort of ten horse and thirty foot-soldiers inched their way up the long and gradual incline.

'These English bastards grind to a halt at the first wee flurry of snow.' Scott complained bitterly. 'We should have dropped the tree at the foot of the slope. By the time these arseholes reach the top, we'll all have frozen to death and they'll be free to clear the track and carry onto Perth blissfully unaware that we planned to ambush them.'

John grinned in spite of his discomfort. He was used to his younger brother's constant complaints, but found that he could not take him seriously when the snow and frost had turned his hair, eyebrows and beard white, giving him the appearance of a grumpy, little, old man.

'What the hell are you smirking at?' Scott snapped in irritation.

John avoided his brother's eyes and pointed down at the slow-moving wagons. 'Look! The horses are struggling on the hill. The soldiers are having to put their shoulders to the wheels.'

They watched as the foot soldiers placed their spears into the carts and heaved at the heavy, wooden wheels. When progress slowed once again, the horsemen dismounted and joined their fellows in pushing the supplies for the Perth garrison up the snow-covered incline. John nodded to himself in satisfaction. The

Englishmen would be exhausted by the time they crested the summit of the hill and found that their way was blocked. Drained by their exertions and parted from their spears, the soldiers would not be able to enjoy their numerical advantage over the Scotstoun men.

No signal was required, as it had been agreed that the attack would be made the moment the first wagon came to a halt. Nearly half the escort fell to Scots arrows and spears, with some men perishing before their eyes had even registered the silent attackers rising from their hiding places on both sides of the track. More were hacked down from behind as they reached into the wagons to retrieve their spears. Those who tried to escape by running back along the track were met by John, Scott, their cousin Eck wielding a sword in each of his hands and Strathbogie with his great axe already drawn back in preparation for the first blow. Driven by desperation, these men fought bravely, but, in their exhausted state, were soon overwhelmed and cut down without mercy.

John Edward leaned on his bloody sword and tried to catch his breath. 'You'll be a wee bit warmer now.'

His brother grinned back at him from the bed of the last of the wagons. 'We'll all be a wee bit warmer the night.' He responded happily, before hefting a barrel onto his shoulder. 'There's enough English ale to keep us all warm for a week!'

The patriot men set about stripping the wagons and the English dead of anything of use or value. In addition to the ale, the English wagons contained barley, corn, dried meat, chickens crammed into simple wooden cages, bundles of arrows and, best of all, new boots for the men of the Perth garrison. Nothing was left behind. Anything that could not be carried immediately to the camp in the depths of the forest was buried to be retrieved at a later date. Even the wooden panelling was kicked from the sides of the wagons, initially to be used to build litters on which to drag their loot away and then later to be utilised to improve the primitive shelters back in camp. The remains of the wagons were broken, piled together and then put to the flame. A number of the stripped and gory English corpses were dragged onto the pyre and the rest were mutilated where they lay to act as a warning to their comrades when they came to collect their dead.

As John pulled himself into his saddle and prepared to lead the fighters away, his head scout, Al, came to his side and handed him a sealed parchment. 'They found that on the English officer.'

John broke the brittle wax, unfolded the parchment and read the message written upon it. His brow furrowed tightly as he read and he shook his head in disbelief as its meaning became clear to him.

'It seems that our lords and masters are not content now that they have kneeled before the English King, but continue to plot and scheme against each other in the hope that they can win the crown of Scotland for themselves. This message is from John Comyn, Lord of Badenoch, to the English Treasurer, informing him that Robert Bruce has offered him all of his lands in return for supporting his claim to the Scottish crown. He urges King Edward to punish Bruce for his treason.'

Al nodded gravely. 'That is unlikely to be good for us.'

'Right enough!' John agreed. 'Civil war at best, wi' us stuck in the middle. At worst, another English invasion.'

'What should we do?'

'Take this to Bishop Lamberton. He'll know better than us the best course to take.' John handed the folded parchment back to Al as he spoke. 'Be quick! I doubt that our man was the only messenger carrying this news south.'

'Lamberton?' Al asked sourly. 'He swore fealty to the English King just as Bruce and Comyn did. He is no friend of ours.'

'I cannot deny it, Al. There are few of us left who have refused to submit and so friends are thin on the ground for us. It might be no bad thing to keep him as an ally. We may have need of friends before too much longer.'

Al nodded in response, tucked the parchment into his cloak and turned his horse for St Andrews.

Robert Bruce, Earl of Carrick and Lord of Annandale, pushed the parchments aside and gazed deeply into the roaring fire whilst savouring a mouthful of wine from his goblet.

'Do you know why I hate coming to London, Thomas?'

Bruce's young squire looked up, but did not stop rubbing dubbin into his master's boots with a dirty, ragged cloth. 'Is it the stink, m'Lord? The streets here are thick with shit. It has taken me hours to clean your boots.'

Bruce laughed wryly, his eyes sparkling with dark amusement. 'No, Thomas, it's not the foul odour, although I am always happy to leave that behind me. I hate London because every time I am summoned here to court, I find that I am forced to kiss the King's arse while all of his nobles stand by and delight in my humiliation. It is no easy thing to kiss the cheeks of the man who has cheated my family out of the crown that is ours by right. Each time I bow my head, I pray that the old bastard will die. Each time he sickens, I pray that the good Lord will at last carry him off and every time he recovers his strength and calls upon me to travel here and abase myself once again.'

Thomas kept his eyes fixed upon his master's boots and concentrated on rubbing the wax into the leather. He was used to the Bruce's rants and knew that he was expected to listen quietly and provide affirmation only when it was demanded.

'Does he imagine that I will suffer these insults without complaint? That I will suffer his unjust treatment in silence?' He stroked his well-trimmed beard and slowly shook his head in anger. 'It is no way to treat a man when royal blood runs in his veins. He will find that I will not suffer it for long. Not for long at all!'

Thomas jumped up from his stool with a start when a loud knocking from the outer door interrupted his master's train of thought.

'I am not to be disturbed tonight, Thomas!' Bruce ordered tersely. 'I must examine all of these documents most thoroughly before I take to my bed. It seems that King Edward means to reduce Scotland to the status of a province, for I cannot find a single place where it is referred to as a kingdom or a realm. He and his minister seek to render their theft legitimate by shrouding their sin in false legality.'

Thomas left the chamber and returned a moment later. 'It is a messenger, m'Lord. He comes from the Earl of Gloucester.'

Bruce had snatched up a parchment and was examining the tight script in the firelight. 'Take the message from him Thomas. I will read it later.'

'He has no parchment, m'Lord. He insists on seeing you.'

'Very well!' Bruce snapped in resignation. 'Send him in.'

Bruce recognised the slim, round-shouldered man as Gloucester's most trusted retainer. He approached with his head bowed and carefully placed a pair of spurs and twelve silver pennies upon the table.

'My Lord Gloucester sends these with his compliments, m'Lord. He said to tell you that he dined with King Edward this evening in a most convivial manner. He was interested to learn that the King has heard from your good friend in the north and that he means to act on this intelligence at first light tomorrow.'

De Bruce gazed at the spurs before slowly nodding his head and gathering up the pennies in his fist. 'Please be sure to give Gloucester my compliments and tell him that his friendship is valued most highly. These pennies are for you, for your trouble.'

The messenger took the proffered coins, bowed and retreated from the chamber. Bruce waited until the outer door banged shut on Gloucester's retainer and then leapt to his feet. 'Thomas! Go and saddle our horses. I am betrayed and must be away from here without delay. Go quietly and tell no-one of our plans.'

'Shall I gather your things, m'Lord?'

'No! Leave it all. If I am caught here, then I am undone.'

2

Walter Langton loved few things more than his whores and his wine. His ability to exert influence over King Edward and so wield great power in the kingdom came close. So too did the accumulation of vast wealth and property. However, he loved nothing more than to build and was at his happiest when discussing plans with his master builder or instructing masons on just how an archway should be constructed or how high a curtain wall should be built. His duties as Lord High Treasurer and Minister had long kept him away from the construction of the castle on his manor at Eccleshall and he had been forced to make do with fleeting and infrequent visits to gauge progress and issue instructions. To his great delight, the ultimate victory over the Scots had freed him sufficiently from the demands of office to fully immerse himself in the final stages of the project. He was so engrossed in observing the testing of the drawbridge mechanism that he did not register the approach of the captain of his guard until he was at his side.

'Morning Browby.' He greeted the man with an icy chill that matched that in the winter morning's air. He had made it abundantly clear that he was not to be disturbed when involved in the building work and he greatly resented the intrusion.

'Good morning, m'Lord.' Browby replied, his head bowed and his eyes avoiding the Bishop's glacial glare. 'I did not want to disturb you.'

'And yet you have!' Langton spat, his lip curled in annoyance.

'I am sorry, m'Lord. But I thought you would want to know that a group of young gentlemen are charging across the estate on their horses, scattering our sheep and cattle far and wide.'

'Christ, Browby! Then take the men and go and crack their heads! You do not need to seek permission from me. Go now and do what I pay you for!'

'I took the men to chase them off, m'Lord. It is the Prince of Wales and his young knights. They are very drunk and in the highest of spirits. He commanded me to go and I thought it best to consult with you before cracking any royal heads.'

'The little shit! Did you tell him that he trespasses on my lands?'

'I did, m'Lord.' Browby replied, his eyes still fixed upon the frozen ground. 'He said that he is a prince and will take no orders from a bastard bishop.'

Langton's eyes widened in indignation and his cheeks reddened. 'By the blood of Christ! I will not have that vile cockscomb and his drunken fops insult me on my own manor. Bring my horse'

Langton, with Browby following on behind, found the Prince and his fellows dismounted on the riverbank refreshing themselves from skins of wine.

'My Lord!' Langton called out, as he approached the youths. 'You must take care. You have run my cattle off.'

'I must take care?' Prince Edward replied, his tone one of incredulity, his words slurred with wine and edged with contempt. 'It is you who should take care, Lord Bishop. Do not presume to command me!'

'I do not command, my Lord, I seek only to beseech you to respect my office and my property. Your father would be displeased to hear that you have so ill-used me.' Langton delivered his words through gritted teeth and barely managed to keep his temper in check.

Edward snorted in derision and turned to his companions. 'Did I not say that he would go running to the King with his tales?'

'You did indeed, Edward.' Piers Gaveston replied, taking an unsteady pace towards the Bishop and placing his hand upon the hilt of his sword. 'You said that the fat pig would go running to the King like a girl running to her mother's apron.'

Langton's fists were squeezed so tight he could feel his finger nails cutting into the palms of his hands. His rage boiled inside him and would have erupted furiously but for Gaveston's belligerent posture. The handsome youth might well be empty-headed and overly familiar with the heir to the throne, but he was also a skilled knight of great renown who routinely took great relish in humiliating any noble foolish enough to stand against him in the tournaments. This perilous combination of skill and drunkenness was sufficient to persuade the Treasurer to withdraw.

'Your father will hear of this!' He delivered this parting shot as he turned his horse away.

'My father will not always be King, Langton. You should remember that. When I sit upon the throne, it will be you who must take care, Lord Bishop.'

Langton did not turn back to acknowledge the Prince's taunt, but that did not diminish the truth of it.

'Long live the King!' Browby declared solemnly from his side.

'Quite.' Langton replied, his face grim and his morning quite spoiled.

Robert Bruce paced the flagstones beneath the steps to the monastery's high altar. His footsteps echoed back to him from the shadows of the poorly lit chapel. He had ridden night and day to reach his castle at Lochmaben on his hurried flight from the English court, but his arrival there had brought no clarity to his situation. For every rumour confirming John Comyn's betrayal, there was another equally convincing rumour suggesting the exact opposite. He had to meet the Red Comyn face to face to determine if their agreement stood or if his competitor had resorted to treachery. The fact that the Comyn had agreed to meet him in Greyfriars Monastery made him hopeful that their scheme was not undone. Nevertheless, his guts still twisted with anxiety as it seemed just as likely that his plot would crumble and he would be outlawed.

The loud creaking of the monastery door being pushed open startled him and he turned and peered into the darkness. The voices at the door were faint, but he knew that his men would be relieving Comyn of his sword just as he had been required to surrender his own weapon before entering. He pulled himself to his full height as his fellow magnate approached through the shadowed interior of the chapel.

'Lord John!' He said in greeting. 'I did not know if you would come.'

'And why would I not, Lord Robert? Did you think that I would be afeart?'

'I did not know what to think. I was told that you had sent word of our agreement to King Edward. I had to take to my heels to avoid being taken prisoner.'

John Comyn laughed, but the sound was dry and devoid of humour. 'Does the Lord of Annandale jump at shadows? You have the ambition to be king, but it does not appear that you have the nerve for it.'

Bruce bristled, but bit his tongue. 'So, you did not betray our sworn agreement?'

'I did not.'

Bruce did not miss that Comyn laid heavy emphasis on the word 'I' and was suggesting that some other party to the agreement had broken faith. He concluded that Comyn was lying as he would trust the only other two parties to their accord, the Bishops of Glasgow and St Andrews, with his life.

'So, our agreement stands, my Lord? In return for all my lands, you will support me in taking up arms against the English King and claiming the Scottish crown?'

Comyn narrowed his eyes and rubbed at his beard. 'Edward would crush a weak Scottish king and we would both lose everything that we now hold. It might be best for everyone if you were to take the land and I was to take the crown.'

'You think me weak?' Bruce snapped, his eyes blazing with anger.

'I know that you are weak! Ten years of war with England and you did not fight in a single major battle, but instead vacillated between the two sides until no man could tell whether you fought for or against the English. A king must know how to fight. A king would not be satisfied with cowering around the edges and picking over what was left. Cunning you have in abundance, but strength is what is needed.'

'Your family is not fit to wear the crown, Comyn! Look at your uncle! He was given the throne of Scotland on a platter, but his blood was weak and King Edward boxed his ears and sent him off like an ill-behaved serving boy. You would do no better!'

Though thickset and heavy, John Comyn was experienced in combat and moved so quickly that the Bruce was taken by surprise. In one fluid and practised movement, he drew the dagger from his sleeve and drove it hard towards the younger man's guts. Only his reflexes saved him from a fatal blow. He turned instinctively sideways and took the blow on his forearm, the blade piercing flesh and muscle before boring into the bone. He roared in pain and drove his fist hard into Comyn's face before drawing his own dagger from inside his cloak and stabbing it hard into Comyn's chest.

The Lord of Badenoch groaned horribly and his legs collapsed beneath him, sending him crashing down onto the steps of the high altar. He stared open mouthed and bewildered as the blood bubbled from his chest and soaked his tunic.

'You have murdered me!' He gasped, still struggling to take in the seriousness of his injury.

The Bruce stared back at him, his face white with shock from the sudden violence. 'I did no more than you would have done to me if your blade had been quicker.' He looked at the bloody dagger in his hand in disbelief and threw it to the floor. 'But why?' He demanded.

Comyn laughed grimly, the hand pressed to his chest failing to stem the flow of blood which now pooled around him on the stone floor. 'Did you think that I would see you upon the throne? Did you think I would bow to you in return for land? I would rather have the Plantagenets rule here for all eternity than see the crown sit upon a Bruce's head.' He drew in a sharp breath and grimaced in pain. 'At least I can die happy knowing that your ambitions have come to naught. No one will forgive you for committing foul murder in a holy place. You will be cast out from the church and no one will support you out of fear for their immortal souls. You will be outlawed and my kin will hunt you down like the miserable dog that you are.'

'Curse you for your bitterness! You have undone me with your foul treachery.' Bruce's face was twisted with hatred and he stepped towards his prone rival with menace. 'We could have had it all. Between us we would have ruled this land.'

Comyn was fading now, his face pale and ghastly white from the loss of blood, but he still managed a sour smile. 'But for how long, Robert? How long before you regretted the loss of your lands? How long before you changed your mind and decided that you wanted it all? I would trust the devil himself more than I would trust you, for the devil has not changed sides as many times as you. If you would know how it has come to this, you must look to yourself.' The Red Comyn then closed his eyes and fell into unconsciousness.

Robert Bruce now overcame his astonishment and felt panic rising in his breast. He breathed deeply and tried to still his racing heart. He knew that the Comyn was right and that all was lost if he could not take control of events. With one last glance at Comyn's bloody body, he turned and strode unsteadily towards the door. When half the way there, he called out the alarm and heard the clash of arms as his men attacked those of the Red Comyn. By the time he pulled the heavy, wooden door open, three Comyn men lay dead upon the ground and two were being pursued on foot as they attempted to escape the onslaught. Two of the Bruce's men approached him, demanding to know what had occurred within the monastery chapel.

'We must be away, for I doubt that I have slain the Red Comyn.' The Bruce stuttered, still shocked and scarcely able to comprehend what had just occurred.

'You doubt?' Sir Roger Kirkpatrick responded as he drew his sword. 'Then I'll make sure.' He turned and rushed into the monastery with James Lindsay following on behind him.

Peter Davidson arrived in Scotstoun in a dirty and dishevelled state. His clothes were ripped and tattered and his horse had been ridden so hard that bloody, pink foam bubbled from its mouth and nostrils. Some of those who had fought at Falkirk with John Comyn's men recognised him and took him immediately to John Edward's house. John saw that the man was teetering on the edge of exhaustion and waved him inside to sit at his table and asked his wife to bring meat, bread and ale for him to refresh himself. After he had eaten, the Scotstoun men gathered around to hear what had brought him to them in such a deplorable condition.

'Robert Bruce murdered John Comyn under the altar in the Chapel of Greyfriars Monastery!' Peter declared, before nodding in response to the shocked faces around the table.

The Robertson shook his head. 'I cannot believe it! No nobleman would commit such a heinous crime knowing that it would damn him in this life and the next. It makes no sense.'

'Did you see it?' Strathbogie demanded. 'Did you see the Bruce slay the Lord of Badenoch with your own eyes?'

Davidson shook his head. 'I did not see him land the blow, but I did see him stagger out of the chapel door with his hands red with blood and the Comyn's own dagger buried in his arm. He set his men upon us and cut down all but I and one other. I had no choice but flee for my life with the Bruce's men hard at my heels. I took to the forest to shake them off, but their pursuit was a determined one and it was more than a day before I finally lost them.'

John nodded gravely. Davidson's tattered and torn clothing and the livid scratches that covered his face and arms were testament to how hard his flight through the forest had been. 'You must rest a while. You have my word that no man will harm you here. Should the Bruce's men track you to our village, be certain that we will drive them off.'

Davidson broke into a smile for the first time since his arrival. 'I do not doubt it, John. I had heard that you were still resisting the English, but had no idea that you had so many men about you.'

John returned his smile. 'Aye. The village has grown these last months. Since your master and Robert Bruce kneeled before the English King, every desperate and dispossessed soul with a sword at his waist seems to have found his way here to us. There are other pockets of resistance

21

around the country, but they are sadly few and far between.'

'It's just as well, for they will be needed soon.' Davidson replied. 'There will be civil war now and the Comyns will need every man they can get if we are to defeat the Bruce and his allies once and for all. You must join with me and march north.'

John met Peter Davidson's gaze unflinchingly and slowly shook his head. 'I have no interest in the magnates' squabbles and will not risk my men's lives to help any noble win the crown. I will fight the English, but I will not take up arms against my own countrymen.'

Davidson sat back in surprise. 'Have you forgotten that we fought side by side at Falkirk under the Red Comyn's banners? Does our great victory at Roslin mean nothing to you? I cannot believe that you would abandon the Comyns now!'

Eck Edward leaned across the table, his hands held out before him with open palms. 'We fought at Falkirk under the Wallace's banners and were glad to have the Red Comyn at our side. The victory at Roslin was indeed great and we are proud to have played our part in what Comyn and Wallace achieved together. But it was the Lord of Badenoch who abandoned us when he gave up the fight and submitted to King Edward's superiority in return for keeping his lands and titles. Now we fight the English alone and that is what we will continue to do. Let the nobles fight amongst themselves. We will have no part of it.'

Davidson scowled heavily, but found that he could not deny a word that had been spoken. 'You may have no choice but pick a side. A civil war seldom leaves much room for neutrality.'

John Edward reluctantly nodded his head in agreement. 'Then we will do what we have to in order to survive, but until the choice is forced upon us, the English are our only enemies.'

Peter refused all invitations to stay and rest, as he was keen to get away north and join up with his kinsmen. The Scotstoun men stood and watched as he rode away.

'This is bad.' Scott Edward opined, his face screwed up in contemplation. 'Both sides will expect us to join with them and will declare us their enemy if we refuse.'

'And while the Bruces and Comyns hack one another to pieces, the English King will ride in unopposed and take the kingdom for himself.' The Robertson's wrinkled brow was deeply furrowed as he spoke and his voice betrayed his weariness.

'I don't doubt that Langshanks will seize his opportunity and send a massive force across the border, but, as long as we stand, he will never do so unopposed.' John Edward's face was set in determination and he met the gaze of each of his companions.

Strathbogie snorted loudly and shrugged his shoulders. 'Alone we can harass the castle garrisons and attack their supply lines, but a full invasion will sweep us all away.'

'That is true.' John replied. 'But if we are not prepared to falls to our knees, then we have no choice but to die on our feet.'

3

William Lamberton, Bishop of St Andrews, declined all offers of refreshment and demanded to be taken straight to the chamber of the Bishop of Glasgow. His cloak was sodden and heavy from the rain and his boots were still muddy from the hard day's ride. One look at Robert Wishart's anxious and fearful expression caused his stomach to knot tightly.

'It's true then?' He demanded, too overwrought to attend to normal ecclesiastical etiquette.

'I'm afraid so.' The Bishop of Glasgow responded with a loud sigh. 'It could hardly be worse.'

'What in Christ's name possessed him? If he had murdered John Comyn in the street I could understand it. Has he lost his mind? He has desecrated a chapel. This sacrilege will damn him in the eyes of all those who might have supported him. His enemies will use it against him. Any chance of uniting the kingdom against the English has gone.' Lamberton took off his gauntlets as he spoke and threw them to the floor with all of the force that he could muster.

'You must calm yourself, Lord Bishop.' Wishart entreated the younger man. 'We must have cool heads if we are to prevail.'

'I should have listened to you when you counselled me against encouraging Robert to make a pact with Comyn. You told me that it was too early and that I should have patience. If I had listened, we would not now be faced with this disaster.'

'If you listen to me now, then we may be able to salvage something from the ruins of our hopes. If you cannot pull yourself together, then we must throw Robert Bruce to the wolves.'

The older man's words caused Lamberton's face to crease in confusion. 'I did not think that we had a choice. The Pope will excommunicate him. He will be outside the church.'

'But what church, William? Are we not the church in Scotland?'

Lamberton's eyes widened in astonishment and he gazed at Wishart. 'You have already done it, haven't you?'

Though Wishart's eyes had grown dull and milky with age, they sparkled with determination. 'He came to me last night. He kneeled before me and freely confessed his sins. I shrived him of his sins and gave him absolution for his sacrilege. The Pope may well declare him excommunicate, but in Scotland he will not be outside the church. I will write to all the clergy to inform them of this and require them to support Robert Bruce.'

'Then we too will be excommunicated.' Lamberton replied.

Wishart nodded. 'I have fought for the independence of the Scottish church for too long to give it up now. With Comyn dead, Robert Bruce is the only option left to us. We tie our fate up with his and take our chances, or we cut him loose and wait passively for Edward Plantagenet to rape our kingdom and place us under the rule of English bishops. I have made my choice.'

Lamberton shook his head in disbelief. 'But he cannot possibly prevail. Even if the pact with Comyn had held firm, it was not certain that their combined forces could have stood against King Edward. Now that the Bruce will have to fight both the Comyns and the English, the odds against him are enormous.'

'I like the odds no more than you, but have even less liking for the alternative. Needs must when the devil drives and we will just have to see where this path takes us.'

Lamberton's head spun but he nodded his agreement. 'Where is Robert now?'

'He goes to capture the castles which command the Firth of Clyde to ensure that supplies and reinforcements from Ireland and the Outer Isles can reach him. Once these are secure, we will meet with him at Scone to crown him King of Scots.'

'Then our fates will truly be entwined with his.' Now that the decision was made, Lamberton found that his anxiety was replaced with a grim determination.

Wishart returned his smile and laid a reassuring hand on his shoulder. 'I am an old man now, so I will pray for our success. You are a young man and must pick up your sword to fight for it.'

The arrival of the first messenger had not troubled Walter Langton too much. He had learned a long time ago that it was foolhardy to take action on the basis of an unsubstantiated rumour, given that rumours were often wrong and were sometimes even manufactured by one's enemies or by the fevered minds of gossips and fantasists with too little to occupy themselves. The second messenger came from a much more reliable source and had worried him enough to sour the joy he felt at seeing the fourth tower of his castle completed. Within moments of receiving the same report from the third messenger, he was ahorse and on his way to the King's side with all speed. Long experience had taught him that bad news travelled fast and that the only thing worse than delivering bad news to King Edward, was being found to be unaware of momentous events despite spending huge amounts of the King's gold on a network of spies and informants.

He paused briefly to wash the dirt and sweat of the road from his face before being escorted into the King's apartments. Edward seemed to have benefitted from the months of rest since the subjugation of Scotland, as his stoop was less pronounced and his eyes were brighter and less blood-shot than before. He beamed with delight when he noticed Langton's approach.

'Walter! How good to see you. I was told that you were busy with your castle.'

'I was, my Lord.'

'It progresses well, I hope.'

'It does, my Lord, but I have come to you with news.'

'I also have news, Walter. Look here!' The King held out his arm to indicate a table upon which a huge and detailed map of the Holy Land had been unfurled. 'The Pope has promised more funds for the crusade and has asked that I make my plans even more ambitious.'

Langton noticed that the map was covered in little silver ships and knights on their horses and assumed that Edward was using these to make a plan of campaign. He groaned inwardly on realising that he was about to tear the King's most cherished daydreams into tatters.

'I have news from Scotland.' He stated flatly.

The King's face fell and he shook his head back and forth.

'I have it on good authority and from several sources that Robert Bruce murdered John Comyn in the Chapel of Greyfriars Monastery one week ago.'

Edward continued to shake his head. 'No.'

'He then moved to capture the castles at Dunaverty, Rothesay, Tibbers, Dalswinton and Dumfries, capturing Sir Richard Siward in the process.'

The King had turned deathly pale and still continued to shake his head slowly and deliberately from side to side. 'No! Not now!'

Langton felt hot bile burning at the back of his throat, but pushed on to deliver the whole accursed message. 'Even as we speak, he makes for the Abbey of Scone where he is to be crowned King of Scots.'

King Edward's shoulders sagged and he cast his gaze down upon the floor, a little silver ship still clasped daintily in his fingertips. As the heavy silence dragged on, Langton almost wished for one of the King's violent rages. The silence, the defeated posture and the deathly pallor of his skin were unbearable and Langton felt almost as if he suffocated. The first sign of the breaking storm was the horrible bulging and pulsing of the veins at the King's temples. Just as Langton became aware of these, he also noticed that blood was dripping from his sovereign's right hand. It seemed that the little silver ship was now clenched so tightly in his fist that its little silver mast had punctured his royal flesh.

When the King raised his head, his eyes burned with a fury which bordered on madness. Langton found that he could not meet that ghastly glare and dropped his eyes to the floor.

'Not one full year ago, Robert Bruce stood in Westminster and watched me celebrate the final victory over the Scots before the shrine of the Confessor.' Each word was delivered with horribly repressed venom and was spat out through clenched and grinding teeth. 'Not one full year ago, Robert Bruce kneeled before me and begged for reconciliation. He gave his oath! He swore fealty to me! To me! To me! His rightful King and Lord Superior!' King Edward's face was twisted with hatred, fury and frustration as he raged against the dishonourable earl. 'I should have exterminated that whole turncoat clan in his grandfather's day. I always knew that their seed was bad, tainted with corruption and overreaching ambition. I should have had his throat cut when he came crawling to me at Falkirk and begged for my forgiveness. I should have ignored his false tears and rammed his severed head onto a spike as a warning to the others. I will have his head, Langton! I swear it!' The King punched his bloodied fist against his chest to affirm his vow. 'I will have it torn from his body and paraded from one end of Scotland to the other! I will have the heads of his wife, his children, his brothers, his cousins, his kinsmen, his servants and his followers! I will have his strongholds razed and his lands burnt black! When I am finished with the Bruces, no Scot will ever dare to defy me again! No miserable Scot will dare to imperil my legacy!'

Langton then watched in horror as the colour drained from the King's fury-reddened face and he stumbled unsteadily towards a chair. The Treasurer caught him just before he fell and man-handled him onto the seat with some difficulty.

'My Lord, shall I call for the apothecary?' Langton asked, his voice filled with concern.

Edward waved the question away and leaned forward to rest his head in his hands. 'It's just my age, Langton. The weakness overcomes me more often now. I had hoped that rest would cure it, but this business has left me drained.' He glanced across at the table and his eyes filled with a weary sadness that brought a lump to Langton's throat. 'Tell them to clear that shit away. I now doubt that I will ever again set my eyes upon the

Holy Land. That bastard knave has made a liar of me and instead of keeping my vow to Christendom, my last days will be spent turning Scotland to ashes.'

'Do not so easily abandon your vow, my Lord. Robert Bruce is but one man.'

A smile of sad and bitter resignation slid onto Edward's face and he patted the Bishop's arm. 'You know the Scots almost as well as I, Walter. It is never just one man. The rot spreads quickly and we must cut it out and then sear the healthy flesh, or rebellion will fester afresh. We have been too kind-hearted in the past, but we have learned our lesson and will now do what should have been done ten years ago.'

Langton grasped Edward's forearms with both his hands and looked earnestly into his eyes. 'Then command me, my Lord, and I will make it so.'

'There is much to be done, Walter. Summon the Earl of Pembroke. He will carry my Dragon Banner immediately into Scotland in pursuit of the disloyal Bruce. Command him to harden his heart and to advance with all cruelty. His path must be marked by slaughter and devastation so that all will know the price of treason. No quarter is to be given. None are to be spared. Not noble, peasant, cleric, woman, child or beast. He must leave the land soaked red with blood. You must then empty the Treasury so that we may muster and supply the greatest army that England has ever seen. We will lay waste to all of Scotland and let starvation take off peasant and noble alike. I will not allow my merciful nature to be my undoing again. The whole world will hear of our terrible savagery and tremble in fear.'

The loch's surface was as smooth as glass in the still, crisp morning air and reflected the clear blue of the cloudless sky like a mirror. The last of the winter's chill was not enough to stop the sun from gently warming their skin. John Edward pushed himself harder against his Lorna's back and pulled her further into his embrace.

'I could stay here forever.' She sighed happily. 'I just wish that you did not have to go.'

John leaned his head forward and kissed the soft, warm skin at the base of her neck. 'The English will no' kill themselves.'

She reached around and slapped his thigh in admonishment. 'None of your nibbling, John Edward. We'll no' be doing any of that here! It's too cold!'

'You never used to care about the cold. I mind coming down here in winter, away from my parents.'

'I'm a respectable mother with three children now. I cannae be lifting my skirts at the Lochside these days.'

'More's the pity.' John murmured, burying his face in her hair and drinking in her sweet scent. John sighed contentedly and gazed off into the distance. Despite life's hardships, he could not deny that he was a fortunate man. He had a beautiful wife, two healthy infant sons and an eight-year-old daughter with the mind and cheek of a twenty-year-old. The gold and silver pillaged from England's northern territories and from its defeated armies was buried beneath the floors of Scotstoun's houses and would be enough to keep the villagers for many years to come. His exploits against the English had won him some renown and near two hundred men who would fight at his command. There had been sore losses too, but he put these to the back of his mind. There was time enough to brood on them during the long hours spent waiting in ambush for unwary Englishmen.

Lorna turned her head and looked up to meet his gaze. 'I'm thinking that we might have nephews and nieces for our children to play with before too long.'

John nodded and smirked knowingly. 'Aye. My brother cannae keep himself away from that McNaughton girl. He blushes like a bride on her wedding night at the mere mention of her name.'

Lorna returned his smile. 'Aye, but I'm no' just talking about Scott.' She then turned her gaze back to the loch and said no more.

John tried to ignore the bait but curiosity won out. 'Alright. None of your teasing. Out wi' it!'

Lorna was tempted to taunt him further, but could not restrain herself from sharing her gossip. 'I've seen Eck talking wi' the Andrews girl and he cannae keep his eyes off of her in the kirk.'

John narrowed his eyes. 'I heard that she was raped when the English soldiers came here and murdered the steward in the square. That's how she's in early twenties and still no' married.'

Lorna's eyes flashed with challenge. 'And what of it?'

'Eck cannae marry a girl who has been damaged like that.'

'And Eck's no damaged himself?' She retorted.

John looked away from her as he considered his reply. He had to admit that Eck was still much changed from his brush with death after the battle at Stirling Bridge. He had been hauled back from the very brink of death and had brought some of its darkness back with him. Plagued with nightmares when he slept and black moods when awake, he was only at peace when battle raged around him and only his skill with the sword stood between him and death. If there was any chance of happiness for him, then maybe he should take it wherever he could find it.

'I'm no' my cousin's keeper.' He finally responded, carefully avoiding the need to admit, yet again, that he might not be the sole repository of wisdom in their marriage. Though he kept his eyes resolutely on the far shore of the loch, he did not miss the smile of satisfaction that crossed his Lorna's face.

'Speak of the devil.' Lorna said, as she nodded towards the village. 'Black Eck does approach.'

John's heart sank, not at his cousin's serious expression, but at the small square of parchment in his hand.

'We've been summoned.' Eck announced as he came to a halt before them. 'A wee monk brought this.' He held the parchment up for their inspection. 'We are to be at Scone at first light tomorrow.'

'For what purpose?' John demanded with some dread.

'It seems that the time has come for us to pick a side. Robert Bruce has decided to have himself crowned king tomorrow and we are to be there to witness his coronation and then swear fealty to him.'

4

Walter Langton, Bishop of Coventry and Lichfield, Lord High Treasurer of England and Minister to King Edward of England, struggled to control his irritation. His journey to Paris had been a difficult one and he did not appreciate being made to wait for hours in the palace of King Philip of France. When the doors of the reception room were finally opened by the liveried servants and Guillaume de Nogaret, Keeper of the Seal and Councillor to King Philip, wafted into the room with a rat-like grin plastered across his face, Langton had to summon all of his self-control to force a smile onto his lips.

'Lord Bishop.' Nogaret greeted him cheerfully. 'How good to see you again. I do hope that we have not kept you waiting for long.'

Langton gritted his teeth and responded in as light a tone as he could manage. 'Tis no matter, Lord Keeper, I have had much to occupy my mind these last few hours.'

'So I have heard, my Lord. I still cannot believe that the Scots are in open rebellion against King Edward. How many years is it since we last met and you demanded freedom of action so that the King could finally conquer the Scots?'

Langton's smile was genuine, but only because he was imagining how satisfying it would be to thump his fist into the slippery Frenchman's face. 'It must have been nearly four years ago. Yes, it was just after that terrible business in Flanders where King Philip lost half of his nobles in a battle with Flemish peasants.'

Nogaret's smile did not falter, but he narrowed his eyes and glared icily at his English counterpart. 'That was indeed a tragic day for France. However, King Philip has worked tirelessly to bring Flanders back under his control with, it would seem, more success than your own King has enjoyed in his northern territory.'

'I cannot deny that we have suffered a small setback in Scotland. But it is just one isolated noble who has broken faith. We will soon apprehend him and bring him to justice.'

Nogaret stroked his beard and considered Langton's words. 'If it is true that only Robert de Bruce has broken faith, then why are you here? I doubt that you have come all this way simply to ensure that King Philip is aware of all of the minor business of your kingdom.'

'I come to ask for your support in ensuring that Robert Bruce is punished for his sins against God. The murder of a fellow nobleman beneath a chapel altar cannot be ignored. Robert Bruce must be excommunicated and his banishment from the grace of God and church proclaimed throughout Christendom.'

Nogaret shrugged his shoulders and waved his hand dismissively. 'That is surely a matter for the Pope.'

Langton laughed with genuine amusement. 'You are too modest, Lord Keeper. It is well known that Pope Clement is your puppet and that one must come to you if one wishes to see the puppet's strings pulled. I will travel on to Avignon to make the request to the Holy Father directly. I come to you first so I can be sure of the answer he will give.'

Nogaret sucked in a long breath which whistled between his teeth. 'You want Robert Bruce excommunicated so that he will be isolated outside the church and so that no good Christian will support him in his rebellion?'

Langton nodded. 'That's pretty much the size of it.'

'And what do you offer in return?' Nogaret sat back in his chair and savoured the moment. 'I seem to remember that you drove a hard bargain when last we met. Do not expect me to be magnanimous now that our positions are reversed.'

'I would expect no such thing, Lord Keeper. I am sure that I can offer something of value to both you and King Philip.'

'Pray tell, Lord Bishop. You have my full and undivided attention.'

Langton leaned towards the Frenchman and lowered his voice to a conspiratorial whisper. 'I hear talk of the debts King Philip owes to the ever more powerful Knights Templar. I hear that the King struggles to repay what he has borrowed to complete the subjugation of Flanders. I have even heard, if you can believe it, that he plots to free himself from these debts by laying false accusations of heresy against the Knights Templar. It is even whispered that he will use his tame Pope in Avignon to outlaw the order and so enable him to escape his debts and seize all the Templar assets.'

To Nogaret's great credit, his expression remained impassive. However, it did not escape Langton's attention that the Frenchman had turned quite pale.

Nogaret cleared his throat before replying most carefully. 'Such rumours and gossip, Lord Bishop, could be highly dangerous. The Knights Templar are very rich and very powerful. It is unthinkable that even a King could act against them. You would be well advised to think long and hard about who you would share these rumours with.'

'I would take great care, Lord Keeper, to share such intelligence only with the closest and most discreet of friends. Only with those that support us and have our best interests at heart.'

Nogaret held Langton's gaze for a long moment before nodding his head curtly. 'You are right, Lord Bishop. Robert Bruce's sacrilege cannot go unpunished. I will write to the Holy Father right away. You should leave for Avignon immediately. Be sure that my message will arrive there before you do.'

John Edward and his men halted at the forest's edge and watched the throng before the doors of Scone Abbey.

'More have come than I expected.' John stated, his eyes still searching the crowd for faces he recognised.

'Aye.' The Robertson replied. 'But many of the nobles will have come to win the Bruce's favour. They'll then scuttle off back to their strongholds and wait the fighting out behind their walls. Only when victory seems certain will they ride out and declare their undying loyalty to whichever side is victorious.'

'You're right, Laird Robertson.' John replied with a sigh. 'I would rather not enter this den of snakes. It is impossible to tell who we should trust and I am inclined not to put my faith in any one of them.'

'But enter it we must. To refuse the summons would be tantamount to declaring for the Comyns.' Laird Robertson paused and looked each of his companions in the eye. 'We must go in and be seen to have attended, but we must keep our heads down and try to slip away after the ceremony without being forced to commit to one faction or the other.' He then jerked his old head towards the Abbey and instructed the Scotstoun men to cover the open ground between themselves and the worthies gathered there to witness the crowning of a king.

John's eyes flicked over the crowd as he walked and picked out those who were known to him. Of the three bishops standing by the Abbey doors, he recognised Lamberton, Bishop of St

Andrews, and Wishart, Bishop of Glasgow. Of the gathered noblemen, he recognised the Earls of Atholl, Lennox and Mar along with Sir James Douglas, Roger Kirkpatrick and James Lindsay. As he strode purposefully forward, he caught sight of the Bruces. The family resemblance was quite striking, as they were all tall, handsome and well built. Edward Bruce, an old friend, nodded a greeting and John returned it before resting his eyes on the man who would be king. Though still undeniably regal in his bearing, Robert Bruce looked very different to the last time John had set eyes upon him. He appeared tired to the point of exhaustion, his hair and clothing were dishevelled and his shoulders were slumped as though he bore the whole weight of the world upon them.

John's lip then curled into a snarl when he saw that Sir John de Menteith stood at the edge of the Bruce circle. John's hand dropped to the hilt of his sword and he took a step towards the man who had treacherously delivered Sir William Wallace to the English for his execution.

A firm hand grasped his upper arm and jerked him back. 'They'll cut you to pieces before you lay a hand on him.'

John turned to find Malcolm Simpson staring intently into his eyes.

'I'll take my chances.' He growled and tried to pull away.

Malcolm tightened his grip and spoke in an urgent whisper so that they would not be overheard. 'Like you, I would gladly risk my life to take revenge for Wallace's death. I fought at his side from the beginning and mourn his loss no less painfully than you. But this is not the time for it and it is certainly not the place. Menteith has sworn himself to Robert Bruce and now has his protection. If you attack his man he will have no choice but to cut you down and, before your blood has soaked into the earth, our friends here will share your fate. Tell me that you are prepared to sacrifice them and I will release you and leave you to your work.'

John followed Malcolm's gaze and the sight of Eck, Al, Scott, Strathbogie and the Robertson brought him to his senses and he shrugged Malcolm's hand away. 'Thank you, my friend. It is truly good to see you.' He spoke these words sincerely and embraced his brother-in-arms. 'It has been too long. You look older.'

Malcolm laughed and looked John up and down. 'You're no young laddie yourself. I see that you carry a few new scars and a touch of white in your hair.'

John grinned in spite of himself and raised his hand self-consciously to his head. 'Away with you. My hair's as dark as ever it was.'

Eck stepped forward and clapped Malcolm on the back. 'Are you still fighting the English or have you taken up the quiet life?'

Malcolm grinned back, his teeth white against his weather-worn skin. 'Did the Wallace no' aye tell us to fight on? That is what I have done, though the successes have been few and far between of late.'

The Robertson interrupted them and pointed towards the Abbey. 'It is time, I think. The priests are waving us inside.'

'Right!' John ordered. 'Let's go in last so we can leave quickly. I am keen to be away from here.'

The Scotstoun men shuffled into the rearmost pew just as the Abbey doors were slammed shut and the priests began the ceremony. Robert Bruce sat before the altar upon the ancient throne of Scotland, resplendent in the few crowning robes and vestments that had been hidden away from the greedy grasp of the English King. The great banner of the Kings of Scotland, with its lion and scarlet lilies, had been unfurled behind the throne to bring solemnity and majesty to the occasion. They watched on as the Bishop of St Andrews delivered the Latin rites, his clear, strong voice reaching all parts of the Abbey and reverberating around its high, vaulted ceiling.

The Robertson scowled at John's side and muttered under his breath as he shook his head. 'This is no' a real coronation. My own faither talked of the crowning of King Alexander. He said that the Abbey was filled to bursting with noble men and women and that they had to leave the doors open so that the lesser knights could peer in and strain to hear the rituals. The pews here are half empty. The crowning stone and all the royal regalia were taken by Langshanks as spoils of war. Even the crown of Scotland was taken.'

As the Robertson spoke, John watched the Bishop of St Andrews bless a simple circlet of gold and place it upon the head of Robert Bruce. When he rose to be proclaimed King of Scotland, the congregation burst into rapturous applause and John found himself joining in. In that moment, even he could not deny that the Bruce looked every inch a king.

On leaving the Abbey, a priest positioned outside each of the great doors informed the witnesses to the coronation that a feast had been laid on nearby and pointed them towards it. The Scotstoun men ignored the instruction and set off in the opposite direction where the safety of the forest awaited them. They had covered just one third of the way there when John heard his name being called from behind.

'Keep walking!' He ordered from the side of his mouth. 'Pretend we didn't hear.'

The next time his name was called, the voice was much closer and its owner was evidently out of breath. John cursed and brought the Scotstoun men to a halt. He recognised the voice as that of Edward de Bruce and, as the man had saved his life after the Battle of Falkirk, he found that he could not bring himself to ignore him.

'Christ John!' De Bruce puffed. 'Ye made me run in all my finery. I can scarcely catch my breath.'

John smiled in spite of his desire to be away from the nobles and all their plotting. He both liked and admired Edward Bruce and he felt small and petty for trying to ignore him. 'You still look good Ed.' He said, with a genuine smile.

De Bruce grinned back and looked down at his cloak of shiny, black fur which reached to the ground. 'I'm brother to the King now, John. I cannae be dressing all raggedy-arsed like you.'

John laughed in response to the good-natured jibe and then jabbed his thumb towards the forest. 'We thought we'd head off now and no' bother with the feast. Given the present difficulties, we did not think that you would have enough to go around.'

Edward let out a long breath and shook his head. 'You don't know the half of it, John. With the English still in Perth, we've had to scour the countryside and extract meat and ale practically at the points of our swords. I doubt that we have won any friends and that is bad when we had so few to start with. With the feast so hard-won, you cannot refuse to join me in a drink and toast the new king.'

John nodded his assent. 'We would never to refuse to drink with you.'

'That is good.' Edward responded in good humour. 'For my brother has requested that you also drink with him and, now that he is King, none of us can say no.'

The Scotstoun men followed on behind Edward de Bruce and exchanged concerned looks with one another. The future of them all hung precariously in the balance and each one of them knew that they would have to navigate a careful course if they were to emerge unscathed.

The sight that greeted them inside the Abbey caused John's stomach to clench painfully and he thought that he would prefer to be in the thick of

battle rather than walking down that aisle.
Beneath the altar sat King Robert of Scotland
upon his throne with the three bishops, four earls,
his kinsmen and retainers and a dozen minor
nobles and knights standing on either side of the
throne. Facing them, with their backs to John,
were almost twenty men, including Malcolm
Simpson and two other Bordermen who had
fought with Wallace, three men of Galloway who
John remembered from the invasion of Northern
England and two men from the North of Scotland
who John recognised as captains who had fought
under Sir Andrew Murray's command at Stirling
Bridge. He did not know the others, but assumed
that they were men like him, commoners who,
through mere accident of war, now commanded
fighting men.

Robert Bruce looked slowly along this line of
men, taking long seconds to gaze into each face
before moving to the next. John returned his gaze
steadily, determined not to betray his discomfort
as the others did through the shuffling of their
feet and the nervous clearing of their throats.
When Robert spoke, his voice was low and deep,
forcing the men to lean forwards to catch his
words.

'As King, I can command you to swear fealty
to me and to commit your men to my cause. It is
my God-given right to do so, but I will not.
Instead, I will ask that you join with me to fight
for the freedom of your country, just as each of
you has done for long years now. Help me to
unite the kingdom so that we can prepare to
oppose the English King when he marches across

our border again.' Robert now rose to his feet and paced along the line, his eyes locking with those of each of the men he addressed. 'He will come, be in no doubt about that!' As he spoke, Robert extended his arm and pointed towards the south. 'His preparations have already begun and he has sworn to burn this land and blacken it from coast to coast. Together, we can stop him in his tracks. Together, we can break his army and send him home in such disgrace that his nobles will never again answer his call. Together, we can secure our nation's freedom for centuries to come. Join with me and we will overcome all the odds that are stacked against us! I will knight any man who swears to join with me this day. I will do it now before my coronation throne! What say you?'

Three men instantly and enthusiastically agreed and King Robert went immediately to thank them and take them into his embrace. The others, including all of the Scotstoun men, stayed silent and kept their eyes fixed firmly on the empty throne. The tension hung heavily in the air and John found himself praying for the excruciating ordeal to be over. Robert Bruce was a charismatic, persuasive and determined man and John knew that he would have to remain calm and draw on all of his diplomatic skills if he was to succeed in keeping his men out of the coming civil war. He decided that the best course was to stay silent, as experience had taught him that to speak was to open a door to your opponent.

'Who else will swear to me?' Robert Bruce demanded, his eyes travelling up and down the line of men. He left the silence hanging in the air until it became heavy and oppressive once more. The eyes of the bishops and earls added to the weight of the expectant and intimidating silence and it was only moments before a Galloway man buckled beneath it and fell to his knees and swore loyalty to the new King. A northerner quickly followed him and received Robert's grateful blessing.

John was still praying for an end to the Bruce's gentle yet effective coercion when a movement caught his eyes. A figure had approached the gathered nobles from behind and was inserting himself into the line between the Earl of Atholl and Nigel Bruce. As he was shorter than the other men by at least a head, John could not make out his features until he stepped forward into the space opened up by his fellow members of the Bruce's court. Recognition hit the Scotstoun man like the warhammer of a charging knight thumping into his chest. All of his determination and resolve to leave Scone on peaceful terms evaporated in that very instant. His carefully composed and impassive expression transformed into a savage snarl and his eyes bored into the oblivious Sir John de Menteith.

Robert Bruce held his arms out and repeated his entreaty. 'Is there no other among you who would swear loyalty to his King?'

John stepped forward with his fingers on the hilt of his sword. 'And why would any man swear loyalty to one who was so recently on his knees before the English King and who still keeps company with rancid, rotten, traitorous dogs?' He then turned towards the man who had delivered William Wallace to his death and growled at him with ill-concealed fury. 'If it was not for all these nobles here, I would fly at you and butcher you like the dog you are. Do not think that your vile treachery has been forgotten. Be certain that you will pay the price, false Menteith. You cannot hide behind your master's skirts for ever. I have vowed that I will slaughter you in bloody revenge at my first opportunity and I make that same oath here today. I will spread your guts across the ground and watch you chew on your own tongue as death carries you away!'

All men there stood in open-mouthed astonishment as John stood menacingly and glared at his mortal enemy. Robert Bruce was the first to react and he moved to put himself between John Edward and the white-faced Menteith.

'Menteith is under my protection and no man may harm him whilst I still live. I will not have blood shed in this holy place on my crowning day.' Robert spoke with calm authority despite the sudden and violent outburst. 'I am King here and command that you retract your threats and beg Menteith's forgiveness.'

John met Robert's eyes and slowly shook his head. 'You have placed a circlet of gold upon your head, but that does not make you King. A crown must be earned through deeds, loyalty, integrity and constancy. I have seen none of these from you, only blind, self-serving ambition. Until you have earned your crown, you will not command me to kneel before a traitor or to fight against my own countrymen just so you can perch upon a throne.'

'I told you!' Menteith hissed. 'They are Comyn men. We should cut them down before they do the same to us!'

John shook his head in derision. 'You will never understand the men who stand before you. We are not for Comyn or for Bruce. We fight not for riches or honours, but for the good of our countrymen. We have fought the English ceaselessly these past years. Never once have we yielded to them or their King. Not one of you can say the same. We will go and battle on and leave you nobles to feud and squabble. We want no part of it and will take no side.' He then turned his head to Robert Bruce. 'The odds are stacked heavily against you. If you are wise, you will work to unite the kingdom behind you to face King Edward when he comes. Beware! If you think only of keeping that crown upon your head, it is likely to slip down and slowly strangle the life from you.'

Menteith jumped forwards, his finger pointing at John. 'Seize him! He has threatened the life of the King.'

Edward Bruce grabbed Menteith roughly by the shoulder and pushed him back into line. 'Shut your mouth, you useless piece of shit! My brother may see fit to shield you, but if you speak again I will let John Edward cut you into pieces.'

'Words pour like shit from between his lips, but he will never face me with a sword in his hand.' John's eyes blazed with fury as he spoke.

Robert Bruce looked John up and down, his cheeks red with anger. 'I did not ask you for your lectures or your insults, I asked you for your sword. If, as you claim, you fight only for your country, you will heed my call and pledge it to me so I can unite the kingdom and protect it from the greed of the Plantagenet King.'

'You demand my sword, King Robert?' John retorted, pulling at his sword belt. 'Here! Have it! May it do you much good!' With those words, John dropped his sword at the feet of Robert Bruce and let it clatter onto the Abbey's stone floor.

There was a second of stunned silence before Laird Robertson's sword clattered to the floor beside John's. The weapons of Eck, Al, Scott, Strathbogie, Malcolm Simpson and two of the bordermen quickly joined them. John then nodded curtly to Edward Bruce and led his men out of the Abbey.

The group moved quickly and in silence as they covered the open ground between the Abbey and the forest. Only when they were in reach of the treeline did Scott Edward articulate the thought in all of their minds.

'Fuck's sake, John! Keep calm, you said. Let's keep a low profile, you said. Make sure we don't cause any offence. Christ! I thought they were going to cut us down there in the Abbey!'

John kept walking but could not ignore his younger brother. 'It did not go as well as I had hoped.'

Behind him, the Robertson snorted with amusement. 'It has to be said though, I would pay good gold to see that expression on Menteith's face again. He near shit himself.'

Only Strathbogie failed to crack a smile at this and his eyes were cast down and his expression grave as they made their way through the trees.

Scott Edward clapped him on the shoulder and tried to console him. 'Do not be downcast. We will find a way through this just as we have always done.'

Strathbogie shook his head miserably. 'It's no' that. I just cannae believe that I've just thrown my good axe away at the Bruce's feet. I'll be needing one in the days ahead and that one was my favourite.'

Scott cuffed at Strathbogie's ear but the older man avoided the blow as a grin spread across his face. 'You're no funny!' He spat, before breaking into a wide grin of his own.

They all joined in with the laughter, but their faces soon grew serious again. They had enemies enough already without adding another king to their number.

King Robert had ordered the nobles to join the feast so that he could consult with his most trusted aides. He sank down onto the throne and rubbed at his temples with his fingertips.

'How many now?' He snapped irritably.

Edward Bruce stroked his chin and cast his eyes towards the ceiling as he counted in his head. 'At best, a hundred knights and two hundred foot.'

'And at worst?' The King demanded.

'Maybe half that.' Sir James Douglas replied, his voice heavy with resignation.

'It's nowhere near enough!' King Robert exclaimed. 'If our enemies gather their forces quickly, we cannot prevail.'

'The Bordermen and the men of Perth would have tripled our numbers.' Edward Bruce returned his brother's glare and shrugged his shoulders.

'And what would you have me do? Go on my knees to John Edward and his ilk and beg them to support me. I will never again have a presumptuous commoner preach to me about kingship. I would rather lose five hundred men than owe those brigands one iota of gratitude.'

'You cannot afford to be stubborn, Robert!' Edward replied evenly. 'It is not just the men that he brings. Half the men in the kingdom have fought with him against the English at one time or another. They admire him for his courage and love him for his honesty and integrity. They will follow him if he comes to your side. Without men like him, you cannot win the kingdom, let alone keep it out of the hands of the English.'

Robert Bruce shook his head. 'I asked for his oath once, I will not ask for it again. We will go to the nobles for support. Those who cannot be persuaded to join with us must be subject to persuasion, force if need be. The path before us will be hard, but you will see that I will both win the kingdom and defend it.'

5

Sir John de Seagrave accepted the goblet from Walter Langton's hand and raised it in a silent toast before drinking deeply from it. He regarded the Treasurer through narrowed eyes and smacked his lips as he rubbed an errant dribble from his bearded chin. 'How does it feel, Langton, to wield such power?'

The Treasurer shook his head and took a gulp of the sweet, red liquid before replying. 'I wield no power, Seagrave. I simply advise the King and then do as he commands.'

Seagrave dismissed Langton's words with a wave of his hand. 'Your false modesty does not wash with me. From the day he was crowned, the King has struggled with his nobles. I doubt that more than half of them have supported him at any given time. Now, when he is in danger of losing his greatest prize, the crown of Scotland, you have every noble in England, Ireland and Wales gathered in Westminster eager to kneel before him. The streets around here are so crowded with them, my men had to beat them back to make way for me. I heard that a viewing platform outside the Abbey collapsed under the weight of onlookers and left several people dead.'

Langton nodded reluctantly before replying. 'It is true that I suggested that the King should knight the Prince of Wales and invite any noble who wished to receive the same accolade to attend. I hoped that some noble families would wish to see their sons so honoured alongside their future king. I had no idea that so many families would respond with so much enthusiasm.'

'Bollocks!' Seagrave replied with a grin. 'You knew exactly what you were doing. The magnates loyal to the King are either dead, or like the Earls of Surrey and Norfolk, are in the process of dying. You have sought to tie a new generation of nobles to the King by offering them fellowship with the heir to the throne. I applaud you. You have lost none of your cunning in your old age.'

Langton abandoned his pretence to modesty and instead basked in his friend's admiration. His skills were so often hidden from sight, it was a rare treat to have them appreciated so openly. 'I cannot deny that you are right, Seagrave. The King grows weaker and is determined that the Scottish question be settled before his reign is over. This is likely the last roll of the dice, so we must be sure that the conquest is final. The support of all the nobles is required if the outcome is to be certain.'

Seagrave held up his hand to bring Langton to a halt. 'How can you be sure that knighting them will do the trick? There is nothing to stop them from receiving the accolade and then refusing to serve when called.'

Langton nodded his agreement. 'That is where the King must do his part. I have brought three hundred young nobles here, it is up to him to bind them firmly to our cause.'

The door to the chamber creaked open and Langton's apothecary limped stiffly to his master's side.

'How is the King?' Langton snapped, betraying his nervousness. 'Have your potions worked?'

The apothecary nodded enthusiastically. 'It took a massive dose, but he is as lively as I have ever seen him. It should last for an hour or two.'

'Then we must not waste it. Come Seagrave, let us take our places.'

The Temple feasting hall was full to bursting and Langton and Seagrave had to elbow their way to their places at the foot of the King's table. Seagrave leaned in close to Langton's ear to make some comment, but the older man could hear nothing above the din of a thousand excited and wine-lubricated conversations. The babel was deafening and Langton worried that the King might not be able to make himself heard above it.

His fretting was misplaced. He was only alerted to the King's presence by the hush that fell over the front few tables and then spread quickly to the back, leaving only a few isolated, drunken discussions, which quickly fell to silence when their inebriated participants sensed the change in the atmosphere. Langton found himself smiling at the King's flair for the dramatic. Easily the tallest man in the room, Edward Plantagenet stood in silence, his face impassive and his eyes moving slowly and deliberately across the hall as if subjecting each and every guest to close scrutiny. Langton knew that the King could see no further than the first few rows of tables, but the gathered nobles did not and they stood transfixed, certain that the King gazed upon them and them alone. King Edward looked every inch the conquering monarch of legend in his crown of gold and his royal vestments. Langton doubted that any of the open-mouthed young nobles who gazed adoringly at their warrior king realised that it had taken hours to tease his thinning hair into a semblance of more youthful curls or that the rosiness of his cheeks had been achieved through the application of various juices to royal skin.

With his audience firmly in the palm of his hand, the King stretched the silence out until it seemed that every man there held his breath in eager anticipation. When he began to speak, his voice was light and gentle and the whole hall leaned forward, the better to catch his words. His voice deepened and grew in strength as he spoke and the words spilled from his lips with increasing speed. He was shouting at the top of his voice by the time he invited his young knights to join him in cursing the perfidious and treacherous Scots and it seemed to Langton that their thunderous response would lift the roof clean off the hall and reduce its walls to rubble. They shouted louder still when the King had two swans enmeshed in golden chains brought before him and invited his nobles to join with him in swearing upon the sacred birds an oath never to rest until the whole of Scotland had been subdued. Their shouting increased in volume and they beat their fists upon the tables when their King vowed before God and the swans that he would avenge the death of John Comyn and the sacrilege of Robert Bruce, after which he would never again take arms against good Christian men, but only against the heathen in the Holy Land.

When Edward finally took his seat, the cheers and stamping continued on for many moments. Each time the King inclined his head or raised his hand in acknowledgement, the hall erupted again in rapturous applause. Langton saw that the King was exhausted, but doubted that any other man there would realise just how much the speech had drained him.

Seagrave leaned in to Langton's ear and shouted to be heard. 'It seems that the King has done his part. When he marches to Scotland he will have the whole flower of English chivalry marching enthusiastically behind him.'

Langton nodded his agreement and could not keep the smile from his face. He doubted that he could be happier in that moment, but then the Prince of Wales took to his feet at his father's side, held his hand above his head and called for silence. Langton leaned back and prepared to enjoy the Prince's humiliation. No sane man would try to follow the King after such an uproarious reception, but it seemed that the vanity of the heir to the throne was boundless and that he could not resist the temptation to take some of the glory for himself.

The Prince's call for silence went unanswered for several minutes, until Piers Gaveston and the other knights of his retinue began to call for it and rattled their tankards on the table.

When silence finally fell, Prince Edward raised his goblet and declared. 'I too will make an oath before this exalted company. Until the rebellious Scots are crushed, I swear that I will not spend two nights in the same bed!'

The applause which broke out was enthusiastic enough, but fell far short of the euphoria elicited by his father's performance.

Walter Langton leaned back and drained his goblet. As he summoned a serving wench to replenish his wine, he poked his elbow at Seagrave to get his attention. 'I do not know what I enjoyed more, the father's triumph or the son's failure. It should be the former, but I suspect that it will be the memory of the latter which will bring me more comfort and amusement in the years ahead.'

Seagrave's lips and teeth were stained red and his words were slightly slurred by the King's wine. 'I surely doubt that you will have many more years ahead of you to enjoy the memory, Lord Treasurer. Uniting the nobles so solidly behind the King can only be attributed to witchcraft. There is no other explanation for it. After tonight's dark work, I have no doubt that you will be burnt at the stake before too many more days have passed.'

They lay naked atop the blankets, all vestiges of modesty abandoned after their urgent though gentle coupling. Eck Edward ran his fingers lazily through Ailith Andrews soft, brown hair, before caressing the smooth, pale skin of her shoulder. He sighed deeply and gazed into her beautiful, wide, brown eyes.

'If the good Lord heard my prayers, Ailith, I would stay here with you forever and never leave this bed. I am only whole when I am with you. My soul is only lifted from darkness when you are in my arms.'

Her eyes searched his face for any sign of mockery, but the intensity of his gaze left her in no doubt as to his sincerity. Her eyes welled with tears and they spilled down her cheeks.

'Hush now! Hush now my bonnie lassie!' Eck crooned gently, as he wiped the tears away with his fingertips. 'You must not cry, for it breaks my heart to see it.'

'I weep for joy, sweet Eck, not for sadness. I thought that no man would ever want me and then you came. My tall, dark warrior, the hero of the songs sung at the village feasts and the subject of a hundred tales of courage and daring. I never dared to dream that such as you would ever look at me.'

Eck unconsciously glanced down at the puckered scar on Ailith's breast. The wound had long since healed, but the mark of the English rapist's teeth could still be seen where he had bitten and ripped away a chunk of her flesh. He felt the darkness rush back into his soul as he thought of what he would do if ever that vile creature came within his reach.

Ailith sensed the change in him and reached for the blanket to cover her nakedness and her shame. Eck gently grasped her hand and tried to soothe her.

'You never need to hide any part of yourself from me. We two are joined now and your pain is my pain. We will bear it together. If that beast should ever cross my path, be sure that I will bring his severed head to you so you can spit upon it.'

Ailith stretched up to kiss him on the lips. She knew that Eck meant what he said and the thought of spitting upon that bastard English head made her love him even more.

'We had better get back before we are missed.' She whispered when she felt him harden against her once more. 'Your cousin will not be happy if we miss the whole of his wedding feast.'

Eck laughed and pulled her closer. 'Scott has eyes only for the McNaughton girl. I doubt if he'd notice if the whole village sneaked away and left just the two of them at the feast together.'

He suddenly sat bolt upright, his head cocked to one side as if listening. 'I thought I heard horses.'

Ailith had turned pale. 'The music has stopped.'

Eck leapt up and began to dress. 'You stay here! Bar the door behind me! I'll come back for you when it's safe.'

He ran for the village square, a sword already in his hand. Between the houses that formed the square, he could see that around twenty mounted horsemen stood at the far side of the village. When he came in sight of the square itself, he breathed a sigh of relief and stopped to sheath his blade. He recognised one of the figures standing in conversation with his cousin at the centre of the crowd of feasting villagers.

A smile spread across his face and he shouted a hearty welcome. 'If it's no' Prior Abernethy! We've no' seen hide nor hair of you since Roslin.'

The Prior's face lit up in recognition and he stepped forward to pull Eck into his embrace. 'The last time I saw you, the English blood soaked you from head to foot.'

'The last time I clapped eyes on you, the priestly robes and wooden staff had been cast aside for armour and a Templar sword.'

'Happy days indeed, Alexander. You look well. Now come and meet the Bishop. I have told him all about you.' With his arm still around Eck's shoulders, he turned to the broad-shouldered and ruddy-cheeked man who stood at John Edward's side. 'This is David de Moravia, Bishop of Moray.'

Eck bowed his head in greeting and noted that the Bishop was now dressed in a tunic of maille beneath a well-worn cloak and not the fine robes had had worn at the crowning of Robert Bruce in the Abbey of Scone. The battered and well-used sword hanging at his waist led Eck to conclude that he had not come to Scotstoun to celebrate Mass.

John waved the two holy men to sit and had ale, bread and meat brought for them. His expression was serious and he was keen to discover the purpose of their visit. 'You should know that the Bishops of Glasgow and St Andrews have already sent priests on Robert Bruce's behalf to persuade us to join with him in his fight against the Comyns. I sent them away with the same answer I gave to the Bruce himself. If you come here with that same purpose, then I am afraid that you have wasted your time.'

The Bishop found this to be most amusing and almost choked on a mouthful of greasy mutton as he threw his head back to bellow with laughter. When he finally managed to clear his throat, he addressed John with a rueful grin. 'You must forgive me, John. If you had known the Bruces for as long as I have, you would know how ridiculous your statement was. Robert Bruce has sent no-one to beg you to join with him, nor will he. He is as stubborn and pig-headed as his father and grandfather were before him. It is a miracle that he asked you the first time. I would wager everything I have that he will not do so again. Like Abernethy and myself, the Bishops of Glasgow and St Andrews have acted on their own initiative and not at Robert Bruce's direction.'

'But the request is the same?'

The Bishop nodded as he took a mouthful of ale. 'It is. You and I are in the same difficult position. Like you, I have led men against the English these last years. Unlike the rest of them at Scone, neither one of us fell upon our knees and swore fealty to the English King. Isolated and without a single noble to lead us, we fought on and refused to surrender our country to English avarice. Now we face a difficult decision. Do we fight on alone or throw our lot in with the only Scottish leader now willing to rebel against Edward Plantagenet? I come to urge you to take a chance on King Robert.'

John nodded thoughtfully and carefully considered the Bishop's words before replying. 'Since the last of our nobles were accepted into King Edward's peace, it has been a comfort to us here in Scotstoun to know that we were not entirely alone in continuing our resistance. We heard word of the patriots in Moray and of your leadership of them. Every man here would be proud to fight alongside you, but I cannot ask them to take arms against men who have fought against the English with us, just to keep a crown on Robert Bruce's head. He has betrayed us more than once in the past and I will not risk him doing so again.'

The Bishop returned John's steady gaze. 'As I have great respect for your courage and integrity, I will not press my arguments further. I have decided to gamble and throw my lot in with the Bruce. Only time will tell if I have chosen wisely. Your friend, William Wallace, once told me that, in the struggle against the English, we must take our friends where we can find them. Though the odds against him are great indeed,

Robert Bruce is the only friend we have who may be able to unite the country against the English. I would ask that you consider that and would counsel you against returning the Bruce's pride and stubbornness in kind. I can see that he has yet to prove himself to you and I will openly admit that his past conduct has been wanting. Pray keep an open mind and stay willing to ally with him if his deeds do turn out to match his words.'

'If he proves to be wiser, more constant and steadfast than he has been in the past, then my decision might well change. In the meantime, I will not risk the lives of my men just to satisfy his ambition.'

'That is all I ask of you.' The Bishop replied, while nodding his head. 'Now, the Prior and I have some gifts for you. My gift is that of intelligence. Our spies tell us that an English army has crossed the border and will march north in search of Robert Bruce. You should know that your actions here have not gone unnoticed and I have no doubt that, sooner or later, they will set their course for Scotstoun. You should look to the safety of your people and make whatever preparations you can.'

'I thank you for the information.' John replied graciously. 'Now that we are forewarned, we will decide on what precautions are necessary.'

'I see that you appreciated the Bishop's gift. I hope that mine will be as welcome, although it comes in the form of a request for a favour.' Prior Abernethy grimaced as though it pained him to ask for anything from his host.

John grinned and shook his head at Abernethy. 'If you but knew how many nights we have sat around our fire and drank toasts to good Prior Abernethy for his courage and deeds during the battles at Roslin, you would not hesitate to ask me for anything, for you would know that I could refuse you nothing. I would tear the very clothes from my back and throw them at your feet if you did but ask it. Tell me what you need and I will tell you how quickly I can provide it.'

Abernethy seemed to be genuinely moved by John's words and bowed his head in acknowledgement. 'You do me great honour, John. What I ask of you requires great secrecy and I would not ask if I did have absolute trust in you and your men. You know that I was once sworn to the Knights Templar?'

'How could I forget it? The image of you wielding your sword in their colours will stay with me until my final breath.'

'It seems that there may be dark days ahead for the Poor Fellow-Soldiers of Christ and the Temple of Solomon. The Grand Master has heard that the King of France and his captive Pope make plans to curtail the power of the order. Though he does not know what form this plot will take, he has decided to take action and put some possessions and members of the order beyond their reach. I have been asked to hide away a number of my brothers in Scotland. I would ask for you to agree to take ten of them to live in Scotstoun. They will provide for themselves and will spend much of their time in prayer.'

John interrupted the Prior with good humour. 'The answer is yes, Abernethy. No further persuasion or justification is required. I will take them gladly for you. Now call them in so we may meet them.'

Though they were dressed plainly, it was evident that these were not ordinary men. Dressed in worn and rough garments, each man wore a broadsword at his hip and a beard that reached to his chest. All were strong and stern-faced and gave the merest of nods when they were introduced. John thought that he might remember the names of the first three, Guillame, Jacques and Geoffroi, but he doubted that he would be able to recall the rest, especially if they remained as mute as they were during Scott Edward's wedding feast.

6

Aymer de Valence, Earl of Pembroke, felt happier than he had for many months as he led his three thousand hand-picked knights through the southern Scottish countryside. His herald held King Edward's Dragon Banner high at his back and it snapped noisily in the breeze. He had been entrusted with capturing Robert Bruce and bringing him to justice and he relished the prospect of the hunt much more than he had the suffocating atmosphere of the King's court. With no baggage train to slow them, his column would forage for their supplies as they went and fly into Scotland like no other English army before them. The King had commanded him to proceed with all speed and brutality to apprehend the traitorous Earl of Carrick and he had no doubt that he would succeed and return to England to receive great riches, honours and acclaim.

The devastated villages and hamlets he had ridden through told him that Rank had lost neither his skills nor his enthusiasm for ensuring that the ordered brutality was duly delivered. The thick, black smoke rising from just beyond the hill to his front led him to conclude that he was about to be reunited with his ferocious subordinate. The horrific efficiency of Rank's work was evident when he reached the top of the hill and saw that every structure in the small village had been reduced to smoking ashes. In the midst of the charred ruins, he found Rank stripped to the waist, his long, matted hair plastered to his skull with sweat and his torso splattered in blood. The ground at his feet was strewn with naked, mutilated corpses and several more hung lifelessly from the branches of the gnarled and ancient tree at the centre of the village square. He seemed oblivious to Pembroke's approach, as he was intent on hacking away at the fingers of a bloody, jerking figure who was suspended from the tree by his neck. Pembroke assumed that it was a man, although it could well have been a woman seeing as the genitals had been removed, leaving only a ragged, bloody cavity in their place.

Pembroke reined his horse in and shouted to Rank in greeting. 'King's Knight! You told me that you would never set foot in Scotland again. Yet here you are.'

Rank turned his head and wiped at the sweat running into his eyes. 'It doesn't mean that I am happy to be here! The King commanded me to come to make sure that you do your job properly. Given that he knighted me with his own hand, I was told that I could not refuse.'

Pembroke dismounted and handed his reins to his squire. 'That's what happens when you make yourself indispensable. Now tell me, have any of these poor souls been persuaded to give away the location of Robert Bruce? The quicker we catch the bastard, the quicker we can leave this place and go south to collect our reward.'

Rank spat upon the ground and wiped the gore from his fingers on his leather trews. 'The villagers knew nothing, of that you can be sure. No sane man would endure such agonies without giving away their secrets.'

'Have you beheaded them all?' Pembroke asked, casting his eyes over the headless corpses.

'Better than that.' Rank replied with a grin. He stepped behind the tree and retrieved a bloody, metal implement, before holding it out for Pembroke's inspection. 'It was a present from the Prince of Wales.'

Pembroke peered more closely at the weapon. 'Ah! It is a very fine mace. See how the flanges have been worked so that they form a star at the top.'

'The Prince told me that it is a bludgeon. It was a gift to him from the King of France. He thought that I would have more use for it than he.'

'Take care!' Pembroke teased. 'I don't want you becoming one of the Prince's favourites.'

'Go fuck yourself!' Rank retorted with a sneer.

'Go fuck yourself, my Lord.' Pembroke shot back with a grin. 'Just because we are on campaign does not mean that we should forget all social niceties.'

'Social niceties my arse!' Rank retorted. 'Watch this!'

He turned and raised the bludgeon high above his head and brought it crashing down upon the head of one of the battered corpses hanging from the tree. The force of the blow caused the skull to disintegrate, leaving only a stump and a bloody mess of gore and brains.

'Christ!' Pembroke exclaimed, swallowing down the bile which now burned at the back of his throat. 'But it is effective.'

Rank nodded and examined the weapon once more. 'I think I prefer it to the sword. I never thought that I would, but it has impressed me.'

Pembroke nodded his agreement before turning back to the purpose of their campaign. 'So, you were saying that you have been unable to gather any intelligence regarding the whereabouts of Robert Bruce.'

'Not from the villagers.' Rank responded. 'But this fucker here is a priest.' He jabbed his thumb in the direction of the hanging man he had been mutilating when Pembroke rode up. 'He was just in the process of giving me some interesting information when you interrupted me.'

Pembroke looked quizzically at the battered and bloodied figure. 'Well, he's not going to tell us anything now, is he? He's being hanging there the whole time we've been talking. He stopped jerking and kicking several moments ago.'

Rank rolled his eyes and muttered something under his breath before taking several paces towards a nearby fire and extracting a metal rod from the flames. He held the glowing metal against the rope until it burned clean through it and sent his victim crashing into the dust. He then rammed the red-hot metal into the cavity between the man's legs and pressed it home, causing the clotted blood and flesh to sizzle and spit, sending great clouds of steam and foul smoke into the still, evening air. At first there was no reaction, but then the man began to scream and kick as he fought to escape the pain.

Rank turned to Pembroke, his face impassive. 'It seems that he has quite recovered. Give me an hour and I will come to you with everything he knows.'

The priest proved to be less resilient than Rank had anticipated, but he was most talkative during his last tortured and tormented moments. Pembroke had watched the King's Knight work and marvelled at the effectiveness of his technique, though it lacked the finesse of the torturers in the King's employ. Those men could reduce a prisoner to a screaming, broken mess with nothing more than a small dagger. Rank's approach, on the other hand, was vicious, savage and bloody and required the use of rope, blade, bludgeon and fire.

Pembroke tore a strip of cloth from the priest's discarded robes and threw it to Rank so that he could wipe away the worst of the gore coating him from head to waist. 'So, it seems that the Bruce is intent on drumming up support in the south, before moving into the lands of his supporters in the north east. We must divide our forces to thwart his plans. You will go ahead to Perth and cut off his route to the north. I will advance from the south and we will trap the bastard between us.' Pembroke brought his hands crashing together to show how the Bruce would be crushed between them.

Rank grinned malevolently. 'I have never killed an Earl before. I will be sure to do it slowly.'

Pembroke laughed in response, but something dark in the King's Knight's eyes caused his merriment to die away. 'You can torture him, but he must be delivered to King Edward alive and in a fit condition for his trial.'

Rank nodded curtly before turning away. Though his order had been perfectly clear, Pembroke hoped that the Bruce would fall into his hands and not into those of his subordinate.

In the days following the departure of the Bishop of Moray and Prior Abernethy, the people of Scotstoun had spent many an hour discussing exactly what precautions should be taken ahead of the expected arrival of the English army. Some of the fighting men argued for preparing to defend the village with force. Others favoured a more cautious approach and suggested that the best course was to abandon the village and flee into the depths of the forest until the danger had passed. John and Scott's father, Andrew Edward, joined with the other village elders in hearing the views of both camps. Both extremes were quickly rejected and all efforts were directed towards finding a middle path. Three days of frustrating debate were brought to an end when Esmy, Lorna Edward's mother and Lady of the Glen, asked if they might use some of the gold buried under their houses to buy their safety.

Many of the villagers were wary of Esmy and the whiff of witchcraft which hung about her and were therefore quick to dismiss her. Andrew Edward, now bound to her through the marriage between his son and her daughter, was less quick to leap to judgement.

'We have gold enough.' He stated, as he considered the idea. 'Can it somehow be used to buy title to the land from the English?' His eyes flitted from side to side as he tried to imagine how such an arrangement could be made. He then shook his head. 'They will not make such a bargain with us. They would take our gold and then attack us just the same.'

Sir Nigel Thwaite seldom spoke at village gatherings. After being taken prisoner following the Battle of Stirling Bridge, he had taken up with Esmy and had decided to remain with her in Scotland rather being ransomed to his family in northern England. The villagers only tolerated the presence of an Englishman in their midst because he had the protection of the Edwards. Sir Nigel stood and cleared his throat, causing all present to turn in his direction. 'You are right, Andrew. The English administrators will never make such an agreement with you. They would, however, entertain such a proposal if it was to be made by an English noble.'

Andrew Edward gazed at Sir Nigel in silence for a long time, before slowly nodding his head.

The finer details were decided quickly and, less than two days later, John Edward and his men watched from the Raploch Wood as Sir

Nigel rode his horse towards the gates of Stirling Castle.

Sir Nigel remembered the castle layout from the Earl of Surrey's council of war the night before the English defeat at the Battle of Stirling and made his way quickly towards the great hall. He groaned inwardly when he found the hall busy with petitioners waiting in line for their petty grievances to be heard. A great table stood on the dais at the far end of the hall and Sir Nigel recognised the azure and silver stripes of the Earl of Pembroke's flag and what he assumed was King Edward's Dragon Banner. He thought it unlikely that Pembroke would have the patience to listen to the complaints of all those waiting in line and so took action to speed his way to the Earl's table.

He approached the scribe sitting at a rickety desk just inside the doors of the great hall and hefted his bag of gold onto the parchment the man was scratching away at with his quill. A scowl began to form on the scribe's face, but it melted away as the chinking of coins within the bag alerted him to the presence of gold or silver.

Sir Nigel leaned down and spoke to him in a whisper. 'I have gold here for the Earl of Pembroke. If I can present myself before him without delay, you shall have gold of your own.' He lay his fist upon the table and let the man see the three coins in his palm.

The scribe's eyes grew wide at the prospect of more gold than he could earn in two years of scratching and he leapt from his chair. 'I will take you to him immediately.'

Sir Nigel slipped the coins into his hot and sweaty hand and followed him towards the dais. The scribe scuttled behind the Earl's chair and whispered in Pembroke's ear while Sir Nigel stood before the table. Pembroke's gaze rested fleetingly on Sir Nigel, before dropping to the heavy bag at his side. Pembroke's appetite for gold was no less than that of any other noble and he waved Sir Nigel forward with one hand, whilst simultaneously waving away the unfortunate and less lucrative petitioner he had been engaged with prior to this welcome interruption.

'You have urgent business for me, sir?' Pembroke enquired, his eyes less concerned with Sir Nigel than with assessing the weight of his bag.

'I do, my Lord, and I thank you for your attention. I am Sir Nigel de Thwaite. You might remember my father, Edmund de Thwaite. He served with you in Flanders along with my cousin Hugo. They both speak well of you, my Lord.'

The Earl of Pembroke narrowed his eyes as if in pursuit of an elusive memory. 'Thwaite you say? Edmund? Ah yes! Not much on top!'

Sir Nigel inclined his head. 'That is right, my Lord. My father is quite bald.'

Pembroke broke into a smile. 'You must send my regards to your father.'

'I shall, my Lord.' Thwaite replied as he hefted his bag onto the table. 'I had hoped that you would be able to help me. I campaigned here with the Earl of Surrey and took lands to the north of Perth. I have held them ever since, but, due to the chaos of the Scottish rebellion, I hold no paper title to those lands. Now that the kingdom is under King Edward's authority, I should like to rectify that so my ownership cannot be challenged.'

'Is there any competing claim to the land?' Pembroke demanded, his eyes once again set on the Scotstoun gold.

'There is no competing English claim to the land, my Lord. And none from any Scottish noble loyal to King Edward.'

Pembroke grinned. 'Then tis an easy matter. Have my man here draw up the particulars and I will set my seal upon it.'

'Thank you, my Lord.' Thwaite replied, pushing the bag across the table. 'I hope that this will be sufficient to cover any costs of administration.'

Pembroke grasped the bag by its neck and hefted its satisfying weight. 'Quite sufficient, Sir Nigel. Now you must join me for lunch while the document is drawn up. I will not have Sir Edmund say that I sent his son away with an empty belly.'

Pembroke led the way from the hall into an antechamber where a table had been laid with cold meats, cheese, and bread. 'I apologise for the plain fayre, Sir Nigel. I travel without baggage or servants and so cannot entertain as lavishly as I would like.'

Nigel's eyes were drawn to a man already at the table with a full platter before him. His fair and curly hair, slim figure and fine features were familiar to him, but he could not recall precisely where they had met. He rose at their approach and greeted Pembroke with familiarity.

'Allow me to make the introductions.' Pembroke boomed jovially. 'Sir Nigel Thwaite, this is Sir Tarquil de Trasque. He is a close confidante of the Prince of Wales and is here to keep an eye on me.'

Tarquil tittered at Pembroke's teasing and offered Nigel his hand. 'It is complete nonsense of course. Prince Edward would trust Aymer with his life. I am here merely as an advisor, given my long experience of Scottish affairs.'

'I am surprised that you two do not know one another.' Pembroke said, as he heaped meat onto his platter. 'You were both here before the battle on the far side of the Forth, were you not?'

Tarquil unconsciously reached up to touch the livid scar which stood out against the otherwise flawless, pale skin of his forehead. 'I did think that you looked familiar, Sir Nigel. Were you here with the Earl of Surrey?'

'I was, Sir Tarquil. I was fortunate enough to escape with my life.'

Tarquil crossed himself and shivered at the memory. ''Twas a terrible slaughter, Sir Nigel. I count myself lucky to have come away with only this scar upon my head.'

'You must tell us how you survived the massacre, Sir Nigel.' Pembroke said through a mouth filled with half-chewed beef. 'I am sure that you must have quite a tale to tell.'

Sir Nigel told his tale as his companions filled their bellies. Some parts of it were true, but most were invented on the spot. He did not tell them how his horse had bolted and, with him clinging on for dear life, had galloped across the field, clean through the Scottish lines and off into the countryside. Neither did he mention that his nervous mount's premature charge had destroyed the discipline of Cressingham's heavy horse and sent them out in in a ragged formation that was broken on the Scottish spears. Despite these omissions, his companions enjoyed his story and plied him with wine and ale to reward him for his entertainment. He had almost cleared his plate when the scribe quietly entered the chamber and placed a parchment, his seal and a pot of melted wax before the Earl of Pembroke.

Pembroke read the agreement over and then sealed it with a smile. 'You might want to hurry home, Sir Nigel. I have already sent a force north to Perth with instructions to hunt for Robert Bruce and to lay waste to any settlement not in loyal hands. This Scotstoun is not far from Perth and I would not like to think that it might be attacked in your absence.'

Neither Pembroke or Tarquil seemed to notice that Sir Nigel paled visibly at the Earl's words. Neither did they find it odd when he quickly made his excuses and left them to their business.

Pembroke broke out into laughter when the door had closed upon his back. 'Christ! It would be a pity if the King's Knight was to beat him to his village. He has paid five times more than it is worth and may arrive to find that he is left with nothing more than ashes.'

'I am sure that you would return his gold to him if that was to be the case.' Tarquil retorted, before both men roared in appreciation of his wit.

7

The young scout emerged from the undergrowth and trotted to Rank's side. He had brought the boy north with him partly because of his tracking and scouting skills and partly because his father was steward on his manor in the south and he felt sure that the man would be less tempted to cheat him of any of his revenues while the boy was in his clutches. Though no more than ten or eleven years old, he was the best scout Rank had ever encountered. He nodded to give the boy permission to speak.

'They have let the track become overgrown, but the village is there, just as you described it.'

'You saw the muddy square with hovels on each side?'

'I did, m'Lord. And there is a well on the far side of the square.'

'Any horses?'

'Only four.'

Rank dismissed the boy with a flick of his head and turned to his captain. 'The last time I was here, the place was crawling with traitors. It seems that the menfolk are away, so we should have an easy time of it.'

The man did not meet his gaze and stared off into the distance. 'The men don't like it, m'Lord. Look there on the trees. Them's witches' marks. We'll be cursed if we don't heed them.'

Rank cleared his throat and spat a huge gob of phlegm onto the ground. 'That's shit! You think we should turn around and go back to Perth just because some scrawny, demented, old whore has made some scratchings on a tree? If that's really what you're suggesting, I'll cut your balls off here and now.'

'I don't know why we're here in the first place. The Earl ordered us north to hunt the Bruce, but you've got us raiding some shithole village.'

'Like I said, I have unfinished business here. I was chased off the last time I came. I don't like to be chased. I was interrupted while I was raping a haughty, French bitch. I like to finish what I start. That same bitch stuck a knife in me and lived to tell the tale. No one else has ever laid a hand upon me without paying for it with their life.' Rank again leaned over and spat thickly onto the ground. 'And a man with one arm threatened me and he also lived to see another dawn. By my reckoning, that's four good reasons for being here.'

The captain's sour expression suggested that he had not been persuaded by his master's words.

'You know, you remind me of myself when I was younger. I was a real cunt back then. Just remember that there's only room for one cunt here and that cunt's me. Got it?'

Rank's tone clearly communicated that his patience was growing thin and his captain quickly nodded his agreement. 'Got it.'

'Good! Now let's get on with this. Same as always. Get everyone in the square, find their valuables, burn their hovels and then slaughter every last, man, woman, child and beast. Go!'

The winding track had become overgrown, but the horses were able to push through the foliage and overhanging branches. More difficult to navigate were the rocks and tree trunks which had been dragged across the path and the great thorn bushes which completely blocked the lower part of the track. Rank ordered his men to dismount and hack their way through. He cursed as he realised that the din of their approach would have given the villagers the time to run into the forest and hide. He did not particularly relish the prospect of hunting them down one by one, but he had the hounds for the job and would do it if he had to. When he emerged into the square, he was surprised to find that it was not empty as he had expected. The villagers filled the farthest third of the square and faced the Englishman as he led his horsemen to a halt at its centre.

Rank calmly examined the crowd just as they nervously assessed the threat posed by him and his men. He could see some fear there, but there was defiance too. A smile crept onto his face as he recalled what had become of all the defiant peasants who had faced him as he progressed north leaving a trail of destruction and slaughter in his wake. He found himself salivating at the prospect of turning the facial expressions before him from contempt to terror, agony and despair. His smile broadened when he recognised the man at the front and centre of the crowd of villagers. His face was more lined and his hair greyer, but there was no mistaking the arm that hung uselessly at his side. This was the bastard who had ordered him away the first time he had come to Scotstoun. He decided that he would kill him last of all. He briefly flirted with the idea of leaving him alive with only his useless arm intact, but quickly decided that he would burn him instead. He then caught sight of the woman who had stabbed him. He had thought of her every time he had looked at the scar on his ribs. Time had not been kind to her and, although she still had that haughty look that had so enticed him all those years before, she had sagged and wrinkled enough to dull his interest. Nevertheless, he would still rape her, as honour demanded that he take what had been refused to him before. He thought that he might choke her as he rode her to sweeten the experience and so that her final spasms would bring him to his finish.

He was aware of his captain speaking to him, but he did not catch his words as his gaze had alighted on another face and the sight of it caused his blood to run cold. He blinked and narrowed his eyes the better to examine the face that stared back at him. Though battered and scarred, there was no doubt that a corpse stood blinking before him in the weak afternoon sunlight. He was only certain when he saw fear reflected in those eyes.

Tom Figgins had been his commanding officer back at the start of the war in Scotland and he had developed a deep and lasting hatred for the man. He had brutalised and tortured him only to be cruelly denied the pleasure of killing him. Figgins had been sent to Stirling to be hanged for desertion and Rank had always assumed that he had died at the end of another man's noose. The sight of him here today sent a pulse of white-hot fury through his very core.

He kicked at his horse and roared at the top of his lungs. 'Figgus!'

Tom Figgins turned pale at the sound of this old taunt and turned and ran for his life. Rank kicked his horse on into the crowd of villagers and, as it was trained to do, it kicked and bit viciously to clear a path for its master. The English horsemen followed their leader through the scattered villagers and out into the forest beyond. Only Tom's intimate knowledge of the woodland around the village enabled him to stay ahead of his pursuers. He headed first for the thickest part of the forest, as he knew that they would be forced to abandon their horses and continue the pursuit on foot. This, he was certain, would enable him to make good his escape. He was forced to revisit this assumption when the howling of hounds reached his ears. His rising panic threatened to overcome him and he had to draw in deep breaths in a bid to control his fear. With the hounds drawing ever closer, he decided that his only hope was to head for the cliffs at the centre of the forest. Fear of falling to his death on the ragged rocks at their bottom had always prevented him from climbing the cliffs, but his fear of capture, torture and death was much greater and it drove him onwards.

His fingernails were torn and bloody by the time he had climbed to the height of three men and, from that point onwards, the hand and footholds were few and far between and his progress slowed. He tried to ignore the baying of the fast-approaching hounds and concentrated only on pulling himself further up the cliff-face. A loose piece of rock broke off under his weight and left him hanging by one hand with his heart pounding in his throat and only his frantic and desperate scrambling saved him from plummeting to his death. Sweat ran down his forehead and stung his eyes, but with no free hand to wipe his face, he could only blink to clear his blurred vision. He pulled himself gratefully onto a pitifully narrow ledge and clung onto it with what little strength he had left. Only then was he able to rub at his stinging eyes with his sleeve. He cleared his vision just in time to see the hounds arrive beneath him.

The slog through the forest had done nothing to improve Rank's temper and he growled up at the prone figure of Tom Figgins high above him. 'Cut him down!' He ordered tersely.

It quickly became apparent that his men's hunting bows were inadequate for the task. The arrows clattered against the rocks around Tom Figgins, but they had little power behind them by the time they reached that height and they neither harmed nor dislodged him.

'I need a man to climb up there and knock that bastard down.' Rank growled. 'A purse of gold for the first to reach him.'

The cliff was steep and its surface treacherously smooth and not one man stepped forward to claim the gold. Rank glared angrily at his men and they, in turn, studiously avoided his gaze. Some kept their eyes fixed on the trembling figure of Tom Figgins high above them, others busied themselves with retrieving their arrows and the rest developed a fascination with the ground at their feet.

'I'll do it!' The boy offered, his hairless chin jutting out in defiance.

Rank looked down at his slight figure and shook his head. 'Is there no man here with courage enough to knock the bastard down? Will you leave a boy to do your work for you?'

He let the silence drag on for a moment, before grunting in disgust and turning back to the boy. 'How would you do it?'

The boy pointed up at the cliff. 'I'll climb up around him and then come at him from above. Once I'm close enough, I'll kick down at him. Look! He's shaking and is too scared to move. He'll fall with the slightest of taps.'

Rank nodded brusquely and the lad scampered to the base of the cliff and began to pull himself upwards. His little fingers and toes made deft use of every tiny crack and fissure and he was soon high above the forest floor. The eyes of every Englishman stayed fixed on the slight figure as he climbed past Tom Figgins to his left and then edged sideways to position himself above his quarry. The boy then turned his head and peered into the distance.

'Horsemen!' He yelled, his voice thin and high-pitched.

'How many?' Rank demanded.

'More than us. They are coming from the direction of Perth and will soon reach the village.'

'Do you see the pennants of the Earl of Pembroke?'

The boy was silent and screwed his eyes up in order to better focus on the approaching horsemen. 'No pennants or flags. The horses are smaller than ours.'

Rank cursed furiously. 'The menfolk return in force. We must be away! Be quick! Kick the bastard down!'

The boy was nimble and seemed to slide rather than climb down towards the cowering Tom Figgins. His first kick was tentative and did no more than thump Tom's shoulder and cause him to cling more tightly to the ledge with every sinew in his body. The second kick was harder and Tom's terrified moan caused the men below to smile up at him in anticipation. His third kick was too slow and deliberate. Tom saw the foot coming and flayed wildly at it with his right hand, his fingers leaving the rock only for a panicked second, before clamping back onto the surface of the cliff.

The boy seemed to hang in the air for a moment before plummeting down towards the rocky ground, the frenzied flapping of his arms doing nothing to slow his descent. Rank had to step back sharply to avoid being hit. He then stared down at the boy's broken body with an uncharacteristic sadness in his eyes.

'I'll be needing a new scout, I suppose.' He stated flatly.

'We need to go!' His captain exclaimed from his side. 'I can hear the horsemen.'

Rank nodded his acknowledgement. 'Leave the boy! There's no time to take him.'

John Edward sighed heavily in relief when he caught sight of the tops of Scotstoun's roofs through the trees. They had ridden hard from Stirling with their hearts in their mouths for fear of returning home to find the village destroyed. He could not recall how many settlements he had seen reduced to smoking ashes these past few years and he thanked God that Scotstoun had not suffered that same fate. His joy died the moment he led his men into the square and found it all in chaos. He was quickly surrounded by panicked villagers, all attempting to tell him of the English attack. Bombarded with too many frenzied accounts all at once, he shouted them to silence and bade one of the Cumming girls to tell him what had occurred. Though visibly alarmed and shaken, the Cumming girl wasted no words in telling John what had happened. He only needed to ask her a few questions to know how best to deploy his men. He ordered Eck to lead half of the force to the road to cut the English off and he instructed the rest to follow him into the forest in pursuit.

He turned to cross the square and found his path blocked by his mother. He was so intent on hunting down the Englishmen that he did not immediately notice that she was drawn and ashen, her eyes fat with tears.

'You must come, John. Let Scott lead the men.' Her voice was firm, her accent unmistakably Scots, but tinged with the French of her youth.

John grasped her shouldered and tried to gently ease her aside. 'Later, Maw. I'll come to you once we have cleared the forest.'

Isobelle Edward did not move and grasped her eldest son's upper arm. 'Come now, John! You must come now!' She then locked eyes with her younger son and nodded her head in the direction of the forest. Scott Edward's heart lurched at the terrible intensity of his mother's gaze. He simply nodded in reply and led the men out of the square at the run.

John was confused and a little angered by his mother's behaviour as she pulled him through the crowd of villagers at the edge of the square. His irritation and his questions died in his throat as the villagers parted to let him through as, when each of them turned to gaze at him, their faces were deathly pale and full of pity. His heart seized in his chest as the last of them moved aside and he saw his Lorna lying in the mud, her face unnaturally white and her lips blue. Her mother kneeled in the dirt at her side with silent tears streaming down her face.

He shook his head in disbelief. 'What happened?' He stammered. 'What happened here?'

Andrew Edward came to his son's side, concern etched into every inch of his face. 'The Englishman rode into the crowd, John. He trampled her to the ground and crushed her ribs.'

John dropped to his knees and cupped his Lorna's face in his hands. Her breath was coming in short pants and tiny spots of blood dotted her lips. Though his face was almost touching hers, her eyes were sightless.'

'Can you no' do anything for her?' He demanded.

Esmy's despair matched his own as she shook her head. 'She's all broken inside, John. Even I can do nothing for her.'

Tears welled up in John's eyes and fell to the ground in fat droplets. 'Can you no' just try? Will you no' just try?' He begged in desperation.

Esmy sobbed softly and had to take several deep breaths to steady herself. 'If I try, I'll only hurt her more. I'm no' going to hurt her more. I'm going to sit here and comfort until she goes.'

'She's going nowhere!' John snapped, rubbing his tears angrily away. 'She's stayin' here with me.' He leaned close to her and tried to force a smile onto his lips and a lightness into his wavering voice. 'Hi now bonnie girl, what's happened to my lovely lassie, what's happened to my beautiful girl? You're alright, you're alright. Everything's going to be fine. I'll look after you.' He stroked her hair and cheeks as he spoke and fought with all his might against the hysteria growing in his breast. 'I'm here now, I'm here now.'

She spoke so softly, he almost missed it. 'John.' She gasped. 'Is it you?'

'It is, my love. I am here now. It's going to be alright. Your mother's here too. It'll all be fine. I promise you.'

A single tear ran slowly down her cheek and she smiled weakly. 'I am glad that it is you. I am glad that you are here, my love.

'And where else would I be, but by your side?' He replied, with tears again flowing from his eyes. 'Now, we must carry you inside so you can get better.'

Another tear ran down her cheek and she reached weakly for her husband's hand. 'I'm dying John. Let me lie here. Just stay with me.'

'Hush now, my lovely! Nobody's dying here. I'll not allow it.'

She squeezed his hand with what little strength she had left and tears now streamed from her eyes. 'I'm all broken inside, John. I can feel it. My breath grows shorter and my strength is going. It will not be long now.'

'No! No! No! You cannot go. You must stay here with me. I've had so little time with you. I'm no' near ready yet.'

'I cannot stop it, my love, though I sorely wish I could. I thought that we would grow old and grey together and it breaks my heart that we will not.' A shiver ran through her body and she grimaced with pain. 'Do not leave me, John. I am frightened now and would not die alone.'

John shook his head and fought to choke back the sobs which shuddered through him. 'You will not die alone, my dear. As you draw your last breath, I will cut open my own veins and we will ascend to Heaven together. I want no part of a world that does not have you in it.'

Lorna's small fingers grasped tightly at her husband's hand. 'You cannot! You must stay to protect our children, I would not have them left alone. Promise me, John! You must promise!'

'I promise you, my bonnie lass. Though I will count the days until I can be with you again. Each one will be an agony and I will wish them all quickly away.'

Lorna's grip now loosened and a sickly smile came to her quivering lips. 'It will not be long, my love. It will seem like mere moments until we two are reunited. Tell our children about me. Do not let them forget me.'

John smiled back at her through his own veil of tears. 'I promise, my love. I will speak of you each and every day. They will know that their mother was beautiful, that she loved them more than the earth and sea and that I loved you more than any man has ever loved a woman.'

But Lorna was already gone. That last smile remained upon her lips and the pain and suffering of her last moments had been lifted. John kissed her gently upon the lips and rose shakily to his feet.

'I will bury her down by the loch. In the place she was happiest.' His shoulders were slumped forward and his eyes cast down upon the ground.

'Will you put her in the dress she wore when we were married? I will go now and dig her grave.'

Isobelle Edward nodded as she wiped the tears from her cheeks. 'Aye, John. Her mother and I will wash her and dress her right. There is no need for you to dig her grave. The men here will do it gladly.' She reached out and clasped her son's shoulder, only to have him violently shrug her hand away.

He stared at her with eyes filled with misery, desperation and desolation and shuddered as though he struggled to stay in control of himself. 'Do not be kind to me, Mother! For I will break if you do. I am half mad with grief and my sanity hangs by a thread. If it falls and shatters, I do not think it could be repaired.' He turned on his heel and walked off towards the loch.

Andrew Edward put his arm around his wife's shoulders. 'Leave him to dig the grave. It is the last thing he can do for her.'

Isobelle sobbed as she watched her son's retreating back. 'Oh Andrew, it breaks my heart to see him so when I can do nothing for him.'

'He must find his own way to heal and, painful though it is, we must leave him to it.'

John dug like a man possessed. Sometimes he sobbed, but mostly he attacked the earth with furious anger and frustration. By the time the sun began to set, he had removed the thick and heavy surface clay and pulled out rocks and stones enough for a shallow grave. By the time the moon rose high in the sky, he was exhausted, sweaty and filthy from head to foot and his fingernails were torn and bloody from pulling rocks from the earth. Only when he fell to the ground did the village men approach with their flaming torches and set silently about their task. Every man in the village took his turn as the excavations continued throughout the night. By the time the sun touched the horizon's edge, Lorna Edward's grave was as deep as the last resting place of any queen and had been painstakingly and lovingly lined with stone.

John stayed at the graveside long after the service was concluded and the menfolk had filled the grave in and gone off to the wake. Eck, Scott, Al, the Robertson and Strathbogie came and stood beside him without speaking. Eck pressed a skin of ale into his hands and they stood together and drained the ale whilst staring out across the surface of the loch.

'What now?' John asked, his voice flat and listless.

'First we drink.' Eck replied. 'We drink a lot.'

'What then?'

'Then we hunt down the bastard who did this and we kill him. We kill him long and we kill him slow.'

John nodded slowly. 'How will we know him?'

'We know him, John. He has been here before. He is the pock-marked whoreson who slaughtered the Steward in the square. He is the one who despoiled my Ailith when she was just a girl. He's the cunt who attacked your mother at her own hearth.'

'I must be the one to end him, Eck. You must give me that.'

Eck dropped his eyes to the fresh earth on Lorna's grave and nodded. 'I will give you that. You can finish him. I will only take a thousand cuts and then leave him to you. I will need his head though. I have promised it to Ailith.'

John turned to face his cousin and looked directly into his eyes. 'Will it kill the pain, Eck? My heart is breaking and I feel that I cannot stand it. Where once my heart was light, all is darkness now. Will it take the hurt away?'

'Aye.' Eck replied. 'For a while. For a wee while.'

'And then?'

'And then we scour the land and clear it of every last bastard Englishman, so that their presence does not infect and pollute the good, Scots earth that Lorna is now buried in. We'll cleanse the kingdom of their filth and send them all to Hell. The doing of it will not bring her back, but I promise you that the righteous slaughter will soothe our souls awhile. We can ask no more than that.'

John returned his gaze to the far horizon and nodded slowly. 'I want only to be reunited with her, but I must wait if I am to keep my promise. If English blood will soothe my soul while I wait, I will bathe myself in rivers of the stuff.'

Eck laid his hand upon his cousin's shoulder. 'The darkness lifts when swords fly, John. I can tell you that. It will be just enough to keep you from madness and despair. But first we drink. We drink a lot!'

8

The French Templars stood apart from the Scotstoun men and watched them go about their work. Three weeks had passed since boredom had driven them to accept the Scotsmen's invitation to accompany them on their campaign against the invading English. Prior Abernethy had warned them that they should not be drawn into the struggle, but they had all agreed that not one of them could stand the tedium of spending another week in the village. They were used to the hard, physical labour, but missed the constant hustle and bustle of Paris.

Jacques Flammier's bushy, black beard stretched from high on his cheeks down almost to his belly. Although only his eyes were visible, it was clear that his facial expression was surly and sour. 'This is shit!' He complained in his native French. 'Abernethy said that these men were soldiers, but they are little more than animals. Look! They torture that messenger though it is obvious to any idiot that he has given up his secrets. They now torment him only for their savage pleasure.'

'And why do they hang the corpses of the escort from the trees? Do they not know that they cannot be killed again?' Geffroi Barreau shivered as he spoke, though it was hard to tell whether it was from revulsion at the macabre scene before him or from the damp, cold air.

'I think the shitty weather has driven them all mad.' Guillame Albinet stated, with an emphatic nod of his head. 'Their leaders are suicidal. Did you see those two charge down the hill? The dark one with two swords and the miserable one with the limp? It is a wonder that the archers did not cut them down. They have the luck of the Devil.'

Jacques Flammier nodded his agreement. 'No sane man would charge in without a shield.' He then pointed to the group of men hoisting a naked and bloody corpse into a tree by its neck. 'I can make out little of what they say, for they speak some kind of strangled, mongrel English, but it seems that they expect an English army to march this way and they mean to use the murdered bodies of their countrymen to warn them off.'

Albinet let out a short and bitter laugh. 'Once they are done with their ropes, we will no doubt be made to run and hide in the forest again like common brigands. There is no honour here. Prior Abernethy has abandoned us to cowards!'

Barreau hushed his companion. 'Look out! The miserable one is coming.'

'Do not piss yourself, Geffroi. These ignorant savages cannot understand our tongue. Just smile and nod and he will go off and leave us be.'

John Edward came to a halt before them, his face expressionless. The Templars' eyes grew wide in astonishment when he addressed them in perfect French. 'An English army marches here and will arrive before too much longer. I have no doubt that brave and noble knights such as yourselves will want to stay and face them, but should your courage fail you, please feel free to flee into the forest along with us ignorant savages.' He then turned without another word and ordered his men to leave.

'Well done!' Barreau spat, as he and the other fugitive Templars followed the Scotstoun men into the Forest of Perth. 'Now they will come to cut our throats while we sleep!'

Robert Bruce drew his men up within sight of the walls of Perth and awaited the arrival of his scouts. The months since his coronation had been both hard and frustrating. The recruitment of men had been much more difficult than he had anticipated, as many of the nobles of Scotland were reluctant to break peace with Edward Plantagenet while the odds were stacked so heavily against the self-proclaimed King of Scots. Coercion, persuasion, bribery and reliance on old loyalties had brought only one hundred mounted, noble knights to his side and, with them, near four and a half thousand foot. His intention had been to use them to defeat the Comyns and their allies to remove the enemy from his back and so enable him to then turn and

101

face the English. The speed and brutality of Aymer de Valence's progress into the heart of Scotland had necessitated a change to those plans.

Edward de Bruce sat mounted at his brother's side. 'I see the Earl of Pembroke's colours upon the walls.' He pointed to the left of the gate and his brother nodded when he spotted them.

'If I am not mistaken, King Edward's Dragon Banner hangs to the right of the gate.'

Edward laughed heartily. 'If Pembroke does come out to play, we will wipe our feet upon those banners and feast in Perth before this day is done.'

'Ah!' Robert Bruce exclaimed. 'Here are our scouts now!'

Edward watched the horsemen approach and shook his head. 'They're not ours. If I am not mistaken, that's John Edward and his captains.'

A look of disgust crossed King Robert's face and he grunted dismissively.

'Do not be so quick to dismiss them, my brother. Though our forces have grown, we are not yet strong enough to be able to turn good men away. Be civil and you just might have another two hundred battle-hardened warriors at your back.'

The scowl on Robert Bruce's face softened slightly, but it did not altogether disappear. 'John Edward.' He said, in cold greeting. 'I did not think to see you here.'

John inclined his head and nodded a greeting to Edward Bruce. 'I have been here since we last met and have harried the English wherever we have been able.'

'Good for you.' Robert replied dryly. 'I have not come to ambush wagons and unwary travellers. I have come to give battle to the Earl of Pembroke. I was just about to ride up to the gates of Perth and invite him to either give up the city or come out and face us. I mean to finish him here.'

'You intend to meet him here in open battle?' John asked in surprise. 'He outnumbers you by almost two to one.'

Robert Bruce snorted dismissively. 'If you use your eyes you will see that I have near five thousand men upon the field. Pembroke rode across the border with barely three thousand men. My spies counted them as they left Carlisle.'

'That is true, m'Lord.' John replied. 'But he has spent weeks in Stirling urging the Scottish nobles still loyal to his king to join with him. My scouts counted them as they marched along the road to Perth. He has near six thousand foot and his horse outnumber yours by more than ten to one. I would counsel you against facing him in open battle.'

King Robert's cheeks reddened with anger. 'Am I to take another lesson from a commoner who has no grasp of the codes of chivalry? A king does not win battles by skulking in the hills. A king must be victorious upon the field if he is to keep his crown.'

'You are right, m'Lord. I know nothing of crowns, but I do know that a defeat is a defeat, no matter how honourably it is arrived at. I stood on the field at Courtrai with Robert of Artois before the battle there and gave him the same counsel as I give you now. Like you, he dismissed my advice and chose the way of chivalry. He was an honourable and courageous man, but at battle's end he lay dead upon the field along with half the nobles of France just the same.'

'Look behind me!' Robert Bruce snapped. 'How many nobles do you see? A handful! Do you think that they will stay with me if I run now? Do you think that other nobles will rally to my standard if I scurry away like a frightened peasant? If you do not wish to join us, then begone and let us be about our business. Go back to your wagons and your messengers!'

King Robert then signalled to his retainers and they rode off towards the gates of Perth. When they had covered almost half that distance, he turned to his brother.

'I cannot believe that a man like that was at Courtrai giving counsel to a French noble. He surely lies.'

'It is true enough, Robert.' Edward replied. 'Bishop Lamberton told me that the French King sent John Edward to Count Robert to counsel him before the battle.'

Robert's face twisted in disbelief, but his brother spoke before he could form a retort. 'Ah! Here comes the Earl of Pembroke. Let us hope that his mood is as foul as yours, for then we shall surely have a battle.'

It was soon clear that the Earl of Pembroke was in the finest of spirits and was pleased to see his fellow nobles.

'King Robert!' He boomed in greeting. 'Together at last. I was starting to think that you were avoiding me. Every time I arrive in a place, it seems that you have only just left it. Most unfortunate! Since your hurried flight from Westminster last year, it would seem that you have developed a taste for the hasty retreat.'

The Scottish King took the Earl's ribbing in good humour. He had spent time with him at court and both liked and respected the man. 'I find that I have grown tired of running and will rest my army here. I do not recall inviting you into my realm and must now insist that you either leave this city or come out to face me in battle.'

Pembroke held his hands up in apology. 'It is far too late in the day, my Lord. It would be dusk before my men were in formation and I do so hate to fight in the dark.'

King Robert nodded his agreement. 'It is better that we engage while it is light. What say you to meeting on this field when the sun is at its highest on the morrow?'

'That would be splendid, my Lord.' King Robert had begun to turn his horse when Pembroke slapped his forehead with the palm of his hand. 'I almost forgot! Your friends asked that I give you their regards.'

'My friends?' The Bruce responded.

'Yes, my Lord. The Bishops who placed that crown upon your head proved far less elusive than your good self. The Bishop of Glasgow was captured at Cupar Castle. The old boy had thrown off his robes and donned armour to seize it from its English garrison.' Pembroke shook his head in admiration. 'We chanced upon the Bishop of St Andrews nearby in Kinross, where he was urging the peasantry to take up arms in your name.'

It was a painful blow to the King of Scots, but he attempted to feign indifference. 'I have other Bishops.' He said, with a shrug of his shoulders.

Pembroke's grin spread wider across his face. 'I hear different, my Lord. I hear that you are left with only the Bishop of Moray and he is pursued night and day by the men of the Earl of Buchan. The Earl seems to be quite cross with you for the murder of his cousin and with the Bishop for supporting the perpetrator of such an act of sacrilege. I doubt that he will remain at liberty for long.'

King Robert turned his horse without another word and crossed the field towards his troops.

Pembroke rode back through the city gates and then climbed the wall to watch the Scottish army turn and march away.

Rank stood at his side and tried to prise a scrap of gristle from between two of his blackened molars with a ragged and dirty fingernail. 'Even though we outnumber them, it'll still be a bloody business. When their commanders can stop them from running, these Scots fight like devils.'

'There will be no battle, my friend. My scouts will shadow them and locate their camp and we'll march through the night so we can fall on them at dawn.'

Rank grinned with delight. 'So much for chivalry.'

'The stakes are too high for chivalry, my friend. If I defeat Robert Bruce and deliver him to King Edward, he will shower me with honours, lands and gold. If I lose to him, the King will shower me with shit and ram my head onto a spike.'

'We'll slaughter them in their beds!'

'I care not where they die, so long as we finish them.'

The Scotstoun men had ridden away from Perth for around an hour before positioning themselves across the road to Stirling. They lit fires, cooked whatever game they could catch and then settled down upon the hard ground wrapped in their cloaks. Though discomfort and anxiety about what the day would bring kept many from their slumber, the stillness of the night was soon filled with the snoring and snorting of fighting men. John Edward could seldom sleep the night before a battle and he was still sat staring into a crackling camp fire when the witching hour had passed and the night had reached its darkest point. He kept his eyes fixed upon the glowing embers when Jacques Flammier approached and sat down at his side.

'You will fight with the Scottish King tomorrow?' The Frenchman asked.

'No.' John replied.

Flammier nodded and stroked his long beard. 'We thought that you would. We thought that your hatred for the English would compel you to join with him.'

John turned and looked at him for a moment, before returning his gaze to the fire. 'I find it best to stay away from ambitious nobles, for their ambition is seldom matched by their wisdom. The last time an ambitious noble persuaded me to join with him in battle against the English, near ten thousand of my countrymen were slaughtered. The flesh had barely rotted from their bones when that noble crawled before the English King and begged for his forgiveness. The King admonished him most fiercely before restoring his land and titles to him. He defied his King and lost nothing. The bones of the peasants still lay scattered across that field. I put my faith in an ambitious noble and put my men in harm's way. I am in no hurry to make the same mistake again.'

'So, you will do nothing?' Flammier asked, disdain clear in his tone.

'We will wait here. If the Bruce prevails, the remnants of the English force will flee towards us and we will cut them down. If Pembroke is victorious, his cavalry will pursue what is left of Bruce's army and we will do what we can to impede that pursuit so that our countrymen can escape. Never fear, you will have action enough tomorrow, no matter which way the battle goes.'

John could not tell if the young man smiled, for his lips were hidden beneath his thick beard, but the glint in his eyes confirmed that the news was welcome. The Frenchman seemed about to respond, but was cut short by the thundering gallop of a fast-approaching horse. John leapt to his feet and raised his arm in greeting to the leader of his scouts.

'Trouble?' He enquired urgently, though he already knew the answer. The expression of concern on Al's face told him that he brought no glad tidings.

'The English move on Bruce's camp at Methven. Their main force marches from the east and two hundred horse circle around the camp to the west.'

'They seek to take him by surprise, but they will encounter his pickets and the alarm will be raised.'

Al shook his head and used his sleeve to wipe the sweat from his eyes. 'The Bruce set no pickets. The only scouts creeping through the darkness are English ones.' The blood on Al's dagger and tunic suggested that not every English scout would be returning safely to the main body of the English force.

John cursed. 'Damn the Bruce and his noble honour! He has relied on the word of his fellow noble and so has led his men to ruin. He will be overrun and his men will be slaughtered!'

Al nodded his agreement. 'The smaller force now encircling his encampment must be intended to cut off any who try to flee. It will be a bloodbath.'

'Can you lead us to the west of the camp so that we can come up behind this encircling force?'

'Aye!' Al replied simply. John would have trusted no other man to find his way through the forest hills in the treacherous darkness. Experience had taught him that this shy and slightly stooped figure could navigate through the harshest of terrain when other men would be quickly lost and left blundering around in the dark.

'Send your fastest man to warn the Bruce! I doubt that the disaster can be averted, but even a few moments may allow them to don their armour and so lessen its severity. I will rouse the men!'

Rank had been on the verge of strangling the useless scout when his eye alighted on a distant, flickering flame. He brought the column to a halt and peered into the impenetrable darkness. By moving his head slowly from side to side he was able to determine that the flickering came from a group of fires rather from a single one. They had not veered as far from their intended course as he had feared. The Bruce's camp lay at the foot of the long slope before them. He craned his neck to examine the horizon and smiled grimly to find that no light yet showed at its edges. There was still sufficient time to move closer to their quarry and then spread his men out across the hill. He would have preferred to be charging into the encampment with the main force to enjoy the panic as the hapless Scots tried to rally before collapsing and fleeing in panicked disarray. He could not blame the Earl of Pembroke for reserving that pleasure for himself. He would have to satisfy himself with cutting down those who survived the onslaught and tried to escape with their lives. He relished the thought of seeing the horror on their faces when they realised that their way was blocked and that all hope was lost.

He turned to the quivering scout at his side and watched him quail beneath his glare. 'You brought us too far, you useless shit! We should be further down this slope. Now go quickly and find an area where the trees are thinner, so we can spread out the better to catch them all. Be quick about it or I'll snap your scrawny neck!'

The scout kicked his heels and immediately rode his little horse out into the darkness.

Rank then turned to his captain, his silhouette barely visible in the murk. 'We will advance slowly and with care. If any man makes a noise which alerts the Scots to our presence, he will answer to me when the slaughter is done. Understood?'

'Understood, m'Lord.' The captain replied, before passing the order along the line in an urgent whisper.

The English line crawled down the slope one careful step at a time. They had covered one quarter of the distance when the first light touched the very edge of the horizon. The sound of raised voices travelled through the darkness and Rank cocked his head to listen.

'The Earl attacks!' The captain exclaimed.

Rank cursed. 'No! The horn was to be sounded to signal the charge. Pembroke's approach has been detected. The Scots run to arm themselves!' Even as he spoke the flickering fires in the Scots' camp dimmed and disappeared.

'They douse their fires!' The Captain exclaimed. 'They mean to impede Pembroke by denying him the light of their fires to guide him through the gloom.'

'Then let us disrupt their efforts to repel the Earl. If we bang our swords against our shields the Scots will think that they are attacked from all sides. Their hurried preparations will turn to chaos and Pembroke will trample them underfoot.' Three horn blasts then sounded from the far side of the camp and the air was filled with the thunder of hooves and voices roaring to the charge. Rank lifted his shield from where it hung at his back and rattled it with his bludgeon. His men quickly added to the cacophony and banged hard on their shields to sow discord within the Scottish ranks.

Such was the din, not one of the King's Knight's men so much as turned their heads when the Scots horsemen charged down the slope towards their backs. Rank only paused in battering at this shield when he saw his captain jerk forward in his saddle. The sight of the arrow jutting from his neck in a spray of blood was so unexpected that his mouth fell open and he did no more than stare in disbelief. Only his men's dying screams and the clash of metal on metal wrenched him from his confusion and he pulled his horse around to face the onslaught. The first Scot fell upon him so quickly he had no time to swing at him. He blindly jabbed the bludgeon towards the man's throat with insufficient force to do him much harm, but the man's forward momentum drove him hard onto the weapon's end and snapped his neck like a twig. The Englishman took a blow to his shield from the left, but could not risk even the merest of glances in his attacker's direction as another snarling Scot lunged at him with his sword from his right. He parried the strike and then swung at him with all of his might. Even above the din of the battle, he heard the man's arm snap with a terrible crack. With the man unable to so much as lift his sword arm, Rank took the time to land his blow with precision and roared with joy as he caved the poor bastard's head in.

A hurried look along the line told him that the fight was already lost. The Scots had no numerical advantage, but the element of surprise had enabled them to cut down the greater part of the English force before they even realised that they were under attack. He reckoned that three quarters of his men had already fallen and saw that those who still fought were assailed from all sides and would be struck down within a matter of moments. He turned his horse and kicked the beast on across the slope towards the forest the scout had led them through less than an hour before.

The frightened Englishman cowered down beneath his shield and made no move to strike

out with his sword as John Edward rained blow
after blow down upon him. The man was frozen
in terror and could scarcely believe that his
fellows in the King's Knight's column had been
ripped to ruins in moments by the Scots'
surprise attack. The orderly advance of a few
moments ago was now reduced to a few pockets
of desperate and despairing defence. John
hammered his sword down hard in a bid to
dislodge the shield, but looked away as a
movement across the slope caught his eye. The
dawn was strengthening and a shaft of light
illuminated the retreating figure momentarily.
The red shield bearing the symbols of an upright
broadsword resting upon three skulls and three
sets of crossed bones meant nothing to John, but
the man's pock-marked face turned his heart to
ice. The cowering Englishman peered around
the edge of his shield and watched in
astonishment as his attacker turned his horse and
galloped away from him. He raised his head and
cast his eyes around in bewilderment and found
that not one Scots savage looked in his direction.
His heart hammered in his chest and he kicked
at his horse to make good his unexpected escape
from death. His silent prayer of thanks to God
for his deliverance died on his lips when the
arrow pierced his skull and tore into his brain.
His eyes were dead and lifeless before his body
hit the ground.

Rank growled in anger when he sensed the
horseman's approach. A glance over his
shoulder confirmed that only one of the damned
Scots had pursued him and he turned his horse

to face him. The Scot roared as he charged in and Rank threw his shield to the ground and raised his bludgeon high above his head, gripping it firmly in both of his hands. As the howling savage came within range of his weapon, he arced it down viciously with all of his considerable force. When the downward swing connected with a thick tree branch, all of that force shuddered through his arms and seemed certain to rip his shoulders from their sockets. The shock of the impact left him stunned for only a second, but that was time enough for his attacker to thrust his sword blade deep into the side of his chest as he charged past. Rank reeled back in his saddle and blinked furiously as light flashed at the edges of his vision. Though he could see the blood pulsing from the wound, there was no pain, only a sickening numbness.

John dragged his horse to a halt and turned it back towards the big, pock-marked Englishman. His face was contorted in fury and hatred as he spurred the beast onwards, determined to unhorse the bastard so that he could begin the long, slow work of drawing his innards from him. The Englishman was slow to turn and was still sideways on when John leaned forward to make his strike. He saw his opponent heft his mace above his head and he grunted with satisfaction when he saw that the wounded man had misjudged his approach and had unleashed his blow fractionally early. Rank stretched every sinew to breaking point and drove his weapon down into the skull of his attacker's horse with every ounce of might he could muster. The force of the blow jolted his arms painfully, but it felled the horse instantly and sent his attacker crashing into the earth.

Though black spots now danced before his eyes, Rank saw that two more Scots horsemen were crossing the slope towards him. His attacker still lay upon the ground, though he was groaning and making feeble efforts to push himself up. A wave of dizziness and nausea persuaded him that he did not have the strength or the time to dismount and cut the bastard's throat. For the second time that morning, he turned his back on the battle and rode away from danger.

9

As always, it was the peasantry who suffered the worst of it. Pembroke's charge tore through the eastern side of the camp first and his knights scythed down the commoners bivouacked there as they ran for their spears or struggled to pull their boots onto their feet. The Scotstoun messenger had arrived only moments before the English horns were blown and the alarm had been too late to avert the disaster. Those few nobles who had managed to mount their steeds before the English charged in, did so without saddling the beasts or donning their armour. Those who did not fall at the first onslaught, rallied to their King and fought desperately to hack their way out of the trap the Methven camp had become. Many of the English noblemen, including Pembroke himself, would later claim to have unseated the Bruce himself or to have cut his horse out from beneath him. The truth of it was that the battle and the slaughter were conducted in confusion in the murk of dawn and it was the resulting chaos that enabled the Bruce and his most loyal followers to cut their way through their attackers and escape up the slope to the west of the camp. With so many

Englishmen engaged in the slaughter of the Scottish foot, only thirty of their knights charged after them in pursuit of the day's greatest prize.

Eck Edward pulled his cousin to his feet and tried to dust him down. His collision with the earth had left him dazed and winded, but apart from a swollen eye, a scratched and dirty face and a torn tunic, he was relatively unscathed.

'I had the bastard!' He snapped in frustration. 'I could smell his stench I was that close to him.'

Eck retrieved John's sword from where it had landed amongst the moss and stones. 'He might be dead already.' He opined, as he examined the blood smeared along the blade. 'You must have cut him deep.'

John spat and rubbed dirt from his mouth. 'I pray that he is not, for he does not deserve such an easy death.'

'Look!' Eck instructed, pointing down the slope. 'We must be away. The English come for us!'

John shaded his eyes against the rising sun and peered down at the near twenty horsemen galloping up from the foot of the hill. 'It's no' the English.' He snorted. 'It's Robert Bruce fleeing the results of his chivalry.'

'I doubt that he'll get far.' Al interjected from behind them. 'See there! The English are hard at their heels.' They watched as around thirty English knights streamed out of the trees and spurred their horses up the slope after the fleeing Scots.

'Should we help them get away?' Eck asked, his eyes never leaving the two sets of horsemen.

John shrugged ill-naturedly, still furious at losing the pock-marked Englishman and still irked by the Bruce's dismissal of him the previous day. 'He made his own bed, maybe we should let him lie in it.'

Eck was already pulling himself into his saddle. 'Edward Bruce rides at his side. Have you forgotten that he saved our lives when we ourselves ran from the English after the defeat at Falkirk? Our bones would yet moulder in that field at Auchterarder if he had not run down the men from the garrison there.'

John cursed in frustration, but called for a horse even as he did so.

Edward Bruce reined his horse in and turned it across the slope. 'Ride on Robert! I will hold them here a while. Go now! Take yourself away!'

James Douglas, Neil Campbell and Gilbert de la Haye quickly followed his example and turned their mounts.

Robert Bruce turned his head and watched impassively as the English knights closed the distance between them. The blood coating the left side of his head and the gore-soaked blade in his hand were testament to the ferocity and desperation of the fight to escape the camp. 'You know that some call me the Summer King because they think my reign will not last the summer? It seems that they are right. I have already lost my army to treachery. I would rather end it here with true and valiant friends than run a single step further.'

'You must come now, my Lord!' The Earl of Atholl implored him. 'They are too many for us and will surely cut us down.'

'So be it!' King Robert declared, as he hefted his sword. 'It will be enough to know that some of them will not live long enough to see my reign brought to an end.'

James Douglas cried out and pointed along the slope. 'Look! More of them charge down upon us. We are lost! They will sweep us all away!'

Edward Bruce turned his horse to face his pursuers and roared with joyful laughter. 'You are mistaken, my young friend! Those are not English knights who charge down upon us. It would seem that the good Lord has not forsaken us this day. He has sent John Edward and his men as instruments of our salvation. Be quick or they will leave no glory for us.' With that, he spurred his horse most viciously and plunged down into the fray.

The English knights were so intent on capturing the new-crowned king that they did not see the Scotstoun charge until it drove hard into their column from the side. Assailed from front and side, they were quickly surrounded and no armour could protect them from the sword thrusts which came in from every angle.

Having hacked down the last of the Englishmen, John found himself soaked in gore and trying to catch his breath beneath the steely gaze of Robert Bruce.

'It would seem that I owe you a debt of gratitude, John Edward.' He said, his tone betraying a certain reluctance.

'You owe me nothing, m'Lord.' John replied. 'I owe my life to your brother. I came simply to repay that debt.'

The Bruce nodded curtly. 'Be that as it may, know that I will not forget this. My brother delights in reminding me that I never forget a slight, however small it may be. He also knows that I never forget a service. I am in your debt.'

'My Lord!' The Earl of Atholl pleaded. 'We must be away. I see more horsemen gathering at the forest's edge.'

The Bruce nodded and began to turn away. 'If you are ever in need, you must come to me. If it is within my power, then you shall have it.'

'Give me your cloak!' John demanded, his voice reflecting the urgency of the situation.

Robert Bruce smiled and shook his head in bewilderment. 'A cloak seems a poor reward for saving the life of your King.'

'No.' John replied. 'I will wear it and lead the English after me. They will assume that they chase the King. We will lose them in the forest while you make clean away.'

King Robert reached for the clasp on his cloak. 'My debts to you seem to multiply the longer that we speak.'

Aymer de Valence, Earl of Pembroke, strode through the ruins of the Scottish camp and surveyed the hellish scene with satisfaction. Bloodied and mutilated corpses lay scattered across the ground on the outskirts of the camp and were heaped in piles towards its centre, where the Scots had made their last, despairing and futile stand. They had been all but defenceless against the sudden onslaught, with most of the dead clad only in their underclothes. His captains were diligent in the execution of their orders and saw to it that every commoner who threw down his arms was cut down without mercy and that the wounded were dispatched with a sword thrust to the throat. The army Robert Bruce had taken months to assemble had been destroyed in less than an hour. Pembroke found that he could not keep himself from smiling, despite the carnage which surrounded him.

He paused before the handful of captured Scottish nobles who sat upon the ground with their arms bound behind their backs. Dirty, battered and bloodied, they stared up at him with eyes filled with defiance and contempt. He crouched down on his haunches and examined the bloody wound in the belly of Sir Hugh de la Haye.

'What on God's earth possessed you to risk all for this king of straw? You have thrown away your lives and your children's birthright for nothing? You cannot have hoped to prevail against such odds.' Pembroke looked into the eyes of each of the captives and shook his head in disbelief.

'We did it to be rid of foul bastards like you!' Sir Hugh spat, his eyes burning with hatred in a face now deathly pale from the loss of blood.

'There is nothing worse than being ruled by such dishonourable men. We would do it all again.'

Pembroke's grin widened still further. 'But you won't, will you?' He then pointed at Sir Hugh. 'You will not live to see the morning out. The blood pumps out of you so fast I am amazed that you have not died already. So, we need not fear further rebellion from you. The rest of you will be sent south to be executed on English soil and, as we have just slaughtered most of your men, we will have little to fear from you or your kin. Your lands will be granted to English nobles and, before too long, you will be forgotten. Such foolishness, such folly!'

Sir Hugh spat towards Pembroke, but the blood-flecked spittle hit the ground at his feet. 'You will be cursed for this morning's work. You broke your word and will be damned for it!'

The Englishman frowned before leaning forward and thrusting his index finger deep into Sir Hugh's wound. He gasped in pain and grabbed at Pembroke's hand, but did not have the strength to push it away.

'I doubt that God will condemn me for defeating a man who slew his rival at the foot of an altar. I am certain that he will reward me for my work. Now! Where is Robert Bruce?' He pushed his fingers harder into Sir Hugh's wound and twisted the torn flesh viciously. Sir Hugh's eyes rolled back in his head, his legs beat a tattoo against the ground and he groaned in agony.

'Let the man die in peace, you despicable piece of shit!' Alexander Scrymgeour growled, his eyes full of malice. 'Your false promise has won this poisonous victory for you, but King Robert is away. I saw him and his bodyguard cut their way through your knights. He is beyond your reach and you will have cause to regret allowing him to slip between your fingers!'

Pembroke did not remove his fingers from the wounded man's guts as he laughed at Scrymgeour's defiance. 'He has no army now. I have killed them all. What do I have to fear from a fugitive with a few ragged men behind him?'

Scrymgeour now took his turn to laugh. 'You will see soon enough, my faithless Lord. He is a better man than you and will fight relentlessly for his crown. If you think that you have finished him here, then you are as stupid as you are unscrupulous. I have no doubt that this day will come to haunt you and you will count yourself accursed that you could not take him despite your low trickery.'

Pembroke returned Scrymgeour's stare impassively for a moment and then grimaced as he clenched his fist inside Sir Hugh's guts and ripped a handful of his bloody innards out and threw them into Scrymgeour's lap. Sir Hugh let out a mournful, high-pitched squeal and collapsed into unconsciousness.

'Robert Bruce may well haunt me, but it will be his ghost which does so. He will not stay ahead of us for long.'

Pembroke then turned as one of his men came to him at the run. 'My Lord! The King's

Knight has fallen. He is wounded most grievously and asks for you.'

Pembroke followed the man to the west side of the camp where Rank lay upon the ground. He was ashen, shivering and his face was coated in sweat.

Pembroke's eyes widened with the shock of seeing the King's Knight laid so low. He had seen him emerge from combat and a dozen tournaments without so much as a scratch. He now looked as close to death as it was possible to be. He grabbed at the neck of the man who had led him here and locked eyes with him. 'Bind him! Then get him back to Perth as quickly as you can. I will take your eyes if he loses so much as one more drop of blood on the journey there. If he dies, you will share his grave!'

'My Lord.' Rank gasped weakly. 'Robert Bruce and his men rode into the forest to the west of here with forty of our men at his heels.

Pembroke kneeled down at Rank's side and grasped his hand. 'You are certain?'

'Aye, my Lord. I was weakening, but I saw quite clearly the same cloak he was wearing when he rode before the gates of Perth.'

John Edward lay flat on the brow of the hill and watched as the English knights slowly ascended the slope. 'What do you think?' He asked without shifting his gaze.

'We can finish them long before their fellows get here.' Al replied. 'We have time enough for that. There's thirty-two of them. Mostly nobles judging by the quality of their horses and their armour. Their horses are too big and heavy for this rough terrain. See how their breathing is already laboured. If we let them climb right up to us, they will scarcely be able to stand.'

John watched on as he considered the best course to take. 'Tom. Can your bowmen take them down? I am loath to lose men in a close quarters fight against trained knights.'

Tom Figgins sucked in a sharp breath which indicated that it might be no easy task. 'We might take down some of them, but with their shields and plate, we would be lucky to take out five or six.' Tom's throat had been damaged years before when English soldiers had tried to hang him and he could do no more than croak his answer out.

'We'll just have to hit their horses then.' Eck concluded. 'Then run in and finish them when they are helpless and weighed down by their armour upon the ground.'

John nodded in agreement. 'It's a pity though. I would like to have one of those big English chargers again.'

'It would be too risky.' Eck replied. 'A mounted knight could easily fell three men before we could unseat him. We could lose half of our men for the sake of horses that are of little use in the hills.'

'Right!' John replied. 'We'll place the bowmen to their right at the top of the slope. I want every man with a spear lined up behind the bows so they can down any horse still standing once Tom has done his work. Then we charge down and finish them.'

The English approach was painfully slow and the Scotstoun men had to lie down flat against the ground without daring to lift their heads for fear of giving away their position. Slowly but surely, the sound of birdsong was drowned out by the steady thumping of heavy hooves onto earth, the horses' snorting and laboured breathing, the creak of leather and the rhythmic clanking of metal on metal. It was hard to resist the urge to lift their heads and check on the knights' progress as the din grew louder and louder and it seemed that they must already be upon them. Great courage is required for a man to hold his nerve in such situations, but not one of them gave into the feeling of panic rising in his breast and they stayed frozen in place until the first twang of a bowstring signalled that the trap had been sprung.

When John Edward leapt to his feet with his sword in his hand, he saw the English column explode into bloody chaos. The Scots bows were deadly at such close range and there was scarcely one beast not wounded by that first volley. Several had already fallen to the ground and others had reared up in fright and pitched their masters hard onto the ground. The second volley inflicted more injuries and the air was filled with the screams of panicked and wounded horses and the voices of shocked and confused men. Some knights fought to control their chargers and turn them towards the archers, but then the spearmen advanced across the slope and a hundred patriots charged screaming down towards them and hit them while they were still in disarray. While those with swords went immediately to finish the knights who had been unhorsed, those with axes charged at the horses that were still standing and smashed at their hindmost legs to bring them down. Those few knights who had been able to regain their feet found themselves assailed from all sides and those who did not throw down their arms and beg for quarter were soon separated from their souls. A handful of knights who had stayed in their saddles saw that the situation was hopeless and they spurred their steeds back down the hill so that they might live to fight another day. A few brave souls kept their courage and retained their honour by fighting on until felled by spear or axe.

John Edward fought ferociously and with no regard for his own life. His fury drove him on to knock one knight's sword from his hand and then finish him with a thrust to the throat. Another Englishman perished when John hacked into his face as he struggled to regain his feet against the great weight of his armour pinning him to the ground. He then advanced on a knight who hacked down at the heads of his attackers, sending several Scotstoun men to their graves. John dropped his sword and grasped the man's shield in both his hands and ripped him sideways from his saddle with his arm still trapped inside his shield by its straps. He then finished him as he hung upside down from his stirrups by kicking viciously at his head.

Eck joined him as he struggled to regain his breath after all of his exertions. They stood side by side and panted as they surveyed the scene before them and wiped the worst of the gore from their hands and faces.

'Christ!' John exclaimed. 'I must be getting old. I am exhausted and there is no part of my body which does not protest. I know that I will be even worse tomorrow.'

Eck laughed and wiped at his lips, which were burst and swollen from a knight kicking him in the face as he tried to pull him from his saddle. 'Well, you better recover quickly for the forest will be crawling with English by then. By donning the Bruce's cloak, you have brought the whole of Pembroke's army into our territory.'

John shrugged in response. 'How are we to kill them if they do not come to us?'

Eck snorted with amusement. 'Aye! There is that. Though it might be better if they came in slightly smaller numbers. Al reckons that there are five hundred more of them making their way towards us as we speak. We'd better no' hang about.' Eck then turned and pointed down the slope. 'What do ye want to do with our prisoners?'

John looked in the direction his cousin had indicated and caught sight of the three young knights being manhandled up the hill towards them. The young knight at their front was handsome, with long, curly, brown hair and a smile which would undoubtedly charm any young lady lucky enough to come within its range. He seemed unperturbed by his predicament and oozed with the confidence which came from a background of nobility, great wealth and privilege. He looked directly into John's eyes when he came before him and he greeted him most courteously.

'I am Sir Stephen Lamphey, nephew to the Earl of Pembroke. I have yielded my sword and asked for quarter. My uncle will pay a handsome ransom for my safe return and will be grateful to hear that I have been well-treated.'

John returned his steady gaze, but his expression remained grim. 'I have no use for ransoms and even less for your uncle's gratitude.'

Sir Stephen's smile did not so much as waver when faced with such hostility. 'Perhaps you did not understand me, my good man. The Earl will meet whatever price you should choose to set. He will want to see me returned safely to my family. He will make you rich.'

'Aye.' John replied, through gritted teeth. 'He will make me rich with the silver he has looted from my countrymen. He will shower me with gold torn from the dead fingers of those he has murdered since crossing our border. I have no yearning for such tainted riches and no desire to see his family kept whole while my own has been ripped from me by those under his command.'

'So, what then?' Sir Stephen demanded incredulously. 'You mean to murder me and shun such riches just so you can continue to lurk in the forests and hills?'

John nodded, 'Aye! I mean to murder you and then fight on until not one Englishman remains within this kingdom.'

'Then you are a fool! You will remain a peasant caught up in a war you cannot win. You will die for this!'

John nodded again. 'Aye! But not today, Sir Stephen. Not today.'

He thrust his dagger deep into Sir Stephen's throat and then withdrew it with a flick which opened up his veins and sent blood gushing from the wound. The young man looked about himself in shocked disbelief for a moment and then collapsed to the ground.

Scott Edward gazed down at the nobleman's jerking corpse and cursed. 'Could you no' have waited until I got that maille and breastplate off of him? I'll have to fucking clean it now.'

John pointed at the two remaining white-faced knights. 'Take theirs before you kill them. It'll save you the trouble.'

10

Walter Langton watched with concern as the servants helped King Edward into the chamber and lowered him gently into his chair. The King appeared even thinner and more frail than he had when Langton met with him a few weeks before. The rebellion in Scotland had, in many ways, sparked him back to life, but it had also drained him. He was absolutely determined to lead his army into Scotland for the final campaign, but the journey north had seen him plagued by ill-health and progress had been painfully slow, both literally and figuratively speaking. When the servants had finished with their fussing and left the room, Langton approached the King and bowed his head.

'Are you certain that you are up to this, my Lord? I am happy to deal with the matter if you would rather rest.'

The King lifted his eyes to Langton's and glared at him. His gaze seemed to burn into the Bishop of Coventry and Lichfield for a long moment before the ghost of a smile crept onto Edward's lips. 'I would not miss this for all the world, Walter. I have been looking forward to this ever since I received word from Pembroke.

Now, give me a goblet of wine and have the bastards brought before me. I am going to enjoy this.'

When the doors opened and the three men were escorted into the room, Langton was shocked by their appearance. They were filthy, barefoot, half-starved, dressed in dirty rags and weighed down by the chains which restrained their arms and legs. All three bore the evidence of mistreatment, with faded bruises covering their faces and their limbs. Worse still was the stench of rancid piss which hung about them so strongly that Langton felt it nip at his eyes.

None of this appeared to trouble the King. He seemed to come alive at the sight of them and his eyes sparkled with mischief and delight as he looked to each of them in turn with a smile upon his face.

'So!' He exclaimed loudly. 'How goes the rebellion? Ah! Not so well I hear. It cannot be when I have the Bishops of St Andrews and Glasgow and the Abbot of Scone in chains before me. No sooner have you crowned a king and sworn loyalty to him, than you are captured and sent south to answer for your treachery to the last king you swore an oath to. But surely King Robert will march his great army across my border and rescue you.' Edward stopped and slapped at his forehead. 'But how can I be so forgetful? He lost his army, did he not? Every last traitor slaughtered at Methven! Pembroke told me that he marched you there so that you could see the wages of your sins for yourselves. He told me that you, Wishart, and the good

133

Abbott wept at the piles of corpses there. Only Lamberton here was able to hold back his tears. Who could tell that he would so hard-hearted and not be moved by the destruction he brought upon them? Now Robert Bruce lurks in the hills like a common vagabond and is hounded day and night by both the Earl of Pembroke and a host of loyal Scots nobles.'

Wishart, who seemed bent under the weight of his captivity, now raised his head and hissed at the English King. 'But you do not have him yet! So long as he is free you cannot claim the crown of Scotland as your own. From the look of you, I doubt that you will live long enough to secure it.'

Edward rocked back in his chair and laughed in delight. 'I may be close to death, my dear Wishart, but I have yet to become as stooped and piss-soaked as you. As the good Lord has seen fit to smile down upon my campaign against the Bruce, I am certain that he means to keep me alive long enough to see his rebellion crushed and his head struck from his body.'

'If you are going to kill us, then get on with it. None of us has the slightest desire to hear you crow.' Lamberton's voice was strong and steady, but heavy with bitterness and rancour.

Edward shook his head and adopted an expression of mock concern. 'No, Lamberton, I have no intention of executing you, though I must confess that I ordered Pembroke not to spare you if you were to fall into his hands. I was displeased when I first learned that he had disobeyed me, but Langton here persuaded me that it would be better if our hands were not stained with the blood of men of God. He felt that it would be in our interests to avoid such a sacrilegious act when facing an opponent who has been declared excommunicate. It leaves us unbesmirched whilst Robert Bruce's claim to Scotland is forever tainted by the foul murder of John Comyn.'

'It is true.' Langton interjected. 'The Pope has ordered that the Bruce's sins be condemned from the pulpit of every church in Europe each and every Sunday until he is brought to justice. He can expect no aid from the continent.'

'And the Holy Father has already indicated that he will not intervene on your behalves. Like Robert Bruce, you are excommunicate and outside the protection of the church!' The King announced with no small relish. 'Your tonsures will save your necks, but you will not enjoy the same comforts extended to you when you were last held prisoner for your treachery. You will each be taken to a different dark and damp dungeon and will be held in chains. If the conditions should carry you off, then that will be no fault of mine and no-one will lay any responsibility at my door. They will say that you only had yourselves to blame. But before the keys are thrown away, you will travel to Newcastle to witness the executions of Sir David Inchmartin and Alexander Scrymgeour, who were taken at Methven and Sir Christopher Seaton, who was captured after the fall of Loch Doon Castle. You will then be transported to London to watch on as Sir Simon Fraser is hung, drawn and quartered. I have ordered that his head be rammed onto the spike beside that of William Wallace on London Bridge. I thought that would be a fitting end seeing as they fought alongside one another in years past. It will do you good to see the ruin you have brought upon the nobles feeble-minded enough to be persuaded to join your cause. Only a handful of men remain with Robert Bruce now. We will whittle that away to nothing soon enough.'

John of Lorne was stony-faced as he watched the battle unfold beneath him. His men had tracked Robert Bruce and his party since they entered Argyll three weeks before. Macdougall eyes were constantly upon them as they rested and recovered in the heather and awaited those few stragglers who had survived the defeat at Methven. John the Lame was both a cautious and a patient man and, though he outnumbered the Bruce by two to one, he had waited until his father-in-law's murderer and his men crossed terrain which provided the best opportunity for an ambush. He had signalled the attack the moment the last Bruce horseman reached the head of the pass.

He watched as the half-naked Macdougall clansmen rose suddenly to their feet on the slopes to either side of the false king's party and swarmed down at them, filling the air with their blood-curling battle cries. The Bruce men suffered badly at first, as the clansmen used their long Lochaber axes to rip at the bellies of their horses and brought them down by smashing at their legs. He smiled with grim satisfaction to see that near seventy men and their horses fell under that first onslaught, reducing the Bruce's strength by more than a third. But the Bruces did not reel for long. They rallied and backed away from the head of the pass and retreated along a narrow defile between a treacherously steep hillside and a loch. The Macdougall men pursued them, but the track was so narrow they were forced to advance two abreast and could no longer bring their numerical superiority to bear. The Bruce men took turns covering the rear of their diminished column and struggled to fend off the relentless clansmen. John of Lorne watched on from the top of the slope as James Douglas, Gilbert de la Haye and Edward Bruce were wounded and as Robert Bruce himself was twice unhorsed.

John of Lorne scowled when Angus MacIndrosser spoke at his side. 'They can fight. You cannot deny that.'

'I'm in no mood for grudging admiration of a worthy adversary. They leave a trail of my dead kinsmen in their wake.'

'Aye.' Angus responded. 'I did say that it was a mistake to attack them so close to the entrance to the defile. We should have let them advance further and so cut off their retreat.'

John bristled at the criticism. The insolent wretch would not have dared to point his finger at his father, the Lord of Argyll, in this way. Since an axe had taken off half of his left foot and left him crippled, some lesser men had smelled weakness and had been emboldened to challenge him in a manner that would have been unthinkable when was whole.

'It is good that you are so wise in the ways of battle, Angus. I will be needing you to bring Robert Bruce down before he kills many more of my men. If he falls, the rest will lose heart and be easily overcome.'

Angus MacIndrosser did not miss the bile in John's tone. 'And how I am to do that, when five hundred Macdougalls cannot?'

'Take your sons to where the path narrows. Then watch as our enemies pass below in single file and fall upon the would-be king as he passes below. The three of you should be just about able to manage that.'

'Aye!' Angus replied. 'We're certainly able-bodied enough for that.'

John of Lorne let the barb pass. It was enough to know that he undoubtedly sent the contemptuous pig and his sons to their deaths. 'Go then! Before I lose any more good men.'

The three men leapt down at Robert Bruce with their daggers drawn. The defile was so narrow at that point that no man could turn and come to the aid of their King. James MacIndrosser held onto the horse's bridle and stopped it in its tracks, leaving Robert Bruce even more isolated. His brother Stuart pulled at the mounted man's leg and tried to unseat him. Angus landed at the Bruce's back and reached around to drive his dagger into his heart. John of Lorne held his breath in anticipation of the traitor's inevitable death. He did not care that Angus MacIndrosser would be the hero of the hour, it was enough that he was in command. If he had forgotten that Robert de Bruce was known as one of the finest knights in all of Christendom, the next few seconds showed him the level of skill and viciousness required to win such an accolade. The Bruce drove his head sharply backwards, rocking Angus with its force and reducing his nose to bloody splinters. Grasping the blade of the father's dagger in his left hand, he swung his sword down with his right and cut away James MacIndrosser's shoulder and arm both. Stuart screamed in rage at seeing his brother cut down and wrenched harder at the Bruce's leg. The father now pulled at the Bruce's cloak and held it so tightly against his body that he could not wield his sword against the younger son. Robert pulled his leg tight against his horse so that Stuart's arm was trapped between beast and stirrup. Unable to free himself when the Bruce spurred his horse on, the poor lad was dragged along the jagged rocks which lined the defile until only ragged strips of flesh clung to his back. Robert Bruce then repeatedly rammed his head back into Angus MacIndrosser's face until his grip loosened and freed the Bruce's arm enough for him to drive the pommel of his sword backwards into his skull with enough force to pierce the bone. The Bruce then turned in his saddle to face the advancing Macdougalls.

John of Lorne cursed and decided that he had lost enough men for one day. He signalled to his captains that they should halt. He then watched the Bruce's back until it disappeared into the gathering gloom. He was a cautious and patient man and was confident that the days ahead would offer more opportunities to put an end to the traitor and he was content to wait for them to present themselves.

Aymer de Valence pointed to the chair on the opposite side of the table and invited Walter Langton to sit. 'What brings you to Aberdeen, Lord Bishop?' He asked, his voice dripping with acid. 'Can I assume that King Edward has sent you to scold me?'

Langton grinned and reached for the goblet on the table before him. 'Well, I did not come for the climate, my Lord. What the Scots call summer is considered to be winter in more civilised lands. I left the King resting at Hexham Abbey. He so wanted to see you in person, but was too ill to cross the border. He will come when he is quite recovered.'

'You bring letters from him?'

'I do.' Langton replied as he placed three folded parchments upon the table, each of them adorned with the King's seal.

'Why don't you tell me what's in them? I have no doubt that you took a hand in the writing of them. It seems that a new one arrives each day and each one berates me more foully than the last.'

'I have no doubt that you understand his concerns. It is a half year since the Bruce had himself crowned. Nearly two months have passed since you destroyed his army outside Perth.' Langton now shook his head in unconscious mimicry of King Edward. 'How can it be that he is still at liberty when you have three thousand knights and three thousand Scots horse at your command for the sole purpose of apprehending him? How can one man elude so many pursuers?'

'Do not underestimate Robert Bruce, my Lord Bishop. He is a very determined and resourceful man. You must tell the King that he stays ahead of us only by the skin of his teeth. Each day his following is diminished and the number of nobles willing to support him is reduced. He cannot evade us for much longer. Not two weeks past, John of Lorne, son of the Lord of Argyll, put his hands upon him, but was beaten off by superior numbers. His luck will not carry him much further.' Pembroke then signalled to his manservant. 'Bring John of Lorne before us. I would have him relate his tale directly to the Bishop.'

Langton shrugged his shoulders. 'You have been singing the same tune since Methven. Each time you tell us that it is only a matter of days and then those days pass with no word of his capture or death. The King wants this business done.'

'It will be done, Lord Bishop. You have my word on that. I will not sleep until I place the traitor's head into King Edward's own hands.'

Langton leaned forward and dropped his voice conspiratorially. 'Then you best be quick. The Prince of Wales has completed his work recapturing the castles in the south. He already marches north and he and his favourite Gaveston boast to any man who will listen that they come north to achieve what the Earl of Pembroke has failed to do.'

Pembroke leaned back in his chair and sighed. 'That is all I need, but I thank you for the warning.'

Langton waved his hand to show that no thanks were required. 'Then there is the other matter. The King believes that you do not follow his instructions with sufficient vigour.'

Pembroke laughed without real humour. 'I have left a trail of corpses and destruction wherever I have gone. I have ignored every rule of chivalry, denied quarter where it has been asked and slaughtered more rebellious nobles than I care to think of. What more would King Edward ask of me?'

Langton waved Pembroke's protests away and pointed to one of the parchments on the table before him. 'The King has heard that you pardoned a Scots noble who had sworn loyalty to Robert Bruce as King of Scotland.'

'Thomas Randolph is my friend. I pardoned him because I believe that Robert Bruce coerced his oath from him. He has now sworn loyalty to King Edward and to join with us in our fight against the rebellious Scots.'

'It must be your last act of leniency. The King was very clear on that.' Langton then pointed again at the parchment before him. 'He commands you to have your heralds make a proclamation throughout the country that all of the wives and daughters of rebellious Scots are to be treated as outlaws. Any man who wishes to rob, rape or murder them can do so with impunity.' Langton turned when a voice sounded in the chamber behind him.

'That is good to know. Elizabeth Bruce is most comely and I have never stuck my cock into a Queen before.' John of Lorne limped across the chamber and bowed his head to Langton and Pembroke in turn, before sinking into a chair.

'This is the man who put his hands on Robert Bruce?' Langton asked, his voice thick with disbelief.

'It is.' John of Lorne replied, as he reached into his cloak and pulled out a large silver brooch with a stone of quartz at its centre. 'I tore this from his cloak in the struggle.'

Langton examined it for a moment and then looked John of Argyll directly in the eye. 'I have seen Robert Bruce fight in many tournaments and know that he would have little trouble dispatching a cripple. I struggle to believe that you were able to engage with him and live to tell the tale.'

John glared back at the Lord High Treasurer and spoke through gritted, yellow teeth. 'I care little about what you believe, Lord Bishop. If you should wish to test my skills, you need only ask. My limp would not stop me from spilling your guts upon the ground.'

'Enough of this!' Pembroke snapped. 'Each of us has an interest in capturing the traitor, so let us not waste our time fighting amongst ourselves. Now John, I was told you want my help to flush the bastard out.'

'Aye!' He replied, pulling his eyes away from Langton with some sour reluctance. 'He has divided his party into two. His brother Nigel and the Earl of Atholl have taken the women and the horses and head for Kildrummy Castle. A small group of knights has stayed with Robert and make their way towards the lands of the Earl of Lennox on foot. We know the area they are hiding in, but need something to draw them out.'

'Tell me what you need.' Pembroke instructed him urgently.

'If you parade your knights along the roads, they will not be able to resist the urge to crawl out from their lairs to watch you. The moment they break cover, I will release my hound and hunt them down.'

'A single hound?' Langton demanded incredulously. 'You mean to hunt him with a single hound?'

'Aye!' John of Lorne replied.

'Is it a magic hound?' Langton asked, his voice heavy with sarcasm. 'Pembroke here has hunted him for months without success. He has used countless men, horses, hounds, spies and informants without ever laying so much as a finger upon his person and you propose to achieve what no other man can with a single hound?'

'This is a very special hound.' John replied, the grin on his face spread so wide that both Pembroke and Langton momentarily feared that he had lost his mind. 'It is Robert Bruce's favourite hound. Before his rebellion, this dog would follow on behind him from dawn until dusk each and every day. They say that he fed it from his own hand. I am told that it has been inconsolable these past few months and howls day and night for his master's return. Once he has his master's scent in his nostrils, he will not stop until he is reunited with him, no matter how far or how hard the Bruce might run.'

Langton roared with laughter and beat his fists upon the table until tears ran down his cheeks. 'My God!' He declared, as he struggled to recover himself. 'That is the funniest thing I have heard for a long, long time. I think I may have underestimated you, John of Lorne.' He then dissolved into laughter once more. 'Can you imagine?' He gasped. 'Can you imagine Robert Bruce's face when he sees that it is his own, his favourite hound that has chased him down? My God! I would pay a king's ransom just to see the expression on his face!'

Pembroke joined in with the hilarity. 'Would that not be a fine tale to tell? A fine tale indeed.'

11

Arwel Ap Owain did not turn his head to look
back as he rode out from Aberdeen. The place
was as filthy and as cold as its people. The city
was supposedly a bastion of loyalty to King
Edward in Scotland, but Arwel felt the surly and
resentful eyes of the local people fall upon him
each time he ventured out from the castle as one
of the Earl of Pembroke's messengers. He had
no doubt that they would do him serious harm if
they thought they could get away with it. He had
barely slept due to the excitement of hearing that
he was to take letters to King Edward at
Hexham and then ride back to Pembroke Castle
with a letter for the Earl's wife. He smiled at the
thought of surprising his own wife and family
after his long absence. If God looked favourably
upon him, the Earl's business in Scotland would
soon be done and he would not be required to
make his way back across the border. The only
fly in his broth was the escort which rode with
him for his protection.

The four Rhydderch brothers were dirty, foul-
mouthed and sullen. He would trust them no
further than he could throw them. In the village
beneath the walls of Pembroke Castle, the whole

Rhydderch family were known to be nasty, light-fingered and dishonest. Anyone foolish enough to lend them money when they pleaded hardship would find it impossible to ever recover the debt. Polite enquiries would be met with a shower of plausible excuses and assurances that the coins would be forthcoming very soon, if not the very next day. More urgent demands for repayment would be met with obscenities and threats. Arwel's own grandfather had never forgiven them for the theft of three chickens back when he was little more than a boy. The Rhydderch brothers' own grandfather had denied the accusation and swore until his deathbed that a fox had carried them away. Arwel knew that he would have to sleep with one eye open if he was to arrive at the border with all of his possessions intact.

He was jolted from his surly reverie when he caught sight of a horseman in the trees. The man rode a small, grey horse, a black dog trotted at his side and they moved at a pace that matched that of Arwel and his party. He glanced over his left shoulder and felt his heart sink when he saw that more than ten horsemen now filled the road behind them. There was still some distance between them, but their pursuers were closing fast upon them. He dug his spurs into his horse and shouted a warning to the Rhydderch men. They had barely reached a gallop when the Scotsmen charged out from the trees, blocking the road ahead and cutting off any possibility of an escape into the forest. Arwel recognised that they were hopelessly outnumbered and threw his hands up in surrender.

The Rhydderch family were known for their ferocity and propensity for violence, just as much as they were for their dishonesty and their willingness to help themselves to the property of others. All four brothers drew their swords and wheeled their horses around to face the assailants now emerging from the trees.

The eldest of the brothers glared at Arwel with contempt and snarled at him. 'Coward! Just like your father!'

Arwel opened his mouth to protest. It had been claimed that his father was amongst the first of the Welsh archers to turn and run at Stirling Bridge and the accusation stung him as much today as it had when it had first been voiced all those years before. Dewydd Rhydderch spat thickly in Arwel's direction before turning and kicking his horse on towards the advancing Scots. Two of the brothers were felled before they reached their attackers. They wore no armour and the spears thumped into them with sufficient force to knock the first brother from his mount and rock the second so far back in his saddle that his head hung down at the tail of his horse as it galloped away in fright. Dewydd reached the Scots and hacked down at them in an attempt to cut his way to freedom. Three times his sword clashed against Scottish metal before a large, white-haired Scot chopped viciously at his horse's hind legs and brought the beast crashing to the earth. Trapped beneath his flailing steed, Dewydd died under a flurry of sword thrusts, cursing until the very end when a sword-point was rammed into his throat.

The youngest of the Rhydderch brothers proved to be either the most skilful or the most fortunate of his brood, for he found sufficient space between his assailants to break through their line and spur his horse on into the forest. Arwel watched with mixed emotions as he ascended the wooded slope. The young lad had always been the friendliest of the four and, of them all, was undoubtedly the one who most deserved to survive. Arwel was only kept from willing him onwards by the fear that he would make it back to Aberdeen and tell anyone who would listen that Arwel Ap Owain had thrown his hands up in surrender and left his fellows to fight and die. Despite the fear for his own fate, he still felt some small measure of relief when he saw the arrow pierce the young lad's back and cause him to slump forward in his saddle.

Arwel kept his hands up high as the Scots surrounded him. He found that he was paralysed with fright when the white-haired axeman advanced towards him with a snarl.

'Off! He ordered.

Arwel stayed frozen in his saddle and did not so much as flinch when the man rammed the top of his axe hard into his face, bursting his nose in a spray of blood and sending him thumping to the ground. He lay there dazed and woozy as hands ripped the leather satchel from around his shoulders.

A Scot with two swords hanging from his belt pulled the satchel open and extracted the letters. 'Scott!' He ordered. 'Read these!'

The slightly shorter, but equally dirty man cracked the seal on the first of the letters and quickly read it. 'The Earl of Pembroke sends fond greetings to his wife, Beatrice.' This seemed to amuse him and his companions. 'He asks that she see to it that his good hunting boots are mended as he expects that his business in Scotland will soon be completed.' The man's eyes moved back and forth across the surface of the paper. 'There's something about monies that are owed to him and he asks that she lights a dozen candles in the chapel for those who fell at Methven.'

'That it?' The first man enquired.

'Aye!' Scott replied. 'That's about it, Eck. It's just shit after that.' He tossed the Earl's letter away and broke the seal on another. 'Ah! This one's much more interesting. Walter Langton, Lord High Treasurer and Bishop of Coventry and Lichfield writes to Edward, King of England, Ireland, Wales and Scotland. He is pleased to report that Robert Bruce was recently defeated in battle near Tyndrum by his most loyal servant, John of Lorne. He suffered a great loss of men and is now at liberty with only a small contingent of knights about him. He says that the Earl of Pembroke will not rest until the traitor is in his hands and that he is confident that Bruce and other outlaws will be captured before the month is out.' Scott paused while he scanned the remainder of the words on the parchment. 'He says that the Prince of Wales and the main English army have secured all castles recently lost to Robert Bruce and his supporters and then goes on to enquire after his health.' He held the letter out towards another of the foul-smelling Scots. 'You should read it yourself, John.'

John took the letter and turned to where Arwel lay upon the ground. 'What's no' in the letters?' He demanded. 'What did you hear in Pembroke's camp that's no' written here?'

'I'm just a messenger.' Arwel stammered nervously.

John laughed mirthlessly. 'That's what they all say, at least at first.' He crouched down and leaned his face close to that of the cowering Welshman. 'You have ears. If you do not want them hacked from your head, you will tell me all that they have heard.'

Arwel's mind raced as he struggled to recall anything that might satisfy the grim-faced savages. 'Ah! The Earl of Pembroke and all of his men have marched west to scare Robert Bruce from his hiding place.'

'What else?' John demanded, his gaze never leaving Arwel.

'Em, uh, the Earl is angry that the Prince of Wales and his army now head north. He fears that he will try to capture Robert Bruce from under his nose or that he will pursue his brother and the Bruce womenfolk who have fled to Kildrummy Castle.'

John exchanged a glance with Scott and Eck. 'How soon is the Prince of Wales expected?'

'Two, maybe three days. The last we heard, his army was at Perth.' Arwel sniffed constantly, but the blood still flowed freely from his shattered nose.

John delivered a vicious slap to the side of his head. 'Is there anything else we should know?'

Arwel shook his head in panic. 'No! That is all I know. I swear it.'

John nodded slowly and bent even closer to him. 'Now tell me this. Is there a knight amongst Pembroke's men who carries a shield with a sword and bones painted on it?'

Arwel nodded furiously.

'What colour is the shield?'

'It is red.'

'And what does this knight look like?'

'He is a big, broad-shouldered man with black hair and a face which is badly marked from the pox. He is the King's Knight.'

'The King's Knight?'

'Yes. King Edward himself knighted him upon the field of bones at Falkirk.'

'Did he fight with Pembroke at Methven?'

Arwel nodded again. 'He did and he was grievously wounded there. He accompanied Pembroke west even although his wounds have yet to heal.'

John locked eyes with his cousin. 'Now we know his name and where he is headed.'

Eck nodded grimly. 'So, we go west?'

'Aye.' John replied. 'With luck, he will fall into our hands.'

'We should warn the Bruce's kin that the Prince approaches from the south.'

John shrugged his shoulders. 'Kildrummy is west of here. It will cost us nothing.'

Eck nodded his agreement and then pointed at the Welshman. 'Let's cut his throat and be on our way.'

John shook his head. 'I will spare him if he agrees to ride back to Pembroke's army and tell this King's Knight that we come for him.' He grabbed at Arwel's hair and tugged it hard enough to make him wince. 'You tell him that John and Eck Edward are coming for him and that we will kill him slowly for the harm he has done to our family. You will tell him of the fate of your fellows here and you will tell him that he will be next.'

'I will. I will tell him all that you ask.' Arwel stammered.

'Then climb into your saddle and begone!'

Arwel scrambled to his feet and quickly pulled himself into his saddle with shaking arms under the hostile glare of the gathered Scots. He expected to be attacked as he turned his horse and he glanced nervously over his shoulder every few seconds until the Scots were lost to his sight.

Arwel did not keep his promise. He did not even return to Aberdeen. He had endured as much of Scotland as it was possible for him to bear. He waited until nightfall amongst the trees and then rode onto the road and made his way south. He rode as far as Newcastle, where he sold the Earl of Pembroke's horse along with its saddle. He used the silver from the sale to buy a share in a dilapidated inn on the outskirts of the

153

city. He never did return to his family, but was said to have devoted himself to drinking away his profits whilst warning travellers not to venture onto the far side of the border.

Robert Bruce brought the remnants of his party to a halt in the forest copse and ordered them to be silent. At first, he could hear nothing above their laboured breathing, but then, in the distance, he caught the sound of the hound's howling.

'Christ!' He cursed in frustration. 'They are still hard on our trail.'

He looked around at his companions and knew that he must look as dirty, sweaty, weary and ragged as they did. They had first heard the hound when they lay in the heather and watched the Earl of Pembroke march his army along the winding track at the foot of the glen below them. They were fortunate enough to reach the forest without coming in sight of their pursuers, but from there all luck had deserted them. Every trick had been employed to throw the hunters off their scent. Burns had been crossed and streams waded through until the frigid waters left their feet numb with cold. The relentless pursuit had brought them to the point of exhaustion and despair by the middle of the afternoon and his brother Edward and James Douglas had persuaded him that they must break into three groups with each one retreating in a different direction to confuse their enemy. He had been reluctant to reduce his force still further, but was persuaded to agree as it gave him at least the chance of escaping those who hunted him.

It saddened him to say goodbye to his brother and his most loyal supporters, even though they promised to reassemble later at an appointed place. It saddened him further when it quickly became clear that the strategy had not succeeded. The hound and the hunters ignored the trails left by Edward Bruce and James Douglas and their fellows and remained doggedly on the heels of the King and his few remaining companions.

'We must scatter into the forest!' He ordered reluctantly. 'We cannot run for too much longer. The hound can follow only one trail, so most of us will evade those who would do us harm.'

The barking was drawing closer, so they could make only the most hurried of goodbyes. King Robert bade young Machar Tait to accompany him and they set off at the run. They ran on until the skies began to darken and still the dog's yapping reached their ears.

'I can go no further!' Machar gasped, as he came to a halt and bent at the waist while he tried to catch his breath. 'My heart beats too fast and my lungs burn. Go on ahead, m'Lord! I will delay them here.'

'Tis too late, Machar!' The Bruce panted. 'Look! They have got ahead of us.'

Machar groaned when he raised his head and saw that King Robert was right. Five men advanced towards them through the forest with malice in their eyes and their swords already drawn.

'They must have sent runners on ahead of us.' King Robert said, still breathing heavily. 'We must finish them here before the hound comes up.'

Machar drew his sword and kept his eyes upon their assailants. 'They outnumber us, m'Lord. I do not see how we can finish them.'

'Their number will be their undoing.' The Bruce replied calmly. 'Because there are five of them, they will have little fear of us. Because there are five of them and only two of us, they will pause when they come upon us. That is when we must attack with all fury. That momentary hesitation will be enough for us to prevail.'

Machar did not seem convinced by this, but had no time to weigh the wisdom of King Robert's words for the five Macdougalls were almost upon them. They advanced steadily and with confidence and, just as the Bruce had said they would, they came to stop just over a sword's length away. Robert Bruce immediately flew at them and hacked down with his sword and Machar leapt forward only an instant later. The first swing of the Bruce's sword sent a Macdougall spinning to the ground with his skull cleaved in two. The second swing brought his sword clashing against a Macdougall blade, but the force of the blow fortuitously took his sword on downwards until it took the man's arm off at the elbow. Machar had not fared so well and was retreating as he fended off a determined assault. A second Macdougall thought to outflank him by circling around to his rear, but

156

his progress was halted when King Robert took his head clean off by striking hard at his neck. The severed head distracted Machar's attacker and the loss of concentration gave the young man enough of an opening to bury his blade deep into Macdougall guts.

The last man standing backed off at the sight of the slaughter of his friends.

Robert Bruce invited him to come at him. 'Come now! Tis not every man who has the honour of being killed by the King.'

The Macdougall growled and his face twisted with hatred. 'You're no king of mine, Robert Bruce. You're cursed before God and will hang before this day is over!'

King Robert nodded. 'I may well hang, my bonnie laddie, but you will not live to see it.'

He attacked the man with such ferocity that he fell back under the force of the blows and parried only four before his blade was knocked from his hand and King Robert stabbed into his guts and sent him to the ground twisting in agony. He still lay writhing and moaning upon the earth when the hound's barking sounded urgently from only a short distance away.

'Come Machar!' He commanded. 'We have no time to loiter.'

They ran on as darkness fell, twigs and thorns tearing at the flesh on their faces and arms as they ran blindly through the black night. They both fell hard onto the earth when unseen roots or rocks tripped them or shifted underfoot and each time they leapt back to their feet and continued on without stopping to see what injury they had caused to themselves. The sounds of the pursuit grew ever closer and torches lit up the forest at their backs. They heard the burbling of the stream before they came to it, but the murk was so thick and impenetrable that they still stumbled down the steep bank and fell into the icy water.

King Robert grasped Machar's wrist and pulled him close. 'We must wade downstream for as long as we can bear the cold. If the hound does not lose our scent here, then we will be taken.'

King Robert turned and dragged the younger man through the knee-deep water at speed, initially not caring how much noise their splashing made. When he judged that some small distance had been put between them and their enemy, he slowed and they progressed with more care and less din. Within a few moments, both Machar and King Robert were numb with the cold and the younger man could not keep himself from shivering. The shouts from above and the barking of the hound told them that their pursuers were at, or near to the stream. They clenched their chattering teeth and moved steadily downwards, ignoring, as best they could, the flickering torches and the shouting at their backs. As they inched slowly away from the torchlight, the night was filled with a sound that filled their hearts with a hope that had been absent since the chase began all those long hours ago. The hound no longer barked. He howled mournfully to the skies so that all would know the despair he felt at losing the quarry he had tracked so tenaciously since the dawn.

King Robert turned and embraced young Machar in his arms. 'I thought all was lost, Machar. We have shaken them off at last.'

'Can we get out of this freezing water now, m'Lord? I can no longer feel my toes.'

The Bruce could feel that the younger man shivered uncontrollably. 'Just a wee while longer, Machar. For your King. Just to be sure. I could run not a step further if they were to regain our scent.'

Machar hissed between his teeth, as he felt that he could stand the cold no longer. 'Yes, my King, but just for a wee while. Any longer and I will shout for the Macdougalls myself.'

Robert Bruce laughed and clapped his companion's shoulder, before turning and continuing on his way downstream.

12

Nigel Bruce stared at John Edward, his eyes
blank as though he was carefully considering the
arguments just put to him. John thought that
Nigel might be the most handsome man he had
ever laid his eyes upon. He was tall, like his
brothers, and he had the same strong chin and
large, intense eyes. He was neither as ambitious
as Robert nor as wantonly reckless as Edward
and John reckoned him to be an honest and
decent man.

'I cannot run!' He said finally, his voice firm
and resolute. 'My brother, the King, commanded
that I protect the Queen and hold this castle until
he comes with a force to relieve us.'

John shook his head. 'There is no force to
relieve you. His army was lost at Methven and
those few knights who stayed with him were
scattered by John of Lorne near Tyndrum. The
Earl of Pembroke now pursues him through the
heather.' John then pointed to the south, their
vantage point atop the high Snow Tower of
Kildrummy Castle providing them with a view
far to the south. 'That smoke upon the horizon
marks the northward progress of the Prince of
Wales and his great army as they burn out all

who would support your brother. They carry with them the siege engines they have used to rip their way into every castle your brother once controlled in the south.'

'Their engines will not reduce this stronghold.' Nigel responded, his arm gesturing towards the high castle walls, the towers, the twin-towered gatehouse, the earthworks and the dry moat. 'With enough men, I could hold out for a year.'

John again shook his head and tried to keep his frustration in check. 'If you keep the Queen and your womenfolk here, these walls will be their prison first and then their crypt.' John turned to the Earl of Atholl and pleaded with him. 'Please speak with him, m'Lord. He does not listen to me.'

The Earl hesitated before laying his hand upon Nigel's shoulder. 'When King Robert commanded you to hold this place, he still had an army at his back. He is alone now and we must act accordingly. We must put the Queen and the womenfolk beyond the reach of the English. We should take them north to the Bishop of Moray where there are men enough to protect them.'

Nigel Bruce shook his head. 'I will not so easily ignore my brother's orders and I will hold Kildrummy just as he has asked.'

The older man looked into his face and sighed at the sight of those eyes set so hard in determination. 'Then let me escort the Queen away. John Edward is right, King Robert would not want them trapped here by an English army.'

Nigel shifted his eyes to the horizon. 'Tis too risky, my Lord. The Earl of Pembroke is to the north of us and in all likelihood already marches here in pursuit of Queen Elizabeth. If I am to defend the castle for my brother, I can spare few men for an escort.'

'I have forty men with me and am headed north. We will gladly act as escort and see the Queen and her ladies safely past the English.' John paused and locked eyes with Nigel Bruce. 'If we encounter them, my men will even don the ladies' cloaks so that the English will pursue us and leave the womenfolk to push north unmolested.'

'So, I should entrust you with their lives? You who would not kneel to my brother and call him King.'

The Earl of Atholl cleared his throat and stepped between the two men. 'This man has stood in rebellion against the English King since before the battle at Stirling. He has lived through the slaughter at Falkirk and inflicted one upon the English at Roslin. He has harried and harassed the English all these long years, even when we all entered into King Edward's peace. No sane man would think that he would deliver the Queen to the English. Your brother Edward told me that he would trust John Edward with his life and I know of no other man who has resisted and evaded the English for so long. If we want the women safely away, we will find no other man more likely to achieve it.'

Nigel again paused as he weighed the options before him. 'Then I assume that you would happily accompany them, my Lord?'

Atholl answered without hesitation. 'Aye! The King ordered you to hold this castle, therefore you must do so. He ordered me to safeguard the Queen and I will keep my word with as much determination as you.'

Nigel nodded his agreement with some reluctance and went off to inform the ladies that they were to depart immediately. Immediacy proved to be a relative concept and two hours passed without sight nor sound of the royal party. When they finally emerged, the Queen proved to be in the foulest of tempers and continued to complain even as she was lifted into her saddle. Nigel Bruce valiantly persisted in his attempts to explain that the Queen's baggage had to be abandoned to allow the party to move quickly, but he did not prevail and their farewells were more perfunctory than either of them would have wished.

Thinking that it would be wise to let tempers cool, John waited until they had been the road for an hour before he brought his horse into line with the Queen's and that of the Earl of Atholl.

'My scouts are fanned out ahead of us. When they have located the Earl of Pembroke's force and found a clear way for you to progress northwards, we will go our separate ways. While you continue on, we will ride towards the English until we come into their sight. Once they begin the pursuit, we will lead them away to the west.'

The Queen stayed silent for a moment and regarded John with a furrowed brow. 'I hope that you will not think me ungrateful, John Edward, but I must ask why you would deliberately invite the English to pursue you? If your scouts are as good as you say they are, why not avoid them altogether?'

John kept his eyes to the front as he replied. 'One of their number murdered my wife and I have sworn on her grave that I will murder him in turn. I can only keep my vow if I bring him within reach of my sword. He will never be within my reach if I hide from the English. I must tempt him out.'

Elizabeth Bruce had been around men of violence all of her life, but something in the Perth man's tone caused her to shiver. She sought to change the subject to something less grim. 'But must you take my ladies' cloaks, John? My Lord Atholl tells me that we will likely have to ride through the night to put miles between us and Pembroke's men. It will grow chilly when the sun goes down.'

'I'm afraid so, m'Lady.' John replied. 'If they believe that they hunt the Bruce women, they will pour all of their men after us, leaving you to make clean away.' John then turned and smiled at her. 'You must take this cloak, m'Lady. It was your husband's. He gave it to me after the battle at Methven. I used it to lure the English away from him as he made his escape.'

Sudden tears jumped into Queen Elizabeth's eyes. 'So it is. I did not see it first.' She turned away and wiped self-consciously at her eyes.

'You seem to be making a habit of saving members of my family, John Edward. Both the King and I thank you for it.'

John bowed his head. 'There is no need to thank me, m'Lady. Now, my scouts return. I must confer with them.'

John kicked his horse on and reined it in at Al's side.

'Pembroke's army is hard by to the east of us. The way ahead is clear to the north.' Al wiped the dust from his face and pointed to the east. 'If we advance to the top of the hill beyond this one, the English will have full sight of us.'

John clapped Al on his shoulder and thanked him for his work. 'If Atholl moves them quickly, then they will be beyond Pembroke's grasp before the sun has set. I will tell him now and we will go our separate ways.'

Rank stood high on the hillside and watched as the Scots broke into two groups. The larger group set off to the east and galloped up the hill opposite him. The smaller group stayed on the road and headed north.

'Which group should we follow?' Rank growled at his scout.

The scout pointed to the east. 'That one. You can see the women with their hoods.'

Rank screwed his eyes up as tight as they would go and stared at the Scots riding up the slope. He then turned his head north and gazed at the riders heading in that direction. He jabbed his finger at them.

'We'll follow them.'

The scout scratched at his head with a puzzled expression on his face. 'Why them? I see no women there.'

Rank pointed at the column as it receded into the distance. 'See that one there, second from the front. That's a haughty bitch if ever I saw one. I've spent the whole of my life being looked down at by haughty bitches. I can spot one from a mile away. That haughty bitch there is Robert Bruce's Queen. I'll wager anything on it.'

The scout did not look convinced, but he had learned that it was unwise to disagree with the King's Knight. 'Shall I ride to the Earl and tell him that we have her in our sight?'

Rank tilted his head to one side and glared at the scout with unconcealed contempt. 'Have you ever fucked a queen?'

'No.' The scout replied.

'If Pembroke captures her, do you think he will let you fuck her?'

'No!'

'Then let us go and take her and give her to Pembroke once we are done.'

Robert Bruce lay flat on the ground and watched the three men make their way across the windswept moor. They were rough-looking fellows, all were armed with swords and the smallest of the three carried a dead sheep across his shoulders.

'What do you think, m'Lord?' Machar asked, as he lay at his King's side. 'Be they friend or foe?'

Robert snorted in response. 'I cannot tell. These days I find that one looks much like the other.'

'I wager that they will roast that sheep when they stop to make their camp.' Machar's eyes were filled with longing and his stomach growled loudly at the mere thought of roasted mutton.

King Robert turned his head and examined his young companion. The long days of running and hiding in the heather had left him gaunt and pale, the physical exertion and lack of food thinning his flesh and leaving his skin stretched tight over his skull. With no bow for hunting, they had eaten no more than a handful of wizened berries and the one small trout they had been able to guddle from a stream in the days since they had escaped the relentless Macdougalls. Machar Tait returned his King's gaze with sunken, dark-ringed eyes. Robert was hit with the sudden realisation that he must look as wretched as the younger man, perhaps worse, given that his greater age would give him less protection from the ravages wrought upon them by their dire circumstances. He turned his gaze back to the three ruffians making their way to the far side of the moor and grimaced as his own stomach clenched painfully at the thought of the feast that they carried with them.

'We have no choice, Machar. We starve here and must eat before the last of our strength is lost.' He laughed bitterly and shook his head. 'Not so long ago, I risked everything to win a kingdom. Now I find that I must risk all in the hope of filling my belly with mutton.'

With the decision made, they rose from the heather and went after the three strangers. They made no effort to conceal their approach and the men soon stopped with their hands on the hilts of their swords and called out a wary greeting.

'Good day, friends.' The Bruce called out. 'My brother and I were on our way to Loch Dee, but we are now lost and hungry. Will you show us the way?'

'What business have you there?' The tallest of the three replied, his eyes filled with suspicion and his fingers still curled around the hilt of his sword.

'I am Donald Kelman and this is my brother Angus. We have kin there and come with news from our family.' The Bruce forced a smile onto his face, but remained alert and ready to draw his blade. 'I would, if it pleases you, know your names and where you are bound.'

The tall man exchanged a look with his fellows and rubbed at his mouth as he replied. 'I am Coinneach Elrick and these are my brothers, Bhaltair and Donnchadh. We are seeking Robert Bruce, for we wish to serve him.'

King Robert noticed that the Elrick brothers looked at him with the same hunger that shone in Machar's eyes as he gazed at the dead sheep. 'If you will share your feast with us this night, I can guide you to him. He hides with my family at Loch Dee.'

Coinneach Elrick nodded his agreement. 'We will make our camp at the forest's edge and you are welcome to join us.'

Robert and Machar followed on as the Elricks crossed the last part of the moor. 'Be on your guard, Machar. I am certain that these men recognise me and that they search these hills in the hope of capturing me and claiming their reward from the English. We will eat and then steal away as soon as the opportunity presents itself.'

They watched warily as the Elricks lit their fire and set the sheep to roasting above it. As the fat dripped and spat into the flames and the air was filled with the most delicious aroma, both men felt dizzy with hunger and their mouths watered like never before. When Donnchadh held out chunks of roasted meat towards them, they snatched them from his dirty fingers and fell to gnawing at them like ravenous animals. Young Machar seemed to swallow the meat without waiting to chew it and his eyes watered from the pain caused by the hot flesh as it burned his gullet on its way to his empty and growling stomach. The Elricks ate with more restraint and their eyes never left the two men as they gorged themselves on the other side of the fire. Each time they finished what was in their hands, Donnchadh rose to his feet and hacked them another portion from the carcass. When their bellies were full and they could eat no more, he held out a skin towards them and bade them drink. The ale was not well-made, but both

Robert and Machar gulped it down gratefully and belched loudly with great satisfaction.

Robert Bruce rubbed at his bulging stomach and groaned with relief. 'I thank you for your kind hospitality. Be sure that you will be rewarded for your kindness when I present you to King Robert.'

Coinneach smiled in response, but the smile was thin and did not reach as far as his eyes. They remained watchful and the Bruce saw that not one of the brothers did so much as touch a drop of ale. The fullness of his belly and the warmth of the fire caused his eyelids to droop and he fought to keep them from closing.

He leaned to his side and spoke to Machar in a whisper. 'I find that I cannot keep my eyes open. Keep guard while I shut them for a little while. If I can rest for only a few moments, I will be much revived and we can make away in the dark.'

Machar nodded and kept his attention fixed upon the Elricks. King Robert's eyes flickered and then closed and his breathing grew deeper and more rhythmic. Machar found that he too struggled to stay alert with his belly so full. Each time his eyes threatened to close, he nipped hard at the flesh on his thigh, so that the pain would keep him awake.

Coinneach, Bhaltair and Donnchadh watched impassively as the young man slumped forward and then jerked suddenly backwards with his eyes opened wide in astonishment. He did this three times before he finally lost his battle and fell into a deep sleep. Even then, the brothers did not move, but remained seated and let more minutes pass. Only when Machar began to snore loudly did they rise carefully to their feet. They had heard tales from the Macdougalls of the Bruce's deadly skill with the sword at Tyndrum and so were convinced of the wisdom of striking him down rather than attempting to take him alive.

Coinneach silently signalled that Donnchadh was to go left and cut down the younger man, whilst he and Bhaltair would deal with the Bruce. He drew his sword slowly and carefully, the blade scraping lightly against its scabbard. The sound, slight though it was, caused the Bruce's eyes to fly open and, seeing the brothers poised to attack, he leapt to his feet with his sword in his hand and kicked at young Machar to rouse him. Coinneach threw himself forward and slashed viciously at the man he knew to be King Robert. This blow was parried, but the next one struck the Bruce hard on his left shoulder. He grunted in pain, but reacted quickly enough to thrust his blade into Coinneach's unprotected chest. The eldest Elrick brother staggered backwards clutching at his heart and the Bruce pushed him aside and came at Bhaltair. The Elrick brother raised his hand high above his head and arced his sword down at the Bruce with all of his might. The King danced nimbly to the side and let him bury his weapon harmlessly into the earth. His own swing was intended to separate his attacker from his head, but the man tried to duck away and instead lost the top half of his skull in a spray of blood, brains and fragments of bone.

The Bruce roared with the savage joy of battle and wheeled around to come to young Machar's aid. His heart clenched painfully when he caught sight of Donnchadh stabbing his blade down into his companion's chest. He could see that Machar was already gone, his life snuffed out before he was able to shake off the fog of sleep and rise to his feet. Donnchadh turned and his eyes widened in shock to see both of his brothers slain. The shock turned immediately to fear as the Bruce approached him with a fierce and murderous expression upon his face. He lifted his left hand as though he was beseeching King Robert to stop. His plea was ignored and he struggled to parry the vicious blows that rained relentlessly down upon him. When his sword was finally knocked from his hand, he fell to his knees and waited for the Bruce to finish him. The end did not come quickly. King Robert let him live awhile and beat him viciously until his frustration and brutal fury were fully spent and only then did he stamp his already broken skull into the earth. He turned from the bloody mess at his feet and fell to his knees at Machar's side. The boy's eyes were still open in fright and he began to weep as he gently closed them. He wept for loss of his friend, he wept for those lost at Methven and at Tyndrum, he wept for himself now that he was alone and he wept for a crown that was surely lost.

13

The Earl of Pembroke smiled when he recognised the approaching rider and brought his column to a halt.

'My Lord Bishop.' He called warmly. 'Tis a pleasant surprise to see you here. Am I to assume that we head towards the same destination?'

Walter Langton gave a grimace as he reined in at Pembroke's side. 'I'm afraid so, my Lord. The King has commanded me to scold his son just as he bade me urge you to greater efforts. If I could avoid that unpleasant duty, you know that I would do so.'

Pembroke laughed heartily. 'You're a braver man than I. I doubt that your message will receive the warmest of welcomes.'

Langton sighed and shook his head. 'My relationship with the Prince of Wales is strained at the best of times. Being the bearer of his father's criticisms is unlikely to enhance it.'

'He will not be in the best of tempers. It would seem that Nigel Bruce and his handful of Carrick men continue to frustrate his efforts to take Kildrummy Castle. He has brought half of England with him along with every siege engine between here and London and still his every assault is repelled.'

Langton made no effort to hide his glee at the Prince's misfortune. 'I may have the answer to his prayers. I have a man within the castle who will, upon my signal, set fire to all the wooden buildings within the castle walls.'

'So, you mean to win his favour by delivering Kildrummy to him?'

Mischief sparkled in Langton's eyes. 'That would be the sensible course, would it not? But might it not be more amusing to use the situation to bring him down a peg or two?'

Pembroke laughed, but shook his head. 'Tell me no more of your schemes. There is friction enough between the Prince and I as we compete to capture Robert Bruce. Your games do amuse me, but this time I would rather keep my distance.'

'Fair enough, my Lord. I will keep you out of it. Now, I must offer you my congratulations. I met your man, the King's Knight, as I left Aberdeen. It seems that he hunts better than the rest of us.'

'I hope that his success will buy me favour with the King. We might not have Robert Bruce in our hands, but I will send his Queen south along with the Countess of Buchan, his sister Mary and his daughter Marjorie.'

'I could not help but notice that the women had been mistreated. Their clothes were torn and Elizabeth Bruce had been quite badly beaten, judging by her bruised and swollen face. The others will not concern the King, but Elizabeth

Bruce is the daughter of the Earl of Ulster. I need not tell you of his importance to us in Ireland.'

Pembroke held his hands up. 'You know the King's Knight. He can be over-zealous, but I will not condemn him for it. If not for him, I would have nothing to lay before the King.'

Langton laughed, his face lighting up with mirth. 'He is a brute. I still remember when he laid out Piers Gaveston at the tournament on the field of bones at Falkirk. Each time that peacock insults me, I close my eyes and console myself with that image of him lying sprawled across the ground, his eyes wide in terror.'

'Twas a fine day.' Pembroke replied, his eyes taking on a far-off look as he too recalled the happy incident.

'Wait a while before you send her south. There will be nothing to worry the King if her bruises have faded.'

'Let us ride on, Lord Bishop. I find that I am in the mood to see you tease the Prince of Wales.'

When they came within sight of Kildrummy Castle, Pembroke let out a long whistle. 'Christ! This must have cost a pretty penny.'

The countryside around the castle was filled with rows of tents, horses, carts, stacked weapons, soldiers scurrying about their business and sacks of provisions as far as the eye could see. The scene was dominated by a dozen siege engines and, even although they were not in use, they must have struck fear into the hearts of every man amongst the castle's beleaguered garrison.

'We have emptied the Treasury for this.' Langton replied miserably. 'Just as we started to repay our debts and build a reserve, we have emptied it so Prince Edward can reduce a few miserable Scots strongholds to rubble. It is such a pity, I can scarcely bring myself to speak of it.'

'Come, Lord Bishop.' Pembroke replied in a soothing tone. 'Let us cheer ourselves by adding to the Prince's misery.'

They soon discovered that the Prince of Wales had long ago proceeded beyond misery and was now in the firm grip of fury and frustration.

'Langton!' He snapped, when he saw the Bishop of Coventry and Lichfield approach. 'If you have come to berate me, you are wasting your time. Messengers arrive from my father three times a day. It would seem that he has nothing better to do than to scold me for my lack of progress while he moulders in the north of England.'

'How goes the siege, my Lord?' Langton enquired cheerily.

Edward scowled and bared his teeth. 'You can see very well how it goes, Lord Bishop. The pits over there are filled with the corpses of the men who have tried to storm the castle walls. The piles of broken rocks at the foot of those walls have been thrown there by my siege engines to no good effect. The place is impregnable!'

'Surely no castle is impregnable, my Lord.' Langton made a great effort to keep any trace of mockery from his voice, but he did not entirely succeed. Only the strength of his will kept him from smiling when he saw the Earl of Pembroke look away to hide his mirth. 'Perhaps I can be of some assistance.'

Prince Edward's brow furrowed and his cheeks turned a dark shade of red. 'You think that you can tutor me in the art of war, counter of coins? Let us hear it then!' He turned to the group of young knights who were his close and constant companions. 'Pin back your ears! The Lord Treasurer means to instruct us in our business.'

Langton ignored the hostile glares and turned his eyes to the castle. He stroked his beard as if deep in thought. 'What you need, my Lord, is a fire. If you can put a flame to the stables, the whole thing will go up like a torch. You need only wait for the gates to burn down and then you can march your men straight in.'

The Prince laughed derisively and his companions joined in with him. 'You fool! You think that we have not tried. The Scots have piled straw on the roofs and soak it with water. The fire arrows do nothing more than fizzle and smoke. The Scots then collect them and use them on us when we assault their walls. If you have nothing better to offer, then be off!'

'There must be a way, my Lord. If you will let me stay for the rest of the day, I am certain that I can find a way to set it all aflame!'

'Do what you want, Langton!' Prince Edward spat. 'Just do it out of my sight.'

Langton turned to Pembroke as the Prince stamped petulantly away. 'We will join him at his table for dinner tonight, my Lord. We must be close enough to see his face when he is told that the castle is ablaze.'

The blacksmith froze in the act of dousing his fire. He cocked his head to one side and listened. The sound came again. He had not been mistaken. The Englishman had told him to listen for the hooting of an owl. He took a deep breath and felt droplets of sweat form on his forehead. His hand shook as he reached for the ploughshare and thrust it deep into the glowing embers of the forge. The signal came again as he waited for the metal to heat until it glowed bright red. He glanced nervously over his shoulder and fought against his fear. He knew that he would die slowly and painfully if he was caught in this act of treachery. He paced the floor and tried to gather his courage. The Englishman had promised him as much gold as he could carry if he set fire to the castle buildings. Such a fortune would not be his even if he were to toil away at his anvil for a thousand years. He closed his eyes and muttered words of encouragement to himself. With gritted teeth, he wound a cloth around his hand, lifted the glowing metal from the coals and strode towards the corn store. Not a single man on the battlements turned to see him open the door and pitch the hot ploughshare onto the pile of bone-dry kernels.

The blacksmith quickly made his way to the well at the far-side of the courtyard and engaged in conversation with the others gathered there, so that they would later testify that he had been with them when the fire broke out. He feigned surprise when the inferno erupted through the corn-store roof and threw himself into drawing of bucket after bucket of water from the well to aid the garrison in their futile efforts to douse the flames. They could do nothing to prevent the fire from spreading to the dry wood of the other buildings and the searing heat and thick, black smoke soon drove them back to the rearmost battlements to watch helplessly as the gates burst into flames.

The Earl of Pembroke and Langton stood at the front of the crowd of excited onlookers and watched in fascination as the conflagration lit the night and sent a great column of smoke into the sky. Pembroke nudged Langton with his elbow and hissed. 'Here he comes!'

The Prince of Wales pushed his way through to the front of the crowd and gazed at the spectacle with his mouth and his eyes opened wide in astonishment. 'But how?' He stammered.

'You are most welcome, my Lord.' Langton bowed his head graciously as he spoke. 'It was a pleasure to be able to help you overcome your difficulties.'

'You should prepare your men for the assault, my Lord.' Pembroke interjected. 'The gates will soon be burned clean through. The stronghold should be in our hands before the first light of dawn.'

Prince Edward nodded in response, but his eyes flitted between the inferno within the castle walls and Langton's expression of smug, self-satisfaction.

'It was obvious, my Lord.' Langton responded to the unasked question. 'I am certain that you will soon work it out. Now you must finish the job.'

The Prince still appeared dazed by events, but set off to rally his men.

As soon as he was out of sight, Pembroke roared with laughter. 'By Christ Langton, you play with fire!'

Langton too, exploded in mirth. 'I know! I know! I shouldn't, but there is a devil inside me that makes me go against my better judgement. He and his companions will agonise over this for weeks trying to work out how it was achieved.'

Pembroke clapped Langton's shoulder. 'Let us drink to the devil in you while we witness the fall of the castle. I doubt that we will have long to wait.'

The gates were breached before their first goblet was fully quenched, but the castle did not fall until late the following evening. Nigel Bruce and his Carrick men refused all calls to surrender and clung stubbornly to the back battlements. The Prince of Wales ordered one assault after another, but the defenders fought stubbornly and inflicted heavy casualties upon the English before they were worn down and finally overrun by sheer weight of numbers.

Langton watched on as the battered, weary and fire-blackened survivors were led out with their arms bound behind their backs. He recognised Nigel Bruce almost immediately, neither the soot nor his injuries being enough to disguise his great height and his fine features.

'This should serve to mollify the King.' Pembroke stated hopefully.

'Aye.' Langton agreed. 'He will be happy that the rebellion is broken and the execution of the captives will satisfy him for a while. But there will be no rest for you until he has Robert Bruce dragged before him to answer for his crimes.'

Pembroke nodded. 'We will have him soon enough. Near every man in Scotland means to claim the reward for his capture. With winter approaching, I will take my men south to Carlisle, where our lines of supply are guaranteed.'

Langton nodded his approval. 'Far enough away to avoid the rigours of a winter campaign in Scotland, but close enough to be able to sally forth when the fugitive is located.'

'Look!' Pembroke cried. 'They are executing the garrison. Should you not find your blacksmith and reward him for his work?'

Langton shrugged his shoulders. 'I promised him all the gold that he could carry. He will be able to carry away none of my riches if he has lost his head.'

In the weeks since Machar's death, Robert Bruce had taken to hiding himself away during the hours of daylight and emerging only once darkness had fallen. He had lost count of the number of times he had heard or caught sight of men searching through the heather or the forests. He had no doubt that the price on his head was high enough to encourage many men to seek their fortune in his demise. The chill of winter was in the air and sustenance was becoming increasingly difficult to find. He had grown thin on a diet of nuts, dried berries and roots and had even found himself reduced to gnawing at the torn remains of a rabbit discarded by a fox or a wolf. That foul meal of raw flesh had poisoned his guts and left him in a much-weakened state. Starvation had driven him to desperation and to risking all for the chance of something to fill his belly.

At first, he had been sure that he was hallucinating. The tiny, distant band of light seemed to float in the darkness, but no amount of blinking or rubbing at his eyes would remove it from his sight. For hours he had stumbled towards it through the murk and the light had grown larger and brighter the further he progressed towards it. It was only when his nostrils detected the merest hint of acrid peat smoke on the breeze that he concluded that he was approaching a dwelling of some kind. When he had crawled forward far enough to make out the dark silhouette of a small cottage, he lay in the grasses and agonized over whether or not he should risk betrayal and capture. All of his instincts told him that he should slip quietly away and continue his slow progress west, but his aching and empty belly argued for the opposite course. Hunger won over caution and sense and he rose unsteadily to his feet and padded quietly to the cottage. He lay his two hands against the weathered wood of the door and listened. No sound reached his ears save for the quiet crackling of a hearth fire. Even at this point, he almost pulled away and only his great strength of will forced him to rap his fingers against the wood.

His knocking echoed through the interior of the cottage and was met with empty silence. He was about to knock again when his ears caught the sound of soft, tentative footsteps approaching the other side of the door. He stepped back one pace and put his hand to his sword, although it did occur to him that he was in no fit condition to defend himself if the circumstances required it. Wood scraped against wood inside the cottage and then, after a short pause, the door opened a crack.

'Who's there?' The small, quiet voice of a frightened woman demanded.

'A weary traveller, good wife.' The Bruce replied. 'All I seek is food and shelter. I would do no harm.'

The door opened a little further and revealed a woman of middle-age, her face fearful and concerned. 'All travellers are welcome here for the sake of one.'

'For whose sake?' The Bruce enquired.

'For the sake of Robert the Bruce who is our rightful King.'

King Robert felt such relief at these words that tears sprang into his eyes.

'I am he.'

The housewife peered out and examined him closely, her scrutiny making him aware of his filthy, ragged and dishevelled appearance. 'Then where are all your men?' She asked, her voice thick with suspicion.

A great sob choked his throat and tears ran down his face. 'I have lost them all. Men, crown and banners. I find myself alone and hunted in my own kingdom.'

The woman's expression softened and she reached out and took hold of Robert's arm, her own cheeks now wet with tears. 'You are alone no longer, m'Lord. I am your loyal subject and, although I am a widow, I have three sons by three different husbands, McKie, MacLurg and Murdoch. They will be your sworn men.' She then fell to her knees and swore herself to him.

King Robert felt himself greatly moved to find such devotion in a world which, only moments earlier, had been so dark, desolate and bereft of any comfort. He reached down and grasped the widow's hand. 'Come now! Rise up! You have given your King new heart just when he feared that all was lost. You alone need never bow or kneel to me or to any other man. Up now, I command you! Should I keep my crown, I will owe it all to you. Be sure that I will not forget it.'

Though severely weakened and dizzy from hunger, King Robert pulled the widow up and bowed to her. She rubbed at the tears on her face and waved him inside.

'Come now, m'Lord! I will feed you and make up a bed so you might rest. Come dawn I will fetch my sons to stand with you.'

King Robert nodded his thanks. 'I must head west into the lands of the Earl of Lennox. He will help me reach Angus Macdonald of the Isles. From there I will be able to rebuild my forces.'

'My sons will get you there, m'Lord. Have no doubt about that.'

14

Walter Langton, Bishop of Coventry and Lichfield and Lord High Treasurer, leaned against the chamber's stone wall and settled back to enjoy the spectacle unfolding before him. The King had taken ill on his way to Carlisle and was forced to stop here at Lanercost Priory until he could recover his strength. He knew that the nobles now crammed into this small chamber had come to see if the rumours of the King's death were true. They had been disappointed to find him alive, if not at his best, and were now suffering his poor temper. It was amusing to see the young Earl of Surrey attempt to exert the same influence over the King that his grandfather had once enjoyed. The callow youth quailed in the face of the King's onslaught, his voice becoming ever more high-pitched as he sought to defend himself from one attack after another.

'Let me be quite sure that I have understood you, my Lord Surrey!' King Edward boomed. 'According to you, I must show mercy to those who have rebelled against me. I must be lenient in my treatment of those who have taken up arms in order to usurp my royal power and deny me my right to rule in Scotland. A right which has been endorsed by the Pope himself, by all of the rulers of Europe and by the greater part of the Scots aristocracy. I am to show compassion to those who are still sworn to the false king Robert Bruce. Is that what you are telling me?'

Langton could not make out Surrey's attempted response as his feeble squeak was cut off in its infancy as King Edward took himself to new heights of outrage.

'When all the wealth of England these past ten years has been swallowed up by the conquest of Scotland, my response to insurrection and treachery should be to show weakness to my enemies? Your grandfather, who himself gave so much in our northern province, would turn in his grave if he could hear such craven blasphemy spill from your lips. I give thanks to God that he is not here to witness this! He came to me for comfort after he suffered the disaster at Stirling Bridge. I have no doubt that he would weep as much if he could hear you now.'

Young Surrey's mouth opened and closed like a fish feeding at the water's surface at sunset, but he made no sound. Langton thought that his face was redder than that of a man dangling from the end of a noose. It was beyond him why the fool persisted when anyone with eyes and ears could tell that his efforts were doomed to failure and that his persistence only further enraged the King and made him less likely to change his mind. He was distracted from this train of thought when Queen Margaret moved to her husband's side and put her hand lightly on his arm. Though she was far from being the greatest beauty Langton had ever seen, he felt a strange attraction towards her. Even after giving King Edward two sons, she remained slim and firm in all the right places. Langton suspected that the attraction was largely driven by the fact that this particular fruit was forbidden to him. Nevertheless, he never tired of watching her or of listening to her gravelly voice and her seductive French accent.

'My Lord.' The Queen purred. 'I believe that the concern is less about the fate of the Bruces and more about that of the Earl of Atholl. Just this morning, the Earl of Surrey pointed out that no English earl has been executed for more than two hundred years. The magnates feel that a man of such high status must be treated differently to more lowly men.'

Langton mouthed a silent prayer thanking God for allowing him to witness such fine entertainment. The young Queen, in her efforts to aid the stuttering Earl of Surrey, had surely condemned him to a tongue-lashing of legendary proportions. He licked his lips in anticipation as the King's face grew more flushed and the thick vein at his temple pulsed horribly.

'So, the Earl of Surrey sends my own wife to do battle in his stead! He drips poison in her ear in the hope of bringing the King to heel. Firstly, my Lord, I am very much aware of how much time has passed since an English earl last faced the executioner. I am also aware that Atholl is no English earl. He is Scots! Secondly, I know full well why this traitor's death does concern the Earl so much. He fears that it will set a precedent.' Edward's face contorted into a snarl. 'If you do not wish to share his fate, my Lord, then do not turn traitor. It is as simple as that!' The King paused to take a mouthful of wine, but his gaze remained fixed on the unfortunate Surrey. 'If you want preferential treatment for the Earl, I will oblige you. Lord Treasurer! You will take down my instructions.'

'Yes, my Lord.' Langton replied, quickly making his way to the King's side.

'In honour of his elevated status, tell them to build the Earl's gallows thirty feet higher than those of the other traitors. Once he is dead, his body is to be burned and his head displayed on London Bridge.' The King paused for a second before continuing. 'Given his high status, you must ensure that his head is spiked upon a pole higher than all the rest. He must stand out in death, just as he did in life.' Edward looked around at the gathered nobles, meeting the gaze of those whose heads were not cast down towards the floor. 'There! Are you happy now? He will be treated differently, just as you demanded.'

'What of the others?' Langton enquired cheerfully, still enjoying the discomfort of his fellows.

King Edward waved his hand in the air as if dismissing the issue as being of no real importance. 'The brother, Nigel Bruce. Have him hanged, drawn and quartered in Berwick and his parts displayed in the cities of Scotland so that all its people will see the price of rebelling against their King. Let it be known that any man taken fighting in the name of Robert Bruce will be executed and disinherited. There will be no exceptions.''

'And the womenfolk?'

Edward's face twisted in fury. 'When Robert Bruce brought them south, each one of them bowed and curtsied to me most prettily. They smiled and blinked their eyes and spoke soft compliments to me. All the while, they nurtured foul treachery in their breasts. Somehow it is worse when a woman turns serpent and bites at you!'

Queen Margaret opened her mouth to speak, but the King waved her to silence.

'Spare me your entreaties. I know that you will argue for their lives. You will tell me that such cruelty is unwarranted when it comes to women, though treachery is treachery whatever the traitor's sex. I will spare their lives, but they will not escape my wrath.' The King turned to Langton, his eyes burning with repressed fury. 'Lord Bishop, you will have cages constructed from iron and wood for these women. The cages are to be suspended from city walls so that their treachery will be known. No provision must be made for comfort or modesty and no protection given against mockery or the elements. Their food must be plain and their company restricted to that of their jailers These women will live, but they will serve as an example to any who would stand against their King.'

This pronouncement produced gasps of horror from the assembled nobles and even

Langton was taken aback by the special cruelty of the measures. He could think of no previous example of any noble woman being subject to such suffering and humiliation.

'Yes, my Lord.' He replied. 'I will see to it immediately.'

John Edward poked at the campfire with a long stick and gazed around the camp. The sixty men he commanded sat around six separate fires, the flickering flames giving off enough light to reveal their exhausted and dirty faces. The weeks since their departure from Kildrummy Castle had been hard, frustrating and filled with danger. They had succeeded in luring the greater part of Pembroke's army away from the fleeing Bruce womenfolk, but the intensity of the pursuit meant that they struggled to remain at liberty and had few chances to inflict harm upon their enemy. There had been neither sight nor sound of the pock-marked King's Knight before Pembroke took his army south across the border. The Scotstoun men had scarcely rested for one day and one night when word reached them that the Prince of Wales was following his countryman's example and was leaving Scotland behind before the first snows of winter fell. The great host that he commanded provided too great a temptation for the patriots and they had harried and harassed them all the way to the border, slaughtering stragglers, messengers and scouts and plundering any supply wagons that fell behind their escorts. Any feeling of triumph from their successes was swept away when a captured scout revealed that the Bruce women had been taken and that Kildrummy Castle had fallen after the English set it ablaze.

With time to rest and with bellies filled with plundered English supplies, John's companions sought to distract him from his melancholy and his brooding.

Scott Edward leaned forward towards the fire, just as he always did when he had a tale to tell. 'Do you remember the night before the battle at Stirling, when the Witch of the Glen breathed in the smoke and told our fortunes?'

John did not lift his eyes from the fire. 'Don't call her that, Scott. She lost her daughter, just as I lost my wife. She grieves for Lorna as much as I and is just as diminished by her loss.'

Scott nodded and raised his hands in apology. 'Fair enough. I did not mean to disrespect her. But do you remember what she said?'

Eck shook his head and attempted to dampen his incorrigible cousin's enthusiasm. 'It was a load of shit, Scott. No more than a wifey's tale told around a fire.'

'That's no true Eck and you know it.' He turned to those around the fire who had not been present in Esmy's cottage all those years before. 'When she had breathed deeply of the smoke, she told us things she could not have known.' He leaned in closer with his eyes wide in wonder and astonishment. 'She knew Al's name, though she had never met him. She repeated words spoken in our camp that even we had forgotten. She even foretold that Eck would be near killed at Stirling.'

'Pish!' Eck exclaimed. 'An auld wife's trick!'

Scott sat back and held his palms out before him. 'Then how do you explain her calling you Eck the Black? None of us called you that back then. Now everyone knows you by that very name, just as she foretold.'

Eck just looked at his cousin despairingly and shook his head.

Strathbogie now leaned forward, always ready for a good tale around the fire. 'What else did she say, Scott?'

Scott looked around to ensure that every eye was upon him. 'When she spoke to John she said that he would make three kings, a saint, a sinner and a fake.' He sat back and slapped his hands against his thighs. 'Think about it. If John hadn't taken down the bridge at Stirling, Wallace would have lost the battle. If he'd lost the battle, he would not have been made Guardian of Scotland.'

'That's no' king though, is it?' Eck retorted.

'In all but name.' Strathbogie replied. 'He was more a king than John Balliol.'

'And think about this.' Scott persisted. 'If John had not ordered us to come to the aid of Robert Bruce after his defeat at Methven, then he'd no longer be a king.'

By this time, John had retreated into his own thoughts. On the night under discussion around the fire, John had first laid his eyes upon his Lorna. He had been less concerned with the telling of fortunes and thought only of exchanging glances with the shy and beautiful creature who had so completely captured his heart. His hand moved unconsciously to his throat and his fingers touched the little bag that hung there. She had given it to him as a remedy for the flechs that had plagued him during that early campaign. The leaves that it had contained had turned to dust long ago, but it gave him comfort to touch what her own fingers had once touched and he sometimes fancied that he could smell her sweet scent on the ragged cloth. A smile had just begun to form on his lips when he was yanked rudely from his reverie.

'John!' Eck repeated. 'Al's back.'

He lifted his eyes just as Al's familiar, skinny and slightly stooped figure emerged from the gloom into the light thrown out by the flames. He waved his friend to a seat by his side and called for hot food and English ale to be brought for him. He watched as his chief scout gorged himself on stew and hard bread whilst feeding morsels of meat to the big, black dog who was his constant companion. He could not help but notice that he teetered on the very brink of exhaustion. It occurred to him that Al had not rested for months. The fighting men might take time to recover themselves while there was nothing to threaten them, but the scouts rode out each and every day in search of possible threats or opportunities for attack. When Al finally discarded his bowl and wiped at his mouth with his sleeve, John set about finding out what he had learned.

'Is it true?' He demanded gently.

'Aye!' Al nodded. 'It is Mary Bruce, Robert's sister. I recognised her from

194

Kildrummy despite the terrible state she is in. They have her in a cage suspended from the battlements. She is kept there day and night with nothing to protect her from wind or rain. Folk come to gawk and jeer at her. Tis a pity to see her so.'

John cursed and slammed his fist into his thigh. 'We should have stayed with the Bruce womenfolk for longer before seeing them on their way!'

Al shook his head. 'I doubt that we could have helped them. I was told that they ran into an English patrol of near two hundred men. There is nothing we could have done.'

'Well.' John replied grimly. 'Then we must do something now.'

'There are too many men, John. She is guarded day and night. Much as I would like us to steal her away, we would be killed if we were to attempt it.'

John glared sternly into the fire, his fists clenching and unclenching at his side. 'Get some sleep Al.' He ordered. 'I will go to see for myself in the morning.'

Roxburgh Castle was an imposing sight. Flanked to the north and south by the rivers Tweed and Teviot, it occupied a commanding position atop a triangular hill, giving its great tower, high curtain walls and sturdy gatehouses an aura of impregnability. John, Eck and Al carried sacks of English grain upon their shoulders and were waved impatiently into the castle by a bored and grim-faced sentry when they informed him that they had come to sell their grain. They caught sight of Mary Bruce as soon as they stepped into the marketplace. The cage of iron and wood was suspended from the battlements at the top of a stone staircase. The young woman was, as Al had reported, in a wretched condition. Even at this distance, they could see that she had been soaked by the night's rain and now shivered in the chill, winter air.

Eck pointed at a figure sitting half-way up the steep staircase. 'That's her jailer.' He stated.

John guessed that he was a veteran of the English King's Scottish campaigns and that he had lost his left leg in some long-forgotten battle or ambush. The frayed and filthy state of his clothes suggested that his position as jailer was an act of charity or a reward for past loyalty that earned him little in the way of coin. The size of the castle garrison ruled out any attempt at rescue, but perhaps something could be done for Mary Bruce through bribery.

The jailer looked up as John approached him, but continued to gnaw at the bone clasped tightly in his hands. John had to force himself to smile and choke back the contempt he felt for the vile creature. His shifty eyes darted in every direction as he scraped his few remaining teeth over the surface of the bone in search of any remaining morsels of gristle. John flipped a gold coin into the air and watched the man's eyes lock onto it. He caught it in his fist and so commanded the jailer's full and undivided attention.

'Do you want to see her pish, sir?' He asked, his expression turning into a leer. 'If you stand down there and look right up, you will see her hairy cunny. You'll have to jump back mind, or you'll be soaked in piss.' He then laughed and beckoned John closer to him. 'Sometimes I forget and look too long, but it is worth it, sir! It is worth it to me.'

John stepped back to avoid the reek of stale urine. It seemed that the jailer did not trouble himself to wash when Mary Bruce's piss rained down upon him.

John held the coin up to make sure that the jailer saw that it was gold and not silver. 'I do not want to watch her pish.'

The man nodded, touched his index finger to the side of his nose and winked. 'You might have to wait to see her make her dirt, sir. If she don't have the squitters, she don't go until the middle of the day.'

John shivered with disgust and concluded that the man was half deranged.

'Not that!' He responded tersely. 'I would speak with her.'

The jailer shook his head and looked around himself in panic, as though he feared that he was about to be attacked. 'Tis not allowed, sir. No one is to speak to her, the Warden commands it.'

'If you were to take this coin to buy yourself meat from the market, no one could blame you if I was to climb these steps while you were absent.' John then held up another coin in his other hand. 'And when you return you could do your duty and order me down and take this coin for your trouble.'

A look of confusion passed over his face, but his eyes remained fixed on the gold. John was starting to fear that the half-wit was beyond persuasion, when he suddenly smiled and nodded. 'Tis not my fault if some rascal scampers up to the battlements when I have gone for food. A man must eat.'

'Exactly!' John replied. 'Go now! Before I change my mind.'

John did not turn to watch him go, but made his way straight to the battlements and called down into the cage. 'M'Lady! M'Lady!'

Mary Bruce peered up and shaded her eyes with her hand. 'My God!' She exclaimed. 'Is that you, John Edward?'

'Aye, m'Lady! I just learned that you were here and came as quickly as I could. I had hoped that the harshness of your captivity had been exaggerated, but I see that it was understated. I am heart sorry to see you in such miserable circumstances.'

'Have you news of my brother?' She asked with urgency.

'The last I heard he had got himself away. I am sure that I would know if his enemies had seized him.'

Mary Bruce began to cry from both relief and misery. 'I am glad that he is yet at liberty. I cannot say the same for all my brothers.' With these words, she pointed along the battlements to where a rotting head sat upon a spike. 'They executed him in Berwick, but King Edward ordered that his head be set upon the wall here to keep me company.'

John felt hot bile burn at the back of his throat when he realised that it was the head of Nigel Bruce. Though the flesh had ripened and blackened, it yet retained some semblance of that man's handsome features. He could not fathom how a king could visit such cruelty upon an innocent woman. To send her brother's head to watch over her incarceration in a cage was beyond depravity.

The sound of the tapping of a wooden crutch upon the stone steps alerted him to the return of the jailer. 'M'Lady, I must go now, but know that I will do all in my power to ease your incarceration.'

'You cannot rescue me?' Mary Bruce asked in desperation.

'Not now.' John replied. 'I do not have enough men for the task. Take heart! You are not forgotten, m'Lady.'

The jailer had now reached the battlements, a dripping, half-chewed chicken carcass in his hand. 'You must go now, sir.'

John held out the second coin, but did not release his grip when the jailer closed his greasy fist around it. He pulled the man forward until his mouth was close to his ear. 'If I hear that you spy upon the lady while she makes her toilet, I will come back and cut your eyes from your head. Understand?'

He then stepped around the vile fellow and made his way down into the marketplace. Eck and Al had done brisk business and were left with less than half a sack of grain. 'Al, you were right.' He admitted ruefully. 'There is no way we can free her. I had hoped that we could bribe her jailer to ease the conditions of her confinement, but he is a base animal and will be of no use to us.'

'I have something that might work.' Al replied. He pointed across the courtyard to where a small, fair-haired boy played beside the stables.

Eck nodded. 'Tis good that our grain was in such demand. This empty sack will do quite nicely.'

Sir Gylmyne de Fiennes reined his horse in and brought his men to a halt. He pulled the scrap of parchment from his jerkin and checked the instructions roughly scratched upon it. He gazed around his surroundings and nodded curtly. 'This must be the place.'

'We should have ridden out in force and hunted the bastards down.' His brother responded angrily.

Sir Gylmyne turned in his saddle and glared at his younger brother. 'That forest stretches for more than twenty miles. If we came in force they would disappear into its depths and I would never see my son again. You may relish explaining his loss to my good wife, but I most certainly do not.'

'This is not merely an attack on you, my brother. As Warden of Roxburgh Castle, it is an attack on the crown itself. The only way to deal with these savages is with the points of our swords.'

'There are men in the trees, Sire.' A guard to his left cried out. 'There! At the edge!'

Sir Gylmyne peered at the treeline and raised his hand to shield his eyes against the setting sun. He counted at least thirty dark silhouettes between the trees, but had no doubt that many more lurked in the shadows behind them.

His brother snorted loudly. 'See! We are outnumbered. I told you that it was a ruse designed to lure us here.'

Sir Gylmyne ignored him and watched as three horsemen broke cover and began to cross the moor.

'Stay here!' He commanded. 'I will go forward alone lest your temper overcomes you and gets my son's throat cut.'

He kicked his horse on and trotted towards the approaching horsemen. He soon saw that his suspicions had been well-founded. These men were not knights, but were ragged commoners mounted on small ponies. Dirty and unkempt, they had the appearance of men who slept in ditches and prowled the forests in search of poor travellers to rob and murder. He hoped that the bags of gold tied to his saddle would be sufficient to satisfy their greed and buy freedom for his son. As they drew closer, he saw that they were armed and that his son sat on the back of the third man's saddle. He also noticed that two swords hung from the man's belt and that his eyes were unnaturally dark.

The outlaw at their centre was the first to address him and he could not help but show his astonishment when he did so in his native French.

'Sir Gylmyne! Your son is glad to see you.'

'Let's get this done!' He snapped. 'Tell me your price. I have brought all the gold that I possess.'

'I am not here for gold, Sir Gylmyne. I am here to moderate your behaviour and teach you chivalry.'

Sir Gylmyne snorted derisively and looked John up and down. 'I am a knight of Gascon. I doubt that I have anything of chivalry to learn from a common man.'

'I disagree. I hear that you treat the people of this area with great brutality. That must stop. I hear that you mistreat women and keep them in cages without the slightest concern for their welfare or their modesty. You must abstain from such cruelty or face the consequences. In short, you must hold yourself to higher standards and adhere to the codes of chivalry. Fail in this and you will lose your son and heir.'

'I can do nothing for Mary Bruce. King Edward has decreed the conditions of her captivity. I cannot deviate from what he has commanded.'

'You rule here, Sir Gylmyne.' John replied. 'King Edward is far away, but your son is here. You must choose between them.'

The Gascon rubbed at his beard in agitation and stared at his young son. 'What would you have me do for her?'

'Warm clothes, decent food and shelter from the elements. If you cannot move her from her cage, you will enclose the end against the battlements so that she can preserve her modesty and be spared the worst of the wind and rain. I doubt that it is beyond your powers to release her each day so she can bathe and stretch her limbs. Her callous treatment should shame you. You will bring an end to it if you want your son returned to you.'

Sir Gylmyne nodded. 'And when would my son be returned to me? How long must I disobey my King before you will release him?'

'I am different to you, Sir Gylmyne. I may be a base commoner, but I would never inflict such suffering upon an innocent. I will release him to you now, in return for your word that you will do all that I ask.' John waved his hand and Eck spurred his horse forward before lifting the boy by the back of his tunic and lowering him gently to the ground. The boy ran to his father and was immediately hoisted up onto the front of his saddle.

John smiled to see the boy's joy at being reunited with his father. 'I have no doubt that you will soon come to the conclusion that there is no need to honour a promise made under such duress. Before you reach this decision, I would counsel you to remember that I was able to walk into your stronghold and spirit your son away in broad daylight while your all your fine sentries looked on. You should remember that I have men and women within your walls and will know if you have broken your word. I will know if Mary Bruce is treated badly. If such news was to reach my ears, be certain that I will take him again. Be certain that I will punish you for your lack of honour and take your wife and son away from you.'

Sir Gylmyne nodded. 'I will not risk my son's life.'

'Good!' John replied. 'Tell Lady Mary that the men of Scotstoun send their regards.'

Sir Gylmyne nodded again and began to turn his horse.

The horseman with the two swords on his belt motioned him to halt. 'We'll take the gold as well. Holding you nobles to higher standards is expensive work.'

15

Edward Plantagenet, Prince of Wales, Count of
Ponthieu, heir to the crowns of England, Wales
and Scotland and to the Lordship of Ireland and
the Dukedom of Aquitaine, was mortal drunk.
He was slightly less drunk than he had been
yesterday, but was more intoxicated than he had
been the day before that. He rose unsteadily to
his feet within the great hall of York Castle and
fumbled at his breeches. His eyelids fluttered
uncontrollably and he emitted a great sigh of
relief as he emptied his bladder onto the stone
flags.

'Christ! That is good.' He slurred, as the
puddle of pish grew at his feet. 'I thought I was
going to burst.'

Sir Tarquil de Trasque lifted his head wearily
from the table and fought to open his eyes. His
beautiful, white curls were plastered to the side
of his face and dripped with ale from the pool on
the tabletop his head had been resting in. He
looked around himself, his eyes bleary and his
face a picture of puzzlement. He did not seem at
all perturbed to see the Prince of Wales pishing
onto the floor at his feet or to observe that Piers
Gaveston lay comatose across the table with a

crust of dried vomit around his mouth. He blinked in surprise when he saw that a well-dressed man was standing silently on the other side of the table with his cap in his hand. He opened his mouth to greet him, but was quite overcome by a wave of dizziness and closed his eyes until it passed.

'There's no wine!' Prince Edward announced, having abandoned his attempts to fasten his breeches. 'Where's that fucking servant with my wine?'

'You sent him away.' Tarquil replied groggily, his eyes still shut against the spinning of the room.

'Why would I send him away? I need wine.'

'You made him dance, my Lord. You ordered him from your sight because his clumsy dancing offended you. You called him a clodhopper and ordered him away.'

The Prince swayed on his feet and his face wrinkled in confusion. 'Did I? I cannot recall it.' His eyes widened when he noticed the silent figure opposite him. 'Who the fuck is this?' He demanded.

'He came the other day, My Lord.' Tarquil responded. 'You told him to come back later.' Tarquil screwed his face up as he attempted to recall the man's name and his business. 'He's back.' He announced, when he found that the memory eluded him.

'My Lord!' The man said, with a bow that took his head to the level of his knees. 'I am John de Askham, Mayor of York.'

Prince Edward shrugged his shoulders and began to shake each of the jugs on the table in a bid to find one that still contained some wine. 'What do you want? Can't you see that we are busy here?'

The Mayor shuffled nervously and fidgeted with the cap in his hands. 'I come about payment, my Lord. You have graced us with your presence for almost three weeks now. The city merchants have provided you with all of the goods, food and wine that you have requested. They tell me that their stores grow empty and they need payment if they are to replenish them.'

The Prince was not distracted from his search for more wine. 'They know that I am the Prince of Wales?' He asked, his tone brusque.

'Yes, my Lord. They are honoured to have the heir to the throne of England in their midst.'

'As they should be.' Edward replied. 'Do they not know that I have only recently returned from Scotland where I fought for the enlargement of their kingdom?'

'They do, my Lord.' The Mayor replied respectfully. 'They have celebrated all of your victories there and revere you for your skill and courage. They request payment with the greatest of reluctance, but your party is very large and your entertainments most lavish.'

The Prince pulled himself to his full height and did his best to stop himself from swaying. 'They would deny me entertainment, sir? I, who have suffered so much and have endangered my own person for their betterment.' He lifted a jug from the table and threw it at the Mayor. 'You insult me at my own table!' He sent a second jug after the first and the Mayor was forced to duck down to avoid being hit. 'How dare you misuse me so!' He shrieked, his cheeks darkening with anger. 'Begone! Get out of my sight you ungrateful, impudent dog!'

The Mayor retreated, bowing and ducking as he backed away. The Prince launched two more jugs after him, but brought his assault to a halt when his hand closed upon one which still contained some liquid. He lifted it to his lips and drained it in three gulps.

'Insolent bastard!' He spat. 'Things will be different when I am King, Tarquil. They will not dare to ask me for gold when that crown is upon my head.'

'Yes, my Lord.' Tarquil replied.

'Oh yes! Things will be different then. I will make earls of my friends and we will rule the country together. Those beggars will be too filled with dread to come before me with their petty demands.'

'Earls?' Tarquil asked, his wooziness diminishing as his interest was piqued.

'Aye Tarquil. You and Piers will stand by my side and we will sweep all before us. You will see. Now! Where's that ox of a servant? I must have more wine to soothe my head.'

The Earl of Pembroke was glad to be away from Carlisle. The past months had been an agony of inactivity and frustration. He seemed to have done little apart from receive messengers who brought no news to cheer him. Most of these came from the King. His proximity at Lanercost Priory had served to increase the frequency of his communications and the sourness of his tone. No fewer than two missives would arrive each day to chide him for his failure to capture Robert de Bruce. The other messengers arrived from Scotland, each one eager to exchange rumours for English gold. A single day could bring reports that the self-made king had been sighted in Ireland, Ayr, Uist, Barra, Turnberry and Rathlin Isle. Each informant would swear to the veracity of his report and hold out his hand in expectation of coin. Pembroke would often comment that the Bruce must be a wizard to be in so many places at once, but he still emptied his coffers and sent good men to investigate each and every sighting.

The messenger from Macdowall of Galloway was the first to immediately convince him that he spoke the truth. He might have been dirty and ragged, but he had commanded Pembroke's attention from the moment he emptied his sack onto the castle floor. The heads, though badly beaten, were still fresh and he had recognised the face of Malcolm McQuillan, Lord of Kintyre, straight away. The man had commanded a fleet of galleys and Pembroke had met him briefly when he was paid to aid the English cause several years before. More than one spy had claimed that he had allied himself with Robert Bruce. The other two heads were not known to him, but he had no reason for disbelief when told that they belonged to two

Irish chieftains with some distant relationship to Clan Bruce. He commanded his men to ready themselves without delay and sent the Macdowall messenger onto Lanercost with the promise that King Edward would reward him for his gifts with the weight of the severed heads in gold.

Looking down at the shore of Loch Ryan, Pembroke could tell that the messenger, though essentially truthful, was not averse to exaggeration. There were fewer beached galleys than he had been led to believe and it was clear that the rebel force numbered far less than the thousand that had been claimed. By his rough count, Pembroke reckoned that no more than three hundred white, stripped corpses lay upon the shore. He pulled his cloak around him against the bitter wind and led his men down towards the gathered Macdowalls. He knew their leader well. Though he was ever loyal to the English crown, Dugal Macdowall did nothing that did not benefit him and his kin. He expected hard bargaining, but was certain that he had brought enough gold to secure his prizes. He was determined to leave with something that would win him some approval from the King and buy him respite from his incessant criticism.

Dugal Macdowall stood on the shore and watched as the English column approached. 'It's Pembroke himself.' He announced to his brothers. 'A more superior, stuck-up fucker you will never have the misfortune to encounter. Just watch! He will look down upon us and wrinkle his fine, noble nose in disgust. He would scarcely give us the time of day if we had nothing to offer him.'

'He'll give up more than his time today.' The youngest of his brothers replied. 'He'll pay handsomely for our prisoners to please his master.'

Dugal turned and spat into the sand. 'Aye! We should give thanks to God for keeping Robert Bruce out of his hands. If he had him already, he would throw us no more than a handful of silver for these traitors. His failure will cost him dearly this day.'

Pembroke groaned inwardly when he caught sight of the Macdowall brothers. Ragged, wild, uncouth and more hairy than beasts, he had no desire to engage with them. The gold King Edward had lavished upon them to ensure their continuing loyalty had most likely been spent on drink, for he could see no improvement in their appearance. They dressed like paupers and lived like pigs. His gold would be wasted on them. He raised his hand in greeting when he came close to them, but received no response from the glowering brothers.

'Good day, gentlemen!' He called out cheerfully, forcing himself to smile. 'You have been busy, it would seem.'

Dugal Macdowall's scowl caused his shaggy eyebrows to knit together, as though two weasels were locked together in a death grip upon his brow. His bushy whiskers and great mane of dark hair concealed his features so completely that only his small, beady eyes were

211

visible. He turned his head and looked along the shoreline at the naked corpses scattered along it.

'Aye! We've been busy right enough. They thought to sneak ashore in the dark and we were on them before their feet hit dry land. Two galleys were able to pull away, the rest perished here on our blades.'

Pembroke followed Macdowall's gaze and examined the carnage at close quarters. 'Your men have stripped them well.' He observed.

'Waste not, want not!' Dugal replied sourly.

'They have been most thorough. They have even taken their underclothes.' Pembroke observed, a slight wrinkle of disapproval crossing his face.

'It gets powerful cold here in winter. The men will be glad of their warmth before too much longer.'

Pembroke shivered in revulsion. His own men would strip the fallen of their boots and armour, but would stop short of looting soiled undergarments.

'Can we see the prisoners?' He asked, suddenly eager to get the business over with.

Dugal nodded and barked an order out. The three men were not bound, but were so battered and badly injured that there was little danger of them escaping their captors. Pembroke could not remember ever meeting Alexander and Thomas de Bruce, but their resemblance to their traitor brother was so strong that he had no doubt as to their identities. Both men were tall, fair of face and in their early twenties. Alexander had fared better than his brother, his only visible injuries being an eye swollen to the size of a fist, burst lips and the loss of his front upper and lower teeth. Thomas, on the other hand, seemed to have lost at least three fingers on his right hand and was nursing a wound to his abdomen which already reeked of decay. The third man was also badly wounded, his shivering and deathly complexion suggesting a great loss of blood. Pembroke recognised him as Sir Reginald de Crawford, an inveterate turncoat and one-time Sheriff of Ayr.

'It would seem that you have changed sides once too often, Sir Reginald.' Pembroke admonished him. 'Whatever could have possessed you to involve yourself in this foolhardy rebellion? You cannot have believed that it would succeed.'

Sir Reginald did not even raise his head, but kept his eyes fixed upon the ground and stayed hard at his shivering.

Pembroke returned his gaze to the Bruces. 'You will be executed for your misguided treachery.' He stated flatly. 'But you may spare yourselves much suffering if you betray your brother to us.'

Thomas Bruce clutched at his guts and fixed Pembroke with a contemptuous stare. 'We will never give up the King. Do what you want with us, we will never betray him.'

'Your brother is no king.' Pembroke retorted. 'No king worthy of the title would hide himself away and run from his enemies like a common coward. He cannot conceal himself in the islands forever. We will hunt him down and execute him. It is but a matter of time.'

Alexander Bruce's eyes burned with both defiance and fear and he spat a bloody gobbet at the Earl's feet. 'My brother, the King, does not hide himself away, he raises an army. He does not run in the islands, but is already back in his kingdom. You English and your Scottish dogs will be swept away before him! You can be sure of that!'

Pembroke could not keep himself from laughing. No threat held any weight when the speaker's broken and bloody mouth caused him to slur and lisp his words. When his mirth had died away, he called a short, squat man to his side. 'You have told me that Robert is back in Scotland. I would know his exact whereabouts and this man here will extract the details from you.' He waved away the traitors' defiant protestations. 'Emery here is most proficient when it comes to the loosening of tongues. An hour with his knives and pincers will have you begging for me to hear you betray your false king.' He ordered Emery to begin his task and turned to Dugal.

'Let us cut to the chase. Name your price for these three.'

Dugal hummed and hawed and spoke at great length about how many men he had lost in the battle. He also wondered aloud if he could expect a greater reward if he took the prisoners to King Edward himself. When he had done all that he could to inflate the price, a settlement was reached. In spite of the exorbitant cost,

Pembroke was satisfied with his purchases. Robert Bruce might still be at large, but the King could not deny that he was whittling away at his family.

Determined to get full value for his gold, he ordered Dugal to furnish him with a wagon to transport the traitors south. The Macdowall leader was so happy with the transaction, he ordered his men to decapitate the corpses on the beach and throw the heads into the bed of the wagon to keep the three companions company on their journey to Carlisle.

'Will King Edward execute the brothers or put them in cages?' Dugal enquired once the wagon was loaded.

Pembroke settled himself in his saddle before he responded. 'I expect that he will have them hanged, their innards drawn out and their heads spiked on the walls of Carlisle.'

Dugal nodded. 'I had heard that the Bruce women are kept in cages and hung from castle walls.'

'That is true.' Pembroke responded. 'Just as the King commanded.'

'It is too much. Even a traitor's women should not be so humiliated. I think the King goes too far.'

Pembroke sat back in astonishment and looked from Dugal to the wagon half-filled with severed heads and then back again. 'I will be sure to inform the King of your sensitivities on the matter. Perhaps he will heed your counsel and choose another course.'

The Macdowalls watched as the English column made its way along the shore. 'I told you he was a snooty bastard.' Dugal growled, before spitting onto the sand.

His brother laughed happily. 'For this much gold, I find that I can forgive his arrogance and much more besides.'

The spy crouched down on the sand and cocked his head against the blizzard. At first, he could make out nothing above the wind and the waves, but then the wind dropped and he heard the rhythmic creaking and splashing of oars. His heart quickened when the weak moon peeked out from behind the clouds to reveal the approaching galleys. Their oars carried them quickly towards the beach and Cuthbert rose to his feet and waved his arms above his head to guide them in. The first galley beached itself on the shingle and a tall figure jumped down and strode purposefully towards him.

The spy fell to his knees in the snow before him. 'God be praised! You have returned to us, King Robert!'

Robert Bruce reached down and pulled the boy to his feet. 'It is good to be back, Cuthbert. Now tell me what you have seen.'

'We must hurry, m'Lord. There are men close to here.'

'The castle garrison?' Bruce demanded.

Cuthbert of Carrick shook his head. 'No, m'Lord. Sir Henry Percy has a hundred men within the walls of Turnberry and another two hundred men quartered outside. These other men are Scots, near eighty of them, as far as I could tell. They are headed here, so we must be away!'

King Robert turned to where his men jumped from their galleys and hauled their meagre supplies ashore. He knew that he would be at a serious disadvantage if he was attacked here, especially if he and his sixty men were outnumbered. He scanned the treeline, but could see nothing other than shadows through the fast-falling snowflakes.

Edward Bruce came to his side and dumped his pack onto the sand. 'Hell's teeth Robert! It is bitter cold. My boots are soaked through and my teeth already chatter in my head. We must get to walking so I can get some heat back into my bones.'

King Robert shook his head. 'Cuthbert has spied a force of men close to here. We must take to the boats and find another place where we can land safely.'

'No, my Lord!' Edward cried in frustration. 'No peril shall drive me back to sea. Here I will take my chances, be they good or ill. You must do as you please.'

'Look!' Cuthbert exclaimed. 'In the trees! Men approach!'

Edward Bruce squinted into the darkness and saw nothing but shadows. He was about to tease Cuthbert for taking fright, when he caught sight of figures advancing through the gloom. He drew his sword and snarled through his teeth. 'If it ends here, so be it. I'll make sure that more blood than mine soaks the sand this night.'

The dark figures advanced steadily and did not hesitate when they came within sight of the King and his party. Edward Bruce hefted his sword and marched towards them. 'Come feel my blade, you'll find its edge is most keen!' He bellowed.

'Good!' A voice retorted from the gloom. 'Then I will use it to shave the hair from my arse!'

Edward Bruce stopped in his tracks and peered into the night, his sword arm falling to his side. 'Christ! John? Is that you? You near frightened us to death.'

'Aye! It is.' John Edward replied, his voice filled with mirth. 'Who did you think it would be? Your messenger reached us ten days past. We've hidden in the forest for the last three days and followed your wee scout to meet with you here.'

John Edward came to a halt before Edward Bruce and they embraced one another happily.

'Just one messenger?' Edward asked. 'I sent three, just to be sure.'

'The others must have been taken.' John replied with a shrug. 'The English pay gold for the capture of any man sworn to your brother. Most of our countrymen seem content to take their coin.'

King Robert joined the two men. 'I did not think to see you here, John Edward. How many are with you?'

John gave a slight bow of his head. 'I have brought sixty men, m'Lord. My brother, cousin, Malcolm Simpson and Strathbogie are among them. Your brother told me that we could kill Englishmen together and so I came. This area is so thick with the English we could make a start this very night.'

'My brothers and Sir James Douglas have also landed in Scotland with men from Ireland and the Isles. We are to meet in the mountains of Carrick and there build our forces. We will not deviate from that course.'

'It would be a pity to miss such an opportunity to strike a blow against Sir Henry Percy and the English garrison who now occupy the seat of your own earldom, m'Lord.' John teased in the hope of provoking Robert Bruce to action.

'I am told that he has three hundred men at Turnberry Castle. He will have set pickets to prevent a surprise attack. I cannot risk the few men that I have in such an impetuous action.' The King shook his head at John. 'Even with your lads, we could scarcely field half as many men as he.'

John jerked his thumb at the man standing at his shoulder. 'Al here will have his scouts silence the pickets. That will leave the two hundred men quartered outside the castle walls open to an attack from out of the darkness. We would carve through them with ease.'

Edward Bruce grasped at his brother's shoulder. 'He is right, Robert. We cannot let this opportunity slip by. Did we not come here to fight our enemies after months of hiding from them? What better way to announce your return?'

King Robert agreed to the plan with some reluctance. He was wary of his brother's impetuous disregard for danger, but could not deny that the prospect was most tempting. 'Such a victory would doubtless encourage men to come to our cause.' He reasoned. 'And that is why we have returned.'

In the days and years ahead, King Robert's adherents would boast of the victory at Turnberry. They painted it as a beacon to rally support for the King and sang his praises for having the courage to strike out at the enemy who thought to conquer his kingdom. They called it the Battle of Turnberry, though it was no battle at all. It was a slaughter plain and simple. The Scots poured out of the darkness and fell upon the unsuspecting Englishmen as they slept. Few had the time to arm themselves and not a single one of them was able to don his armour before being cut down. No Scotsman with a thirst for English blood was left unsatisfied. John Edward himself found solace in his butchery, his broken heart forgotten for a moment as the hated English were massacred. King Robert and his brother vented their own fury and frustration after months of running from their enemies and immersed themselves in the bloodbath most enthusiastically. Only one of the two hundred fine Englishmen escaped with his life. He ran to the castle in his underclothes and ordered the guards to close the gates behind him. Then, along with his fellows and the fearful Sir Henry Percy, he watched impotently from the castle walls as the snow was turned red with blood and King Robert and his men took possession of their warhorses, arms, armour and even Sir Henry's own household plate. They then watched on as the Scots marched off with enough booty to arm a force three times the size of the poorly-equipped corps that had landed with Robert Bruce.

16

James Douglas sat back and fought to keep his impatience in check. In the three weeks since he had landed in Scotland with a handful of loyal men, he had been hidden away in Thomas Dickson's humble cottage less than a mile from his old family seat at Douglas Castle. Thomas, who had been his father's loyal servant, left the cottage each day and would return after dark with two or three supporters from the Douglas lands. Little by little, these clandestine meetings had succeeded in persuading thirty-two of his vassals to join with him in rebellion. James was now tired of the talk and the sneaking around in the dark, but the caution of those now sworn to him was keeping them from taking any action.

Alan Dickie sat on the other side of the cottage's hearth with a look of consternation on his face. 'It would be sacrilege to attack them in the kirk.' He stated, his eyes fixed on those of James Douglas.

'Is it not sacrilege that I have been ousted from my rightful place as Lord of Douglas? Evicted from my family seat and replaced by English placemen. No man here wants to be ruled by them, but they have one hundred and twenty men to our thirty. We cannot attack them in the open. We must use our heads and find a way to make the odds more favourable. I did suggest that we attack the garrison when they are gathered in the kirk on Palm Sunday, away from their walls and in no fear of attack from our men within the congregation. If you can suggest another course, then I would be glad to hear it.'

Alan Dickie shook his head. 'You know well that I have no better plan in mind. I can see how it could succeed, but am not the only one to have misgivings about slaughtering them before the altar.'

'The sin would be mine alone. You are sworn to me and must do as I command. If your lord and master commands you to commit a sin, it is he and not you who will be damned for it. If it will ease your conscience, I'll have the priest give you absolution the moment our work is done.' The Douglas looked around the faces illuminated by the light of the fire. 'What about the rest of you? I cannot hide myself away with Thomas for much longer. With each passing day the risk of being discovered and taken increases. Would you have me in English hands or will you follow me in striking at our enemy?'

Thomas Dickson leapt to his feet and put his hand on the hilt of the sword he had pulled from its hiding place in the thatch of the cottage the night Douglas had arrived at his door. 'To the death, m'Lord!' He cried. 'We will follow you unto death!'

The others stood and pledged their loyalty and even Alan Dickie rose reluctantly to his feet and agreed to the plan.

James Douglas smiled happily and raised his goblet. 'Let's drink to it and then get to work. We have only two short days in which to make our preparations.'

The time passed by quickly and so many men came to confer with the Douglas that Thomas Dickson became fearful that such activity would be noticed and reported to the garrison. Each time that knuckles rapped upon his door, he answered with his sword in his hand lest it was soldiers come to take his lord away. By the time the sun rose on the morning of Palm Sunday, he had barely slept and his nerves were stretched tight.

'All will be well, Thomas.' Douglas reassured him as they lay on the slope behind the kirk and watched the parishioners arrive. 'With thirty men sat alongside the English on their pews and these ten here with us, we will make short work of them and take Castle Douglas back.' He clapped Thomas on the shoulder and tried to coax a smile from him. 'We have too few men to hold the castle, but once we have slaughtered all of the garrison, we will send one man south to warn them that any man who tries to take my castle will suffer the same fate as these men. If our work is bloody enough, no Englishman will dare to take possession of the place and our people will be free of their cruelty.'

Thomas nodded and steeled himself for the task ahead. The castle garrison now arrived en masse and disappeared from sight into the kirk followed by the last of the parishioners. When they had all entered the building, James jumped up and led his men down to the door of the kirk. He placed his hand upon the handle and turned to his men, giving the sign of the clenched fist to indicate that they should ready themselves. Each man returned the gesture and unsheathed his sword.

James threw the door open and ran inside crying 'Douglas! Douglas!' as he went.

There was a brief moment in which no man reacted to the serenity of the kirk being rudely shattered and then all exploded in chaos. The Douglas men already in the kirk pulled out the daggers secreted upon their persons and fell upon the stunned soldiers with all brutality. Men cried out and women screamed in fear and there was a great rush to escape the church. The English soldiers who turned for the door were met with the sight of the snarling Douglas with ten men at his back. They hacked at their enemies with great fury until the floor was strewn with twitching corpses and the aisle ran thick with English blood. With little fear of such an attack on this holy day, many of the Englishmen had come without their swords and they were cut down even as they raised their arms and asked for quarter. By the time the Douglas called for his men to stop their slaughter, only twelve Englishmen remained alive, cowering beneath the altar.

When the prisoners were secured, James immediately led his men to the castle so that its gates could be breached before word of the attack in the kirk reached any guards who had remained behind. They arrived to find the gates still open and only a cook, a porter and servants inside. They also found tables set out for a banquet and the castle ovens filled with meat and bread. To the delight of his followers, the Douglas ordered that the castle gates be closed and the feast served to his men. With both bellies and goblets filled to every man's satisfaction, their victory was celebrated with great joy and gusto. They drank toasts to their young Lord and praised him to the heavens for being handsome, daring and brave. A more sombre moment came when he was informed that Thomas Dickson had fallen during the battle in the kirk. No man there thought any the less of him when he dropped his head into his hands and wept for the loss of his loyal servant. If anything, it further elevated him in their estimation and they took to referring to him as the Good Sir James, a soubriquet that was applied to him until his dying day.

When he had dried his eyes and the feast had been consumed, he declared that they must leave a fitting memorial for the slain Thomas for the English to find when they made their inevitable return. He first ordered his men to pack up and remove as much of the weapons, armour, silver and clothing as they were able to carry away. He then had the well poisoned with salt, the wine casks staved and eleven of the prisoners executed and their corpses thrown onto the corn and malt heaped in the cellar. When all this was done, he set the castle ablaze and dragged the last living prisoner out through the gate.

'Go south and tell every man you meet what you saw happen here. Tell them that the same fate awaits any man foolish enough to occupy my castle.' The Douglas shook the man to ensure that he had understood. 'Now go!'

The Englishman turned and walked unsteadily away. He had seen the madness in the young man's eyes and could scarcely believe that he was to escape the slaughter. The sudden eruption of violence in the kirk would plague his dreams for years to come and would tear him from his sleep, shaking, breathless and soaked in his own sour sweat.

The ghastly smile on King Edward's face caused Langton's stomach to churn and he was almost overcome by the need to defecate. To those unfamiliar with the Plantagenet King, the smile might appear to be entirely genuine. To those who knew him well, the smile was thin and barely served to mask his boiling fury. Langton had little fear of being subjected to the King's wrath on this occasion, as he knew well that the Earl of Pembroke and the Prince of Wales were to be its main recipients, but it was never wise to be complacent when the King was roused to anger. There was always the danger that the King would involve him in the scolding and he had little desire to earn the enmity of either Pembroke or the Prince.

'So, my Lord, how goes it in Scotland?' King Edward enquired, his tone clipped and edged with repressed irritation.

The Earl of Pembroke hesitated a fraction before replying. He knew that being summoned to Lanercost Priory so abruptly did not auger well. 'We remain hard on the heels of Robert Bruce, although he is slippery and continues to elude us. I am confident that we will have him before too much longer. I will deliver him to you, my King. This I swear. You will have his head upon a spike, just as his brothers' heads already sit atop the gates of Carlisle.'

Edward locked eyes with Pembroke, his smile gone and his expression grim. He held his gaze for a long moment before replying. 'Did I ask you to bring his family to me?'

'No, my Lord.' Pembroke responded, his head now bowed towards the floor in the vain hope of avoiding the worst of the King's displeasure.

'Did I not command you to bring me Robert Bruce?'

'Yes, my Lord.'

'Did I not furnish you with an army and my own Dragon Banner to accomplish this task?'

'You did, my Lord.'

Edward's face now twisted with rage and flushed red with anger. 'Then, why do I still wait? How can one man so defeat you, my Lord? Was I foolish to name you as my commander in Scotland? It would seem that the task is beyond your capabilities.'

Colour spread across Pembroke's cheeks as the accusation stung him badly. He dared to raise his head and meet the King's gaze. 'You were not foolish, my King. I crushed the rebellion before it had the chance to spread. Since I defeated Robert Bruce at Methven, he has been nothing more than a fugitive. All of the castles of Scotland are back in English hands and we have harried the Bruce and his allies so much that he has been unable to raise an army to replace that which he has already lost. I have done all that you commanded, save for the capture of this one man.'

'Is that so?' The King growled menacingly. 'You may think that I sit here in my dotage, ignorant of what goes on in my own kingdom, but you are wrong. Very wrong, my Lord! My spies paint a very different picture of the state of my northern province. They tell me that Robert Bruce is very far from being a ragged fugitive who is pursued relentlessly through the heather and is harried from dawn to dusk. They tell me that he skulks in the mountains of Carrick and gathers his forces. They tell me that more men flock to him with each victory won by him and his followers. My garrisons at Castle Douglas and Turnberry are slaughtered and their arms put into the hands of my enemies.' The King clenched his fists and ground his yellow teeth so hard that Langton feared that they would break. 'And all the while, where do you sit? You sit in Carlisle with every comfort of home and hearth and your favourite whore on hand to give you pleasure, only sallying across the border when others have done your work for you. I give you an army and you keep it safe in England while Dugal Macdowall and his hairy savages fight our battles for us. If I trusted the Scots to capture Robert Bruce, I would have ignored you from the outset and handed my gold to the Macdowalls instead!'

'My Lord!' Pembroke exclaimed. 'These were not battles. Men will not flock to the Bruce's standard because he has ambushed soldiers as they sleep or because his followers have slaughtered men as they pray within a church. These are isolated incidents, nothing more. The moment we force him into battle, his tiny force will be shattered and I will deliver his head to you!'

The King shook his head furiously. 'You don't know, do you?' He barked. He then thumped his fist viciously against the arm of his chair when Pembroke shrugged his shoulders and gave only a look of puzzlement in reply. 'A Macdowall messenger reached me yesterday. He told me of a battle where two hundred of his kinsmen were defeated and put to flight by Robert Bruce and a considerable force of men. Our allies are slaughtered while you drink and carouse in Carlisle. You will have your men pack up and leave for Scotland immediately, my Lord. You should count yourself lucky that I do not dismiss you from my service. If I had a capable man close at hand, I would do so without hesitation.'

Langton could not help but feel some pity for Pembroke. He was an honourable man and it was a shame to see him blushing and humiliated before the King. What made it worse was the expression of self-satisfied glee upon the face of Prince Edward. Langton's only consolation was the knowledge that his happiness would be short-lived.

'I would be honoured to carry your Dragon Banner across the border, my Lord Father.' The Prince announced happily. 'I am certain that the men would take great heart from being led by their future King.'

That sickly and horrific smile returned to King Edward's lips. 'Tell me, my Lord, where is your own army now? The one that I emptied the Treasury to muster and equip. The one that was raised after I knighted three hundred nobles at your side at Westminster to bind them to you in loyalty. That army which fought no battles in Scotland. Pray tell me where in Scotland that army now is. It must be far away to the north, laying waste to the lands of our enemies, for I hear no reports of it. I would know its current location.'

It was the Prince's turn to flush red and stammer under the King's terrible gaze. 'Like Pembroke, I have brought my troops south to spare them the hardship of a winter campaign.'

King Edward leapt to his feet, his eyes wild and veins bulging at his temple. 'Thou liest, foul creature! I know well that you have dismissed those barons I assembled for you! They have left Scotland for tournaments in the south and in Europe. Your foot have dispersed and now winter at home so that you can entertain your young men and drown in drink within the walls of York. The Mayor of that city travelled here to demand payment for all that you and your favourites have consumed. Langton! List the expenses I have been forced to meet!'

The Lord High Treasurer flinched at the command. Eager to avoid being caught between father and son, he did not unfurl the parchment on which the Mayor had itemised the costs and instead attempted to minimise his role by giving a few general examples rather than the whole damning list. 'Payment was demanded for one hundred and twenty cattle, seventy sheep, seventy pigs, two hundred rabbits, sixty-five geese, forty swans, a barrel of eels, a hundred cheeses and four hundred loaves of bread.'

'And the drink, Langton!' The King hissed, his eyes never leaving his son's face.

'Two hundred and fifty barrels of French wine, two hundred barrels of English ale and one hundred and twenty flagons of Cornish mead.'

'And the entertainments, Lord Bishop. Do not forget the entertainments.'

Langton felt his own face grow flushed and he studiously avoided Prince Edward's resentful gaze. 'The Mayor sought payments for the services of minstrels, jugglers, troubadours, jongleurs, mummers, bears, mystery players fire-eaters and conjurers.

'Not to mention the tournaments, the jousting, the gambling and the generous gifts for your close companions.' King Edward spat venomously. 'If you fought half as well as you spend, Scotland would be conquered and I could die in peace! But that is not the worst of it, is it you miserable and unworthy piece of shit? The Mayor has told us that you intend to make earls of your intimates!'

The Prince shook his head and held his hands out to placate his father. 'He lies! I would suggest no such thing. I would ask for nothing more than for the county of Ponthieu to be granted to Sir Piers Gaveston. He has served me better than any other man and I would see him rewarded for it.'

The King's colour darkened so much that Langton feared that his heart would seize up in his chest. 'I have no doubt that he has served you well!' He roared in fury. 'The unnatural intimacy between you is the talk of the court! You bastard son of a bitch! Now you want to give lands away, you who never won any for us! As the Lord lives, were it not for the fear of breaking up the kingdom, you should never enjoy your inheritance!' The King then leapt at his son and grabbed at his hair, tearing out great lumps of it until he grew too breathless to continue and ordered the Prince and Pembroke from his sight.

Langton avoided the murderous look the Prince threw in his direction as he left and instead busied himself with pouring a goblet of wine for his wheezing King.

Edward took the goblet with a nod of thanks and wiped the sweat from his brow as he waited for his breathing to slow. 'There is not a day when I do not wish that my elder sons had lived,

Langton. Each one would have made a better king than that foul and foolish beast. We must separate him from those who would lead him astray. See to it that Sir Piers Gaveston and Sir Tarquil de Trasque are exiled within the week, Walter. I will not have them distract my son from his responsibilities.' Edward swallowed a mouthful of wine and sighed deeply. 'I fight to unite the kingdom but fear that he will not be strong enough to keep his crown.'

Langton let out a nervous laugh. 'At least it will fit more easily upon his head now.'

The King looked down at the clumps of hair scattered across the chamber's stone floor and joined in with the laughter. 'By Christ! If I had not run out of breath, I would have left the bastard bald!' When his laughter subsided, he grasped Langton's forearm and shook it gently. 'It comforts me to know that he will have you to counsel him when I am gone.'

'I doubt that he will have me, my Lord.' Langton replied wearily. 'His resentment towards me is significant and his nature is not a forgiving one.'

'Do not fret so, my Lord. When he feels the weight of kingship upon him, I have no doubt that he will turn to you.'

It would not do to tell the King that he was mistaken, so Langton emptied his goblet instead.

'Do you have confidence in Pembroke?' King Edward asked. 'Can he apprehend Robert Bruce?'

Langton nodded. 'He is a capable and honourable man. My concerns do not relate to him.'

'Spit it out then, my Lord Bishop. I do not have the time to dance around the issue. If you have concerns, I would know them.'

Langton stroked his chin while he took the time to choose his words carefully. 'My informants tell me that, although the Bruce has few men about him, a steady trickle make their way into the mountains of Carrick to join with him. That troubles me. Just a few short months ago he could attract few men to his standard. How can he now command such loyalty?'

'I have had you in my service long enough to know that you never ask a question unless the answer is already known to you. Out with it! I sense that you mean to criticise me and you should be sure that I will not take offence.'

'I am told that men now begin to flock to him as a consequence of our harsh policy. Some are offended by our treatment of his womenfolk. Some have lost kin during our campaign and join with him to gain revenge rather than through any great loyalty. Our proclamation that all who have allied themselves with him will be executed, leaves those men with no choice but to throw their all in with his cause. Rebellion is the only alternative to death, so they will not seek our peace. I fear that we are unwittingly driving men into his arms.' Langton paused to gauge the King's reaction. He might have mellowed with age, but he could still react badly to criticism.

King Edward held his Treasurer's gaze for a moment before nodding his head slowly. 'You are telling me that my commanders have interpreted my orders too rigorously. I give you thanks for bringing this to my attention. I will write to them and chastise them for their over-enthusiasm. It would be a pity if their mistake was to strengthen our enemy.'

17

Aymer de Valence, the Earl of Pembroke, stood at the edge of the treeline and gazed across the loch in the direction indicated by his captain's pointing finger. The tree cover was more sparse on the higher ground and this enabled him to make out the distant figures of men and horses amongst the gently smoking campfires. The weeks spent vainly searching the wild Galloway countryside now seemed altogether worthwhile. The terrain provided a thousand hiding places and could well have concealed Robert Bruce and his followers for years to come. Indeed, if his men had not been tempted into attacking the English camp at Clatteringshaws, Pembroke's scouts would not have been able to follow them back to the lair of the self-made king. The loss of six men and some meagre possessions was a small price to pay for this prize.

'We've got the bastard!' Pembroke declared happily.

'They will not be easy to attack, m'Lord.' His captain replied. 'The valley is narrow and the lake is so wide that our only approach is along that narrow defile. The ground before their camp is rocky and strewn with boulders. Tis no place for a cavalry charge.'

Pembroke clapped his captain on the back. 'We'll have no need of our horses. He has no more than four hundred men to our one thousand five hundred knights. We will lay up for the day and advance on foot once darkness has fallen. We'll be upon them before they have broken their fast. Tell the men that we will take our rest here in the trees. No fires are to be set. We must remain undetected. I do not mean to give him warning of our presence and let him slip from our grasp once again.'

John Edward, Robert Bruce and his brother Edward had unbuckled their armour and left it in camp so they could move quickly and without the risk of making any noise that might give away their position. They kept low as they followed Al along the ridge. When the scout dropped to his belly and crawled forward, they followed his example.

'There!' Al exclaimed, his voice an urgent whisper.

Edward Bruce stared hard and then shook his head. 'I see nothing but trees.'

Robert narrowed his eyes and strained them until they hurt. 'There is nothing there.'

'Patience!' Al replied, before remembering who he addressed and hastily adding. 'M'Lord.'

John kept his eyes fixed on the spot Al had indicated and waited. Long minutes passed in silence before he hissed at his companions.

'There! To the right of that old, twisted tree. Do you see it?'

The late afternoon sunshine was weak, but it was strong enough to reflect off the knight's highly polished bassinet. The Earl of Pembroke insisted that his men took great care of their armour and this man had evidently spent many an hour buffing his helmet to the highest of sheens.

Robert Bruce let out a low whistle. 'You were right, Al. It can be no coincidence that they are here.' He turned to his brother. 'They must have followed you back from your raid on their camp! Did I not tell you that it was a foolhardy action when we still have so few men about us?'

Edward Bruce waved his hand dismissively and kept his eyes on the distant knight as he emptied his bladder. 'Pish, Robert! If we stay hidden away, the few men we have will grow dispirited and take themselves away. They must have their excitement and something to show for their discomfort.'

Robert Bruce grimaced in frustration and turned back to Al. 'How many did you see?'

'They rode in single file and the column stretched so far back I was unable to count them accurately. If pushed, I would say that they number between one and two thousand mounted knights.'

Robert Bruce moaned and screwed his face up in distaste. 'Too many for us then. We must break camp and steal away before they reach us.'

Edward Bruce nodded his head in reluctant agreement. 'As much as I hate to agree with you, I must concede that they are too strong for us. We must satisfy ourselves with putting ourselves beyond their reach.'

John Edward locked eyes with his old friend. 'We have other options.' He said, his eyes twinkling as he spoke.

King Robert exhaled sharply. 'Against fifteen hundred hardened knights? There is no other choice. We must run.'

Edward Bruce held his hand up to silence his brother. 'Let us not be too hasty, Robert. We should hear what John has in mind.'

John outlined his plan and answered every question and challenge that the Bruces put to him. King Robert took more convincing than his brother, but the decision was made before the sun had fully set.

The Earl of Pembroke was not at all perturbed that progress along the narrow defile had been slower than anticipated. He was satisfied that stealth was the primary consideration and that their silent approach would give them the element of surprise, even if their attack was launched well after dawn. The narrow track was rocky and strewn with stones and gravel and his men had to move carefully to avoid tripping and falling to the ground in the darkness. Now that they were so close to their objective, the din of an armoured knight crashing to the ground would surely give them away and provide the Scots with enough warning to disperse and slip away. He angrily jerked his head around when a loud scraping sound split the silent, pre-dawn air. He glared backwards along the defile in fury, but could not identify the culprit in the gloom. He was about to command the men to silence in an urgent whisper when the same sound came again. This time it was louder and he sensed that it came from the rocky slope above him and not from his rear. He gasped in horror when his eyes finally discerned that dark shapes skulked further up the slope.

The shouted order rang out and echoed across the valley, causing the head of every English knight to snap upwards. 'Now!'

The air was filled with men grunting and straining and the sound of rock scraping against rock. Pembroke's blood seemed to freeze in his veins as he realised what was about to happen. The first few rocks clattered and clacked as they crashed down towards the ravine. Pembroke drew his sword instinctively, but it was of no use to him against the torrent of boulders which thundered down towards him and his men. The English knights were trapped in the narrow defile and shouts of panic soon joined with the screams of those battered and crushed beneath the falling rocks. Some of the English attempted to scale the steep incline and take the fight to their enemy, but none of them came within reach of the Scots before flying stones sent them tumbling back onto the hard, rocky floor. Pembroke knew that panic and ill-discipline would lead to a rout and he screamed at his men to retreat in good order. With the ravine only wide enough for the men to move in single file, there was an agonisingly long wait before his orders were passed back to the rear of the column and his men suffered terrible casualties before they began to shuffle back towards their camp.

The Scots were now clearly visible as the light of dawn crept around the edge of the horizon. They kept pace with the retreating column and, although they no longer had the time to apply their levers to huge boulders and send them crashing down onto the English, they picked up every large rock in their path and hurled them down at English heads. Pembroke cursed himself as he pushed past his men and stepped over the corpses of those whose skulls had been smashed in spite of their polished helmets. He knew that the valley side became much less steep a little way back and he was eager to get there to rally his men. Although he never looked behind him, the screams of alarm and agony told him that the Scots were making the most of the attack. The snap of bowstrings revealed that Robert Bruce had some archers under his command and that they were being deployed now that there were fewer stones to throw. He had almost reached the place where he planned to rally his men when a great roar went up and echoed across the valley. He turned in time to see the Scots screaming in rage as they slid and skittered down the rocky incline before dropping into the gulley with their swords and axes in their hands.

'Move! Move! Move!' He screamed at the top of his voice. 'If they trap us here they will slaughter us all.'

The crush of men in the narrow gorge was a horrific and claustrophobic experience for everyone there. More than one man had his ankle broken under the feet of his fellows as they pushed, shoved and elbowed at one another in their desperation to escape. Several more were crushed underfoot when they were tripped and fell to the ground. Pembroke heard the clash of swords to his rear and decided that he would not abandon his men. He tried to turn back to join the fray, but found that he could not as the weight of men at his back carried him onwards against his will. Only when he reached the defile's end was he able to turn back towards his enemy and order his men to form up to meet them. Many of the knights ignored his orders and continued to flee from the Scots in panic.

He turned to the few who stood with him and tried to catch his breath. 'Like us, they will have to exit the ravine one at a time. Do not give them time to form up! Cut them down the moment they emerge. We may yet win the day, for we greatly outnumber them.'

They waited nervously with their eyes fixed on the ravine's end. They listened as the clash of blades, the war cries and the screams of the dying echoed around the glen. They listened on as the din of battle ebbed gradually away and was replaced with cheering and singing. They waited for more than an hour and not one single

Scot rushed out to throw himself onto their blades.

Pembroke's captain came to his side. 'It is time to go, m'Lord. The day is lost.'

Pembroke nodded sadly. 'Aye, but there will be other days and I swear that I will not be caught out like this again.'

Edward Bruce wiped the blood from his beard and touched his nose tentatively to explore the damage done by an English fist. 'Not a bad morning's work, Robert!' He announced cheerfully. 'Near two hundred English dead and we lost only eighteen of our own. Two who cracked their heads after falling down the slope and sixteen who fell in the fighting in the ravine.'

King Robert nodded his approval as he examined the torn flesh over the knuckles on his right hand. He had suffered the injury after leaping into the midst of the English in the gulley, but could not recall what had caused it. 'I am glad that I was persuaded to fight. Word of this victory will bring more men to our cause.'

'It will that!' Edward replied enthusiastically. 'It would seem that John Edward has an eye for these things. He has a gift for battle and sees opportunities that are hidden from the rest of us.'

'I cannot deny it.' King Robert replied. 'But did you see him and his men leap into the ravine amongst the English knights? They seemed to lose their minds and charge down when we could have finished them from above without any risk to our men. There was a madness about them, I saw it in their eyes. They cut down every Englishman in their path. Even those who dropped to their knees and asked for quarter were slaughtered.'

'But they can fight, Robert. If we had an army of Edwards and Strathbogies we would have no need of other men. I would march them up that hill right now and finish Pembroke off and to hell with his superior numbers.'

Robert Bruce threw his head back and laughed. 'That is because you are as mad as they are. If my army was made up of men such as you and the Edwards, I would either rule the whole world or lose it all in a single morning. Now, come brother! We must be away. We have stung Pembroke and he will be keen to make amends. Let us put some distance between us before he recovers his wits.'

The Earl of Pembroke considered the six weeks since his defeat in the ravine at Glen Trool to have been amongst the worst of his life. The debacle had caused morale to plummet and he had lost nearly one hundred and twenty men to desertion and had been forced to hang the forty who had been captured as an example to the others. Robert Bruce had somehow managed to evade his scouts and he found himself once again reduced to searching the hills and forests in the vain hope of catching sight of him. His most valued informants reported that a steady stream of men made their way to Galloway to join in the rebellion. Worst of all, messengers arrived daily from Lanercost Priory with parchments filled with the King's threats and stinging criticisms. These lowered his mood so much that he no longer read them himself. He instead asked his captain to do so with the instruction that he was to tell him only of direct instructions or new intelligence. It also caused him great anxiety to know that both Sir Philip Mowbray and the Earl of Gloucester were in Scotland with large bodies of men and were intent on capturing Robert Bruce for themselves. He dared not lose his one opportunity to restore his reputation and his relationship with the King and so pushed his men to the limits of their endurance in pursuit of the outlaw king. It now seemed that these efforts were to be rewarded and that he was to beat his rivals to the prize.

The hairy Macdowall scout pointed up the hill's green and gentle lower slopes, his finger jabbing at the cone of rock at its top. Amongst the few trees growing there, campfires sent thin columns of smoke up into the sky. The scout muttered something, but Pembroke could not make it out.

'Speak up man!' He bellowed. 'How am I to understand your rough tongue if you mumble inaudibly?'

'He says that it is called Loudon Hill, m'Lord' His captain offered from his side.

'I care not what name these savages have given it. I care only that I have him within my grasp.' Pembroke scanned the ground most carefully, his brow furrowed as he carried out his assessment. 'Why has he placed his men there, Ashworth? What trickery is in his mind?'

'It is a strong position, m'Lord. His six hundred men could easily hold off our three thousand from there. We would be on our knees by the time we reached the top and they would cut us down with ease. He could hold out there for months.'

'He does not have enough supplies to hold us off for long.' Pembroke replied with a grin. 'There is no need for us to assault his position on the hill. We will place men around its base so that he is surrounded and cannot slip away. The cavalry will form up on that lower slope and we will wait him out. He will either starve or be forced to come down and face us. Either way, we have him. We have him!'

Robert Bruce stared down as the English formed up on the green slope below him. The sun reflected off the helmets of the formidable ranks of knights and the bright colours of their shields and pennons lit up the field. He could not help but admire the sight even as it filled him with dread. 'We barely scratched him at Glen Trool. By my count, he has near three thousand men under his command.' He turned to the man at his side. 'You are certain that this will work?'

John Edward opened his mouth to respond, but was interrupted by the King's brother. 'It is too late to be asking that, Robert. They surround us now, so we have no choice but to fight. It is up to God whether or not we prevail.'

'Nothing is certain in battle, m'Lord.' John replied, ignoring Edward Bruce's interruption. 'If the men stand when the cavalry charge, then it might work. If they run, they will be slaughtered. When we stood at Stirling, we broke the English heavy horse. When we stood at Falkirk, we broke their charge. When the line broke at Falkirk, they ran us down like dogs.'

King Robert shook his head. 'I understand the strategy, John, but I struggle with the reality when it is laid out before me. How can men with spears defeat all of those mounted knights in their armour? It defies all logic!'

John pointed down at the slope below them. 'The ground is firm at the centre, but turns to bog on either side. The ditches we dug further narrow the field. The charge will be funnelled towards the centre as it advances. The horses will collide and jostle one another, reducing their speed and disrupting their formation. By the time they reach our spears, they will be fighting to stay in their saddles. The second rank will then run into the back of the first. The resulting chaos will allow our spearmen to do their work.'

King Robert nodded but his expression remained pained. 'Perhaps we should wait until morning. If it rains, the ground will be further softened.'

John shook his head. 'We cannot wait, m'Lord. If the wind picks up, it may blow away the grasses we have used to cover the ditches. If the English see that we have been digging, they are less likely to charge at us. That would leave us trapped and outnumbered. We must go now.'

The horn blast brought Pembroke to his feet and he threw the half-eaten bowl of stew to the ground. 'By Christ!' He exclaimed. 'The Scots are coming down from their perch! I thought that they would keep us waiting for days.' He watched on as the Scots made their way down from the rocky summit and began to form up a little way down the grassy lower slope. His lips moved silently as he counted the distant figures. 'He has gained a few men, Ashworth. I make it close to six hundred men.'

'Aye, m'Lord.' His captain replied. 'I make it about the same.'

'He has done well to attract nearly seventy men a week. It is good that we will finish him before he is further strengthened. Now, order the men to their horses! I want both ranks ready before the Scots are fully formed up. We will sweep through them before they are set!'

Pembroke stood with the reserve and watched as the two squadrons of heavy horse began to advance slowly up the slight incline. He shook his head to see how the small band of Scots at the top of the slope was dwarfed by the superior English force. 'By Christ, Ashworth, you have to admire their courage! Few men would stand when faced with such might. I would not blame them if they threw down their arms and begged for mercy.'

'You would give them quarter, m'Lord?' Ashworth enquired.

249

Pembroke shook his head. 'The King was quite clear. None are to be spared. Now sound the attack!'

Three blasts of the horn signalled the charge and the knights spurred their mounts on into the gallop. The thunder of hooves filled the air and caused the ground to vibrate. Pembroke sat back in his saddle and enjoyed the spectacle. The sight of so much horseflesh and so many armoured knights charging into battle never failed to stir the blood and set the heart to racing. The Scots were now lost from his sight and Pembroke waited for the inevitable crash of armoured horse breaking through the meagre Scottish lines. He frowned slightly when the knights on both flanks seemed to slow. His mouth then dropped open as the neat, disciplined ranks seemed to close up and fall into disarray. The clash, when it came, was not as he expected it to be. Instead of cries of terror and pain from the broken Scottish foot, the air was filled with bestial screams of agony and fright from amongst the English horses. Both English ranks fell into chaos and riderless horses galloped off in all directions.

'M'Lord!' Ashworth cried, his finger pointing up the slope. 'Look! The Scots advance!'

'What?' Pembroke snapped incredulously. 'They cannot advance!' The words died in his throat. The Scots were advancing, their long spears forcing the English knights back whilst their swordsmen danced out between their points to hack down at any knights who lay upon the ground. Riderless horses and mounted knights now turned and began to flee the battlefield in panic. Pembroke saw that dead and dying horses and knights were strewn across the green slope. He could also see that three lines of parallel ditches had been dug in front of the Scots line to disrupt the charge. He raised his hand and ordered the fleeing knights to halt, but they had lost their courage and galloped on by.

'Come to me!' He hissed through gritted teeth. 'Come on to me and I will use my reserve to finish you!'

But the Scots did not advance much further down the slope. They halted when they had killed every knight still upon the field and then marched back over the corpses of men and beasts alike and reformed in the position they had previously occupied.

Pembroke struggled to keep his temper as the ragged and dirty rebels taunted him and dared him to come and share the fate of his men. He was sorely tempted to order his reserve to charge the hill, but knew that the horse carcasses would impede their advance and ensure that they would suffer just as badly as the other squadrons had. He stared long and hard at the celebrating savages before turning his horse away.

'Come Ashworth!' He ordered. 'We are finished here.'

18

'So, Pembroke is finished?' Sir John de Seagrave asked, before sipping from his goblet.

Walter Langton sat back and surveyed the interior of the tavern to ensure that no one was paying undue attention to their conversation. 'I'm afraid so. The King intends to dismiss him from his service the moment they come face-to-face.' He shrugged his shoulders and shook his head sadly. ''Tis a pity, Sir John. He is an honourable man and I will take no pleasure in seeing him so humiliated.'

'It seems harsh, Lord Bishop. It was but one small engagement, a mere skirmish. I heard that he lost less than two hundred men.'

Langton pursed his lips and shook his head before lifting his hand with all five fingers pointing upwards.

'Five hundred men?' Seagrave hissed in surprise.

Langton nodded and leaned across the table so that he could reduce his voice to little more than a whisper. 'The most shameful part is that his fine knights broke and ran from a handful of Scottish foot, though they outnumbered them by five to one. When word of this reached the King, he near suffered a fit of apoplexy. If Pembroke had been before him at that moment, I do not doubt that he would have had him executed.'

Seagrave slumped back in his chair. 'It would seem that age has not mellowed his temper.'

Langton allowed himself a sly smile. He had no doubt that Seagrave was thinking of the disaster he himself had suffered on the other side of the border some years earlier. His defeat at Roslin was far greater than that of the Earl of Pembroke on Loudon Hill and he had endured his own humiliation at the King's hands for his failure. He toyed briefly with the idea of raising the subject, but decided to leave it for another day.

He leaned forward again and whispered. 'But that is not the worst of it.'

Seagrave's eyes widened with the curiosity of a man in need of gossip. 'Really?'

Langton nodded gravely. 'Really! My spies tell me that Sir Philip Mowbray suffered a similar reverse, though he has worked hard to keep it quiet. I am told that a ragged Scot appeared at the gates of Bothwell Castle and claimed that he knew where Robert Bruce was hidden along with all his men. Sir Philip, eager to capture the Bruce and claim his reward from the King, rode out with a thousand men. When they were out of sight of the castle garrison, the ragged Scot threw off his cloak, unsheathed his sword and attacked Sir Philip's bodyguard. Men with spears then rushed out from the trees and cut the horses out from beneath Sir Philip's men.

I am told that Sir Philip was unhorsed three times and was lucky to escape with his life. It is said that he rode so hard for his castle that his bodyguard could not keep pace with him.'

Sir John could scarcely contain his glee at hearing of another's misfortune. 'Christ! Is there no end to the Bruce's trickery?'

Langton shook his head. 'It was not Robert Bruce who attacked Sir Philip. It seems that the ragged Scot who enticed him out from behind his walls was Sir James Douglas.'

Seagrave let out a long, low whistle and his eyes opened wide in astonishment. 'Not the son of Douglas le Hardi? He is but a boy.'

Langton was relishing his role as teller of tales and made Seagrave wait for confirmation while he drained his goblet. 'A boy he may be, but he is proving to be an able knight. He has allied himself with Bruce and has sworn to recover Douglas Castle and all the lands seized from his father and awarded to Robert Clifford.'

Seagrave shook his head in disbelief. 'I saw him at court not more than three years ago and he had not a single hair upon his chin.'

'I remember it.' Langton replied. 'He came to beg for the return of his lands and the King chased him off.'

'I'll wager that he regrets that now.'

Langton tapped the side of his nose with his index finger and winked. 'But that is not the worst of it.'

Seagrave rubbed his palms together in anticipation and leaned forward so that he would not miss a single word. 'Tell me all, Lord Bishop. Leave no detail out.'

'Hearing of the misfortunes of Mowbray and Pembroke, the Earl of Gloucester rode out from Ayr Castle with a force of two thousand men in search of Robert Bruce. He came upon the rebels to the north of Loudon Hill and pursued them into the forest. The Scots led them on for a mile or more and then turned on them.'

'Christ!' Seagrave exclaimed, banging his fist on the table. 'He should have known better. The forest is no place for knights, but suits these savages with their axes and their spears. No one knows that better than I.'

Langton allowed himself a smile before replying. 'I have no doubt that Gloucester was fully aware of the fate that befell you at Roslin, Sir John. I suspect that, as can sometimes happen, his ambition overcame his good sense. You can hardly condemn him for it. The man who presents the head of Robert Bruce to the King will be showered with honours and gold.'

Seagrave shook his head. 'How many titles does he need? He already holds the Earldoms of Gloucester and Hertford and the Lordships of Clare and Glamorgan.'

Langton nodded in agreement. 'I cannot deny that he is a greedy bastard, but he has had his comeuppance. He did not withdraw when he should have done and the Bruce inflicted severe injury on his force. My informants tell me that less than half of those who rode out from Ayr made it back to the safety of the castle walls.'

Seagrave waved to the tavern keeper and indicated that he should replenish their jugs. 'It would seem that Robert Bruce is far from being a lone fugitive. These victories will bring more men to his standard. The King must be beside himself with fury to see his conquest so unravel.'

Langton nodded. 'He was furious when word of Pembroke's defeat reached us, but grew disconsolate when I told him of the ambush of Sir Philip's men. He sat before me with his head in his hands and groaned. It took me an hour to coax him from his melancholy. He said that death would be preferable to his present purgatory. With his spirits so low, I must confess that I hesitated to share the news of the Earl of Gloucester's debacle with him. I swore the messenger to secrecy and left it a whole day and a night before approaching him. In the end I forced myself to face him only out of fear that another would bring the news directly to him.'

'I would not envy you that task.' Seagrave interjected.

'But then the most wondrous thing occurred, Sir John.' Langton let the silence hang for a few long seconds to enhance the drama of the moment.

'What?' Seagrave demanded.

Langton's eyes shone with excitement. 'The King, who has been so poorly these past weeks, leapt up from his couch. 'By God!' He cried. 'I must do it all myself! My kingdom will be lost if I leave it to those feckless fools and villains! Order the muster, Langton!' He commanded. 'I will lead the army myself and put an end to this rebellion!' You should have seen it, Sir John. He was quite revived. He pulled himself to his full height and was no longer stooped with age. He sent away his apothecary and left his litter at the doors of Carlisle Cathedral. When he mounted his horse and set off this afternoon, he looked as strong as he did ten years ago.'

'Can he do it?' Sir John asked with a look of astonishment upon his face. 'I was told that he was close to death.'

The Bishop shook his head but could not suppress his smile. 'If you had asked me this a month ago, I would have chided you for your madness. Now that his power has been restored, I believe that he will lead his army north and put an end to the rebellious Scots. He will crush them beneath his heel, Seagrave. I am sure of it.'

Seagrave shrugged his shoulders. 'It will not be the first time that he has confounded all expectations. Do you remember when he took to the field at Falkirk when the battle was all but lost? He took command despite his injuries and turned disaster into victory.'

'You will not, I hope, think less of me when I confess that a tear came to my eye when I saw him mount his charger this afternoon. There is a strength in him that can be possessed only by a King. It reminded me that I am privileged by my proximity to greatness.'

Seagrave raised his goblet with all solemnity. 'To the King!'

Langton toasted the King and drank deeply from his goblet. 'So, Sir John, once again we two set our course north for Scotland. Let us drink to victory this time! We have both suffered enough in that wretched land.'

Seagrave nodded his agreement enthusiastically and drained his goblet. 'I think your man is looking for you.' He informed the Bishop, as he pointed towards the tavern door.

Langton twisted around in his seat and saw that Browby was approaching with his head down to avoid cracking it on the tavern's low rafters.

'Browby!' He called in greeting. 'Come join us! The wine is tolerable if you drink enough of it.' The smile melted from his lips when he caught sight of Browby's grim expression.

'You must come, m'Lord.' Browby stated gravely. 'The King has need of you.'

'Can it not wait until the morning?'

'No, m'Lord.' Browby replied. 'It may be too late by then.'

The King might well have mounted his war-horse as if rejuvenated, but he had made little progress outside the walls of Carlisle, covering only six miles before being forced to halt at an isolated settlement close to the Cumbrian coast. Langton rode into the encampment at Burgh by Sands and made his way into the King's pavilion. The smell of shit and sickness assailed his nostrils the moment he stepped into the tent's dim interior. The King's attendants stood together in the ante-chamber and Langton's worst fears were confirmed by the gravity of the expressions upon their faces. He hesitated as a feeling of dread threatened to overcome him, before forcing himself on into the King's bedchamber. He gasped when his eyes adjusted to the gloom and he saw just how much King Edward had deteriorated in the hours since he had last laid eyes upon him. His flesh had turned an unhealthy shade of grey, his eyes had sunk back into their sockets and the stench of his decay filled the small room. Langton felt tears jump into his eyes and he fell to his knees at King Edward's side. He reached out and took the King's hand in both of his and began to say a prayer. Even as he mouthed the familiar words, he noticed that the King's skin was already deathly cold, though the weakest of pulses told him that he still clung to life.

The King stirred and drew a short, ragged breath and his eyes blinked open. 'Is that you, Walter?' He asked in a breathless whisper.

'It is, my Lord.' Langton replied, his own voice shaky and faltering.

'I am dying, Walter.' The King replied, as tears ran down his cheeks.

'No, my Lord. I will not have you die. I have sent for the apothecary. He will revive you, just as he has done many times before.'

King Edward gave the slightest shake of his head and closed his eyes as if the movement pained him. 'No more potions, Walter. I am close to death and do not want to be befuddled when I come before the Lord. My eyes are blind and my heart flutters in my breast like a broken bird. It will not be long now.' The King's breath now wheezed horribly from his lungs.

The Lord High Treasurer was surprised to find that he was sobbing and shaking uncontrollably.

'Do not weep for me, Walter.' King Edward gasped. 'I need your strength now that I am so weakened. You must save your grief for when your King has no more use for you.'

Langton tried to bring his sobbing to a halt, but did no more than stifle the convulsions by clamping his lips together. He felt the King's hand tighten weakly around his fingers. He raised his head and saw that tears now flowed from the King's eyes.

'The bastard Scots will say that they have defeated me, Walter. You know that it is true. They will say that death carried me away before I could crush them. I will not have that, Walter. I vow before you and before God that I will have them broken and Robert Bruce executed for his treason. I need you to see that my vow is kept, Walter. Will you do this last thing for your King?'

Langton nodded furiously before realising that the King's sightless eyes would not register the gesture. 'I will, my Lord. As God is my witness, I will make sure that your vow is kept.'

The King was now shivering, but Langton was certain that he had heard his words. 'When I am dead, you must do these things for me. Have my heart cut out from my chest and have it conveyed to Jerusalem. Have it buried there so all will know that I kept my oath to return there. Have the flesh boiled from my bones and the bones put into an urn. You will command my son to march my army into Scotland with my bones at its head, so that all will now that I led the final conquest of that accursed, obdurate land and the defeat of the vile traitor Robert Bruce.'

'I will, my Lord.' Langton replied. 'I give my sacred oath that all will be done just as you have commanded it.'

King Edward closed his eyes for the final time and took two shallow, laboured breaths before his whole body was gripped by a violent spasm. Langton had to rip his fingers out of King Edward's death grip before they were crushed. He pushed down upon the King's shoulders in a vain attempt to reduce the ferocity of the fit and spoke words of comfort in the hope that the King would hear them. When the spasm eased, Langton looked down and knew immediately that Edward Plantagenet was no more. All of the great power and strength of his will had gone and only the frail and wizened flesh and bones remained. The Bishop of Coventry and Lichfield prayed for the King's immortal soul and anointed his body. When he was done, he said goodbye to the man who had given him wealth and position and, as far as was appropriate, a modicum of friendship. When he left the King's side, he found the Earls of Lincoln and Warwick in the ante-chamber, their faces pale and their expressions grave.

Langton did not bother to wipe the tears from his face. 'The King is dead.' He informed them, before standing aside so that they could enter the chamber to see for themselves.

When they emerged a few moments later, Langton positioned himself before the pavilion's entrance so that neither they nor the King's servants could leave. 'It is now our duty to ensure that the succession runs as smoothly as possible. News of the King's death must remain secret for now. If word of it should spread, it would be enough to encourage rebellion in Scotland, Ireland and Wales. I will send messengers to the Queen and the Prince of Wales and to no others. Once the Prince is here with his army around him, he will be proclaimed King and the succession will be complete. We will have the King's remains transported in secret to Lanercost Priory so that the flesh can be boiled from his bones as he commanded.'

The two Earls exchanged glances as if they found themselves overwhelmed by the night's momentous events. 'Yes, Lord Bishop.' Warwick replied. 'You can be sure that we will do our duty.'

The Scotstoun men peered down into the valley below and watched as Pembroke's army marched into the distance.

'Once they are through the next valley, we can turn for home and tell the Bruce that we saw them across the border, just as he commanded us.' John Edward rubbed at his eyes as he spoke. The last few days of tracking the Earl of Pembroke's force had been tiring work. John and twenty of his men had shadowed the Englishmen, taking out their scouts and messengers by stealth and falling upon any stragglers or wagons that fell behind the main column. They would be glad to see the back of them and to have the opportunity for much-needed rest.

'We need go no further.' Eck Edward replied. 'We have crossed the border already.' He pointed across to the far side of the valley. 'See that yonder goatherd with the ancient donkey at his side. I saw him when we were here with Wallace. This valley is on the English side, of that I am certain.'

John nodded his agreement. He had no desire to go further if it was not necessary. He pushed himself to his feet and grimaced as he stretched his legs. The thigh injured during the battle at Falkirk was often stiff and sore and the pain was only relieved when he flexed the muscles tight. 'Let's go and question the English messenger Al captured this morning. If we squeeze him hard enough, he may give us a morsel to throw upon the Bruce's table.'

The poor messenger looked as if he had already been squeezed quite hard. His left eye was swollen horribly and dry blood formed a crust around his nose and mouth. The boy flinched when John jabbed him with the toe of his boot.

'He had gold on him.' Al said, as he held up two coins for John's inspection.

'Who gave you the gold?' John snapped.

The messenger shivered with fear but found enough courage to shake his head.

John drew his dagger and held it out towards the boy. 'You will tell me what I ask. You can do it now, whilst you are unharmed, or you can do it once you are cut. I will take your eyes, your ears, your fingers and your balls. Once you have spoken, I will take your tongue. You choose how it is done. An easy death or a hard death. It is all the same to me.'

'Please!' The boy pleaded. 'I only took the gold to put food on the table for my brothers and sisters. My mother is dead and my father has taken to the drink in his grief. If you kill me, then there will be no-one to care for them.'

'Then talk, boy!' John retorted. 'My patience is already worn thin.'

'I carry a message to the King of Scots.' The boy stammered.

John exchanged glances with Eck and Strathbogie. 'Who in England would send a message to Robert Bruce?' He demanded.

'The Bishop of St Andrews.' The boy replied. 'He is a prisoner at Durham. My uncle is his jailer and pays me a penny to empty his pot and change his straw. The Bishop offered me four gold pieces to take his message north. He gave me two before I left and promised two more when I return.'

John shook his head in astonishment. 'What message does he send?'

The boy rolled onto his side and thrust his hand down the back of his breeches. After a few seconds of fumbling and scrambling around in his underclothes, he extracted a small square of stained parchment and held it out to John with trembling fingers. John's nose wrinkled in distaste and he took the scrap between his thumb and forefinger.

'How long have you kept it there?' He demanded.

'These past two days. The Bishop told me that I must keep it hidden.'

John unfolded the damp parchment with care and squinted at the tiny letters scratched upon it. He recognised Lamberton's hand in spite of the poor state of the parchment and the poor quality of the ink. He broke into a smile as he read on.

'What does it say?' Scott Edward demanded impatiently when his curiosity overcame him.

John looked around at his fellows and held the parchment up for them to see. 'God be praised!' He declared ecstatically. 'The Bastard King is dead! The good Lord has struck him down as he rode here at the head of his army! Scotland is free of him at last!'

The Scotstoun men embraced one another and howled with joy. Scott ripped the parchment from his brother's fingers so that he could read it for himself.

'We must celebrate!' Strathbogie cried joyfully.

'I will go down into that village and buy ale and goats for us to roast!' Eck announced happily. 'We must mark the occasion of our prayers being answered.'

'The King's body lies at Lanercost Priory.' Scott announced, as he finished reading Lamberton's message. 'Did we not meet with Wallace there during the invasion of England?'

John nodded in confirmation. 'We did and now we will return there to gain some small revenge for his loss. We will eat and drink and then turn our horses to the south.'

'You're no' serious?' Scott exclaimed in disbelief. 'You'll get us all killed!'

John clasped his brother's cheeks in his hands and looked him in the eye. 'Death has hung about us these past years, yet we have always stayed just beyond its reach. God has placed this opportunity in our hands and we must not forsake it out of fear. Let us strike out and land a final blow upon he who ripped Wallace from us and condemned him to the worst of deaths.'

'I'm in!' Eck interjected with grim determination.

'Me as well.' Strathbogie declared.

Scott broke from his brother's grip and turned to see all of the Scotstoun men step forward and affirm their willingness to join with John.

'There isn't a single sane man among you!' He said disapprovingly with a slow shake of his head. 'I suppose I'll have to come along just to make sure that you don't fuck it up!' He could not stop himself from breaking into a grin when his comrades cheered him and clapped him upon the back.

'What about him?' Al enquired, jabbing his thumb towards the messenger who still lay prostrate at their feet.

John glanced down at the boy before replying. 'Cut his throat! He has already heard too much. The Bishop will thank us for saving him two gold pieces.'

19

Prior Multon was awakened by the sound of a
flint being scraped inside his chamber. The
intrusion did not cause him any undue alarm as
he had grown used to his sleep being interrupted
during the six months King Edward had spent at
the Priory. Scarcely a week would pass without
the royal servants rousing him from his sleep
when the King had need of something in the
small hours of the night. His mild annoyance at
being disturbed turned to fear only when the
candle caught light and the flickering flame
illuminated the faces of the four men gathered
around his bed. Their hard faces, weather-worn
skin and unwashed stink marked them out as
low men who had no honest business within the
walls of the Priory. He pulled the blanket to his
chin in a vain attempt to protect himself from
imminent attack. He peered up at the man
standing closest to him and felt himself relax a
little when he realised that he recognised him.
His head tilted to one side like dog hoping for a
morsel from his master as he tried to recall
where he had seen this man before. It took a few
seconds before his memory did its work and he
flinched in fright.

'You!' He spat, his expression a mixture of horror and astonishment.

John smiled down at the cowering figure. 'I am flattered that you remember me, good Prior.'

'How could I forget?' The Prior replied, his tone acid and filled with accusation. 'Those days were the darkest that Lanercost has ever seen. I thank the Lord that the traitor William Wallace was captured and executed. No Scot has dared to raid across our border since then and our brothers and our treasures have been safe from thieving and murderous Scots!'

'You will remember then, that I came to the defence of both your brothers and your treasures. I chased off a band of brigands and spared you from bloodshed and the loss of your relics.'

Prior Multon nodded slowly. 'I remember it well. Twas when brother Bentley and brother Thomas were murdered in the snow upon the steps and your fellow Scots sought to carry off the sacred finger-bone of St Mary Magdalene.'

'You fell to your knees in that blood-reddened snow and thanked me for sending the rogues away. You said that you owed me a great debt.' John paused until the Prior nodded his head in acknowledgement of that fact. 'Tonight, I have come to collect that debt.'

The Prior's brow wrinkled in confusion. 'I do not understand.' He stammered, before his eyes opened wide in shock. 'You cannot mean! There are guards all around the grounds. You would be cut down before you could get away!'

'The guards are not as alert as you might expect. We shall steal past them just as easily when we go as we did when we arrived. Now, take us to where the King's remains are stored and we will relieve you of them as we relieve you of your debt.'

The Prior shook his head furiously. 'I will not! The King's remains are sacred! I will not allow it!'

The tip of John's dagger pierced the Prior's fleshy jowls, thrusting his head painfully upwards and sending large droplets of blood dripping onto his thin blanket. 'Do not mistake me, Prior. I will have my way in this whether you assist us or not. Refuse me and I will cut your throat and move onto the next brother in line. If need be, I will leave the Priory soaked in blood and hunt for the King's carcass myself.'

The Prior grasped John's wrists to reduce the pressure on the dagger. 'They will execute me if the King's remains are lost. Have mercy, my son. Have mercy on me!'

John shook his head and jerked his blade upwards. 'You must choose, Prior. I can execute you here and now or you can live long enough to fall upon your knees and beg your masters for their forgiveness. Choose now!'

'I will take you!' The Prior cried in desperation. He threw the blanket back and pushed himself up from the bed. He pulled his rough woollen robe over his head and tied it at the waist. 'You know that you will be damned for this. The good Lord will punish you for such sacrilege!'

John gestured towards the door. 'We'll take our chances with God, good Prior. If he is Scots, and I believe that he is, I know that he will look kindly upon us. Now, lead on!'

John, Eck, Scott and Strathbogie followed the Prior along the Priory's narrow, stone corridors, the darkness broken only by the candle in the Prior's hand.

'Something smells good!' Scott exclaimed, as a meaty aroma filled the air. He rubbed at his belly in an effort to stop it from growling and gurgling at the thought of broth.

The Prior stopped before a large, wooden door and cast a contemptuous glance in Scott's direction. 'I doubt that your appetite will trouble you for long.'

John shrugged in response to Scott's puzzled expression and followed the Prior through the door. He froze in fright at the scene before him in the chamber. A massive black cauldron was suspended from chains above a huge, roaring fire. Two monks fed wood into the flames whilst a third, very tall man stirred at the bubbling contents with a wooden paddle. He realised that a man's body was cooking in the cauldron just as Scott pitched forward and spewed the contents of his guts onto the earthen floor.

A faint smile flickered across the Prior's face. 'I told you that your appetite would not last long. King Edward's last wish was that the flesh be boiled from his bones. The brothers here are almost done.'

John belched and felt acid burn at the back of his throat. He drew his sword and pointed at the large monk with the wooden paddle. 'Put the bones in a sack. We'll be taking them with us!'

The monk slowly turned his head towards the Prior. 'Do it now, Brother Cuthbert.' The older man ordered. 'Or they will cut our throats and take them anyway.'

While Cuthbert used his paddle to extract King Edward's bones from the bubbling cauldron, Eck and Strathbogie tore strips of cloth from the monks' habits and used them to bind and gag the Prior and the two monks who had been tending the fire.

Cuthbert was similarly trussed up once his work was done and the four Scotsmen stole off into the night carrying the still-steaming sack with them.

Walter Langton walked the full length of Carlisle Castle's great hall under the Prince of Wales' hostile glare. He fell to his knees before the dais and swore loyalty to him as the new King.

Edward Plantagenet waved his hand dismissively. 'Enough, Langton. There will be time enough for that tomorrow when I am proclaimed King. You will join with the Bishop of Durham, the Earl of Lincoln and the Earl of Warwick in doing public homage and fealty to me as King. Now, I was told that you have requested an audience. Be quick! I have much to do.'

Langton remained on his knees as the King had not given him leave to rise. The smirk on the face of the King's companion, Tarquil de

Trasque, revealed that this was a deliberate slight rather than an oversight. 'I did request an audience, my Lord. I was with the King when he died and he made me swear to pass his last instructions onto you.'

Edward laughed without mirth. 'You mean to command me, Langton? I who am your King? It is not for you to instruct me.'

'I would give you no instruction, my Lord. I would only tell you of King Edward's last wishes as he commanded me to do.'

The King picked up his goblet and waited for it to be filled. 'Very well. Get on with it.'

Langton felt his cheeks redden at being so humiliated. 'He ordered that his heart be cut from his chest and conveyed to Jerusalem for burial there, so that his oath to return to the Holy Land would be kept. He also commanded that his flesh be boiled from his bones so that you could carry them into Scotland at the head of your army. That way, he would keep his oath to win victory over the Scots.'

King Edward now laughed with genuine amusement, though it was clearly edged with bitterness and scorn. 'That sounds just like my dear father! Even in death he expects us to win great victories to bring honour to his name. Perhaps I should renounce my crown and perch it upon his lifeless head so that he can rule even as his flesh turns to dust.'

'It was not meant that way, my Lord.' Langton protested. 'He believed that no army with him at its head could be defeated by the

Scots. He wanted nothing more than to give you victory.'

'No!' King Edward snapped venomously. 'He meant to steal all glory for himself. I'll be damned if I will win battles only for people to say that the victories were won by the power of his bones! His heart stays in his chest and his bones within his flesh! Understood?'

Langton clenched his fists in a bid to control his rising panic. He had not anticipated that Edward would deny his father's dying wishes in such a callous fashion. 'I have already sent his body to Lanercost Priory to have the flesh boiled from his bones, just as he commanded me to do.'

'Then you had better have them unboil him, Langton. I want his corpse paraded from here to Westminster so that all can see that he is dead. You will see to this as your last act for my family.'

'My last act?' Langton stammered.

King Edward's face transformed into a snarl. 'I told you once that I owed you a debt, Lord Bishop. The moment my father's funeral is over, I will pay that debt with interest. I have not forgotten your many insults, my Lord. I recall with clarity each and every occasion when you went running to my father with your complaints regarding my expenditure. I remember too how you whispered in his ear and filled his head with lies about Sir Piers Gaveston until he lost patience and ordered him into exile. Not even the burdens of kingship will dim my memory.

Now, take yourself from my sight! I have matters of state to attend to.'

The ride from Carlisle to Lanercost did nothing to ease Langton's nerves. The captain of his guard, Browby, had tried to soothe him, but succeeded only in bringing him to a temporary state of calm, before he once more erupted in panic and fury. He raged against the young King and cursed him for his cruelty. He asked the same questions a hundred times and was undeterred from repeating them by Browby's lack of answers. 'How am I to restore King Edward's flesh upon his bones? Am I a wizard? Am I a worker of miracles? How can it be a crime to do as my King has commanded me? The bastard has done this so that he has an excuse to execute me!' Only when the Priory came into view did he manage to pull himself from the grip of hysteria and turn to Browby with an expression of desperate hope on his face. 'Perhaps the monks' work is not too far advanced, Browby. Perhaps we can yet salvage something from this disaster.'

He lost both hope and his grip on his panic when the trembling and shame-faced Prior stuttered and stammered his confession that Scots villains had come in the night to steal King Edward's bones away.

'Christ!' Langton shrieked. 'You have condemned me to death! The King will hold me responsible for this!' He flew at the Prior and punched him to the ground, before kicking viciously at his head. The Prior would have perished there and then if not for Browby pulling his master bodily away.

'You must control your temper, m'Lord.' Browby hissed as Langton struggled to free himself from his iron grip. 'We will need all of your wits if any one of us is to emerge from this with our heads intact. You must calm yourself!'

Langton broke away from Browby and hammered at his own head with the heels of both hands. 'There is nothing to be done, Browby! All is lost!'

Browby looked around the chamber in search of inspiration. Three monks were busy sweeping up the cold, grey ashes that were piled around the base of a black cauldron suspended from the ceiling by thick, iron chains. He watched them work for a few moments before turning to the Prior. 'You are skilled in the arts of embalming and the preservation of mortal remains, are you not?'

'I am.' The Prior replied. 'I have long experience of the preservation of relics.'

'Including the bodies of saints?'

'Yes. I have had the privilege of instructing many brothers in these arts and my pupils have gone on to be responsible for the remains of some of the most important saints in England. Some of them are hundreds of years old, but still attract pilgrims from far and wide.'

'But the flesh must still deteriorate with the passing of years, despite your skills.'

'That is true, sir. Most flesh will turn to dust eventually or be corrupted by damp and mould.'

'Then how do you keep the saints presentable enough to encourage the pilgrims to part with their coins?'

The Prior smiled with pleasure at having the opportunity to boast of his skills. 'You would be amazed what I can do with powder and paint, clay and wax.'

Langton grasped the Prior's upper arm and squeezed it hard. 'If we had a corpse, could you make it look like the King?'

A look of astonishment crossed the Prior's face and his mouth fell open. He thought for a moment before replying. 'It could be done, Lord Bishop, but only if the corpse was fresh.' He then shook his head. 'Where would we find a corpse as tall as King Edward? He stood head and shoulders above most other men.'

Browby turned his head and stared at Brother Cuthbert as he swept at the ashes. 'What about him?'

The Prior shook his head sadly. 'He is too short, my Lord. We would have to dislocate his thighs and knees and stretch the sinews to bring him close to King Edward's height.'

'Then you must send the other two brothers away, good Prior.' Langton ordered. 'We have much work to do.'

20

Aymer de Valence, the Earl of Pembroke, restrained himself from rattling Piers Gaveston's teeth. The weeks of snide remarks and veiled criticisms had worn his patience thin. Any joy he had felt at being appointed as commander of the new King's army had long since evaporated and he cursed himself for agreeing to march north with his sovereign to bring Scotland back under royal control. The old King Edward was not yet in his grave and already his son was showing himself to be weak and unable to exert any authority over the handsome, young knights he chose to surround himself with. To have his judgement constantly challenged was one thing, to have his courage questioned by this impudent pup was beyond intolerable.

'I do not make the suggestion because I fear Robert Bruce, my Lord. I counsel the King to retire south because it is a necessity.' Pembroke growled through gritted teeth.

Gaveston waved his hand as if dismissing Pembroke's words. 'Two months have passed since the King led his army across the border. In all that time you have not once engaged with our enemy. You lead the men out through the gates

277

of Dumfries Castle at sunrise and then lead them back in untested and unscathed before the sun has set. You cannot blame me for questioning your courage or your competence. We have given you men and horses enough to finish the traitor and yet you have not so much as scratched him. Now you suggest that we turn for home and abandon our northern province.'

Pembroke ground his teeth together in frustration. 'Perhaps if you spent less time drinking wine and playing games, you might venture out beyond the castle walls and hunt the rebels yourself. Then you would see that they slip away into the mountains and the forests the moment we approach.'

'But why would he do that, Pembroke?' Gaveston shot back with an unbearably smug expression on his face. 'He cannot be king if he does not face us in battle. Brigands skulk in the mountains, kings command on the field of battle.'

King Edward placed his goblet upon the table with the exaggerated care of a drunk trying to maintain the appearance of sobriety. 'He's got a point, my Lord Pembroke. If Robert Bruce refuses to fight us, he cannot beat us.' He shrugged his shoulders and did his best to suppress a belch. 'Therefore, we win.'

Pembroke shook his head impatiently. 'He means to starve us out, my Lord, and he is close to achieving his goal. We must move south before the winter and take our time to gather our strength and deal with other pressing matters.'

Edward took another mouthful of his wine before replying. 'What other pressing matters?'

Pembroke left Langton's letter in his pocket as he had already committed its contents to memory. 'Your father remains unburied, though near three months have passed since his death. The magnates have withdrawn their support from you and the treasury is empty. The administration of the kingdom is in chaos due to your absence and the King of France grows more strident in his demands for you to come before him to swear fealty for your possessions in France. We can leave these matters unresolved no longer, my Lord.'

'You must command the magnates to attend me here, my Lord! I will order them to fill my coffers and to provide me with enough fighting men to enable me to finish this rebellion.'

Pembroke shook his head. 'You know well that they will not come so long as these two men are with you.'

Edward's temper snapped and he threw his goblet from him. 'Bastard dogs! Who are they to tell me what to do? What kind of King would I be if I was to strip Piers of the Earldom of Cornwall and Tarquil of the Earldom of Trasque just because the magnates demand it of me? I will not do it, Pembroke. You tell them that and damn them for their impertinence!'

'You knew that the appointments would enrage the magnates before you announced them, my Lord.' Pembroke replied evenly. 'Now we must deal with the consequences as best we can.'

Gaveston hammered his fist against the table. 'They defy our royal authority, Edward.' He declared viciously with his teeth bared. 'We must teach them a lesson.'

Pembroke could not mask his surprise at Gaveston's open assertion of his possession of a portion of the power of the crown. It beggared belief that he did not realise that it was this very ambition that roused the magnates to fury. 'It would be better if we refrained from the teaching of lessons and concentrated instead on the building of bridges.'

The King patted the shoulder of his scowling favourite in a bid to calm him. 'Tell us what you have in mind, Pembroke. Then we will decide what course to take.'

'If you insist on ignoring the magnates' demands, then we must find other ways to bind them to you. It seems to me that circumstances present us with a unique opportunity to do so. No magnate will refuse to attend the old King's funeral. They will come running to your side if you invite them to participate in the ceremony for your father in some small way. Nor will any lord refuse to attend the wedding of a King. No date has been set for your marriage to the daughter of the King of France. This is an opportunity to win the magnates' favour and to sweeten relations with the French King. If the wedding was to be quickly followed by your own coronation, I have no doubt that every noble in the land would scramble to kneel before you and your Queen and swear undying loyalty. Your reign would begin in unity and strength and we would have funds and men enough to bring an end to the rebellion here.'

Pembroke's heart sank when Edward turned immediately to Gaveston and Trasque. 'What do you think, Piers?'

Gaveston rubbed at his beard and cast his eyes upwards towards the hall's high ceiling. 'I think that we do need to strengthen our hand. Let us leave Tarquil here to watch over the rebellion for us. You and I should make our way to Westminster to make arrangements for the funeral, the wedding and the coronation. If we can gather the magnates around us, we will be better placed to push them into line. We will start our reign in strength.'

King Edward nodded enthusiastically and turned back to Pembroke. 'It is decided then, Pembroke. We will feast tonight with our loyal Scots nobles and then start for London on the morrow.'

Pembroke hesitated before bowing his head in acknowledgement. He saw with terrible clarity that it would be better for the King and kingdom both if he was to draw his sword and plunge its point deep into Gaveston's guts. He wished that he possessed the courage and the selflessness to do the deed, but found that he had neither.

The three horsemen watched as the English column wound its way along the sodden, muddy track. The distance and the falling rain might have obscured their view, but it was still possible to make out the figure of King Edward at the column's head.

The largest of the three turned and spat onto the ground. 'John Edward and his men will harry them until they cross the border?'

Al kept his eyes fixed upon the backs of the departing Englishmen and avoided giving a direct answer to King Robert's question. 'He is not the first king we have chased from Scottish soil.' The evasion was a small one and not an outright lie. The Scotstoun men would indeed shadow the English column and pick off any men foolish or weak enough to stray from the safety of the army, but John Edward was not at their head. He and four others had ridden for Scotstoun to see their families and to dig a new latrine at the back of the village square. Al kept this information to himself, as he did not know how he would explain why the village had such urgent need of a pit for people to shit in. The thought of his wife and family emptying their bowels onto the bones of the English King brought a smile to his face.

'What now, Robert?' Edward Bruce demanded. 'With no army to field against us, the remaining English will huddle behind their castle walls and await the return of their King once the winter is done.'

King Robert laughed, though the sound was cold and hollow. 'The English King may have gone, but he leaves us surrounded by enemies. We must make what we can of this opportunity to reduce their numbers. When the English return, as surely they will, we must be strong enough to face them.'

Edward Bruce shook his head. 'Then we must pray that he does not return quickly. Most of the nobles will wait until they see how events unfold, leaving us alone to deal with the Macdowalls of Galloway, the Macdougalls of Lorne, the Earl of Ross, the Comyns under the Earl of Buchan and the garrisons of every castle in Scotland. Tell me, brother, how are we to deal with them all with only a handful of knights and a few hundred foot soldiers behind us?'

King Robert turned to meet his brother's gaze and paused in contemplation before replying. 'One at a time, Edward. That is how we will deal with them. We will reckon with them one at a time.'

Edward broke into a wide grin and nodded his approval. 'I'll drink to that! Who first?'

It was Robert's turn to grin. 'Dugal Macdowall will be first. He sent our brothers to be executed by the English. He will pay the price for that and then we will head north for the others. The Bishop of Moray preaches tirelessly there and he tells me that the glens now buzz like a nest of wasps ready to fall upon our enemies and sting them with all fury. We will have men enough to face our enemies before too much longer. They must decide whether they perish or bow down before us. I care not which path they choose, just so long as it is finished before King Edward marches north once more.'

Browby silently entered the chamber and made his way towards the Bishop's desk, his face as grave as Langton had ever seen it. 'It is confirmed, m'Lord. The King's men will come for you at first light.'

Langton slumped back in his chair and let out a long sigh. 'Come, sit with me Browby. If this is to be my last night of freedom, you will not leave me to drink alone.'

Browby slipped into the chair opposite his master and watched as he filled a goblet and held it out towards him. 'We could still run, m'Lord. The docks are filled with French ships and their captains will take any cargo in exchange for gold.'

Langton slowly shook his head as he savoured a mouthful of wine. 'I have made as many enemies in France doing the King's business as I have here in England. I might remain at liberty for a week or two, but I would not last long before my throat was slit and my corpse tossed into a ditch. I will take my chances in the King's dungeons.'

Browby sipped at his wine and returned Langton's steady gaze. 'You are calmer than I expected, m'Lord. I thought that you would be angry. I thought that you would curse the King and rage against his lack of constancy and his cruelty.'

The Bishop laughed and lifted his goblet to toast his captain. 'My outlook changed after that business at Lanercost, Browby. I feared that I would be exposed and sentenced with execution each and every day of that damned procession from Lanercost to London. I near cried with relief when the new King took his leave of us after the first two days and I cannot articulate the joy I felt when the King was finally entombed. I could have cried with happiness when that marble slab slid into place and hid the Prior's work from view. He had used so much wax by the time we reached Westminster that I had to order the guards to let no-one approach with a torch lest they caused the old King's face to melt. By Christ, imprisonment is a much less daunting prospect when one has lived under the constant threat of death!'

'You need worry no more, m'Lord. I heard that the Prior and his two attendants were viciously attacked and murdered on their way back north. Only you and I know of brother Cuthbert's fate.'

'Then let us drink to brother Cuthbert, Browby. May he rest in peace.'

Browby returned the toast. 'I understand your relief but I do not understand your lack of anger at being treated so badly after a lifetime of loyalty to the crown. You should be cursing the King.'

Langton shrugged his shoulders. 'There is little point in wasting my anger upon him. He was born with every advantage in life. He is tall, handsome, fearless, skilled with the sword and lance and was born to be King. Despite this, he is weak of heart and mind, so weak that he allows those he sees as his friends to rule him. He allows them to lead him into disaster.' Langton was warming to his theme and leaned towards Browby in his eagerness to make his point. 'I told Pembroke to get him to use the funeral, the wedding and the coronation to bring the nobles back within his embrace and to ease relations with France. What does he do? He gives pride of place to that popinjay Gaveston at the coronation. He has his coat of arms hung upon the walls of the hall alongside Gaveston's and not those of the Queen. He has Gaveston sat next to him at the feast and ignores Isabella of France so much that not a single English or French noble failed to remark upon it. If the Earl of Trasque had not been there to distract her, I have no doubt that she would have wept. The Earl of Lancaster was so enraged by the display that he had to be restrained from taking his sword to the King's favourite before the eyes of the gathered nobles. When the nation should be united behind him, he has somehow conspired to have even less support than he did before. I need not waste my time wishing him ill when he constantly brings misfortune upon himself.'

'Then!' Browby interjected. 'Why do you still attempt to help him? Messengers fly between you and Pembroke so that he may counsel the King more effectively. Why do so when the King is about to strip you of both liberty and fortune?'

Langton waved his finger at his captain. 'You have me there, Browby. I cannot deny it. I have spent so long scheming that I find that I cannot do without it. I will plot and manipulate as long as I am able, even if others are to enjoy the fruits of my endeavours. I have hidden away enough of my fortune to ensure that I will be able to make mischief even from within my dungeon walls. I will keep you busy placing my gold where I wish it to be. Now drink up! I shall be cross if we are not drunk when the King's men come.'

21

The chill morning air caused Dugal Macdowall to shiver in spite of his furs. He groaned with relief as he emptied his bladder and sent a stream of steaming pish onto the frozen earth. He had just begun to shake himself when he caught sight of a lone horseman standing at the foot of the glen with a black dog on the ground at his side. He rubbed the sleep from his eyes with his free hand and tried to bring the figure into focus. He could not identify the man at such a great distance and decided that he would take his men to investigate once he had filled his belly with hot porridge to fortify himself against the freezing temperatures. He was supping at his hearth when the thunder of galloping hooves caused him to leap to his feet in fright and cast his wooden bowl aside. He exchanged a panicked glance with his brother before they both snatched up their swords and burst out into the clear, cold morning.

Dugal knew immediately that the day was already lost. The horsemen had charged into the far end of the village and were now scything his men down as they spilled out from their houses, still squinting their eyes against the brightness of

288

day. The village's single street was already strewn with the dead and the wounded and thick smoke rose from the thatched roofs of several cottages. The columns of smoke now drifting into the sky at either end of the glen told him that all of his territory was under attack.

'Get the horses!' He snapped at his brother. 'We must flee! Robert Bruce has come to avenge his brothers.'

His brother looked back at him in confusion. 'How did we have no warning of this? Where are our lookouts?'

A memory of the lone horseman and his dog flashed into Dugal's mind and he cursed himself for his decision to break his fast before challenging his presence in the glen. 'They are already dead at the hands of better men. Now, get the horses or the Bruce will have the vengeance he seeks. We will run for the forest and gather ourselves there.'

By the time darkness fell, it seemed that all of Galloway was aflame. Dugal watched impotently as his cattle were driven off and every structure on his lands was put to the torch or pulled down. Others had made their way into the forest as the day progressed, but there were too few of them to mount a counter-attack. Misery was piled upon misery as frightened men, women and children arrived with their tales of what they had suffered. The rebels slaughtered all who came into their hands and spared none regardless of age or sex. Dugal would have wept, if he had not felt so numb, when informed that his uncle, brother and three nephews were lost. He did shed a tear when told that the raiders had uncovered the hoard buried beneath his own hearth and had carried the gold away in the sacks the Earl of Pembroke had delivered it in. He had quickly wiped that tear away before it was noticed, but knew that he would feel the loss for a long time to come.

'They will regret this when the English King returns.' He vowed bitterly. 'If Robert Bruce comes within my reach, I will cut him down and the English can keep the reward they have offered for his capture.'

Though he spoke with feeling and strong emotion, all men there knew that he would do no such thing. Vengeance was a fine thing to have, but it was no substitute for coin.

John Edward huddled as close to the fire as he could without setting his cloak alight, but the flames did nothing to warm his aching fingers. 'By Christ!' He exclaimed to no-one in particular. 'I do not think that I have ever been so cold.' None of his companions gave a response, as they were too wrapped up in their own misery and too busy with their own shivering. The march north from Galloway had been hard. The western Highlands offered little in the way of sustenance and the last of the Macdowall cattle had been slaughtered more than a week before. The hard weeks had brought some joy, as men arrived each day to join with them and to swear allegiance to King Robert. This joy was somewhat tempered by the need to feed these extra mouths, even as their provisions dwindled away.

John looked up to see that Gilbert de la Haye approached them. The Baron of Errol was closer to King Robert than any other man, save for his brother Edward, and John groaned at the realisation that he was about to be pulled away from what little warmth the fire offered him.

Sir Gilbert nodded a greeting to the huddled men of Scotstoun and crouched down at the fire. 'By Christ, John! But it is cold. I have lost all feeling in my feet and am too afeart to take off my boots lest my toes come away with the leather.'

John noted with some satisfaction that Sir Gilbert appeared as dirty and ragged as the other men gathered around the fire. When he had first set his eyes upon him at King Robert's coronation at Scone, he had been as finely dressed a man as he had ever seen. The privations of the past year had also seen him grow gaunt and hollow-eyed. 'I must warn you, Sir Gilbert, if you have come to take me away from my fire, you will have to take me by force.'

Gilbert laughed merrily and rubbed at his fingers in a bid to warm them. 'I doubt if I will have to resort to that. King Robert sent me to fetch you because your scout has had sight of John of Lorne.'

'He approaches?' John demanded, his attention now fully upon Sir Gilbert, the fire temporarily forgotten.

Sir Gilbert nodded. 'Aye! He comes with a thousand men at his back.'

'Ah!' John exclaimed. 'He outnumbers us by nearly three hundred men. Will the King fight him here? I almost wish for it. In the heat of battle, I might forget about my frozen extremities.'

'Don't say that to the King, John. He is looking to you for sanity. His brother urges him to attack without delay and gain revenge for the weeks when John of Lorne and his hounds hunted us through the heather. The King will fight him if he must, but would prefer to negotiate.'

John pushed himself stiffly to his feet and groaned with pain as his injured thigh protested. 'Then we must rouse the men, Sir Gilbert. The Macdougalls of Lorne must see us ranged against them on this high ground if the King is to have his way.'

John disliked John of Lorne on his first sight of him. His hair was thin, straggly and greasy and his mouth was filled with thin, yellow teeth which gave him a rat-like aspect. He thought that the three men who rode forward with him for the parley must be his close relations, for they too put him in mind of vermin. John trotted forward at Edward Bruce's side with Robert Bruce and Sir Gilbert on the far side of him. Edward mumbled furiously under his breath as they advanced and John could hear him grind his teeth together in fury. At that moment, John though that a battle was more likely than not.

John of Lorne brought his horse to a halt and glowered at Robert Bruce. He jerked his head backwards in the direction of the ranks of

Macdougall spearmen. 'You will find us harder to surprise than the Macdowalls of Galloway.' He growled.

Edward Bruce snapped back at him with equal venom. 'We will slaughter you just the same.'

King Robert raised his hand to bring his brother to silence. 'I will be frank with you, sir. I doubt that you will bow down and call me King.'

The Macdougall snorted derisively. 'You are no king, Robert Bruce, and I will bow to no man who has murdered my kin. The only question in my mind is whether I finish you now or wait for the return of King Edward.'

'Then you must decide now. You see my army here before you. We are ready to settle this. Just say the word and I will order the charge.'

John of Lorne raised his head and looked slowly along the ranks of Robert Bruce's army. 'You have fewer men than I. Those that you have are ragged and worn. I have no doubt that I would prevail.'

King Robert nodded his agreement. ''Tis true that my men are tired, but they are sharp and battle-hardened. Many of them, like this man here.' The King pointed towards John Edward as he spoke. 'Have fought continuously against the English since Stirling Bridge. Such seasoned men will not die easily. You must ask yourself how much a victory would cost you. You must ask yourself how the remnants of your army would fare when my allies arrive here. You will already have seen that the galleys of Angus Macdonald of the Isles already patrol the Firth of Lorne and Loch Linnhe and threaten you from the sea. I have no doubt that you have heard how the Bishop of Moray preaches and gathers men who are sworn to me. You might well prevail today, but what of the days to come?'

The slight flaring of John of Lorne's nostrils was enough to confirm that he was fully aware of the forces gathering against him. He knew that, even if he was victorious, the battle would leave him severely weakened.

King Robert read the indecision in his countryman's eyes and pressed home his advantage. 'I will give you a truce until Midsummer's Day. I give you my word that no man sworn to me will attack you or do any harm to you before that day. In return, you will lead no army against me. If you do not keep your word, I will turn on you with every man available to me and put an end to you. This I swear before God.'

John of Lorne was a cautious man and thought it wise to keep his army intact until King Edward returned. He had no doubt that the English King would return in the spring, at which point he could break the truce with impunity. 'You have my word.' He replied, as he began to turn his horse.

'Till Midsummer then.' Edward Bruce shouted cheerfully at his back. 'Then we will settle with you!'

'That went better than I expected.' John Edward announced in a tone of mild regret. 'I had hoped that the battle would warm my frozen blood.'

King Robert kept his eyes on the retreating Macdougalls. 'You will have no end of opportunities to warm yourself in the winter frosts, John Edward. With the Macdougalls of Lorne now temporarily immobilized, we must turn to face the Earls of Ross and Buchan.'

The Earl of Trasque grew more disconsolate as the royal column drew closer to Dragan Hall. 'He has not come!' He snapped, his anger failing to mask the fact that he was close to tears.

Lady Ingrede reached out to comfort him. 'I am sorry, Tarquil. I know just how much you were looking forward to receiving him. But you must steady yourself. I see the Queen's carriage and you must not cause offence by welcoming her here with tears in your eyes.'

'I will not tell how much silver I have wasted on poets, musicians and minstrels for the King's entertainment. Each one selected to cater for his particular tastes. I am furious that he has been kept away!'

'It will not be wasted, dear Tarquil. Tis still a great honour to have the Queen beneath our roof. Now force a smile onto your lips, lest your frowning startles the girl and chases her away from us.'

Tarquil did as his wife instructed and stepped forward with a grin plastered across his face and bowed as Queen Isabella of England was helped down from her golden carriage by a liveried coachman. Tarquil bowed lower still and kissed the proffered hand. 'Welcome to Dragan Hall, your Majesty. We are honoured by your presence.'

Lady Ingrede bowed but kept her eyes upon the Queen. Though undeniably beautiful, the Queen was more girl than woman and had scarcely begun to bud. It would be a year or two before she would be capable of producing heirs. She was dressed expensively but her attire was modest and not at all ostentatious. When she spoke, her voice was light but not as frivolous or as childlike as her girlish frame might suggest.

'The honour is mine, my Lord.' She replied, her smile lighting up her face. 'I have been looking forward to this for weeks. It is so dull at court without you there.'

Tarquil bowed his head in thanks and turned to introduce his wife. Queen Isabella reached out and took Ingrede's hands in hers.

'You are fortunate indeed, Lady Ingrede, to have a husband such as this.' She declared, her accent still more French than English in spite of the attentions of the tutors her husband had engaged for her. 'He has shown me such warmth and friendship since I landed on these shores. The King, my husband, has had so little time for me, but Tarquil here has been so kind and attentive, he has kept my spirits high. Now let us go inside, the air is cold and I would warm myself.'

Once the Queen was seated by a roaring fire with a goblet of warm, spiced mead in her hand, she reached out and patted Tarquil on his lower arm. 'Now that we are alone, I must apologise for my husband's absence. He was looking forward to coming here, but was persuaded to be elsewhere.' A frown darkened her face when she paused. 'I will not say who it was that persuaded him.'

'You do not need to say, my Lady.' Tarquil replied. 'I know full well that Piers Gaveston is behind this. He does all that he can to keep me from the King.'

Queen Isabella lowered her voice even although the servants had been sent away and there was no one who could overhear them. 'Tis bad enough that he comes between the King and his friends, but worst still that he keeps the King from his Queen.'

'He is a serpent!' Tarquil snapped, with more venom than he had intended.

Queen Isabella leaned forward towards Tarquil and Ingrede. 'We should not trouble ourselves with him too much. The serpent's head will be struck off before many more days have passed.'

'Really?' Tarquil gasped. 'Pray tell us more, my Lady.'

Isabella cast a glance over her shoulder before continuing in little more than a whisper. 'My father, the King of France, was most furious to hear that my husband is prevented from paying me the attention due to his Queen. He has engaged the support of the magnates of

England and, led by the Earls of Lancaster, Lincoln and Warwick, they are working to force the King to send Sir Piers into exile. The King refuses of course, but he will soon have to yield, as his treasury is empty and they refuse to provide men for his armies.'

Tarquil shook his head in disappointment. 'The King could resist them for years, my Lady. Moneylenders flock to his doors and he can simply continue to move his court from one city to another, stripping the country bare as he goes. I never saw him pay for so much as a barrel of wine when he was Prince of Wales, I doubt that he will start to honour his debts now that he is King.'

The smug, conspiratorial smile on the Queen's face drew Tarquil back under her influence. 'He might well be able to extort wine and pork from fearful merchants, but he cannot raise an army without gold and the support of the nobles. His need for an army grows greater as the situation in his northern province deteriorates. He dares not lose what his father had won and it is that fear which will cause him to cast Piers Gaveston away.'

'What news from Scotland, my Lady?' Ingrede enquired.

'The Earl of Pembroke tells me that Robert Bruce grows stronger with each day that passes. He has defeated the Macdowalls of Galloway and forced the Macdougalls of Lorne and the Earl of Ross into agreeing to truces with him. Only the Earl of Buchan and supporters of John Comyn now stand against him and he has already swept up the Great Glen and seized their castles at Inverlochy and Loch Ness. If the Scots nobles are unwilling or unable to stop him, the King must march north and stamp out the rebellion himself.'

Tarquil was much cheered by this news and excused himself from the Queen's presence to see to the arrangements for that night's feast. When he had left the chamber, Ingrede turned to the Queen.

'As we are sharing confidences, my Lady, I would touch upon a most delicate matter.' The Queen smiled at her and nodded to indicate that she should continue. 'You do realise that Tarquil's resentment towards Sir Piers Gaveston is driven by jealousy? He feels that he has been usurped and wishes only to regain his position as the King's most special favourite.'

The Queen hesitated before answering, but did not break eye contact with Lady Ingrede. 'I know that Tarquil loves the King as much as I, but he is no threat to me. Gaveston also loves the King, but he seeks to control him. That is a threat I cannot ignore. If the King must have a favourite, I would rather that it was your husband.'

Ingrede nodded and thanked Isabella for her candour.

'What of you, Lady Ingrede?' The Queen asked. 'Does it trouble you that your husband has a greater love for another man than he does for you?'

Ingrede smiled tightly and shrugged her shoulders. 'I get by, my Lady, and I am not unhappy.'

The sly smile that crossed Queen Isabella's face belied her tender age. 'I have heard that the King's Knight helps you get by.'

'What have you heard?' Ingrede replied in shock.

Isabella now grinned wickedly. 'I have heard that your youngest son has none of your husband's fine features, but that he is as dark and as square of jaw as the King's Knight.'

Ingrede groaned and her chin dropped to her chest.

Isabella reached out and clasped her fingers around her hand. 'Do not worry, sweet Ingrede. We shall keep each other's secrets and those who whispered it to me will keep it to themselves or I will set the King's Knight upon them.'

22

John Edward kicked the snow from his boots and entered the King's pavilion. The faces of the men who greeted him were as grim as his own. The air inside the tent was as frigid as that outside of it and John pulled his cloak more tightly around him. King Robert lay on his bed at the room's centre, his face pale, his eyes ringed with black circles and his hair and face soaked with his own sweat. His attendants had buried him beneath a pile of furs, but he still shivered uncontrollably.

The Bishop of Moray had paused when John came in through the flap, but he now returned to his argument. 'I did not spend months persuading men to join with us only to see their lives thrown away in some rash attack. We must be cautious. We have few enough men as it is.'

Edward Bruce snapped back at him, his fists clenched tightly at his sides. 'You would rather see them freeze to death on this mountain while the Earl of Buchan and his allies wait for the frosts to do their work for them. They are down on the plains and do not suffer as we do here. They can afford to wait for the spring! Not one of us will be left by then.'

Gilbert de la Haye stepped between the two men. 'We must wait until the King's health is restored and he recovers his strength. He must ride at our head when we face the Comyns in battle.' He lifted his hand and held it out towards John. 'Let us ask John Edward for his opinion. All men here know him to be clear-headed and averse to impetuous acts. Let us hear what he has to say.'

Edward Bruce cursed. 'Christ! It would be better to throw our lives away than to perish here while our enemies watch on in comfort!'

John felt colour rush to his cheeks when all eyes fell upon him. He rubbed at his beard and tried to collect his thoughts. 'The Bishop is right to urge caution, for we are outnumbered by two to one. Edward Bruce is also right. We found four men frozen solid beneath their blankets in the snow this morning and we will find more when the sun rises tomorrow. Our men are starving, the clothes rot on their backs and their plate and maille grow orange with rust. The men of Angus attack our outposts at will and not a single day passes without us losing scouts, pickets and men whose hunger drives them to hunt beyond the limits of our camp. More men desert each night, not from any lack of courage or loyalty, but because their bellies have been empty for too long. Our horses have not eaten for days and will soon be of no use to us. If we do not attack, the Comyns will not need to raise a hand to defeat us.'

Edward Bruce punched the air in delight. 'Christ! It is just as I said. We must be bold!'

'Very well.' The Bishop of Moray conceded with a sigh. 'We will march down and face them just as soon as the King is well enough to ride at our head.'

'We'll ready the men now!' Edward Bruce retorted. 'Leave the King to me! I will tie him to his horse myself if I must.'

It soon became apparent that King Robert was too weak to remain upright in his saddle. Ignoring the pleas of the Bishop of Moray and Sir Gilbert de la Haye, Edward Bruce ordered Sir William Wiseman and Sir David Barclay to ride on either side of the King and use their strength to hold him upright. He then had other knights of Moray ride alongside them with the King's banner and pennants held as high as they were able. 'Let them see that they face King Robert.' He barked. 'It will test their courage.'

John felt his heart begin to hammer in his chest the moment he caught sight of the Earl of Buchan's forces drawn up across the road to Inverurie. Even at this distance, the disparity in numbers was obvious. Edward Bruce ordered the men into two thin ranks in a vain effort to mask his numerical disadvantage. A glance along the line did nothing to soothe John's anxiety. The men were gaunt and ragged and would likely tire within minutes of engaging the enemy. In moments of hopelessness, any sane man will pray for divine intervention. John found himself mouthing a silent prayer and making promises to make changes to his future conduct in return for a miracle upon the field. Edward Bruce seemed to have taken leave of his senses and, instead of resorting to prayer, he galloped manically back and forth along the line roaring at the men to rattle their swords and scream dire threats at their enemy.

When he judged that the distance between the two armies had closed sufficiently, he stood up in his stirrups, raised his sword above his head and cried the charge. John kicked at his mount and urged the beast on after Edward Bruce. With barely half the distance between them covered, John saw the miracle begin to unfold. He blinked furiously to make sure that his eyes were not deceiving him and felt hope rise in his breast. The Comyn foot were breaking. The thundering charge lead by the roaring Bruce had filled the hearts of Buchan's archers and spearman with such fear that a small number of them had dropped their weapons and run from the attack. The panic spread with incredible speed, turning the stream of deserters into a deluge. The armoured men-at-arms held fast for a moment longer and then they too faltered and fled. The Earl of Buchan was quick to realise that the day was lost and he turned his horse and fled the battlefield alongside Sir John Mowbray and Sir David Brechin. Fewer than a third of Buchan's horse remained when Edward Bruce's charge hit their line. Whether they were too slow to react or too courageous and honourable to flee, it is impossible to tell. They fought bravely and stubbornly, but were soon overwhelmed by the rebels' superior numbers and were cut down.

When the last of them had fallen, Edward Bruce turned his horse and held his blood-stained sword aloft. 'Finish them!' He screamed. 'Finish every last one of them!' A great howl of fury went up from the rebel ranks and both horse and foot alike poured over the dead and the dying in pursuit of the fleeing Comyn men.

The enemy foot, as always, suffered the most. Having abandoned their weapons in their haste to escape the charge, they could do nothing to defend themselves when the cavalry caught up with them. John's right arm soon grew tired and sore from scything his sword down at Comyn heads. The English men-at-arms amongst them were more troublesome, as those who had kept their helmets often required more than one blow to finish them off. Edward Bruce only called off the hunt when the sun began to set and they came in sight of Fyvie Castle.

'The Earl of Buchan has taken refuge within the castle.' He informed John. 'We will make camp here and call him out in the morning.'

Some men built fires and others went off in search of game, but most simply fell to the ground in exhaustion and slept upon the bare earth. They were roused from their slumber before the break of day. It seemed that the Earl of Buchan had lost his appetite for battle and had slipped away under cover of darkness. The exertions of the previous day had done little to sap Edward Bruce's strength or energy and he harassed and chivvied mercilessly until his force was ready to renew the pursuit.

John would always remember this day as being the longest of his life. Weak from hunger, saddle-sore and aching from the previous day's fighting, they rode for hour after hour, up hills and down glens, across rivers and streams, over vast stretches of moorland and through thick forests. Edward Bruce never flagged for a moment, nor lessened his pace. He kept his eyes fixed firmly on the horizon and kept them there, even when scouts came in to report on the enemy's position.

'If we do not finish them now.' He explained to John. 'They will come back. If we can run them down today, then we will not have to fight this battle again.'

John laughed despite his miserable condition. 'We have enough battles to fight, Ed, without fighting them twice over.'

'Christ, John.' Edward replied grimly. 'It seems that we are never more than one step away from disaster. Once we are done here, we must turn to face the Earl of Ross, then the Macdougalls of Lorne and then, if we are lucky enough to live so long, we will be just in time to welcome the English King when he returns.'

'If I don't get my arse out of this saddle soon, I'll no' be fit enough to fight anyone.' John groaned, as he tried to stretch his thigh muscles enough to relieve their stiffness.

'You may have your wish!' Edward exclaimed. 'Look there! The Earl of Buchan has finally tired of running.'

John saw immediately that the fleeing Earl had now turned to faced his pursuers. He reckoned that there were around one hundred and fifty horsemen lined up across the valley floor. He glanced to his rear and quickly counted the numbers of rebel cavalry now answering Edward's command to form up. Nearly ninety men were close by, with another twenty or twenty-five still making their way up the hill behind them.

His cousin brought his horse to a halt at his side. 'We will be almost evenly matched when the stragglers come up!' Eck announced cheerfully.

Edward Bruce heard him speak and jerked his head towards him. 'We will not wait for them. We must strike before the Earl loses his courage once more.'

Eck shrugged nonchalantly and drew both his swords. 'Let's finish them then.'

John cursed silently as Edward Bruce grinned manically and drew his own blade. 'At them!' He cried and dug in with his spurs.

John urged his own horse on and followed Edward into the charge. The rebels' horses gained a terrible momentum as they galloped and accelerated down the long slope and they hit the Earl of Buchan's line with enough force to shatter it and send his knights reeling. John saw little of it, for an unseen blow struck him hard in the chest and threw him back from his horse with an impact sufficient to tear his feet from his stirrups. Just as he drew back his arm to strike at a snarling Buchan knight, the ground and the sky tilted horribly and he crashed into the earth hard enough to knock all of the breath from his lungs. Unable to draw breath and fighting his rising panic, he was deaf to the din of battle and had only a slight and peripheral awareness of the

carnage unfolding around him. He pushed
himself to his knees and hammered at his chest
in an effort to drum life and air back into his
lungs. Black spots began to dance before his
eyes and he no longer had the strength to hold
himself upright. He slumped forwards onto the
earth and lay there waiting for death to take him.
He heard voices calling his name, but they were
faint and far away, so he paid them no need. He
remained supine and limp when he was pulled
roughly from the ground and did not react when
his cousin's desperate, frightened face filled his
field of vision. Eck's mouth opened and closed
furiously, but John heard not a word of it. He
saw Eck draw back his fist and punch hard at his
midriff, but that first blow caused him no pain.
His second punch was a different matter
entirely. The instant it landed, John felt
something give within his abdomen and he was
able to take a shuddering, gasping, agonizing
breath. The moment the air entered his lungs, he
was engulfed in a world of pain and noise. He
gazed about himself in confusion. The neat lines
of cavalry were gone and in their place were
scattered corpses and broken, pitiful horses.
Some men still hacked at one another with their
swords, but most had spurred their horses away,
some in desperate flight and some in determined
pursuit.

'Get him in his saddle!' Eck ordered with
urgency.

John, still dazed and not fully comprehending
what was happening, let Strathbogie hoist him

into his saddle and place his feet back in the stirrups.

Eck leaned across from his own mount and took his reins. 'The Earl of Buchan has fled.' He informed his woozy cousin. 'The Bruce has ordered that we ride down every last knight in his service.' Eck pointed to the west and John turned his head to see five knights just cresting a steep hill. 'Those are ours. We must hurry! They have a start on us.'

It took only five minutes for John to recover his wits, take up his own reins and throw himself into the chase. He hunched forward to ease the sharp ache in his chest, but could do nothing to soothe the discomfort in his legs, shoulders, arms, neck and throat. He prayed as he rode. He did not care whether the fugitives evaded them or were cut down, he just wanted it over quickly so he could climb out of his saddle and lay down upon the earth. It seemed that his prayers were not heard, for the Buchan men stayed beyond their reach until the sun began to set. Even then, they might have escaped into the darkness if the river had not been so high as to make the ford too treacherous to cross. They turned their horses upon the bank, drew their swords and prepared to face their pursuers.

It was to be an even fight. There were five of them lined up against John, Eck, Strathbogie, Scott and Al.

Strathbogie hefted his axe as they closed on the Buchan men. 'Let's finish them quickly. I see that they carry provisions with them and I have eaten nothing for days.'

John strained his eyes in the fading light and then exhaled sharply. 'These men are known to us. See their surcoats!'

'Christ!' Eck exclaimed. 'They are the Red Comyn's men.'

John gestured to the others to rein their horses in and he went forward alone. One of the fugitives reciprocated and came forward to meet with him.

'Jesus! It is you.' He exclaimed, when they were close enough to see one another.

'Peter Davidson.' John responded. 'I had hoped that I would not see you here.'

'So, you have thrown your lot in with Robert Bruce?'

'I have.' John responded. 'For now, at least. I am sworn to drive the English out and he seems to offer the best prospect of its achievement.'

Peter nodded wearily. 'What now?'

'That is up to you.' John replied. 'I have no desire to fight against men who stood shoulder to shoulder with us at Falkirk, but neither can I allow you to go free if it is your intention to remain allied with the English. You know this of me.'

'So, we must fight.'

John shook his head. 'You can throw off your surcoats, maille and helmets and join with me. No one will notice if a few more ragged warriors join the ranks of the Scotstoun men. You are sworn to the Comyns, but the Comyns are no more. Your lord is either dead or flees for England. Even as we speak, Edward Bruce ravages Buchan from end to end. He will burn it, harry its people, pull its castles down, salt its wells and render it incapable of supporting armed men.'

Peter Davidson nodded sadly. 'It is true. The Earl is already away. He made for the coast where a ship waits to take him to England. We turned on you in the glen to slow your pursuit so he could make good his escape.'

'Why fight on when you are abandoned by your Lord? You know that other Comyn men have already submitted to King Robert?'

'I will never kneel to that false king!' Davidson snapped. 'He slaughtered the Red Comyn on holy ground! That I can never forgive!'

'That is not a condition of my offer. I ask only that you fight with me against the English. I will keep you as far from the Bruces as I am able.'

Davidson nodded reluctantly but forced himself to smile. 'I suppose that it is the least of two evils. It would be a shame if we were forced to kill old brothers-in-arms.'

John returned his grin. 'That is not the worst of it. If my men are to agree to this, you must share your food with us. Strathbogie is near mad with hunger and I fear that he might well slaughter all of us in order to fill his belly.'

Browby swatted at the flies buzzing around his head in the early evening's summer sunshine. He was thirsty after his long ride and hoped that the Earl of Pembroke would not keep him waiting long. The sound of approaching hoofbeats told him that his hopes were to be realised. The Earl looked shifty and nervous and cast his eyes around him.

'You can relax, m'Lord.' Browby assured him. 'I arrived an hour past and have scouted the area most carefully. No man lurks in the bushes to spy upon us. After working for the Bishop all these years, I know well the precautions which must be taken.'

Pembroke nodded. 'I apologise. It would be ill for me if we were to be seen together. How fares your master?'

Browby shrugged. 'You know the Bishop. He scarcely seems to notice his poor conditions. Even as he starves, he seems only to hunger for information, intelligence, gossip and rumour. With only a damp floor to lie upon, he still sits like a spider at the centre of its web. He grows thin, his hair falls out and his flesh turns grey. I do not know how long his plotting will sustain him.'

'I might have news that will cheer him. You should tell him that his suggestions may yet bear fruit. The Pope was, as Langton suspected, happy to support the nobles by condemning Gaveston's unnatural influence over the King. If he is not deprived of the Earldom of Cornwall and exiled by the end of the summer, he will be declared excommunicate.'

'My Lord Bishop will be glad to hear it.'

'He might be gladder still to hear that the situation in Scotland places still more pressure on the King to bend to the will of his magnates. After defeating the Earl of Buchan, Robert

Bruce has proceeded to lay waste to his lands and has captured and destroyed the Comyn castles of Kinedar, Dundarg, Rattray, Tarradale, Slains and Kelly. He continues to threaten the castles of Duffus, Belvenie, Skelbo, Elgin and Aberdeen, even as he turns to face the Macdougalls of Lorne. In the south, his young adherent, Sir James Douglas makes havoc in his name. Just one week past, he slew the warden of Castle Douglas, the second commander to suffer that fate. It is said that he is in league with the devil and I am struggling to find any man willing to take command of the garrison. He has near total control of all of Douglasdale, Upper Clydesdale and the Forest of Selkirk as far as Jedburgh.'

'You think that the King will comply?' Browby asked.

'He must!' Pembroke replied. 'The situation in Scotland is not yet beyond salvation, but he cannot leave the rebellion to fester for much longer. His reputation would never recover if he was to lose that kingdom.'

'What about the Bishop, m'Lord? Did you raise the matter with King Edward?'

Pembroke grimaced internally and then lied. 'I did, Browby, but the King insists that he must suffer for a while longer. I will ask him again when Gaveston has been removed. He never leaves his side and it is often difficult to tell if the King has a single opinion that Gaveston did not plant in his head. Now! Let's be away. I will send for you when I have anything new to report. Please send the Bishop my regards.'

23

Sir Edward de Cheney made his way through the castle and climbed up onto the battlements. He had a kind word and a smile for everyone he passed, be they lowly servant, hardened soldier or recent recruit. Tall, handsome and resplendent in the finest armour money could buy, he was both admired and liked by every man, woman and child within the walls of Castle Douglas. He was, by some years, the youngest warden to have served here, but the Earl of Pembroke had been happy to overlook his tender years on account of his enthusiasm for the post and the willingness of his father to provide the gold to pay for the necessary men, equipment and supplies. Sir Edward looked out from the battlements and surveyed his new domain. The land was duller and less green than the forests and moors of his native Yorkshire, but he was certain that he could tolerate it for the next twelve months. He expected the coming winter to be hard, but his father's supplies were already stowed in the cellars and he had set his men to gathering more food from the day of his arrival just two weeks before.

The tales he had heard of the black-hearted men of Douglas had proven to be unfounded. He had men enough to ensure that each patrol was too strong to be attacked by common brigands and they had enjoyed great success in parting the miserable locals from their oats, barley and grain. Cattle and sheep had been harder to procure, as it seemed that the peasants had driven them deep into the forests to keep them out of English hands. Sir Edward was nothing if he was not tenacious and optimistic and he had no doubt that his men would succeed in acquiring sufficient mutton and beef to be cured for the winter months.

The autumn sun still had some of its heat and he closed his eyes, the better to enjoy its warmth on his skin. He reached into his jerkin and pulled out the locket which hung from his neck on a chain of gold. He kept his eyes closed and lifted it to his nose. He fancied that he could detect just a hint of her scent from the precious lock of hair enclosed within the locket. Sir Edward screwed his eyes up tighter and conjured up a picture of his sweet Elspeth in his mind. He had known that Elspeth de Seiv would be his wife from his very first sight of her. His heart had been captured the moment he looked into her light blue eyes and he knew immediately that he wanted nothing more from life than to be the man who put a smile upon her face. This ambition had proven to be a difficult one, for she rebuffed his every advance and seemed to frown even more intensely than usual when he came into her presence. His parents, who were utterly devoted to their eldest son, worked tirelessly to make the match. Even when her doting parents were won over by the promise of gold, the fair Elspeth continued to resist most stubbornly.

'Am I expected to give myself to a young knight who is yet unproven?' She had asked, her pretty chin set hard in defiance. 'Am I to deny myself the chance of a match with a lord or an earl and give myself to a boy who is yet to win honour or lands for himself?'

Sir Edward had begun to list the tournaments in which he had acquitted himself quite well, but was brought back to silence by a dismissive wave of her little hand.

'You must prove yourself, if you wish to win my hand.' She said, her tone resolute.

'Tell me how!' Sir Edward had responded, falling to his knees at her dainty feet. 'You have captured my heart and there is nothing I would not do to win your affection!'

Elspeth de Seiv's face flushed red and she seemed to be quite overcome by this display of devotion. Her eyes then narrowed and a sly smile touched her lips. 'I hear tell of a castle in the wilds of Scotland. They say that its master was dispossessed by the old King and made a pact with the devil to win it back. They say that he has sworn to kill any man who dares to take his stronghold and that every man who has tried has been most foully murdered. They say that the place is cursed.'

'I too have heard these tales.' Sir Edward replied. 'Tis Castle Douglas you speak of.'

Elspeth nodded slowly. 'If you have the courage to hold that castle for a year and a day, then you will have proven that you are worthy of my hand.'

Sir Edward had ridden to the Earl of Pembroke that very night. Pembroke had rebuffed him initially, suggesting that he should gain experience under a seasoned commander before seeking a command of his own. He had eventually been persuaded to accede to the request, the boy's begging, the offers of gold and the lack of an alternative candidate all contributing to his capitulation.

Sir Edward was pulled from his reverie by the sound of men's voices shouting in the distance. He opened his eyes and was delighted by what he saw. There, at the edge of the forest, an old drover and three of his sons were driving their cattle away. Sir Edward counted the beasts as he slipped the precious locket back inside his tunic.

He whooped loudly and took the steps back down to the castle courtyard two at a time. 'Gilbert!' He cried at the top of his voice. 'Saddle the horses! There are cattle outside. If we are quick, we will have beef enough to keep us until the feast of Saint Acelda.'

It took Sir Edward and his young men only moments to arm themselves while their squires saddled their horses. All of them were the sons of minor nobles who held lands close to those of the Cheney family and they were eager to make their names before Scotland was fully conquered.

317

The wizened, old gatekeeper hesitated when ordered to raise the bar and throw the gates open. 'You must take care, young sir.' He reasoned in his thick Yorkshire accent.

'Nonsense man!' Sir Edward shot back. 'There are twenty of us in full armour and the drovers have been foolish enough to run their cattle before our walls. Now open the gates!'

The old man gave a shake of his head, but did as he was ordered. The young men of Yorkshire then kicked at their steeds and thundered out into the sunshine, the light shimmering on their new and unblemished plate as they went. The drovers turned at the sound of their approach and ran for the forest in panic. Sir Edward beamed happily at his companions and ordered them to herd the cattle back towards the castle. With so much meat to be cured, he could now be sure that he could hold the castle for a year and then ride south to claim his bride. His happy smile froze on his face when Gilbert suddenly jerked forward in his saddle and fell to the ground with a spear between his shoulder blades. The sight was so sudden, unexpected and horrific that he could only stare in bewilderment with his mouth agape. His stomach turned to water when the air was filled with the sound of men screaming 'Douglas!' at the tops of their voices. He flicked his head around in time to see men armed with spears, swords and axes rushing out from the forest's edge. A glance towards the castle told him that the gatekeeper had watched the ambush unfold and had already closed and barred the gates to keep the rebels out. With his sole avenue of retreat cut off and five of his men already down, Sir Edward took the only course left open to him. He drew his sword and rode into the midst of the men of Douglas. His father's sword, gifted to him on the morning of his departure for Scotland, served him well and sent three disloyal Scots spinning to the earth with their skulls split open. More would surely have followed if one of them had not come up on him from behind and used his long axe to rip his horse's belly open and send its steaming guts spilling onto the ground. Sir Edward cut down at his attackers' heads even as his mount faltered and fell. The blow that dropped him also came from behind. It clattered his helmet and left his head ringing so that he had to fight the waves of nauseating dizziness to remain conscious. He lay there helpless, his leg trapped and crushed between the hard ground and the weight of his dying mount. He looked up as a sword-wielding figure loomed over him. Dark, well-built and handsome, he had no doubt that the dispossessed Lord of Douglas had come to finish him. He closed his eyes when the sword-point was pressed against his throat and tried desperately to bring his fair Elspeth's face to his mind. In his panic, he found that he could not recall her beauty and, as he choked and began to drown in his own blood, the last face he saw in this life was that of the grinning, demonic James Douglas.

When word of Sir Edward's sad demise reached the county of Yorkshire, the father of Elspeth de Seiv did scold her quite severely.

'You sent that young boy to his death!' He raged. 'If you were not going to have him, you should have told him to his face, instead of sending him off on some fool's errand!'

The fair Elspeth surprised her father and mother by declaring that she did, after all, love poor Sir Edward. She protested her devotion to his memory, even though they reminded her that she had often declared that she did not want him and considered him to be a pest. She took to dressing all in black and spent all of her time hard at mourning and prayer. Though she lived to a ripe old age, she would give herself to no other man and always kept a candle burning in eternal memory of poor Sir Edward de Cheney.

The summer had been kind to King Robert. His illness had passed and the slow work of capturing and reducing the Comyn and English castles had given him the opportunity to gather his strength. His spirits had been lifted when the good citizens of Aberdeen rose up against the English garrison and threw the gates open so that the rebels could run in and slaughter the occupying force. With a great seaport now in his hands, supplies had begun to arrive from Flanders, the Hanseatic towns and from Scandinavia. His army of starving, haggard vagrants was slowly transformed into something much more menacing and the unbroken series of victories brought new men flocking to his standard each day. John paused to look at him before approaching. He thought that he once again looked as powerful as he had when challenging the Earl of Pembroke before the walls of Perth.

The King turned and waved him forward. 'John Edward! I hope that you have good news for me. Have your scouts found another way into the heartland of the Macdougalls of Lorne?'

'They have, m'Lord.' John responded. 'But the approach is no better than this. Our men will have to march much further and will still be in danger of ambush.'

King Robert nodded and continued to study the landscape before him. 'See how John of Lorne has blocked the pass and formed his men up on the slopes of Ben Cruachan. With the mountain on one side and a sheer drop to Loch Awe on the other, we can only approach along that narrow and hazardous track. He cannot think that I would be foolish enough to charge in and let him pick off my men from above.'

'I doubt that he thinks you foolish, m'Lord, but he may still pray that impatience will encourage you to risk the attack. I think it more likely that he is happy to create an impasse. If we are not reckless enough to attack, we must wait here until we are driven off by the English King or by the snows of winter.'

Robert Bruce now laughed with rare and genuine amusement. 'They have waited for King Edward to save them all these months. I doubt that he will come now. He does not have his father's appetite for winter campaigns. The discomfort does not agree with him.' He turned again to John. 'So, if we are not to withdraw, what are we to do?'

John looked into the distance and examined the Macdougall positions, even although he already knew them well. 'We must do exactly as he has, m'Lord. We must block the Pass of Brander so that his cavalry cannot advance and we must position our men on the slope above the Macdougalls.'

King Robert nodded. 'If we send archers and spearmen up that far slope under cover of darkness, they could take the Macdougalls by surprise. If I also send my Highlanders at them from the mountain's foot, they will not be able to stand.'

'Our men have recent experience of throwing rocks down at their enemies, m'Lord.' John replied with a grin.

'Good! Your men will join the attack from above.'

John bowed at the King's command and began to turn from him.

'Stay, John Edward!' He ordered brusquely. 'We have other matters to discuss. Once we are finished here, you will go south with my brother. The Macdowalls of Galloway have gathered themselves and are soon to receive reinforcements from over the border. We must scatter them before they become a threat.'

John narrowed his eyes. 'You will divide our forces when the Earl of Ross still threatens us?'

The King shook his head. 'If my judgement is sound, we will not have to fight him. I know him to be a frightened and greedy man. If we defeat the Macdougalls, he will be afraid to face us. If I promise him more land, greed will persuade him to swear himself to me.'

'And you will accept it? Even though you know that he helped to put your wife, daughter and sisters into the hands of the English.'

King Robert stared hard at John before replying. 'As a man, I want nothing more than to fly at him with my sword and cut him into bloody ribbons. As King of Scotland, I must deny myself that satisfaction. I cannot fight everyone. The more men I can bring to my side through persuasion and negotiation, the stronger I will be when the English come. I think that my country has seen enough of blood, if I can spare it more, I will.'

'Then you are a better man than I, m'Lord. The English killed my wife. I will avenge her death each day until the last of them have been killed or driven from this land.'

The King nodded his understanding and turned his eyes back to the Pass of Brander. 'What of the Comyn men amongst your ranks? It would seem that you found it in your heart to forgive them.'

John briefly considered denying the accusation, but quickly decided that lying would be futile. 'They are good men, m'Lord. I fought with them at Falkirk. I am loath to slaughter those who have stood with me against the English and, just as you said, we cannot fight them all.'

'Did you disobey the orders of William Wallace, just as you ignore those that I have given?'

'I was ever loyal to Sir William, m'Lord. I only ignored his orders when I judged that they were wrong.'

King Robert laughed, but the sound was thin and lacked real mirth. 'I know well that you think that you can judge your King. I have forgotten not a single word of the scolding you gave me at Scone. If any other man had so disrespected me, I would not hesitate to cut him down. But you!' The King raised his hands and shook them in frustration. 'You, I do not understand. Just when I am told that you take Comyn men into your camp, I hear that you did my sister a great kindness when she was chained up in a cage on the walls of Roxburgh. Any other man who did such a thing would come rushing to my side to lay claim to favour or reward. But not you! I hear it only from others.'

John said a silent prayer of thanks. He had feared that he was about to be punished for harbouring the Comyn men against the King's orders and could not believe that he was saved thanks to a forgotten kindness done many months before. He did not know how word of it had reached King Robert's ears, but he was glad that it had. 'I ask for nothing, m'Lord.' He replied with his head bowed. 'I live only to kill the English.'

'Go and ready your men, John Edward.' The King demanded, with a shake of his head. 'They have a long climb ahead of them this night.'

John of Lorne hobbled to the galley's side and leaned heavily upon his crutch. He still burned hot with fever but had forced himself up from his cabin below deck at the sound of the battle horns.

'See Father!' His young son squealed in excitement. 'They come!'

John of Lorne rubbed at his eyes as if he could not quite believe what he was seeing. The galley was anchored a bow-shot from the shore, giving him a clear view of the narrow pass, his knights blocking the way through and his warriors positioned on the slope above the pass. He could also make out the figure of Robert Bruce at the head of his cavalry.

'By Christ, Somhairle!' He declared in disbelief. 'I never thought that he would attack. He must have lost his mind! His men will be trapped in the defile and we will massacre them from above!'

Only his poor health and his natural caution kept him from dancing a jig in his excitement. He had been in despair when he received news of the defeat and the flight of the Earl of Buchan. He had been the strongest of the Comyn faction and it had seemed certain that he would destroy Robert Bruce and his rebel army. The loss had been a heavy blow to bear and he had slept little as he awaited the inevitable Bruce advance. He rubbed his hands together in anticipation of winning a victory that had been beyond the Earl of Buchan.

He narrowed his eyes when the sound of three horn blasts travelled across the still waters of the loch. For an instant, he could see no response to the call, but he then caught sight of men rushing out from the rebel ranks and swarming up the steep slope towards the Macdougall lines. The futility of the Highland charge brought him to laughter.

'The slope is too steep, Somhairle.' He informed his young son. 'Our archers and spearmen will cut them down long before they reach our lines. A warrior must be brave, but he must always use his head. Those men have great courage, but they charge to their deaths.'

'I will remember, Father.' Somhairle replied dutifully. 'Look there! More of our men are charging down the mountain. They will sweep these fools away!'

John of Lorne felt the colour drain from his face and his heart seemed to leap into his throat. He knew fine well that he had no men positioned higher up the mountainside. He opened his mouth to shout a warning, but it was already too late. Cries of alarm were immediately replaced with screams of agony as the Bruce's men poured arrows, spears and rocks into the backs of the men of Lorne. They stood long enough to meet the Highland charge and fill the air with the ring of sword on sword, but they could not withstand the simultaneous assault from above and below for long. The sight of the men of Lorne turning and running from the field of battle brought a great roar from the rebels and caused tears to form in the eyes of their defeated leader. He watched on in helpless agony until the pursuit and slaughter of his men continued beyond his sight.

Young Somhairle was ashen and shocked into silence. The sight of tears on his father's cheeks was almost as horrific as the slaughter he had just witnessed. It broke his wee heart to see his father so dejected and broken. John himself found that he could not bring himself to look his son in the eye.

'We must be away now.' He croaked, unable to keep the grief from his voice. 'We'll come back with the English King and make the Bruce pay for his work here today.'

Somhairle nodded but kept his gaze fixed upon the deck of the galley. In spite of his tender years, he knew well that his father's defiance was hollow and that he did not believe his own words.

24

The Scotstoun men had learned long ago that it was best to keep silent when Edward Bruce decided to hold forth. He had an uncommon love for the sound of his own voice and, when there was wine enough to lubricate it, he did not like to have its sound diluted by the voices of others. In a less likeable and less entertaining man, this would have been a detestable characteristic. In the case of Edward de Bruce, his charm, sense of humour and propensity for mischief served to make his self-absorption quite tolerable. Indeed, both men and women flocked to be in his company and this morning was no exception. While the Edward men, Strathbogie, Robert Boyd and Sir James Douglas sat around Edward's campfire at their breakfast, a wider circle of men leaned in and hissed at others to hold their wheest so they too could capture his words.

'My brother thinks that I am only good for the burning of hovels and for the stealing of cattle.' He complained, his voice still slightly slurred from the previous night's pilfered ale. 'He orders me to burn Buchan from end to end and no sooner have I done it than he sends me to do the same here in Galloway. And while we chase sheep and throw Macdowall crones from their cottages, where is King Robert? He is in the north preparing to do battle with the Earl of Ross. Must he have all the battles and all the glory for himself? Can he spare no small piece of honour for this poor knight to win?'

'Tis a shame!' John Edward said with a smile. 'Poor wee Edward is left with nothing and has only the promise of the Earldom of Carrick to comfort him.'

Edward pointed his finger and shook it at John in mock admonishment. 'He would say that, would he not?' He asked the assembled company as he crouched down at Scott Edward's side and slipped his arm around his shoulders. 'Young Scott here knows exactly what I mean. He too has to suffer the indignity of being the younger brother. Admit it Scott, it does pain you to be commanded by your brother. To be required to obey his every command, even when you know that he is mistaken.'

Scott laughed merrily in spite of the swollen and broken nose he had suffered during the worst of the fighting at the Pass of Brander. 'It is painful.' He agreed.

Edward Bruce opened his eyes as wide as they would go. 'If it is bad for you, just think how I suffer. You can still disagree with John, I have heard you do it a thousand times. There have been occasions when some of us have grown fed up with your constant bitching and bickering. But I cannot. My brother is King and

329

is therefore right, even when he is wrong.' He paused to shake his head in a pretence of dejection and to elicit appreciative laughter from his audience. 'I do not know how I bear it.'

'Here's our scout!' Strathbogie announced, as he pushed himself to his feet

'Al!' The Bruce shouted in greeting. 'Pray tell me that we have more than the burning of a few mean settlements ahead of us this day. If you have nothing more to offer, then I will surely die from the tedium of it all.'

Al climbed down from his saddle and accepted the skin of ale John held out towards him. 'You will have your wish.' Al responded, before drinking his fill. 'The Macdowalls are less than an hour from here.'

Edward Bruce clapped his hands together in excitement. 'How many?'

Al wiped at his mouth with his sleeve. 'About twelve hundred, maybe slightly more. There's Macdowalls there, but others too. Men-at-arms and armoured knights, might be English.'

'Did you see their colours?'

'Aye.' Al replied. 'A red shield with a white shield at its centre.'

'Ingram de Umfraville!' Sir James Douglas exclaimed. 'It must be him.'

Edward Bruce nodded his agreement and roared at the men to break camp and make ready for battle.

'They greatly outnumber us, Ed.' John said firmly. 'We should not rush in!'

Edward Bruce laughed cheerfully and took John by his shoulders. 'This is what I like most about you, John. You will urge me to caution, but once the charge is ordered, you will fly at our enemies with more fury than any other man and you will cut at them until the last of them is dead upon the ground. That is how it will be today. I will fall upon them before they slip from my grasp and damn the consequences. God himself will decide if we are to prevail.'

Dugal Macdowall had felt uneasy from the moment he left his tent to take his morning pish. Dawn had just begun to light the far horizon and the air still held the chill of the night. The distant figure had been indistinct in the half-light, but he was certain that he saw a black dog walking at his side. A gust of wind had shifted the morning mist and the figure had been lost from his sight. He tried to convince himself that his mind was playing tricks and conjuring threats out of the mist, but he found that he could not shake off his discomfiture. The hours of marching had done little to improve his mood. He knew well that Sir Ingram de Umfraville and the Englishman, Aymer St John, both looked down at him. His depleted ranks were ragged and poorly equipped after long weeks encamped in the forest, leaving him with no choice other than to soak up their contempt and ignore their jibes about him being surprised by Robert de Bruce. If he was to regain his lands, he would need their men in their pretty surcoats and shiny new armour.

Sir Ingram brought the column to a halt just short of a shallow ford over the River Dee to receive the returning scout. The man reported that the rebels approached, he confirmed that they had no more than seven hundred men and that they carried the banners of Douglas and Edward de Bruce.

'We shall deploy here!' Sir Ingram ordered loftily. 'They can line up on the far bank and cross the river to parley.'

'They're sneaky bastards!' Dugal spat with venom. 'We should make our lines further back on the plain, so that they have no opportunity to outflank us.'

Aymer St John's nasal laugh made a honking sound which set Dugal's teeth to grinding in annoyance. 'Not to worry, Dugal. We have outriders on all sides. We shall not be taken unawares.'

Dugal fumed silently when Aymer and Sir Ingram exchanged a smug glance. Dugal was a man who seldom missed an insult, however slight it might be, and he did not miss their mockery.

They had waited for only a few minutes when the rebels began to fill the clearing on the far side of the ford.

'My God!' Aymer St John declared. 'If this is the army of Robert Bruce, I can scarcely believe that he remains at liberty!'

Sir Ingram shook his head in derision. 'I know. They have a handful of ragged knights, some peasants on horses and an unruly mob armed with their wooden poles. I have half a mind to charge in and finish them here.'

'Do not forget that they have defeated the Earl of Buchan and the Macdougalls of Lorne.' Dugal said with some urgency. 'We would be foolish to underestimate them.'

Aymer St John kept his eyes on the rebels as they formed themselves into two ranks. 'I have not forgotten that you suffered at their hands Dugal, but that was because they managed to take you by surprise. If they had not caught you still abed, I have no doubt that you would have seen them off. They must have surprised the Earl and the Macdougalls in a similar fashion. You really must take greater care to secure your positions.'

'Ah!' Sir Ingram announced. 'Here comes their delegation. We shall soon see what they have to say for themselves.'

'That's no delegation!' Dugal exclaimed, his voice quavering in fright. 'They're charging at us!'

Sir Ingram started back in amazement. The rebel cavalry were indeed charging across the ford and their spearmen were following in their wake.

'Do they mean to form up on this side of the ford?' Sir Ingram enquired in disbelief. 'They cannot mean to attack us here. Only a mad fool would assault such a superior force.'

'Perhaps it is their intention to charge past us and escape into the forest.' Aymer St John suggested. 'They will know that we are unlikely to follow them there.'

'Command your men to attack!' Dugal roared desperately. 'Or they will sweep us away.'

Sir Ingram finally overcame his shock and gave the order, but it was already too late. Their knights had barely reached a canter when the rebel cavalry hit them at full gallop and tore bloody holes in their ranks. The knights then rode onto the spears of the rebel foot that followed on behind and those who were unable to turn in time saw their horses impaled on the spikes and were pulled from their saddles to die under rebel blades. The men-at-arms fresh from England and the bedraggled Macdowalls fared little better. The rebel cavalry cut down at them with fury and then ran them to ground when they threw their arms aside and tried to flee the field. Dugal Macdowall fought on until his horse was cut out from underneath him. He would have fallen as the rebel foot advanced if Aymer St John had not offered him his hand and pulled him up onto the back of his mount. They then joined Sir Ingram and the remains of their army and ran for the safety of Buittle Castle with the rebels in dogged pursuit.

It is said that a man learns more from a single defeat than he does from a thousand victories. Dugal Macdowall and Sir Ingram de Umfraville learned that they were no longer willing to risk all to defend the rule of King Edward in Scotland. They crossed the border with their families and took refuge on their manors in England to await more favourable developments. Aymer St John learned that he took defeat quite personally, especially when his own stupidity had contributed to the disaster. He chose to stay in Scotland to form an army from the remains of that broken on the River Dee and from fresh recruits raised in England. He prayed only for the opportunity to redeem himself by defeating the Bruces and claiming his reward for winning the province back for King Edward. He worked hard to drill and equip his troops and paid good gold for reports on the activities of Edward Bruce as he tore a path of destruction across all of Galloway in a bid to extinguish all resistance to his brother's illegitimate rule.

The spy who came to him was a Macdowall who had been able to infiltrate the enemy camp. Aymer was convinced of the veracity of the man's account by his refusal to accept any coin for his information and by his insistence that he be allowed to join the ranks of his army to take revenge against those who had done so much injury to his kin.

'You are sure that they can only exit their camp through this narrow defile?' Aymer asked for the third time.

'Aye.' The dirty Macdowall replied, his tone betraying no uncertainty. 'There is no other way their horses can go. A man on foot might be able to scramble away over the rocks, but they would not be able to carry away the great piles of loot they have stripped from Galloway. If we trap them there, I have no doubt that they will fight to keep all that they have taken.'

'And the defile is too narrow for more than one horse at a time?'

'You could fit two at a time, but it would be tight.'

'We must move quickly then. It would be a shame to see them slip away.'

The Macdowall shook his head. 'We have time enough. Edward Bruce amuses himself with drink and dice and is in no hurry to move on. He will stay where he is until his brother comes down from the north to seize hold of his gold.'

'Very well!' Aymer replied. 'I will send my best scouts to watch over them. When the moment is right, we will spring the trap.'

Edward Bruce was groggy and not at all pleased to have been pulled from his bed while it was still dark. He called for water and splashed it around his face in the hope that it would be cold enough to revive and refresh him.

'Christ! My head throbs like it has been hit with an axe.'

Sir James Douglas groaned in sympathy from his side. 'It is that bitter Galloway ale. If you drink enough of it, it leaves you close to death in the morning.'

John Edward's condition was not much better, but the urgency in his old friend's eyes forced him to put his own suffering aside. 'They are already at the foot of the glen?'

'Aye!' Al replied. 'I could not count them in the dark, but it is a significant force. More than what we faced at the ford over the Dee. They have heavy horse, men-at-arms and spearmen.'

'You think that they might stop to make camp?' Sir James asked, perhaps more in hope than expectation.

Al shook his head. 'This is a forced march. They come with the purpose of trapping us here. By the time the sun rises, they will have formed up at the end of the ravine. We will be left with the choice of fighting them or scattering into the hills.'

'No!' Edward Bruce boomed. 'There's no way in hell I'm leaving all of our loot. My brother is in dire need of coin and he expects me to deliver it. I will die rather than let some English bastard come in here and take it for himself.'

'Do we have time to get our men formed up before they arrive at the defile?' John asked, his eyes fixed on Al's.

'Aye!' Al responded, with reassuring certainty.

'Right!' John declared. 'Let's rouse the men and get them into place. These bastards will not find us asleep when dawn breaks.'

Sir James Douglas pointed towards Al. 'If there are as many of them as he says, then it is likely that we will be overcome. Is there nothing we can do to even the odds?'

John rubbed at his beard in concentration and tried to picture the approach up the glen's long, gentle slope. 'Al, could you find your way through the darkness and the fog well enough for some of us to circle around behind the English?'

Al thought for a second and nodded. 'Aye. But we would have to go now. There is little time left before the dawn.'

'Right!' Edward Bruce commanded. 'Every man with a horse is to follow Al. Every man without a horse is to make his way to the bottom end of the ravine and form up. Angus Macdonald has command of the foot. Let's move!'

Al moved slowly and carefully through the darkness, taking time to check each step as the steep hillside was treacherous due to the abundance of loose rocks hidden beneath the thick carpet of moss. The men followed on behind with their horses creeping forward nose-to-tail. It seemed that an age had passed before Al brought them to a halt and hissed at them to be silent. At first the dark and foggy night was filled with an eerie silence, but then came the faint sounds of hooves thumping into damp earth and the creaking, clanking, metallic sound that is heard only when large numbers of men march in maille and armour.

John moved forward and clapped at Al's shoulder. He had never doubted his friend but found that he never failed to be amazed by his skill as a scout.

Confident that any sound they made would be drowned out by the din of the English advance, Al moved forward once more and they continued their gradual descent. As the rattle of armour and the thud of hooves receded into the distance, they reached even ground and Al turned and led them across the slope. There was no need for him to say anything when they reached the path taken by the English. The grasses had been churned to mud by the passage of the heavy horse and the boots of a thousand Englishmen.

When all fifty of the rebel horsemen were clear of the trees, Edward Bruce silently gestured at them to mount up and follow on behind him. He kicked his horse into a canter and advanced for a few moments before bringing the column to a halt so that he could listen. He repeated the manoeuvre several times before he judged that they were close enough to the English to attack them when they charged at the rebel foot, but far enough back to avoid being discovered too early. John thought that the sky was beginning to lighten, but the thick fog hung heavily in the damp air and kept them hidden from the sight of any Englishman who might happen to glance to his rear.

As they tracked forward in silence, the tension in the air was almost as thick as the fog. The rising sun turned the world from black to grey and John felt as if he was shadowing an army of phantoms with only briefing sightings of faint, ghostly silhouettes to confirm that a great army marched less than a bow-shot to their front. The plain widened as they ascended and Edward Bruce made urgent hand gestures to command his men to spread out and be ready to charge. The first gust of wind was not particularly strong and it did little apart from cause the thick fog to swirl around in the air. The second gust was much stronger and it cleared the fog away from the hillside. All at once, the grey wall that had concealed them was gone and only clear, morning air separated them from the English force. If one Englishman had cast an inquisitive glance over his shoulder, they would have been discovered. There was a moment in which no Scotsman did anything other than gape in astonishment at the sudden appearance of the English column. John glanced along the line and saw the same expression of shocked indecision on almost every face. Only three men reacted differently. The faces of Edward Bruce, Sir James Douglas and Eck Edward were filled, not with concern, but with the joy and the fury of battle. They did not hesitate or look to others for instruction. All three of them kicked at their horses, unsheathed their swords and screamed their battle-cries at the tops of their voices. In a matter of seconds, the silent, protective cocoon provided by the fog was replaced by the chaos and the din of battle.

John kicked his own horse to the gallop and saw the frightened English faces as they turned their heads at the sound of battle-cries and the thundering of hooves. He screamed his fury at them as they struggled to turn their steeds to face the fast-charging Scots. The contest was unequal. There is nothing to match the majesty and power of the charge of the heavy horse. At rest, however, the beasts are slow, ponderous and difficult to manoeuvre. Not one English knight had his horse fully turned when the Scots cavalry tore through their lines. A few managed to turn around far enough to parry blows from Scottish weapons, but many were cut down or bludgeoned from behind. The smaller horses favoured by the Scots were nimble enough to turn quickly and they tore back through the disordered English knights, leaving a trail of blood and slaughter in their wake.

When Edward Bruce ordered his cavalry to wheel around and charge for the third time, the English broke in panic. Most ran up the slope to escape the charging cavalry, but were met by Angus Macdonald of the Western Isles leading the Scottish foot downhill to join the battle. Finding themselves trapped and unable to run, they tried desperately to form up and make their last stand. Though they fought bravely, they were thrown back by the furious momentum of the Scottish charge and, assailed from all sides, were soon put to slaughter.

When the last of the knights had been unhorsed or chased from the field, John leapt down from his saddle and joined with the foot. The field was littered with corpses and he picked his way between them as he hunted for men to fight. Some of the English knights threw their swords away, fell to their knees and begged for quarter before he cut them down. Not a single Macdowall made such a plea. They fought like cornered beasts and did not yield until injury or death meant that they could no longer stand. John's battle rage was so strong that he was not aware of the wounds to his left shoulder and right forearm until he sat down to catch his breath when he could find no more enemies to kill. He was examining the gash in his shoulder when Sir James Douglas threw himself to the ground at his side and offered him a skin of ale.

'Christ!' He exclaimed. 'There is no better way to start the day!'

John nodded his agreement and drank greedily from the skin. 'This Galloway ale tastes delicious when accompanied by a victory!'

Sir James grinned back at him, his teeth unnaturally white against a skin darkened by drying blood. 'Did you see their armour?' He asked excitedly. 'Much of it is new, undented and unscratched before this morning.'

'I might get some for myself.' John replied.

'You should.' Sir James replied with a grin. 'It might save you from getting so full of holes.'

John decided that he could drink to that and he poured the last of the ale down his parched throat.

25

The Earl of Pembroke gazed at the King and fought to mask his contempt. His father would have erupted in fury when faced with such intractable problems, but the young King Edward reacted only with petulance and sulked like a scolded boy.

'It cannot be.' He whined miserably.

'It is true, my Lord.' Pembroke replied firmly. 'He has defeated the Comyns, the Macdowalls and the Macdougalls and has forced the Earl of Ross and others to swear fealty to him as King of Scotland. He has held a parliament attended by all of his nobles and clergy and has declared the independence of Scotland. He has made his brother Lord of Galloway and restored the estates of Sir James Douglas. He rules as King and grows stronger with each passing day. Our hold on the country is now limited to our castles and those beleaguered garrisons are either besieged or too afeart to venture out lest they be attacked. They stay huddled behind their walls and pray for the day when you will lead an army to relieve them.'

'I cannot save them when the nobles of England refuse to support me with either gold or with men. The Treasury is empty and I have to bow and scrape just to pay my own household.'

'Then you must appease them.' Pembroke retorted. 'A King cannot rule without the support of the magnates. If this stalemate continues for much longer, Scotland will be irretrievably lost. To lose the province will make you seem weak and the nobles will push for still more compromise. You must act now, my Lord. Put aside the minstrels and the feasts and seize your kingdom before it is lost.'

'The magnates are jealous of us.' Piers Gaveston said lazily, as he leaned across the table towards Pembroke. 'We shall never relinquish our royal power to them. There must be another way.'

'You could step aside, my Lord.' Pembroke suggested helpfully. 'Their enmity towards you is the greatest barrier to gaining the magnates' support. If you were to take your leave, in the best interests of the King, he would have all the gold and men that he could wish for.'

'Why should I?' Gaveston snapped, his face contorted with bitterness. 'I have done nothing but serve my King loyally.'

'That's not quite true, is it, my Lord?' Pembroke replied. 'They do resent your close relationship with the King, but you have not helped matters. You taunt them, force them to kneel before you when you represent the King, you take great pleasure in knocking them or their sons from their horses in the tournaments and you mock them so openly that word of it reaches their ears.'

King Edward, as he did so often, leapt to his favourite's defence with more energy and passion that he could summon for his own kingdom. 'That is not true, Pembroke. I have never heard Piers publicly mock any of the magnates.'

'Burst-belly?' Pembroke retorted.

King Edward could not help but laugh. 'Alright, that one is true. But you cannot blame Piers for that. The Earl of Lincoln's belly grows fatter and rounder each time we see him. I hardly dare to invite him to feast with me for fear of his guts exploding.'

Pembroke ignored the King's mirth. 'Whoreson?'

Gaveston now joined in with the King's laughter. 'That was harsh, but Gloucester's mother did secretly marry a squire. I cannot be blamed for her willingness to spread her legs.'

Pembroke paused until Piers met his glare. 'Joseph the Jew!'

Gaveston's cheeks now burned red and he could not hold Pembroke's gaze.

'Oh!' King Edward exclaimed uncomfortably. 'You have heard that one? Piers should apologise for that, though I know that he did not mean it to be as harsh as it might sound.'

'They have all heard these insults.' Pembroke growled in response. 'It is little wonder that they refuse to support you when they feel so disrespected. Something must be done.'

Edward pulled himself up to his full height. 'You are right, of course, but I will not throw Piers to the wolves. There must be another way.'

'I may have the answer.' Gaveston answered with a sheepish glance in Pembroke's direction. 'I have recently sounded out the Earls of Surrey and Hereford. They are willing to support a campaign in the north and are certain that a call to arms will bring a whole host of minor nobles flocking to our standard. Sir John de Seagrave and Sir Robert Clifford have already indicated their willingness to take commands.'

Pembroke found that Gaveston's wide-eyed enthusiasm caused him great irritation. 'With such support, we could indeed raise an army to equal any that has crossed the border before. The harder question is how you will find the gold to pay, supply and equip it and keep it in the field long enough to bring the Bruce to battle.'

'That is the clever part, my Lord.' Gaveston replied with glee. 'I have contacts in Florence with the Compagnia dei Bardi. They have already agreed to provide us with as much gold as we would like.'

'The Bardi!' The Earl exclaimed. 'Such a loan will prove to be most expensive.'

'What does the expense matter?' The King asked happily. 'Once Scotland is conquered, we will have riches enough to settle our debts with much left over besides. Piers, you are so clever! What could possibly go wrong?'

Pembroke chose to keep his own counsel and left the King and his favourite to wallow in their orgy of self-congratulation.

The months of winter and spring had passed by peacefully for the men of Scotstoun. With his enemies in Scotland defeated or persuaded to swear loyalty to him and with the English King too busy fighting with his own nobles, King Robert set about the business of government and sent his commanders to besiege those castles still held by the English. Sir James Douglas was sent to the south, Edward Bruce was given responsibility for the strategically important Stirling Castle and John Edward was charged with keeping the Perth garrison safely behind their walls. With no siege engines to breach the walls and no prospect of success for any surprise attack on the vigilant garrison, little more than guard duty was required from the Scotstoun men.

Boredom was the greatest enemy and John sought to alleviate this by changing the guard each Sunday. With half of his men left to discourage the garrison from making any excursions, the other half were able to return to the village and spend time with their families. John took great pleasure in helping his children with their writing and telling them stories to fire their imaginations or to lull them off to sleep. The evenings he spent at table in conversation with his parents, his uncle, Father MacGregor and the Robertson. Each sunset was spent by the loch and he would sit at the graveside and tell his sweet Lorna about all that had happened that day. He would sometimes break the monotony by riding for Stirling or Galloway. Though it was always good to see Edward Bruce and Sir James Douglas, he never stayed for long, as he soon tired of their complaints, for they suffered under the yolk of inactivity even more than he did.

The arrival of the messenger from King Robert was the cause of no small excitement in the village and John found himself surrounded and jostled before he had finished reading the parchment.

'What does it say?' Scott demanded impatiently.

John paused as if he was in deep thought and kept silent just long enough to torment his bother. 'King Robert has summoned us to Cambuskenneth Abbey!' He announced loftily. 'The English King has mustered a great army and marches towards our border!'

The village was soon abuzz with activity and men gathered up their possessions and their arms and prepared to depart for Stirling. John did his best to appear solemn, but was secretly delighted at the prospect of seeing old comrades again and at the possibility of renewing his fight with his enemies. The garrison at Perth shouted and jeered from their walls as the Scotstoun men marched past and it was clear from their taunts that they knew that the English King had returned. John waved back at them with a cheery grin, but could not help but wonder how the news had reached them when his men had let no man in or out of the city for months.

The roads grew busier with horses, carts and men on foot the closer they drew to Stirling. By the time they had passed beneath the heights of the Abbey Craig, it seemed that every man in Scotland was set upon entering the meander of the River Forth in which the Abbey sat. John did not have the patience to wait as the crowd inched forward and kicked his horse on so that those on foot had to make way for him. A line of monks blocked the Abbey gates and directed people to their appointed places. A young monk took John's reins and pointed him towards an ancient, hard-faced monk who sat at a table with an open ledger before him.

'Name!' He demanded without bothering himself to look up.

'John Edward.'

The monk scowled more fiercely and ran his finger down the list of names on the parchment before him. When his finger reached the bottom, he looked up and shook his head. 'Your name's not here. You can go to the Abbey gardens and listen from there. I doubt if you'll hear anything, but only named guests can enter the Abbey.' He waved John to the side and asked for the next man to step forward.

'Are you sure?' John asked. 'The King wrote to command me to come.'

'You?' The old monk asked in astonishment, as he looked John up and down with distaste. 'You had a letter?'

John nodded and watched as the old boy huffed and pulled another parchment from beneath the first and scratched his fingernail down the list of names. His finger jerked to a halt about a third of the way down the page. 'John Edward?' He demanded, his disapproval and disbelief evident in both his tone and the expression on his face.

'Aye!' John replied. 'Of Scotstoun.'

The monk's eyebrows shot up his forehead in delight. 'I have no Edward of Scotstoun! I only have a John Edward of Perth here. Now, if you'll make you way round to the side, you can listen in from the gardens.'

'No!' John insisted. 'They know me by that name as well. I have just come from besieging the garrison at Perth, just as King Robert commanded me to do.'

The monk did nothing to hide his disappointment and turned to gesture a young novice forward. 'Third pew, left hand side!' He barked, before dismissing John with a wave of his hand.

The boy asked John to follow him and he took him to his place in the Abbey. The rearmost pews were already filled and he was aware that heads turned as he was led to the front. The feeling was not an unfamiliar one, as he had experienced the same sensation when he stood as witness for William Wallace when he was knighted in the Kirk o' the Forest. He had little time to dwell on this, as he found his old friend, Malcolm Simpson, already seated in his designated row. He embraced him warmly and they exchanged news as the Abbey slowly filled and the din of a thousand conversations echoed around the walls and the high, vaulted ceiling. The whole place fell to a whispering hush when the Abbot took to the platform set up before the altar and raised his hands for silence.

The Abbey then exploded in noise and cheering when King Robert entered at the head of a procession containing his brother Edward, the Bishop of Moray, Sir James Murray, Thomas Randolph, Angus Macdonald of the Isles and the Bishops of Dunblane, Dunkeld and Ross. The Abbot was aghast at the disturbance and frantically gestured for silence, but was forced to wait until his unruly congregation tired of their screeching and clapping and of stamping their feet. When calm had been restored and seats retaken, the Abbot punished the gathered men for their behaviour by launching into a prayer that was as dry as it was lengthy. John took the opportunity to study the men standing upon the platform. Edward Bruce looked much the same as he always did, clean, well-barbered and dressed as perfectly and as stylishly as it was possible to be. The greatest change was in the appearance of King Robert himself. His face was no longer gaunt and pale as it was in Buchan. The months of relative peace had obviously seen an improvement in his diet and his cheeks were fuller and he glowed with good health. The ragged garments of his time as a fugitive had been replaced with robes fit for a king and the crown lost at Methven had been improved upon with a thicker and more ornate circlet of gold. John could not help but think that he now looked every inch a King.

When the Abbot was done, he gave way to the King. Robert Bruce stepped forward and did not speak. The reverential hush seemed to hang more heavily in the air with each moment of silence as King Robert took the time to slowly pass his eyes over every last man crammed into the Abbey pews. John found himself smiling, for he had seen William Wallace use the self-same technique to heighten his audience's anticipation while they waited for him to speak. The device was simple, but highly effective. By the time King Robert began to speak, every man in the Abbey was leaning forward in his pew, the better to hear the King's words.

'I, Sir Robert, by the Grace of God, King of Scots do give thanks to every loyal lord, knight and subject who has answered my summons. Know that I will not forget those who answered the call when my kingdom was threatened. King Edward of England and his army are already at Carlisle and they will march on our border before many more days have passed. We patriots are gathered here to draw up our plans to ensure that the English King will not prevail. He marches here in strength with the Earls of Surrey, Cornwall, Gloucester and Hereford at his side. He marches here with three thousand armoured knights, thirteen thousand foot and two thousand archers under his command.' King Robert paused and waited for the low whistles, whispers and sharp intakes of breath to subside. 'I know well that we cannot match such a force in open battle. It would be folly to attempt it when all the Lords of Scotland could only hope to raise one tenth of their cavalry and a quarter of their foot.' A few defiant voices cried out, but King Robert waved them to silence.

'We will withdraw beyond the Forth and deny him the opportunity to defeat us. Then, as we have done many times before, we will wait for starvation and want of supplies to force them home.' The King seemed to wince at the murmur of protest that swept across the hall. 'I too would prefer to defeat the English upon the field, but we are not yet strong enough and I will not throw away what has been so hard-won in some grand, futile gesture of defiance. You will bring all fighting men across the Forth. You will command your tenants to gather up their stores of grain and herd their cattle here, so that the English will find no sustenance as they progress north. There will be no engagement with the enemy, save for the four flying columns I will send south to harry and harass them. Those four columns will made up of the men of Carrick, under the command of my brother, the Lord of Galloway, the men of Douglas, under the command of Sir James Douglas, the men of Moray, under the command of Sir Thomas Randolph and the men of Perth, under the command of John Edward. All other men are commanded to keep themselves beyond the reach of the English. If we deny them battle and sustenance, their invasion will fail and we will be free of them once more.'

If there was any who disagreed with the King's strategy, their voices were not heard. The moment King Robert had delivered his orders, Edward Bruce stepped forward with his sword held aloft and cried, 'God Save the King!' The congregation leapt to their feet and took up the cry with great vigour. King Robert was swept from the Abbey on a wave of adulation.

'Christ!' Sir John de Seagrave cursed, as the sodden, leather saddle strap came apart in his hand. He threw the buckle away from him across the courtyard of Bothwell Castle in fury and frustration. 'How much longer must we moulder here? Six months at Biggar, four at Linlithgow and another four here! While Robert Bruce hides in his caves, the incessant rain rots our saddles and turns our armour to rust while our horses starve. Look!' He exclaimed angrily. 'This beast was the finest that money could buy when we left Carlisle. Now it is reduced to skin and bone and I dare not ride it in my armour for fear that it will not bear the weight.'

The Earl of Pembroke shrugged his shoulders. 'What can we do but wait, if he will not come out to face us?'

'What kind of knight fights a secret war such as this? They watch from the hills and sweep down the moment a footman, messenger, scout or hunting party strays too far from the camp. I lost near thirty men last week when they foolishly ventured out in search of loot, but the cowardly Scots ran from the slaughter the moment I rode to their aid.' Sir John spat onto

354

the mud at his feet in disgust. 'There can be no value to a crown if it is held without honour or chivalry. I cannot understand why a single Scots noble would follow such a mongrel king.'

'We share some of the blame for our own predicament.' Pembroke replied dryly. 'Robert Bruce was not alone in abandoning of the codes of chivalry. It was the old King who commanded that we should lay all honour aside in the last campaign of his reign. We left a blackened and bloody trail from south to north, we executed his followers, noble and commoner alike, we held his women in cages and I myself refused his challenge to meet with him in open battle at Methven and instead fell upon his camp as he slept.'

'That does nothing to cheer me, my Lord.' Seagrave retorted bitterly. 'I have eight hundred men with me. Every last one of them marched north intent on gain. A year has brought them nothing but mildew and starvation. If they were not so afraid of the Scots lurking in the forests, they would have deserted long ago.'

'Would it cheer you to know that you will not have to suffer for much longer?' Pembroke enquired. 'The King is assailed from all sides and cannot remain here for many more days. He has exhausted his funds and can no longer pay the men or procure supplies. The great barons of England have joined forces against him and have called him to Westminster for a parliament where they will demand a reduction in his powers and the banishment of the Earl of Cornwall.'

355

'Gaveston!' Sir John hissed. 'No one will mourn his absence. He insists that men must bow lower to him than they do to the King!'

'The King has also incurred the enmity of the King of France. King Philip has written to chide him for neglecting his daughter, the Queen, in favour of the bold Piers. He has also urged him to make peace with Robert Bruce and so secure his kingdom. The King resists all of these demands, but the pressure grows with each passing day. He clings on here in the stubborn hope that Robert Bruce will come to his salvation by kindly leading his army onto the field to be defeated.'

Seagrave snorted derisively. 'So, once again we will trudge back across the border with our tails between our legs.'

'When we do.' Pembroke replied, lowering his voice and casting a glance over each of his shoulders. 'Be sure to have your own carts at the head of the baggage train along with my own.'

Seagrave leaned towards the Earl, his curiosity piqued. 'How so, my Lord?'

'I have heard that Robert Bruce has been busy importing great quantities of English arms through Ireland.'

'You think that he means to fall upon us as we retreat?'

Pembroke nodded. 'I also know that the King will ride on ahead with the cavalry so that he need not endure a night of discomfort under canvas. He will push on at all speed to reach the next castle and leave the baggage with scant protection.'

'I thank you, my Lord.' Seagrave replied gratefully. 'I will ensure that my wagons are not at the rear of the column.'

26

John Edward did not see Scotstoun again until three full months after the English army had scuttled back across the border. His homecoming was a joyous event for the village, as his men came with wagons heavily laden with spoil. Part of this had been taken when the forces of Sir James Douglas, Edward Bruce and the men of Scotstoun had fallen upon the rearmost half of the English baggage train at a place where the road south wound its way through a narrow glen. Tom Figgins had commanded the archers of Perth and Douglas to bring down one horse in each wagon team so that its dead weight would prevent its fellows from pulling their load forward. Those men of the escort who did not run were soon cut down by spear and sword and the Scots horsemen buzzed around the English column to hurry them on their way. The dead beasts were then cut from the cart shafts and the carts were turned around to make their way back north.

The greater part of the spoil had been taken when King Robert ordered his army to sweep into the northern counties of England to take the gold he required to administer his kingdom and equip his soldiers. With no army to oppose them, Bruce, Douglas and Edward tore through the north and took an immense booty of stores, armour, horses and hostages from as far afield as Lanercost, Hexham, Corbridge, Durham, Chester-le-Street, Hartlepool and a great many towns and villages in between. They often looted with impunity while timorous guards did nothing but watch on from the tops of their walls as those they were paid to protect were stripped of everything of value. The invasion was different to that of Wallace many years past. There was no burning or wanton slaughter and only those who resisted with arms were cut down by Scots swords. Those past crimes of violence and destruction were replaced with those of intimidation and extortion, with towns and cities being coerced into paying huge sums of money in exchange for a guarantee that no Scot would attack them so long as their payments were made. In this way, silver flowed into the Scottish Treasury and the King's men were rewarded with great plunder.

It was early afternoon when the feasting began in the square and John Edward and his men revelled in the celebrations. He filled his belly with roast meat, satisfied his family's ravenous appetite for tales of his exploits and danced with his squealing, happy children. It was sunset before he was able to slip away and walk down to the lochside to sit at his Lorna's grave. It did not surprise him that the mere sight of the cairn that marked her resting place was sufficient to bring him to the brink of tears. No matter where he was or what he was doing, she was always there at the edge of his mind, almost as if she was stationed at his shoulder to watch over him. He spoke softly as he added the stones he had collected on his travels to her cairn. He told her where each piece of rock had been found as he pushed it into place. Stones from Cambuskenneth, Stirling, Durham and Corbridge were carefully placed alongside pebbles from Lanercost, Carlisle and Chester-le-Street. In this way, he told her where he had been and showed that she had never been far from his thoughts. When he was done, he said a prayer for her soul, told her that he missed her and that he could not wait to be with her again. Then, as was his custom, he wiped the tears from his cheeks and stared out across the loch as the sun shrunk to a narrow strip of gold on the far horizon. A quiet voice startled him from his bittersweet thoughts of better days.

'I thought to sit with you, but you must send me away if I intrude.'

John turned at the sound of the Robertson's voice. 'Never, Laird Robertson.' He replied warmly. 'I see that you have brought a skin of ale for each of us. I would not insult you with a refusal. Come, sit with me upon the bank!'

The two men sat in silence and drank as the sun slipped from view and the world darkened around them.

'I would like to be buried here.' The Robertson stated suddenly. 'It is so peaceful. So beautiful.'

John nodded his agreement but kept his eyes fixed on the horizon. 'Very well. I will see to it that you are buried here. Just let me finish this ale and then I will do it myself.'

The Robertson made to cuff at John's head but could not keep himself from laughing. 'You've always had the cheek, I'll give you that. But look how far you have come. I can scarcely believe that the man now at my side was that wee boy who arrived at my camp in the woods all those years ago. Little did I think that the lad I set to scrubbing my pots would walk with Kings and be renowned as a warrior across the land.'

'I think that you are getting sentimental in your old age, Faither.' John replied, though his chest had swollen with pride at the older man's praise.

'Aye, that might well be true, but I know that I would have had no old age in which to grow sentimental if you had not given me shelter. You took me in and built me a house here so that I could recover from the wounds I suffered at Falkirk. I have known great happiness in this village and I came down to the loch to thank you for it. I am no kin of yours, yet you have shown me such kindness.' The Robertson reached out with a trembling hand and took a hold of John's wrist. 'I can never repay what I owe you, but would have you know that I am grateful. Thank you, John!'

John was surprised to find that his eyes had filled with tears and his chest had swelled with emotion. He kept his eyes to the front and pointed at the Robertson with trembling fingers as he fought to keep his voice from wavering. 'You do not say that to me! You need never say that to me. Of all men, you owe me the least! If there is a debt that cannot be repaid, it is that which I owe to you. I cannot count the times that you have saved my life, but neither do I forget. We may not be related by blood, but I count you closer than kin. Wherever I am, there is a place for you. You need not ask for it, for it is yours by right. If you ever try to thank me again, I will dig your grave there and then.'

The silence hung in the air for a moment before the Robertson replied. 'But you would bury me here, just as I requested?'

John burst into laughter and roughly embraced the Robertson even as he cursed him.

'So, what do you think tae King Robert now?' The Robertson asked in a characteristically unsubtle attempt to change the subject.

John had to think before he answered. 'I cannot forget that he was once sworn to the English King and I am not yet certain that he would not change his colours again. However, I cannot deny that he has some admirable qualities. He is courageous in battle and is one of the most skilled knights that I have ever encountered. He has also shown that he will put the needs of the kingdom before his own. He took the Earl of Ross into his peace when a lesser man would have cut him to pieces for his part in betraying his wife and his sisters to the English. It is to his credit that he put his personal enmity aside in order to avoid further bloodshed and so strengthen the kingdom. He has been strong enough to hold the country together whilst a great English army sat in our midst.'

'You are warming to him then?'

John shrugged. 'I cannot be sure that he will not betray us again. For now, he gives us the best opportunity to clear the English from our lands. I will stay with him until that changes.'

The Robertson turned and gazed at Lorna's cairn for a moment. 'I know that you promised to clear the English out, but you also promised to make a better life for your children. A strong King will make for a secure kingdom and such security would mean that your children would not have to face the same dangers and sufferings that have beset us. Might it not be time for you to put your doubts aside and throw everything in with him?'

'It might.' John replied. 'But he is still cold with me. He does not forget that I scolded him when he crowned himself king.'

The Robertson nodded. 'Aye! It might take him a while to forget that. Few Kings like to be scolded.' He paused to drink from his skin. 'What next?'

'King Robert has set three priorities. The supply of silver must continue to flow in from the north of England. He has set Sir James Douglas the task of ensuring that it does. The Scottish castles still occupied by the English must be taken. He has commanded his brother to oversee the breaking of their walls. His legitimacy as King of Scots must be recognised.

He has ordered me to accompany Sir Thomas Randolph to France to seek support from the Pope and the King of France. If they can be persuaded to so recognise him, it will greatly strengthen his position.'

The Robertson raised his eyebrows as high as they would go. 'I have never been to France.'

'Are you not too old to make the journey?' John asked with an impish grin.

'You did say that I would always have a place at your side, wherever you might be. You also said that I would not have to ask for it.'

John shook his head in exasperation. 'I hope that the sea makes you as sick as it makes me.'

The Robertson took to life aboard ship with great gusto. He spent his days regaling the galley hands with his tales and the nights dining with Sir Thomas Randolph and his retinue and the small party from Scotstoun. He took great pains to ensure that he did not neglect John and often came out onto the deck to engage him in conversation.

'You must recover yourself and join us at table.' He insisted cheerily. 'Sir Thomas will deny himself none of the finer things in life. His wine is strong and sweet and the venison he took aboard at Wick is as tender as any I've ever had.'

The mere mention of food was enough to set John to puking again and he stayed hunched over the gunwale as the galley made its way to the Orkney Islands and then onto the Shetland Islands. The voyage across the North Sea caused him great suffering, for the galley was constantly buffeted and tossed by the great, grey swells. There was some relief for him when they put into Bergen, for they were met by servants sent by Isabel, the Dowager Queen of Norway and sister to King Robert of Scotland. The three days spent ashore in the sumptuous accommodations provided by the Dowager Queen were enough for John to quite recover himself. He had hoped and prayed that the larger Norwegian ship commissioned to take them south would make for a more comfortable journey, but he found himself again overcome with nausea before the Norwegian coast was even lost to sight. The long voyage through coastal waters all the way to Calais was a nightmare of nausea and dizziness and John felt close to death when he finally staggered down the gangplank and set his feet upon French soil. He groaned when he saw who had come to meet them.

'John Edward!' The horseman called from his saddle, his wide smile displaying his great amusement. 'This is the most pleasant surprise! I had no idea that you were returning to France. I count myself blessed to have stumbled upon you in this place.'

Sir Thomas Randolph was clearly discomfited by the exchange, as he had made no arrangements for an escort. 'Who is this?' He demanded.

John grimaced as his stomach had not yet stopped its painful cramping. 'This is Captain

Marsaud of the Palace Guard. He has no doubt been sent to escort us to Paris.'

Sir Thomas shook his head in confusion. 'But our arrival was not announced. How could he know that we would arrive here today?'

'He always knows.' John groaned. 'Even when I arrive in secret and under cover of darkness, Captain Marsaud is always there to greet me.'

Marsaud continued to beam with pleasure. 'I could not have you wandering the streets of Calais without protection. The port is full of English traders. I would never forgive myself if one of them was to cut your throats or seize you as prisoners to present to the English King. That would not do at all, my friends. Come now! We will escort you to Paris.'

The days spent riding south to Paris were sufficient for John to regain his health and he was able to take pleasure in the company of his companions and the meals they took in roadside inns along the way. He also found that he enjoyed his conversations with Marsaud as they discussed their past adventures together. Sir Thomas listened on in astonished silence as they shared tales of the attempted assassination of Wallace in Paris, of John's dinner with King Philip of France, of the visit to the chateaux of the deposed Scots King, John Balliol, and of their presence at the Battle of Courtrai where the flower of French nobility was scythed down. When they found themselves alone together on the evening of their arrival in Paris, Randolph turned to John with a shake of his head.

'There is much that I do not know about you, John Edward. What other surprises do you have for me?'

John smiled as he met Randolph's gaze knowing full well that it was the revelation of his meeting with John Balliol that preyed on the mind of the nephew of King Robert. 'You need fear no unpleasant surprises from me, Sir Thomas.' He replied in an even tone. 'Just so long as you are never tempted to again swear fealty to the English King.'

The colour rose instantly to Randolph's cheeks. He did not like to be reminded that he had kneeled before the old King Edward and had begged for his life after he was captured upon the field at Methven, only to then again swear allegiance to Robert Bruce when he was captured by Sir James Douglas at Peebles. 'I would never betray my uncle!' He protested.

'Good!' John replied. 'But know that I will watch you just as carefully as you watch me. I have no doubt that we will both have many chances to prove our loyalty.'

There was little opportunity for them to dwell on this awkward exchange, for they were summoned to the palace of King Philip of France the very next morning. John paced around the great antechamber and could not help but recall the long days he had spent there with Wallace as they awaited their audience. The hours passed no more quickly this time around and he waited with Randolph with growing impatience and watched the shadows lengthen as the sun set and the skies above Paris grew dark.

He had been on the verge of suggesting that they return to their lodgings when a palace clerk instructed them to follow him. The passageways they passed through were narrow with walls of bare stone. John realised that they were being confined to the passages used by palace servants and were being deliberately kept away from the wide, ornate palace corridors and the curious eyes of courtiers and fellow petitioners. The clerk opened a door and indicated that they should enter.

Guillaume de Nogaret, Keeper of the Seal and Councillor to King Philip of France turned to greet them with a smile. 'Gentlemen! Welcome!' He extended his hand with his fingers pointed daintily towards the floor and let Randolph and John take turns to bow and kiss it. John noted that the Keeper had grown a little more grey around his temples and a little more white of beard since he had last seen him. Otherwise, he was unchanged and his smile still put John in mind of a wolf who is about rip open the throat of its prey. 'Please sit!' He instructed them as he waved his hand towards the couch opposite him. Randolph took the seat closest to Nogaret while John remained standing as befitted his subordinate status. It had been agreed beforehand that he would support Sir Thomas by carrying the satchel containing the letters to the French King and the Pope from King Robert, his magnates and his bishops.

'I bring you salutations and felicitations from that magnificent prince, Sir Robert, by the Grace of God, King of Scots.' Sir Thomas began. John let his mind wander for he had already heard the speech several times and knew that he was in for a long wait before they reached anything of substance. 'He has commanded me, Lord Keeper, to convey his thanks to you for granting us this audience and asks only for an audience with His Majesty, King Philip and with the Holy Father. I bring letters for them from King Robert himself and from all the nobles of Scotland.'

Nogaret's expression grew more pained as Randolph's speech progressed and he now waved him to silence. 'I am afraid that there will be no audiences, Sir Thomas, nor can I accept any letters from you. Both you and Robert Bruce are in open rebellion against King Philip's son-in-law, King Edward of England. We cannot ignore the fact that both you and Robert Bruce have been declared excommunicate by the Holy Father. It would be impolitic for either the King or the Holy Father to engage with you in any way.'

Randolph attempted to move on to the part of his speech which detailed the legitimacy of Robert Bruce's claim to the throne of Scotland, but Nogarct again indicatcd that hc should stop.

'I cannot hear your case, Sir Thomas. It would be highly inappropriate even for me, a humble servant to the King, to speak with you of such matters. If word of it was to reach King Edward's ears, it might well sour relations between our two nations. I have only met with you today away from the eyes of the court out of courtesy to John Edward.' He turned to John with a smile. 'Come, John! You should sit. I would take some time to talk with you.'

John took a seat next to Sir Thomas, acutely aware that he was staring at him in astonishment. 'What would you like to talk about, Lord Keeper?' John asked warily.

'Ah!' Nogaret declared. 'I could talk with you of many things. The King still speaks of you and your heroics at the Battle of Stirling Bridge. He so enjoyed that evening in your company and that of William Wallace. Such tales you told! You know that the King's offer is still open? There is always a place for a skilled officer in the ranks of our armies. You should consider it!'

'Please offer my humble and most heartfelt thanks to King Philip, Lord Keeper.' John replied. 'I would be honoured to accept, but cannot do so until my country is at peace. Only then would I be free to take up such a commission.'

'That is what we all want, is it not?' Nogaret asked. 'King Philip is most eager to see hostilities brought to a close. He would welcome peace between England and Scotland so that his son-in-law no longer has to face a threat to his north. He has troubles enough within his own borders, does he not?'

John knew Nogaret well enough to know that he was baiting a hook. He resisted for a moment before giving in to his curiosity. 'To what troubles are you referring?'

Nogaret rearranged his features into a well-practised expression of surprise. He was aware that John recognised his small deceits, but it did nothing to lessen his enjoyment of them and in no way discouraged him from persisting with them. 'You have not heard? It would have happened while you were still at sea.' The Keeper leaned forward and lowered his voice, though it was unlikely that they would be overheard in this back-chamber hidden in the depths of the palace. 'While Robert Bruce raids the north of England and holds its cities to ransom, the magnates of England have taken arms against King Edward. They have seized his favourite, the Earl of Cornwall, and now close in on the beleaguered King and those few Earls who still stand with him. The whole kingdom teeters on the very brink of civil war.' Nogaret paused to allow the Scots to take the news in. 'It would please King Philip if a peace settlement could be reached. If only there was something we three could do to bring that about.'

'If King Philip was to influence the Pope.' Sir Thomas began, only to be cut off by Nogaret.

'No!' He snapped. 'He will not oppose King Edward so publicly. John, I thought that you were about to speak. Have you some suggestion to make?'

'I cannot speak for King Robert.' John began. 'But I think that he would be more receptive to peace negotiations if his legitimacy as King was recognised. Without such recognition, he is left with no alternative but to defend his crown with force.'

Nogaret tilted his head to one side as if he was contemplating the idea for the first time. 'I do not know if I can persuade the King of the wisdom of this course, but I will mention it when we next meet.' He then pushed himself to his feet. 'Now! I must get back before my absence is noticed. I will wish you bon voyage now, as I know that you will not tarry in Paris now that you are aware that your presence might prove embarrassing to His Majesty.'

Nogaret made his way to the King's apartments the moment John and Thomas left his presence. King Philip lifted his head from the parchment in his hands as he approached.

'So, Lord Keeper, how were our Scots savages?' He asked.

'Just as we expected, Majesty.' Nogaret replied with a bow. 'If you write to Robert Bruce and address him as King, he will receive peace envoys from England.'

'Then I must also write to King Edward and persuade him to send those envoys.'

'It would be better if you did not mention to him that you have addressed the Bruce as King of Scots.'

King Philip nodded his agreement. 'I agree. The little shit will resist and try to cling onto that northern province even though he barely hangs onto his own throne by his fingernails. What of the Scots? Did they ask that I intercede with the Pope and have the excommunication of Bruce and his supporters lifted?'

'They did, Majesty. I refused to consider it.' King Philip raised an eyebrow to indicate that further explanation was required. 'The Scots are best treated like dogs, Majesty. You feed them a morsel with one hand, but let them see that you have another in your pocket. That way they will stay loyal and obedient and will perform all manner of pretty tricks for us.'

27

The long months in the frigid, dank cell beneath Wallingford Castle had provided Walter Langton with ample opportunity to contemplate his own death. Indeed, there had been many occasions, particularly during the freezing winter months, when he had actively prayed for it in order to bring his suffering to an end. He had even grown used to the regular beatings and did not resist when the guards threw the metal grate open and pulled him out to administer the physical punishments mandated by the King. His current condition proved that his belief that he had conquered his fear of pain and death had been an illusion. His arms and legs had shaken uncontrollably from the moment his goalers had pulled him from the dungeon and loaded him into a wooden cage tied to the back of a cart. His tattered and frayed robes gave him no protection from the rain and wind, but he knew that he shook from fear more than he did from cold. His shivering increased each time a castle came into view, as he feared that each one was to be the place of his execution.

His terror did not subside as the cart continued to rattle and clatter its way north,

stopping only for his jailers to empty their
bladders and bowels, fill their stomachs and rest
their horses during the hours of darkness. They
ignored his questions and left him to fret and
shiver in the filth of his cage. His heart set to
beating hard in his chest when he saw the walls
of York in the distance. He sobbed to think of
the times when he had approached those same
walls in the company of King Edward. Gone
were the fines robes, polished armour and the
power and invincibility brought by his proximity
to the crown. Now he came paralysed with fear,
dressed in rags, smeared in his own shit and
soaked in his own stale piss. His humiliation
was tempered by the fact that no living sole
would recognise him as Lord High Treasurer
and Bishop of Coventry and Lichfield. Years of
neglect had conspired to hide his features behind
dirt, grime and a wild and untamed beard. A diet
of thin gruel and rotten fruit and vegetables had
stripped away the thick layers of fat built up
through years of feasting and indulging himself
in the finest of wines and strongest of ales.

He tried to summon his courage as the cart
passed through the Micklegate Bar and on into
the city, but found that, in his weakened
condition, he could do nothing to prevent
himself from trembling. He prayed that few of
his enemies would be there to bear witness to his
execution, but knew well that King Edward's
cruelty made it unlikely that he would miss the
opportunity to torment him, even as he took his
life away. He pushed himself back hard against
the rear wall of the cage when the goalers came

for him, but they simply seized him by his ankles, pulled him roughly from the cart and let his emaciated body thump onto the hard-packed earth. When his legs refused to support his weight despite the encouragement of their boots and their fists, they lifted him bodily by his oxters and dragged him into York Castle's great hall.

The tears in Langton's eyes prevented him from recognising the tall figure at the far end of the hall until the goalers had dragged him the full length of the chamber. His tears, his fear and his poor state of health did not prevent him from recognising the fury and hatred burning in the eyes of the Earl of Pembroke.

'You bastard son of a dog!' The Earl roared as he drew his fist back.

Langton's mouth dropped open in astonishment, not because he was about to be struck, but because of who was about to land the blow. Pembroke was the nearest thing to an ally that he had and he could not fathom what he had done to incur his displeasure.

Pembroke brought his fist crashing down with ferocious and vicious force, sending the larger of the two goalers crashing to the ground with blood flowing from his ruined nose. The second jailer fared worse when Pembroke's elbow smashed into his mouth, tearing all of his front teeth from his gums.

'Out! Out!' The Earl shrieked. 'I commanded that he was to be brought to me and you have misused him badly. Fuck off out of my sight before I call for my sword and spread your guts across this floor.'

The goalers required no further encouragement and scrambled to their feet before running from the hall as fast as their legs would carry them. Pembroke leaned down and helped Langton to stand, his face full of concern.

'I had no idea, Lord Bishop, that you were in such poor condition. Browby told me that you had grown thin, but I see now that they have starved you. Come, let me sit you down and call for meat and bread. You must build your strength.'

Langton looked about himself in confusion while Pembroke barked orders at the servants. He fell upon the bread and mutton like a ravenous hound and gulped at the wine the Earl had poured for him.

Tears poured down his face as he emptied the goblet. 'By Christ, my Lord!' He declared when he had drained it. 'I never thought that I would taste such sweetness again. I know not why you have brought me here, but I thank you for it. Even if this is to be my place of execution, I will go to the block quitc happily now that my belly is full.'

'By God!' Pembroke retorted in horror. 'You thought that you were brought here to be executed?' Not so, Lord Bishop! Not so! I brought you here because I have need of you. The King has need of you!'

Langton stared at Pembroke for a moment before breaking into hysterical laughter. 'The King has need of me? The man he has had

377

locked away and mistreated all these years? What disaster has befallen him to bring him to this unhappy place?'

'He is in danger of losing his crown. The Earls of Arundel, Gloucester, Warwick, Hereford and Lancaster have mobilised their armies. Only Surrey and I now stand with him. The kingdom teeters on the brink of civil war.'

'Then he must treat with them.' Langton replied. 'He must know that he cannot prevail when all of the kingdom is against him.'

'He is deep in mourning and is in no fit state to treat with them.'

'Mourning?'

Pembroke dropped his eyes to the floor in shame. 'I took Piers Gaveston prisoner at Scarborough and handed him over to Warwick. I thought it best that he be removed from the King's side, as it was his presence that had most soured relations with the magnates. Though they gave me their word of honour that Gaveston would not be mistreated, Warwick and Lancaster had him executed. The King now wallows in his grief and the whole land holds its breath for fear of what he will do next.'

'Gaveston dead?' Langton replied in shock, before erupting into laughter once more. 'Forgive me, my Lord! I have prayed for this moment a thousand times over the years of my incarceration. I know full well that it was he who prompted the King to treat me so horribly. You will not deny me my moment of joy.'

'If the circumstances were not so grave, I would join you in your celebrations.' Pembroke replied. 'The future of the kingdom hangs in the balance, Lord Bishop. Will you come to our aid in this darkest of hours?'

'I did not spend the best years of my life keeping the crown of England upon a Plantagenet head just to see it snatched away by that greedy dullard Lancaster. Take me to the King! We have work to do!'

'Perhaps you should bathe first, Lord Bishop. I will have a servant trim your hair and beard and bring fresh clothes for you.'

Langton shook his head. 'Let him see what he has done to me. If I am to save his crown, I will need to employ every tool of manipulation to bend him to my will. Guilt at my mistreatment might strengthen my armoury.'

Pembroke saw the change in Langton. The fear in his eyes had been replaced with a calculating hardness and, while his appearance was still most wretched, his posture was already becoming less stooped and more upright. The transformation gave the Earl of Pembroke a sense of hope that had been absent for the past few days. 'Very well, Lord Bishop. I will take you to him. He is in the chapel.'

Langton heard King Edward of England long before he saw him. His sobbing, wailing and moaning echoed through the castle corridors. On entering the chapel itself, he saw Edward on his knees at the side of a plain wooden catafalque. The body of Piers Gaveston, Earl of Cornwall, was laid out on its top draped in fine gold cloth. The King turned his head at the sound of Langton's footsteps and looked up at him, his

379

face red and wet with tears and snot. The King was so deep in his misery that he was oblivious to Langton's haggard and emaciated features and to his filthy, malodorous condition.

'Langton!' He bawled. 'Look what they have done to poor Piers! Look at what those bastards have done to him.'

The cloth draping the corpse was gossamer thin and did nothing to hide the injuries inflicted upon the King's favourite. An attempt had been made to stitch his head and body back together, but the thick, black thread did nothing to detract from the horror of the ragged flesh where his throat had once been. The wound told Langton that the sword used to behead Gaveston had not been chosen for its sharpness. The many cuts and black, purple and yellow bruises covering his entire body and all of his limbs spoke of vicious beatings and mistreatment over a number of days. The gash in his stomach made it plain that he had been grievously wounded before his life had been taken. The gaping, torn and bloody gash at his groin was the clearest evidence of the vicious cruelty meted out to him by his torturers. Langton searched his heart for some modicum of pity for his suffering, but could find none.

He crouched down so that he could look directly into the King's eyes. Edward continued to sob and keen mournfully. Langton held him in his dispassionate gaze and felt nothing but contempt for the pathetic and miserable creature before him. He slapped him hard across the cheek and ignored the shocked gasp that came from Pembroke.

'Do you want to lose your crown?' He demanded.

The King blubbered harder but shook his head.

Langton slapped him again, his every sense tingling at the pleasure it gave him to hit out at the monster who had tormented him these last few years. 'Then you must pull yourself together! Every moment that you sit here crying like a child is a moment your enemies use to plot against you. Up! Be a man and rise to your feet!'

Edward responded with a high-pitched cry that roused Langton's irritation to still greater heights. His third slap was the hardest of all and it rocked the King's head to the side.

'Do you mean to let them away with Gaveston's murder?'

'Piers!' Edward wailed.

'Aye! Piers. Do you not wish to avenge his death?'

Edward now returned Langton's gaze and jutted his bottom lip out in trembling defiance. 'I will ride out and cut those bastards down!'

'Then you will die! Ride out against your enemies and the man who killed poor Piers will take your crown for himself. Is that what you want? To lose your crown, your favourite and your own life? Tell me that this is what you truly desire and I will strap you into your armour myself.'

Edward gritted his teeth and tried to choke back his sobbing. 'I want revenge, Langton! I want to see them all dead for what they have done!'

'If you listen to me you will have your revenge and keep your crown, but you must be prepared to be patient. Your current position is so fragile, it will take us months to recover our strength. Will you be guided by Pembroke and I?'

'If you swear that I will have Lancaster's head at the end of it.'

'I swear it, my Lord. It will take time, but you will have your revenge.'

King Edward nodded and pushed himself to his feet. 'Then tell me what I must do. My father always said that you could scheme and plot your way out of anything.'

'First of all, we must avert the immediate threat. You will never have vengeance against the Earl of Lancaster if your crown is lost. Pembroke will go to the magnates to negotiate peace. He will offer them pardons for their parts in Gaveston's murder. In return, they must swear to support a fresh campaign in Scotland.'

Pembroke nodded his approval. 'That way they will expend their military strength in the north and their threat to the King will be reduced.'

'Aye, my Lord.' Langton replied. 'And while their eyes are upon Scotland, we will be hard at work strengthening his position at home and abroad. I will make for France to gain King Philip's support and to gain loans from both him and the Pope.'

'And what shall I do, Lord Bishop?' Edward enquired, his grief laid aside for a moment.

'You must see to the Queen, my Lord. If King Philip is to give his support, he must know that his daughter is not neglected. You must devote all of your attention to her. If you put an heir in her belly you will find your father-in-law more amenable and your nobles more willing to support you.'

'So, my part in this is to tup my wife?' The King asked, his tone full of distaste.

'Aye, my Lord!' Langton replied with a smile. 'Tup her well and tup her often. Then prepare to make for Paris. If King Philip is to support you against the magnates, he will want you to come and be seen to kiss his arse in his own palace.'

In the long months since his return from Paris, John Edward and the men of Scotstoun had sunk back into the dull tedium of blockading the garrison at Perth. Though the close proximity to home had obvious advantages, the crushing boredom was hard to bear. They tried to amuse themselves by inventing ever more fantastical schemes for breaching the city walls. Spirits were raised temporarily when news reached them of successes elsewhere. Feasts were held beneath the walls of Perth when they heard that starvation had forced the garrisons of the castles at Banff, Dundee, Ayr and Loch Doon to surrender to their besiegers. These improvements in morale were short-lived, as the well-stocked cellars of Perth Castle kept the garrison frustratingly well-nourished. There had been some excitement when King Robert ordered half of the Scotstoun men to join with him in an assault on the walls of Berwick. This too had provided only a temporary diversion, as a barking dog had alerted the garrison to their attempt to scale the walls and they had been beaten back without ever seriously threatening the stronghold.

Boredom is the enemy of discipline, so John kept his men busy honing their fighting skills. Men practised with sword and bow each morning, with the exception of the Sabbath. He had also taken to running schiltrom drills in the afternoon, as it improved the way the men worked together and wielding the heavy poles served to build their muscles and keep them strong. He had hoped that these displays of martial prowess would serve to test the resolve of the garrison, but they seemed to enjoy the spectacle and would line the walls to good-naturedly cheer and jeer at the combatants. He was putting his spearmen through their paces when Al rode in to report that a force of cavalry was approaching from the direction of Stirling.

'How many?' John demanded, as Al dismounted and kneeled down to pat the Black Dog's head.

'Fifty.' Al answered, as he scratched at Dugal's chin.

'Any idea who it is?'

Al's eyes sparkled with amusement. 'We are about to be honoured with a royal visit. I saw the King's standard.'

John groaned. 'I doubt that he has ridden so far just to honour us. In my experience, great men only make such efforts when they come to chastise or to ask for something. Set a table! King Robert will require refreshment.' John then grimaced and waved his hand below his nose. 'Christ Al! That dog's guts grow more rancid with each passing week. Keep him away from the table while we talk with the King.'

Al rubbed harder at Dugal's chin. 'Just you ignore him Dugal. He's no' as old as you and his guts don't smell much better. Come away and let's see if I can find a bone for you.'

John shook his head as he watched Al walk off. He rubbed the worst of the dirt and dust from his tunic and trews and awaited King Robert's arrival. It was quickly apparent that the King had not come to honour him and his men.

'It would seem that the English barons have reached some kind of settlement with their King.' King Robert informed him between mouthfuls of venison. 'I doubt that they will muster before winter, so we should expect them to come in the spring. The key strongholds of Berwick, Bothwell, Stirling and Perth Castles remain in English hands. They must be taken before King Edward marches north. How fares the garrison here? Are they close to surrender?'

John shook his head ruefully. 'No, m'Lord. I see nothing to suggest that they starve. Their sentries do not grow thin as they did at Dundee.'

The King tapped his fingers impatiently against the top of the rough, wooden table.

'Have you identified any weaknesses in their defences that we could exploit?'

John shook his head again. 'Nothing that would not carry the risk of heavy casualties.'

'I think that now is the time for us to take risks, John Edward. If we are to survive another invasion, I would rather do it without having to worry about the Perth garrison at my back.'

John leaned forward and rubbed at his beard. 'There is one place where the moat is just shallow enough for a man to cross.'

'But how would you scale the walls?' King Robert demanded. 'Surely a wooden ladder would sink into the mud?'

John hesitated, unsure as to whether or not it would be wise to share a strategy that had been both formulated and dismissed as unrealistic around an ale-soaked campfire. 'A wooden ladder would not work, m'Lord. A ladder constructed from two ropes and ten or twelve wooden slats would stand a better chance of success. The iron cleeks from our campfires could be used to hang the ladder from the walls.'

King Robert stared back at John as his fingers continued to drum upon the table. 'How would you get the hooks to the top of the wall?'

John turned and gestured towards the men going through their schiltrom drill. 'Those spears are long enough to reach the top. We need only strap them to the cleeks and the whole ladder could be pushed up into place.'

King Robert was silent for so long that John feared that he thought his plan to be the work of an imbecile. It was a relief when he finally spoke. 'We should break camp now and retire to Scotstoun. It will take us a few days to fashion the ladders and that should be long enough to lull the garrison into a false sense of security.'

The presence of the Scottish King caused great excitement in Scotstoun. John could not help but be impressed by the way he conducted himself. He did not shut himself away with his aides, but wandered the village talking with commoner and noble alike. He took an interest in everything from the types of fish to be caught in the loch, to the best fields for the cultivation of crops, to the techniques used by Angus Edward in his forge to put an edge on a blade. He was even more taken aback when the King approached him during the afternoon of their planned assault on the walls of Perth and asked if he might say a prayer at Lorna's grave. John was surprised that he even remembered that he had lost his wife and was choked with emotion when he fell to his knees before the cairn and spoke a prayer of beauty and compassion.

The King then rose to his feet and turned to John, his eyes sparkling with tears. 'We, who have lost so much, must ensure that something good is built on all this suffering.'

Those words stayed with John as he crawled through the darkness at King Robert's side, each of them pushing a pole towards the moat. They eased themselves into the frigid waters and moved slowly towards the base of the wall, using the poles to steady themselves and check the depth of the water.

Jacques Flammier, one of the Templar Knights hidden in Scotstoun by Prior Abernethy, watched on as King Robert stood shoulder deep in the moat and used his great strength to lift the cleek high enough to hook it over the rampart. 'Mon Dieu!' He purred in admiration. 'What shall we say of our nobles in France who think only of stuffing their bellies, when so renowned a knight will risk his life for such a miserable hamlet.' He then slipped into the moat and hurried across so that he might scale the ladder behind the King and John Edward.

Robert Bruce turned to John on the rampart and gripped his shoulder. 'Most men here are Scots sworn to the English. Any man who asks for quarter is to be spared. Understand?'

John nodded and waved his men up the ladder. With twenty Scotstoun men at his side, John left the King to guard the rampart and set off to range through the town. The garrison were taken by surprise and were overcome before they could gather themselves sufficiently to mount a meaningful defence. Before the sun had risen, half of them had perished at the hands of their attackers and the remainder had thrown down their arms and begged for mercy. Sir William Oliphant was found amongst the prisoners. As the man who had held Stirling Castle for long months against the siege engines of Edward I, King Robert was most anxious to speak with him. Sir William explained that the English had only released him from imprisonment when he swore that he would fight for the English Crown. King Robert offered him pardon if he would swear loyalty to him and agree to go and assist Edward Bruce in the siege of Stirling Castle. The Earl of Strathearn was also discovered amongst the prisoners and he too was forgiven when he fell to his knees and swore himself to King Robert.

It took longer to raze Perth Castle to the ground than it did to capture it. Without sufficient men to garrison it himself, King Robert ordered it torn down to deny its use to any invading English army. He left this task in the hands of the Scotstoun men and ordered them to go and reinforce his brother in besieging Stirling Castle when they were done.

28

John Edward could think of nothing he had
enjoyed less than the siege of Stirling Castle.
The worsening weather did not help, as the
constant rain made it impossible to dry boots,
clothes or tents. The garrison was less benign
than that at Perth and would shoot arrows down
at any man foolish enough to stray too close to
the castle walls. The very height of the
stronghold was enough to lower men's spirits,
for it always loomed over them as a mocking
reminder of their essential impotence. The worst
part of it was to be under the command of
Edward Bruce. There was never a man born who
was less suited to sitting patiently whilst waiting
for events to unfold in his favour. The forced
inactivity brought him close to madness and his
sullen, brooding presence was enough to drive
reasonable men to drink. He did, it is true, try to
occupy himself in the town, but he quickly tired
of the same whores and the same errant,
unfaithful wives. The men of Stirling similarly
tired of the Bruce's ill-temper when the dice did
not fall his way and his search for gambling
partners was seldom rewarded with success. His
appetite for wine and ale was also problematic,

for it was impossible to maintain discipline and keep men from drink when they saw their commander leave camp each night only to stagger back again in the small hours of the morning.

'Come John!' He would often implore. 'Let's mount up and ride south to raid the North of England! We must keep those bastards on their toes and we can fill our purses as we go.'

John would shake his head in amused resignation. 'We cannot leave, Ed. Your brother has ordered us to remain here to ensure that not one bag of grain reaches the garrison.'

'Fuck my brother!' Edward would curse. ''Tis alright for King Robert. While we rot here, he takes the Earl of Moray to conquer the Isle of Man. He will already have landed at Ramsay and I doubt that Castle Rushen will hold out for more than a week. He and Randolph will have all the glory, while we do nothing but grow fungus between our toes.'

John tried to always take his ill-tempered ranting in good part, although he found it tiresome in the extreme. He expected more of the same when he was summoned to meet with him in a tavern within sight of the castle gates. He was relieved to find him in high spirits at a table beside the inn's fire.

'John!' Bruce roared. 'Come and join me! Landlord! Bring more ale! My friend and I have much to celebrate.'

John took his place at the table and returned Edward's grin. 'What are we celebrating? Have you parted some poor from his silver?'

Edward Bruce shook his head with the exaggerated care of a man deep in his cups. 'Tis not silver that I have liberated, John. It is us.' He slurred. 'I have freed us from the bondage of this siege. No longer must we moulder away in this muddy shithole. We may now go wherever we please.'

John blinked in confusion and was overcome with a sense of foreboding. 'What have you done, Ed? How are we freed from the siege?'

Edward Bruce leaned forward and attempted to tap the side of his nose with his index finger. Such was his level of inebriation, he missed his target. 'I made a pact with Sir Philip Mowbray. If no English army has relieved him by midsummer next year, he will freely yield the castle to me. He has pledged his honour on it. So, there is no need for us to starve him out. We need only wait a year and the castle will be ours.'

John felt the blood drain from his face. 'Your brother will be furious!'

'He's always furious, John, but it is not him who has to spend months sitting around when there is fighting to be done. Now drink! My cunning must be celebrated.'

They did not have long to wait for King Robert's fury. Two weeks after the pact was made, he arrived in Stirling, having left Thomas Randolph in command of the newly conquered Isle of Man.

'Christ Edward!' He growled through gritted teeth. 'Have you lost your wits? Never have I heard so long a warning given to so mighty a

King as the King of England. You have given him a full year to prepare an invasion. You have thrown down a challenge that no King could ignore. I cannot even disown your vow, as I must treat my brother's pledged troth as if I had made it myself. Foolish knave! You have undone all that we have won.'

Edward waved his hand dismissively. 'He will not come. Our spies tell us that he is still at odds with his magnates. He cannot raise an army without their support.'

'At odds with his magnates?' The King snarled. 'He will be at odds with them no longer when they hear of this pact. This challenge will unite them where all else has failed. They will rally behind him and march here to defend the honour of England.'

'We would have to fight them at some stage, Robert. They would never be content to leave you perched upon your throne. Better that we do it sooner than leave it until they have grown stronger.'

Sir John de Seagrave smiled broadly as he looked Walter Langton up and down. 'You look well, my Lord.' He exclaimed in wonder. 'There is twice as much of you as there was when last I saw you!'

Langton laughed in delight and patted at his ample belly. 'I thought of little else but food throughout my incarceration. The more I starved the more I dreamed of pottage, pork pot pies, honey-mustard eggs, malardis, venison, roasted swan and cheese. Ah! The very thought of cheese would have me salivating like a dog.'

'So, you have been indulging yourself to make up for what was denied to you?'

'I stuff myself with every delicacy I can think of and eat until I can barely move. I then wash it down with ale and wine until I fear that my guts will split under the weight of it all.'

'Then I bring glad tidings. King Edward and the Earl of Pembroke have ordered me here to Eccleshall with gifts for the Lord High Treasurer and Bishop of Coventry and Lichfield. Your servants are already busy in the courtyard unloading the carts I escorted here. The grateful King and Earl wish to reward you for your good service with wine, ale, gold, silver and household plate. I have been commanded to express their gratitude for the part you played in improving relations with the King of France and with the magnates of England. The King still raves about the extravagance of his reception in Paris and Pembroke often expresses his astonishment at how you brought about reconciliation with the nobles and gained their support for the new campaign in Scotland.' Seagrave paused to wink at Langton. 'He even tells me that you had a part to play in Queen Isabella falling pregnant, though I did not dare to ask for details.'

Langton laughed and ushered Seagrave towards a small table. 'They owe me gratitude for all those things and for much more besides. Come! Let me show you what came into my hand this very morning!' The Bishop lifted a parchment from the table and put it into Seagrave's grasp.

Seagrave's eyes grew wider as he read on. 'My God!' He exclaimed. 'Our prayers are answered!'

Langton nodded. 'I could not have asked for more. Once I make this known, there is not a nobleman in England who will refuse to answer to the call. Edward Bruce's impatience has provided me with the lever I require to unite the whole country behind the King. We will build an army so mighty that it will sweep Robert Bruce and his band of traitors from the surface of the land.'

'Such a victory will greatly strengthen King Edward's position.'

'More than that, Sir John.' Langton replied. 'It will make him more powerful than his father ever was. It will make him the most powerful ruler in all of Europe.'

'And you will stand at his side.'

Langton drew in a great breath. 'Nothing intoxicates like power, Sir John. Nothing comes close. Now, come and help me with this letter. I must amend it before I set the priests to copying it and distributing it to every noble family in England, Ireland and Wales.'

'Amend it?' Seagrave asked. 'Surely it requires no amendment. Sir Philip Mowbray could not have been clearer. Stirling Castle will be lost if the garrison is not relieved by the coming midsummer. The nobles will not be able to stand idly by and suffer such a blow to English prestige.'

'This army must be the mightiest ever fielded by an English King, Sir John. I will leave nothing to chance. If I add a passage or two detailing how Robert Bruce taunted the English nobles for their disunity and cowardice, they will respond more furiously and commit more men to the enterprise. I will have my priests scratching away night and day until every last noble has seen evidence of these insults to English honour.'

King Robert ensured that his brother had ample opportunity to reflect on the consequences of his rash decision to enter into a pact with the commander of Stirling Castle. Declaring loudly that he wanted him far from his sight, he set Edward Bruce the task of razing every captured castle to the ground. His instruction was that every wall should be broken down so that no single stone was left standing upon another. He further stipulated that the stones were to be scattered so widely that any future castle builders would be forced to transport their own materials to the sites of the previous strongholds. Edward soon found himself harking back to his days of laying siege to castles with some fondness. The work of breaking walls was slow, dirty and beset with practical difficulties. The miserable nature of the task only increased as autumn turned to winter and the bitter winds and frosts tormented men and beasts alike. Although innocent of playing any part in the making of the pact, John Edward and the men of Scotstoun found themselves sharing in the younger Bruce's punishment. John started his day by cursing the Lord of Galloway's impetuous nature and he ended his waking hours in much the same way. Much of the time in between was also spent berating him for his foolish impatience.

Always keen to make the best of every situation, John found that the work offered some small advantages. The physical labour required to topple great blocks of stone, to break them up and load them into carts served to harden his men and greatly increase their strength. He had not spared himself from wielding lever, hammer or pick and he took great satisfaction from seeing his muscles and sinews grow hard and tight. He also kept an eye out for any materials that could be reused in Scotstoun. He and his brother Scott had long talked about building a hall and houses for themselves in the village and they had loaded several wagons with oak beams, lintels, flag stones and tiles. Though these acquisitions did bring them some small measure of satisfaction, it did not come close to compensating them for their months of misery and toil.

Their suffering was the greater for having to listen to Edward Bruce's constant complaints. 'I am treated no better than a slave!' He would moan to anyone who came within earshot. 'Can it be right that the King's brother is reduced to this? A noble knight forced to toil like some common labourer.'

Eck Edward reckoned that it was a miracle that no man had yet inadvertently sent a rock crashing down upon his head. On the worst days, when the wind was viciously cold and cut through men's clothes like an icy blade, he doubted that a single man would have mourned his loss if an accident had brought his whining to an end.

When spirits were as low as they could go and the days so cold that water could not be brought to the boil on the fires around the camp, news of the successes of others brought all men there closer to despair. A messenger brought them word of the fall of the castle at Linlithgow. He told them how a local farmer called William Bunnock had driven a loaded haywain into the entrance of the castle gate and there cut the horses' traces so that the portcullis could not be closed. Patriots hidden amongst the hay had then leapt from their hiding place and attacked the garrison unawares. Other men were concealed close by and, on hearing Bunnock's cries, they too rushed in and soon had the castle in their hands. The men cheered on hearing of the heroics of their countrymen and applauded warmly when told that King Robert had given Bunnock a rich reward, but they could not hide their melancholy at being denied the opportunity for glory and reward for themselves. They grew even more disheartened when they learned that it was they who were to have the task of breaking down the walls of Linlithgow.

'Damn him!' Edward Bruce raged. 'If Bunnock has taken his reward, let him be the one to reduce the walls. I'll be damned before I will topple a single stone.'

His mood was no better after three hard weeks of turning Linlithgow Castle to rubble. It could not be denied that the castle boasted a superior level of craftsmanship to any of the other strongholds they had destroyed, but all men there soon came to curse it on account of the effort required to bring it down. The job was not even half-way to completion when they learned that Sir James Douglas had captured Roxburgh Castle despite being heavily outnumbered by the English garrison. Edward Bruce grew more enraged as the messenger told of the audacity of the attack, as the Douglas men had scaled the walls using rope ladders and had surprised the garrison while they sang and danced in celebration of Shrove Tuesday. The details of the daring and heroism of his rival proved too much for the Lord of Galloway and he snatched a heavy hammer from one of his men and threw it so far into the forest that it was never recovered.

'If Douglas has captured it, then he must break it down. I have walls enough to deal with. Let some other fool deal with Roxburgh!' He roared defiantly.

John found that he enjoyed the demolition of Roxburgh Castle. This might have been due to a reduction in the severity of the frosts or to the beauty of the views across the Rivers Tweed and Teviot. It might also have been because he associated the place with the cruel and inhuman incarceration of Mary Bruce. He took the greatest of pleasure in sending the very battlement her cage had been suspended from crashing to the ground below. They had scarcely begun their work when another messenger arrived to test the sanity of Edward Bruce to its very limits.

'What is it this time?' He barked. 'What hero has claimed a victory while I chip away at stones?'

'The Earl of Moray has captured the Castle of Edinburgh!' The messenger announced with glee. 'He scaled the castle heights under cover of darkness with only a handful of Moray Highlanders at his back. They hacked their way to the castle gates and threw them wide to admit his main force. The garrison were so afeart by the ferocity of the attack that those who did not slip away through the open gate, instead scrambled over the walls and took themselves away.'

'Thomas fucking Randolph!' Edward Bruce cursed. 'The most cautious man in the kingdom is hailed for his acts of daring while I push and pull at stones. My life could not be more miserable.'

'I have letters from the King, m'Lord' The messenger announced timidly.

'I did not doubt it.' Edward replied in unhappy resignation. 'I suppose that my brother commands me to Edinburgh as soon as my work is done here.'

'Yes, m'Lord.' The messenger replied. 'I also have orders for John Edward of Scotstoun. He is to attend King Robert at Stirling.'

'Once the castles are reduced?' The Bruce demanded.

The messenger shook his head. 'No, m'Lord. He is to go immediately with all of his men.'

John could not keep the smile from his face. He thought it just that Edward would be forced to complete his punishment without him.

'Grin all you like, John Edward.' The Lord of Galloway growled. 'But I will not forget this moment. Remember that I am my brother's heir. If anything should happen to him, my first act as King will be to appoint you as Breaker of Castles. You will end your days coated in dust and bent under a lever.'

John began to take his leave and waved at him with the cheeriest of grins spread across his face. Edward responded by looking about him, but he could find nothing that could be thrown.

29

'By God, Lord Bishop.' Sir John de Seagrave declared. 'Have you ever beheld such a host?'

Walter Langton leaned against the battlement and gazed out over the mass of men, horses, carts and tents that filled the land around Wark Castle for as far as the eye could see. 'I have laboured long and hard for this, Sir John.' Langton replied. 'I have emptied the Treasury and borrowed heavily from the Pope, the King of France and most of the Italian banking families. The Genoese, Antonio Pessagno, now holds more title to English lands than the King himself. In the King's name I have issued writs to eight earls and ninety barons summoning them to muster here on the banks of the Tweed with their contingents. Sixteen thousand foot soldiers have been levied from thirteen English counties and five thousand archers from north and south Wales. Those few Scots still in opposition to Robert Bruce have also been summoned. John Comyn, son of the Red Comyn, Sir Ingram de Umfraville and the Earl of Angus have already arrived. Knights from France, Brittany, Poitou and Guienne have accepted the King's invitation to share in the spoils.'

'I had heard that King Edward had ransomed Sir Giles d'Argentan from the Emperor of Byzantium.'

'That is true, Sir John.' Langton replied. 'That cost us dear, but it was worth the outlay. The knights of Europe flocked to our side when they heard that the finest knight in all of Christendom had joined with us. Nothing has been left to chance. You will not find a ship between here and Dover that is not in our service. The granaries in the south of England have been emptied so that our soldiers cannot be starved into retreat. I have made all the blacksmiths of England rich to equip every foot soldier with helmet, sword, shield and spear. Never has an English army been so well accoutered.'

'And what of the cavalry, my Lord?' Seagrave enquired. 'I see the banners of Gloucester, Pembroke and Hereford alongside those of the veterans of the old King's campaigns, Sir Ralph de Monthermer, Sir Robert Clifford, Sir Henry Beaumont, Sir Maurice Barclay and Sir Marmaduke de Tweng.'

Langton nodded grimly. 'The old boys have come out in force. Tis shameful that the same cannot be said of Lancaster, Warwick, Surrey and Arundel. They offer their excuses and send only the minimum number of men required by their feudal obligations. We will deal with them once our victory is won. Despite their craven disloyalty, we can still field four thousand heavy horse. The mightiest king in Europe could not stand against them. When Robert Bruce has sight of them, he will throw his tainted crown aside and beg for mercy.'

'Will the King take him back into his peace if he submits and begs for forgiveness on bended knee?'

'No.' Langton replied, his face set hard. 'The time for forgiveness has long since passed. Any man who has sworn fealty to the false King will be executed and his family dispossessed. Every noble here has been promised lands in Scotland as reward for his service. The old lords must be cleared out so that loyal lords can take their place. We must purge and purify mercilessly to stamp out every last vestige of defiance and resistance. This will be our last campaign. We do not go to subdue the Scots, we go to crush them.'

King Robert sat at the far end of the chamber within Cambuskenneth Abbey. An attendant had ordered John to wait until he was summoned and he took the opportunity to study Robert Bruce while he waited. The King looked tired and bleary-eyed as he worked away at the parchments piled high upon his table. John smirked to himself, happy to see that King Robert suffered under the weight of his duties as King, just as he himself had suffered during the past months of hard labour. Long minutes passed before King Robert looked up and registered the Scotstoun man's presence. He fixed him in his weary gaze before waggling his fingers to indicate that he should approach.

'How fares my brother?' He enquired, as John came to a halt before the table. 'Has he learned humility?'

John knew that Robert Bruce had little time for frivolity, but he could not keep himself from smiling at the suggestion that a few months of breaking stones would be sufficient to make a humble man of Edward Bruce. 'He understands the meaning of the word, m'Lord.' John replied. 'Whether or not he has acquired the characteristic, I could not say.'

King Robert rubbed at his tired eyes with his fingers. 'No doubt he still complains that I have treated him badly.'

'Only during his waking hours, m'Lord.' John responded with a grin. 'He finds the work tedious and yearns for excitement.'

Robert pointed to the heaped parchments and groaned. 'Even the King must see to matters that are tedious. No matter, he will soon have excitement enough. The English King has crossed the border at the head of a great army. I doubt that we will have more than two weeks to prepare. That is why I have summoned you.'

'I am yours to command, m'Lord.'

The Bruce hesitated as if was trying to decide if there was some trace of mockery in John's tone. He gave a slight shake of his head as if dismissing the thought before he continued. 'I want the English advance tracked and its progress reported back to me. I am told that your man is the best scout in Scotland.'

John nodded. 'He is, m'Lord. His name is Al.'

'Then set him to work. He will send reports three times a day. I want to know where the English are, what they do and how many of them do it. Understood?'

'Yes, m'Lord.'

'Should he require messengers, horses or anything else, they will be provided.'

'I will instruct him immediately, m'Lord.' John replied, as he turned to take his leave.

'Wait!' King Robert commanded. 'I have other orders for you. I am told that King Edward has engaged a great fleet of ships to supply his army. It seems that he has bought such great quantities of barley, grain and oats in England, Ireland and France, that vast granaries have been constructed on the border to store it all.'

John grimaced. 'He means to deny us the opportunity to defeat him by waiting until winter comes and his army is overcome by starvation.'

'Aye!' The King replied. 'But I think that it is worse than that. I think that he does not come to defeat our army, he comes to occupy our kingdom. If even half of the reports are true, he has purchased sufficient supplies to maintain his army for two years or more.'

'It would be hard to withstand an occupation of such long duration.'

'That is precisely my point.' The King replied grimly. 'I have learned that it is wise to avoid meeting the English in open battle, but it may be the lesser of two evils if they can withstand the frosts and snows and winter in our midst. We must prepare to melt away into the hills and forests and live to fight on a day when the conditions suit us better. However, if they truly have the means to wait us out for two years, or even more, we must also prepare for the possibility that meeting them in battle might be the wiser course.'

'I see the sense in what you say, m'Lord. What will you have me do to aid these preparations?'

King Robert stroked his well-trimmed beard and paused before replying. 'When I met with you before the walls of Perth, you were drilling your men in schiltrom formation. I could not help but notice how nimbly they manoeuvred. It set me to wondering if such a formation could be used offensively rather than in a purely defensive manner.'

John nodded. 'I have seen it used for both defence and attack. At Courtrai, the Flemish spearmen broke the charge of the French heavy horse and then advanced to push the remaining knights and men-at-arms from the field. The Scots under Wallace and Murray at Stirling Bridge similarly used the schiltrom to force both cavalry and foot back against the banks of the Forth, where they were slaughtered.'

'I have no heavy horse and the few light cavalry that I do possess would be swept away by the English knights. If I am to fight, I will have to fight with spearmen. Can you drill our foot so that they can deploy with the same agility as your own men?'

'Give me long enough, m'Lord, and I will make them dance for you.'

A faint smile crossed the lips of the King of Scotland. 'It is good that you are confident, John Edward. You have two weeks. I will be amazed if you can tame our wild and wilful Highlanders in so short a space of time. They fight like devils and do not take kindly to discipline, least of all when it is a stranger who seeks to impose it.'

The Earl of Pembroke was furious and did nothing to hide his agitation from the Lord Treasurer and Bishop of Coventry and Lichfield. The two men had broken away from the main column and ascended a hill so that they could talk privately and assess the progress of the English army from their elevated position.

'I can bear the ingratitude.' Pembroke snarled. 'God knows I have been around kings long enough to have grown used to it. It is the wilful stupidity that tests my temper. He spends weeks at Berwick playing games with his young knights and ignores all pleas to advance. Now, when he finally deigns to lead the army we have built for him, we will only reach Stirling before the castle is surrendered under the terms of the pact through long, forced marches. Both men and horses will be exhausted by the time we are in sight of the castle.'

Does it really matter, my Lord?' Langton asked in the most soothing tone he could muster. 'I doubt that Robert Bruce and his ragged band will trouble us much. A little tiredness will not make much difference one way or the other.'

'It matters because it could have been avoided. I had some sympathy for him after Piers Gaveston was executed, but now I think that there is something rotten at the very core of him. To waste any small advantage for the sake of minstrels and jugglers is unforgiveable. And look at the column! It stretches back near twenty leagues!'

'He has promised so many castles and estates that our nobles have added their wagons to the column so that they can immediately furbish their new houses with tapestries, plate and furniture. I hear that he has promised the lands of Thomas Randolph, the Earl of Murray, to young Hugh Despenser. I am told that he alone has brought ten wagons to slow the column further.'

Pembroke growled. 'Do not mention that bastard's name to me. I see him more and more in the King's company. I fear that he will come to occupy the space once filled by Piers Gaveston.'

'That would be most unfortunate.' Langton replied, his brow wrinkling at the thought. 'Gaveston was bad enough, but he was a mere fop and a fool. Despenser is quite different and could be all the more dangerous.'

'He is like his father, all ambition and greed. It would be no bad thing if he was to fall in battle.'

'You worry too much, my Lord.' Langton replied with a smile. 'Enjoy the sunshine. In a few short weeks, the Scots will be crushed, the crown will be secure and we shall have our rewards.'

'I do not worry enough!' Pembroke shot back. 'Look! See on the opposite slope. That scout and his damned dog are seldom out of my sight. Robert Bruce will know every detail of our advance. When I send men to chase him off, he runs from them and then returns the moment they rejoin the column.'

'There, there, Pembroke.' Langton crooned with a smile. 'I will not have you upset. I have a man in my employ who excels in the hunting of men. I will set Odde on his trail and leave you with one thing less to trouble you.'

King Robert had gathered his commanders around him on the hillside so that they could watch the troops complete their drills. He remained impassive as the schiltroms responded to the horns and made their manoeuvres in time to the beating of the drums. He made no comment while the massed spearmen advanced, retreated and then traversed the slope. He was not even moved to speak when the four phalanxes shuffled together to form a single, massive schiltrom. An eyebrow was raised slightly when the men responded to a series of short horn blasts and snapped from a rectangular formation into a wedge. A second eyebrow was elevated when the horns sounded again and the men arranged themselves into a perfect circle.

Edward Bruce was, as ever, much less reticent than his older brother. 'Bravo!' He cried. 'Bravo, John! You have made them dance most prettily.'

Thomas Randolph, the Earl of Moray, also offered his congratulations. 'You have worked miracles in the little time you had. Christ! Just weeks ago, I struggled to stop them from fighting amongst themselves. Now they jump together when horn and drum are sounded.'

John kept his eyes on the troops below and tried to appear nonchalant, though, in truth, the praise had caused him to straighten his back and puff out his chest. He took pride in the performance of the men and could not help but reflect on the difficulties he had faced. The men of Moray in particular, had seemed more intent on settling ancient scores and animosities between themselves than on preparing to face the English.

'We have King Robert to thank for that.' John informed the gathered commanders. 'By attending the drills each day and talking with the men, he gained their trust and loyalty. They have put old rivalries temporarily aside because they want to fight for him and win him a great victory.'

'Don't be in such a rush to kiss his arse, John.' Edward Bruce replied, his face full of mischief. 'He has won nothing yet and so can offer you no reward.'

King Robert ignored the laughter and remained impassive. 'It is as agreed then. Randolph will command the men of Moray and Ross on the left, Douglas will lead the second division, my brother the third and myself the reserve. Sir Robert Keith will command our five hundred light horse to prevent the English from deploying their archers. We will form up here when the English come up, just as we have this morning.'

Sir James Douglas cleared his throat and spoke when King Robert turned to him. 'What of the men who stream into our camp each day? They come from all over the kingdom, sometimes a hundred in a day.'

The King shook his head. 'If we do choose to fight, only disciplined men will stand when the heavy horse charge in. I cannot risk having undrilled men within our ranks. If one man loses his courage and runs, others will follow and lead us into rout. Any stragglers should be sent to the back and join with the grooms, camp followers and other small folk on Gillies Hill. They will retreat ahead of us if we refuse to give battle. John Edward will instruct them. They must be prepared to flee in an orderly fashion.'

'Aye, m'Lord.' John replied in confirmation. 'I will see to it.'

'Now, let us hear from that scout of yours. Is he here?'

John waved Al forward and stood at his side as he hesitantly made his report under the eyes of the most powerful men in the kingdom.

'The English column left Edinburgh at dawn. They march here with all speed. By all counts, there are twenty-five thousand of them in total. Sixteen thousand of these are common foot, all of them armed with shield and sword. There are five thousand Welsh archers followed by carts piled high with bundles of arrows. Near four thousand knights ride at the head of the column, all with great lances aloft and pennants flying. Tis a dreadful sight to behold.'

'It is just as we thought.' King Robert replied. 'They outnumber us by more than four to one and outclass us in arms by an immeasurable degree.'

'But we will still fight!' Edward Bruce insisted. 'We have trained, we have chosen the place of battle. We have dug trenches at the side of every track and road to prevent them from outflanking us. If they are to relieve the castle, they must come here to our chosen ground. We will never have a better opportunity to defeat them.'

The King turned to his brother. 'I have never shared your love of the dice and I cannot lightly gamble with the lives of all men here. I will wait until the last moment to make my decision. We will fight only if the good Lord gives us some advantage.' The King turned back to Al. 'When do you expect the English to arrive?'

'They will be close by the end of the day. They will be upon us by the morning.'

Robert Bruce nodded. 'They advance in good order?'

'Yes, m'Lord.' Al replied. 'I have never laid my eyes upon a more fearsome sight.'

King Robert sighed and momentarily rested his chin on his chest. 'Let us not spread panic in the ranks. We will tell the men that the English advance, but let it be known that they do so in great disorder. They will see the lie for themselves soon enough, but at least it will not disturb their rest. Whether we stand or flee, both will be done better after a good night's sleep.'

30

Pembroke breathed a sigh of relief the moment he caught sight of Stirling Castle atop its high, rocky crag. He celebrated by wiping the sweat from his brow and slaking his thirst from the skin of wine tied to his saddle. The forced pace of the advance over the last seven days had left him exhausted. He had no doubt that the foot-soldiers had fared much worse.

'Tis s sight for sore eyes!' Walter Langton declared from his side. 'We have made it here with more than a day to spare before Sir Philip Mowbray is due to hand the castle keys to Edward Bruce.'

Pembroke wiped at his beard with his sleeve. 'Aye, my Lord Bishop. Robert Bruce must now relinquish it to us or he must fight for it. I'll wager that he rues the day that his brother made the pact.'

Langton's reply was interrupted when King Edward came up to trot at their side with young Hugh Despenser following on close behind.

'You see, Pembroke!' The King declared happily. 'I said that you worry too much. We have reached Stirling with time to spare, though that fact does not seem to have done much to cheer you.'

'I am pleased, my Lord.' Pembroke responded. 'I just suffer in this heat. I have never known Scotland to be so warm.'

'You are too hot?' King Edward retorted. 'Look at me! I am only the only knight here who has donned armour, maille, surcoat and cloak. My flesh will be roasted by the time I strip it all off!'

'I told you not to wear it all, my Lord.' Hugh Despenser laughed, gently scolding the King. 'You will be poached before the day is out.'

'But I must wear it all, for the men are so inspired to see their King ride at their head in all the regalia of war. See! I am the tallest man here and no knight is more finely armoured.'

High Despenser put his hand to his mouth but failed to stifle his giggle. 'Apart from Sir Giles d'Argentan. His armour has been so highly polished, it shimmers in the sun.'

The King shook his head dismissively. 'He is such a peacock. I did not expect a knight of such renown to spend so much time primping and preening himself.'

Langton exchanged a glance with Pembroke before clearing his throat. 'We should make camp before too much longer, my Lord.'

'Nonsense!' The King retorted. 'The sun will not set for another two hours. We should advance to where the Bruce awaits us and give battle before he can prepare himself.'

Pembroke's eyes widened in astonishment at the King's words. 'My Lord! We must take the time to survey the land before we sound the charge. Our scouts have told us that Robert Bruce has positioned himself betwixt us and the castle at Stirling. He has assembled his foot in strong and marshy places that will be difficult for our horse to penetrate.'

'Christ, Pembroke!' The King snapped. 'Look behind you! I have mustered an army of a size never before seen in these islands. The column stretches over so many miles that it is impossible to see the tail from the head. Such a company is more than sufficient to penetrate the whole of Scotland. In truth, if the whole strength of Scotland was gathered here before us, it could not halt our charge. We must advance and finish this business.'

'It will be dark before we are fully formed up, my Lord. It would be wise to bivouac and then reconnoitre the Scottish positions tomorrow. We must halt to allow the men to rest, for they have marched hard since dawn and must recover their strength before they fight.'

'I doubt that they will have to fight.' Edward replied. 'Only a fool would stand against all the might of England.'

'Then I pray that Robert Bruce is a foolish man.' Langton interjected. 'For the Scots are more proficient at running than they are at fighting. If they stand, we will finish it here. If they run and hide, it will take months to flush the last of them out. Nevertheless, I agree with Pembroke. Whether tomorrow brings battle or pursuit, our men will do better if they are rested.'

King Edward groaned and rolled his eyes. 'Hugh! Halt the column and order the men to make camp. Tell them that the Earl of Pembroke is too tired to continue and is in need of his bed. They must wait for the morning for their King to lead them to glory.'

Al crouched at the edge of the treeline and squinted into the distance. Though he was at too great a distance to make out individual figures, he was able to observe the English army spread itself out on both sides of the road and set about making its camp. He watched on until tiny columns of smoke began to rise into the clear, blue sky. Al reckoned it would be close to midday before the English could break camp and march to the Scottish positions in the marshy ground in the valley of the Bannock Burn. Something caused him to freeze and made the hairs on the back of his neck stand up. He turned his head and slowly scanned the thick forest to locate the threat his instincts had alerted him to. He jerked at the sound of a bow-string being released, but did not so much as see the arrow that tore into his ribcage with enough force to splinter bone and throw him backwards onto the ground and drive all of the air from his lungs.

Al began to panic and beat at his own chest when he found that he could not draw breath. He could hear the blood hammering in his ears and was convinced that his heart was about to burst in his chest. Only when he raised his shoulders off the ground, was he able to take in short, rapid breaths. The relief was fleeting for, in this raised position, he saw that a dark figure was stalking through the trees towards him with his bow still in his hands. He pushed desperately at the ground with his hands and feet but was rooted to the spot. His heart sank when he realised that the arrow that had pierced him was pinning him to the ground. He pulled at the shaft in desperation, but every movement caused him to feel dizzy with pain and the shaft could not be moved. He fixed his eyes on the hunter and pulled his dagger from his belt.

Odde approached the Scottish scout with the utmost caution. He could see that his arrow had caused him great injury and was certain that he would soon die from his wound. However, he was aware of the dagger clutched in his shaky hand and was keen to avoid any injury to himself. He was loath to waste another arrow on finishing him, but was even less keen on loitering in such close proximity to the Scottish army while the poor wretch bled out amongst the leaves and twigs. He reached over his shoulder to pull an arrow from his quiver, but was stopped short by the sound of an animal rushing towards him from the depths of the forest. The black dog would have been lost among the shadows if it had not been for the white around its muzzle and the yellow of its great fangs. Even as he fumbled the arrow onto his string, Odde saw that the dog was old and that it moved with astonishing speed for a hound of such great age. It was close enough for him to hear the low, menacing growl reverberating in its throat as he hurriedly drew back the bowstring. The moment the shaft was loosed, the dog launched himself at Odde and was not deflected from his course by the bodkin point ripping the flesh on his back so badly that white bone was visible for an instant before blood poured from the wound. The Black Dog's teeth might have been old and yellow, but they tore flesh just as efficiently as they had in his youth. Odde's scream of terror was choked off when the old dog snapped his jaws tight shut around his throat and shook his head with every ounce of strength left to him until he tore Odde's throat clean out and left him jerking and spasming on the forest floor.

Al's eyes filled with tears when the Black Dog came to his side and nuzzled at his hand. He was moaning now, for the pain was worsening just as quickly as his strength was fading. The Black Dog stayed with him until he fell into unconsciousness and then, still bleeding heavily from the gash along his back, he turned back into the forest.

John sat with his back against a tree and drank heavily from a skin of ale. The afternoon had been so taxing he felt that he deserved a drink. The weeks of dealing with the bickering men of Elgin, Nairn and Forres now seemed easy in comparison to his new responsibility of organising the sma' folk so that they would retreat in good order if so required. The grooms, camp-followers and assorted late-comers were reluctant to accept that they were too poorly armed and too poorly trained to fight in the schiltroms. Even though he had invoked King Robert's name a hundred times, they would not cease their arguments. He had finally given in and won their cooperation by lying to them, telling them that they should ready themselves to be used as a reserve. He instructed them to arm themselves and be ready to fight when they were called upon and ready to retreat should the circumstances require it. His mind was still reeling from the hours of listening to their pleas and complaints and he wanted only some little peace to recover himself. Dugal's howl snapped him to immediate attention. He knew that something was far wrong, for he had never before heard such a mournful sound. Dugal stood soaked in his own congealing blood, raised his head to the sky and cried out his misery so all would know that some disaster had overcome him.

When his howling was done, he turned for the forest and did not once turn his head to check that he was followed. The Edward men, John, Eck and Scott, Strathbogie and the Robertson struggled to keep pace with him through the thickness of the forest, but, soon enough, they came upon him standing guard over his stricken master.

John felt tears jump unbidden into his eyes, for he could see that Al's injury was bad. His skin was as white as winter snow and his breath came in ragged pants. John dropped to his knees and took his old friend's hand in his.

'Al!' He said gently. 'It's John.'

Al's eyes blinked but only half-opened, as if the effort to open them fully was beyond him. 'John!' He gasped, his lips twitching in a feeble attempt at a smile. 'I am glad that you are here. I'm dying John. I'm dying here.'

John squeezed his hand and shook his head furiously. 'Naebody's dying the day, Al. We'll get our horses and take you to the Lady of the Glen. She saved Eck and I from worse than this. She'll have you better before you know it.'

Al squeezed at John's hand, but he was so weak that he barely felt it. 'Don't move me, John. I've bled too much already.' He wheezed.

Strathbogie leaned down and patted John's shoulder. 'He's right, John. Look at the earth around him. It is soaked with his blood. I doubt that he would survive the ride to Stirling, never mind Scotstoun. Let him die here with his friends around him.'

John nodded his agreement and let fat, silver tears fall onto his friend's chest. 'It's alright, Al. We'll no' move ye. We'll just stay with you. Just lie quiet.'

Tears now flowed from Al's eyes. 'My sons will now grow up without a father, just as I did.'

John shook his head and choked back a sob that threatened to overcome him. 'I will look after Mary and the boys, I promise it. I will treat them as my own, as will every man here. Your sons will know that their father was a great man, a patriot and warrior. We will tell them of your courage and skill and of how Kings and Guardians counted you amongst their most valued men. They will grow up proud of their father and all that you achieved. Do not doubt it, for I have given my word and you, of all people, know that I will not break it while there is still breath in my body. I am just sorry that I was not here to protect you.' John then wept for he could see that his friend was close to death.

Al's eyelids flickered uncontrollably before focusing on John once more. 'Don't cry John! You have nothing to be sorry for. I had nothing when first we met. I was outcast and despised. You offered me friendship and my life was transformed. These last years I have lived a life I would never have dared dream of. I had a wife, sons and friends. You need never apologise to me.' Al groaned horribly and grimaced in pain. When he spoke again, his voice was less than a whisper. 'Keep my Mary safe for me! She has suffered much and will be feart without me to protect her.'

'I will, Al. You need not worry. I will keep her safe.'

But it was too late. Al was already dead and John wept for him.

'Let's get him back to camp.' Strathbogie ordered when John had spent his grief. 'Once we are done here, we'll take him back to Scotstoun and bury him there amongst his ain folk.'

'That's if any one of us is still alive to do it.' Scott Edward said with a shrug of his shoulders. 'Do you see what Al was scouting out?'

They all looked out across the plain and were awed into silence by the sheer scale of the English camp. The sun was now low in the sky and the twinkling lights of the enemy campfires seemed to stretch for miles in every direction.

Eck was the first to break away. 'It's just as well that they have come in such great numbers. Maybe now there will be enough of them to kill for us to avenge Al and all the others that they have taken from us. I've had enough of sieges and breaking walls. It is high time that my blades were once more soaked in English blood. Now, let me cover Al with my cloak and you can carry him away. Strathbogie and I will deal with this cunt here.'

John had been so intent on Al that he had not noticed Odde's throatless corpse until now. It made him smile wryly to know that Al's attacker had died in the Black Dog's jaws. He did not even ask what Eck and Strathbogie intended to do with his corpse. He trusted them to do what was appropriate.

The Earl of Pembroke rubbed at his right temple with his fingers, but the gentle pressure did nothing to ease his throbbing head. He could scarcely believe that the King's every decision served to drain strength from the English army. It had begun with his insistence on dawdling at Berwick for so long that the army had been forced to march at pace through the summer's heat to arrive at Stirling in time to relieve the castle. Now his foolishness was threatening to throw away more of their advantage over their enemy.

'We shall advance at dawn and attack Robert Bruce on his chosen ground. It will take more than his pits and trenches to bring all the might of England to a standstill!' The King still wore his armour and strutted amongst the gathered nobles as he spoke.

Pembroke could not tell if his cheeks were flushed red from excitement, from the day's heat or from the wine he had consumed as the evening progressed. The King raised his goblet to acknowledge the cheers of the younger, more inexperienced nobles, Gilbert de Clare, the Earl of Gloucester, and Sir Henry Beaumont foremost amongst them. Pembroke cleared his throat to intervene, but was beaten to it by Humphrey de Bohun, the Earl of Hereford.

'The men are tired, my Lord.' He began. 'Might it not be wise to let them rest for a day to recover themselves after the hard march from Berwick. I know from my long experience of campaigning here that they will fight all the better if they are not weary.'

The smile on King Edward's face froze and he glared at the Earl of Hereford with barely disguised contempt. 'If you are afeart, my Lord, you must retire. We have sufficient men of courage around us and will manage just as well without you.'

Hereford jerked back as if he had been slapped hard across his face. 'I must protest, my Lord! I am not afeart and think only of the men.'

'Not all men here are as old as you and Pembroke. A few hours rest and we will be refreshed enough to scatter the Scots. Idle here if you must, but you will not keep your King from battle.'

Langton laid his hand upon Pembroke's arm to forestall his furious protests. 'Might we prevail upon Sir Philip Mowbray to share his opinion with the company, my Lord. Unlike like the rest of us, he has kept watch on Robert Bruce and his army from Stirling's high walls. I am certain that his observations will prove quite instructive.'

Pembroke exchanged a glance with Langton which conveyed his appreciation of the Bishop's skill in steering the conversation in a more fruitful direction and away from imminent, open conflict.

'It would be my pleasure, Lord Bishop.' Mowbray replied with a smile. 'We need do nothing. The pact made with Edward Bruce was quite clear. Now that an English army is encamped within three leagues of the castle, he has no claim upon it under the laws of chivalry. Nothing compels us to do battle.'

King Edward shook his head. 'I have not brought this mighty army so far north only to allow my enemies to elude me once again. We will finish them here and then march in triumph through the gates of Stirling Castle.'

'Very well, my Lord.' Mowbray replied. 'I have studied the disposition of the Bruce's troops, both from the castle heights and from close quarters when I circled around them on my way here. It is my opinion that we need not concern ourselves with open battle or with resting our soldiers. The Scots will not stand and fight us. They will run at our first approach. We should be more concerned with how we stop them from fleeing, for should they disperse, it will take long months to run them down. We must cut off their retreat before it has begun.'

King Edward did not look entirely convinced but stroked his beard in contemplation. 'And how, Sir Philip, would we accomplish this?'

'Much as you had already proposed, my Lord. Send a body of knights directly towards the Scots along the main road to Stirling and set them to flight. A second body of knights should advance past the Kirk of St Ninian and take up a position behind Gillies Hill. Robert Bruce has already placed his camp-followers there in preparation for their retreat.'

'Hah!' The King exclaimed. 'Then we cut them down as they run! Whether they stand or not, we finish them here and spare ourselves the trouble of having to pursue them through the hills and forests. I will do it! The Earl of Gloucester will command the vanguard and march against the Bruce. Sir Robert Clifford and Sir Henry Beaumont will take six hundred knights and position themselves behind Gillies Hill. We shall have our victory in time to take our lunch at Sir Philip's table.'

The Earl of Hereford's face turned purple as the King issued his commands. 'My Lord!' He spluttered in anger. 'As Constable of England I should have command of the vanguard.'

The King shook his head and sneered derisively at the Earl. 'Not five minutes past you were telling me that you were too tired to fight. I thought to spare you from this task by according the honour to a man of greater youth and energy.

Now you complain and claim precedence. Which is it to be? Such indecision is not becoming, my Lord!'

Hereford quailed under the King's venomous onslaught, but steeled himself to take what was his by right. 'I did not say that I was tired, my Lord. My concern was for the men.'

'Christ!' Edward exploded. 'Must I suffer this self-serving bickering! If you insist on your ancient rights, then I must give you joint command. You will have your rights and your glory, but you must share them with Gloucester.'

'Would it not be wiser to have a unified command, my Lord.' Pembroke suggested tentatively. 'A single commander has the benefit of ensuring unity of purpose. There is confusion enough in battle without asking men to obey two masters.'

Edward now turned his fearsome glare upon the Earl of Pembroke. 'That would have been my preference, my Lord.' He spat. 'But it seems that my older commanders lack the vigour required for battle. Necessity demands that command of my divisions is shared between those with experience and those with the stamina to apply it. Now be off! Hector me no longer. I must prepare for the morrow!'

Langton walked with Pembroke until they were safely beyond the hearing of the other nobles.

'Christ!' Pembroke exclaimed. 'What manner of sin have we committed to deserve such a foolish and witless King? Even on the eve of battle he cannot help himself from favouring his young knights. He has learned nothing from almost losing his crown over his love of Gaveston!'

Langton nodded. 'He is punishing Hereford and Clifford for their part in Gaveston's death.'

'This is not the time for the settling of scores. Those young fools have little experience of war. They are so eager to charge in to win glory that they will leave their sense behind.'

'How much harm can they do?' Langton replied. 'Robert Bruce will run at his first sight of Gloucester and Hereford. Clifford and Beaumont need only run them down as they flee. It is difficult to see how even those young fools could turn it to disaster.'

'You speak true, Lord Bishop.' Pembroke replied sullenly. 'But it does not auger well for the future if our King allows his head to be turned by young and pretty knights in matters of such import.'

31

Leading fifteen hundred English knights against the army of Robert Bruce should have been the proudest moment of Humphrey de Bohun's life. Instead, he was sullen and full of resentment as the column of heavy cavalry followed the road towards Stirling Castle under a clear, blue, morning sky. The cause of the Earl of Hereford's animus rode at his side in the form of Gilbert de Clare, the young Earl of Gloucester. Even his maille hood and great helm did not hide the smug smile that had been upon his face since he had mounted his destrier just after dawn.

'The office of Lord High Constable of England has been held by my family for nine generations!' Hereford snapped when he could contain himself no longer. 'I am commander of the Royal Army and Master of the Horse by right. Your presence here is an attempt to usurp my rightful office!'

The Earl of Gloucester turned his head towards Hereford and smiled more broadly still in a deliberate attempt to antagonise the older man. 'My presence here is at the command of His Majesty, King Edward. If you seek to usurp his royal authority by ordering me to relinquish my command, you will find that your wishes carry less weight with me than those of the King. I will execute his orders with the very vigour he has demanded.'

'I shall not allow such a callow youth to lead the King's horse into disaster. You will obey my every command or you shall answer for it.'

'I will answer for my actions.' Gloucester replied, the smile on his face still present but more forced than it had been previously. 'But I will answer to the King and to no other. If you wish to curb the enthusiasm of callow youth, then perhaps you should start with your own nephew and order him to rejoin the ranks rather than have him galloping on ahead like some indisciplined fool.'

Hereford snapped his head back to the front in irritation and set his eyes upon the distant figure of his nephew, Sir Henry de Bohun. He thought that the boy cut an impressive figure with his tall, slim frame encased in full armour. He knew that he ought to call him back, but decided to let him roam ahead simply to cause Gloucester some small annoyance.

'Look!' Gloucester declared from his side. 'The Scots have captured some poor scout and hung him from a tree.'

Hereford saw that the corpse had been stripped, mutilated and suspended from a rope tied to a tree branch which overhung the road. As they drew closer, he noticed that the man's hands, feet and genitals had been hacked away and his throat torn out as if by some wild and savage beast. He counted a total of ten arrows protruding from the corpse's head, chest and stomach.

'They have hung it here as a warning to our men. They hope that its gruesome spectacle will sap their courage for the fight.' Gloucester shook his head in disgust. 'I will ride ahead and cut it down!'

'Leave it!' Hereford growled. ''Tis well that they see it, for they will know that they will suffer the same fate if the Scots have their way. They will fight all the harder for knowing the cost of defeat or capture.'

'I doubt that they will have to fight, my Lord.' Gloucester declared in excitement. 'Look there! Through the trees! I see Scots scurrying away. They have seen the might of England and they flee! We must pursue them and cut them down.'

Sir Henry de Bohun was nearly a hundred yards further along the road and he too saw the Scots running in the forest. He did not hesitate and spurred his horse on into the trees. His advance quickly brought him out into a long, sloping meadow with a deep stream at its bottom. He reined his horse in and saw that the whole Scots army was formed up at the far end of the long, gentle slope. He could see that the rebel force was made up almost entirely of spearmen and that they had been marshalled into four divisions arrayed across the full width of the open ground. With only a fraction of the men the English could field and with no knights or archers, he knew immediately that they could not hope to stand against the fifteen hundred knights under his uncle's command. He also knew that they had left it too late to flee and would soon be cut down. He had just turned his horse to gallop back to Hereford with this news when a movement on the far side of the meadow caught his eye. A mounted knight on a grey palfrey had emerged from the trees with five or six men on foot around him. They were so intent of examining the ground at their feet that they did not detect his presence. Sir Henry concluded that he had happened upon them whilst they surveyed the field on which they expected to give battle. He again made to turn but stopped suddenly when he noticed that the knight riding the palfrey wore a circlet of gold around his helmet.

'Praise be!' He whispered to himself as his heart began to beat hard in his breast. By the grace of God, he now had Robert Bruce, the self-proclaimed King of Scots, unguarded and within reach of his lance. He inhaled sharply to steady himself. The Bruce had no lance and was mounted on a smaller, inferior horse, but Sir Henry thought nothing of the codes of chivalry as he couched his lance and spurred towards him. He closed his mind to any thought of the renown and fortune he was about to win and instead concentrated only on keeping the steel tip of his lance pointed at Robert Bruce's heart. Such was his focus on his quarry, he was unaware that the Highlanders of the Scottish King's division had read his intentions accurately and were now pouring over their fieldworks and charging down the slope towards him to defend their King. Neither was he aware that his uncle and the Earl of Gloucester had entered the field and were beginning to hastily line their knights up further down the slope.

Sir Henry had covered a quarter of the meadow's width when he saw Robert Bruce's head snap up and turn in his direction. The Scots leader hesitated for only a second before pulling his axe from his belt and spurring his palfrey towards his attacker. Sir Henry knew that Bruce, with neither shield for his defence nor lance for the attack, was as good as dead already. The distance between them closed quickly and Sir Henry tensed himself for the impact of his lance striking Bruce's chest. He saw the Bruce pull hard at his reins and stand up in his stirrups. The little horse was so fleet of foot that it responded instantly to the command. It swerved to take its master away from the lance's lethal tip, before turning back in towards the great, English destrier, bringing its rider in close enough to chop his axe down at Sir Henry's head with sufficient force to cleave through helm, skull and brain.

The Earl of Hereford cursed at the sight of his nephew's body twitching its last at Robert Bruce's feet, but he was unable to dwell on how close the boy had come to bringing glory to his family. The screaming, half-naked Highlanders now streamed past their King and charged at the half-formed English line with their long spears held out before them. He screamed at his men to advance, but the Highlanders were on them before they had even reached a trot. Without momentum, the heavy cavalrymen were thrown backwards by the Scots, their long spears pitching a great many knights from their saddles before they could strike a blow. The Earl of Gloucester was thrown to the ground when his mount was impaled on a Scottish spear and reared up in its agony. The impact had stunned him and he was only saved from the Scottish blades by his squires who grabbed him by his ankles and dragged him away to safety. With the deep stream to their rear and with no hope of forming up for the charge, Hereford ordered that the retreat be sounded. More knights were felled as the heavy horse turned and lumbered back the way that they had come, but the Scots did not pursue them far, for their King rode ahead of them and ordered them to halt.

Hereford remained grim-faced as he led his men back towards the main army. He did not relish the prospect of facing the King, for he knew that he could expect no leniency after suffering such humiliation at the hands of the ragged, Scots rabble. He was also dreading the prospect of facing his sister-in-law with the news of the death of her favourite son. If anything, he feared her shrewish scorn more than he did that of the King. His only consolation was that he no longer had to suffer the Earl of Gloucester's smug and superior demeanour. The young Earl was pale of face and badly shaken by his brush with death. He rode at his side but was mercifully silent and seemed too stunned to wipe the dirt from his face or to

435

brush off the clumps of earth and grass that had been jammed into the joints in his armour when he was thrown onto the ground.

Edward Bruce reached his brother's side just as the last of the Highland warriors had been persuaded to abandon the pursuit of the English knights. 'For Christ's sake, Robert!' He shouted angrily. 'You scold me for taking unnecessary risks but throw caution to the wind yourself. Do you think these men would stand against all of England if you had fallen? We would have lost everything and our house would have ended upon this field. Bethink you, Sire, the fate of all Scotland rests upon you!'

King Robert leaned down and tried to pull his axe from the head of Sir Henry Bohun. 'Damn it!' He cursed, when the shaft came away in his hand. 'I have broken my good axe!'

Edward Bruce now laughed heartily. 'At least it was not wasted, brother. Look at his shield! You have ended a Bohun! Tis payment for when the old English King awarded that family our estates in Annandale, Carrick and Essex. This one at least will enjoy them no more.'

'I could have done nothing different, Edward.' King Robert said in reply to his brother's scolding. 'If I had turned from the challenge the men would have been disheartened to see their King run from the very danger that he himself asks them to face. If they are to face the English, they deserve a better King than that.'

'Listen!' Sir James Douglas declared from his saddle. 'They seem happy enough with the King that they have.'

They all turned at the sound of cheering and saw that all of the men in the schiltroms were shaking their spears in celebration of their King's triumph upon the field.

'This will give them heart if we decide to stand.' Thomas Randolph, the Earl of Moray, declared happily.

'They will need it.' Edward Bruce replied. 'The force our Highlanders have just chased from the field was fearsome enough. The English King can field more than double that number of knights.'

'I see some of them now!' King Edward cried out in alarm, whilst pointing in the direction of St Ninian's Kirk. 'Look! There! They must have ridden along the Carse under cover of the bank. Now they make for our rear!'

'They will outflank us!' Sir James declared in horror.

'Lord Moray!' King Edward snapped. 'You have that flank. You must march out and cut them off!'

Edward Bruce threw his head back and laughed. 'Look! Your schiltrom already marches out to meet the English. John Edward has not waited for your orders, my Lord. He has seen the danger and now advances to face it.'

The Scottish commanders then watched as the schiltrom marched out at double-time and put itself between the English horse and Gillies Hill, effectively halting their advance.

'Go now!' King Robert snapped at Randolph. 'If you leave it to John Edward, he will kill every Englishman who falls into his hands even if they beg for quarter. You know well how he conducts himself. Go quickly or you shall have no knights to ransom when we are so sorely in need of gold.'

Randolph hesitated no longer. He mounted his horse and galloped off in pursuit of his schiltrom. Edward Bruce's laughter echoed in his ears as he went, for he seemed to take great amusement in his predicament.

John Edward rode at the head of the schiltrom with Eck, Strathbogie and the Robertson at his side. The body of English knights came to a halt at some distance away.

'I count six hundred of the bastards.' Strathbogie announced, before leaning to the side in his saddle and spitting onto the ground. 'They hesitate because they are not keen on throwing themselves upon our spears.'

John shook his head. 'They have halted while we deploy. They wait to see if we will leave them room enough to ride around us.'

'Not today, my English friends, not today.' Eck Edward growled between his clenched teeth. 'Come to us so we may cut you down.'

John turned his horse and rode along the schiltrom's front rank. 'Form square! Form square!' He shouted as he went. 'Three ranks! Three ranks!'

The men fell into line with the speed and ease of well-drilled men and John returned to the centre before dismounting and sending his horse away with a sharp slap to its rump.

'Three ranks?' The Robertson asked with one eyebrow raised high. 'That's fell thin is it no'?'

'It is.' John replied with a shrug. 'But if the line is any shorter, I fear that they will charge past us and cut off our retreat. We must halt them here and force them to engage.'

'They engage now!' Eck cried, pointing towards the English.

'Tis only a single knight.' Strathbogie exclaimed in disbelief. 'He cannot mean to throw himself upon our spikes.'

The Scots watched in open-mouthed astonishment as the English knight charged across the open ground with his lance couched and a red shield bearing a white lion rampant held tight against his body. The Scotstoun men stepped through the three ranks of spears and shook their heads in wonder. The horse ran straight onto a spear, its weight and momentum causing it to be impaled and lifted momentarily into the air. The pole bent horribly before snapping with a crack loud enough to leave a ringing in the ears of every Scotsman in the vicinity. Both knight and horse crashed to the ground with horrific force, the knight groaning groggily and the horse neighing horribly in its agony and fright. Eck Edward stepped between the spears and, taking care to avoid the beast's thrashing feet, went to put an end to the Englishman.

'Stop there!' Thomas Randolph cried out as he jumped down from his saddle. 'You must give him quarter if he asks for it.'

'He has not asked for it, m'Lord.' Eck replied. 'He is terrible dazed and has not yet recovered his senses. He has not asked for mercy and so will not be given it.'

Randolph stepped forward and peered down at the semi-conscious knight. 'Tis Sir Thomas Gray. He is my prisoner now.'

'Then take him, m'Lord!' John Edward exclaimed. 'For here come the rest of them. Take care of your friend from the English court. We will see to the slaughter of his fellows.'

John then ordered Tom Figgins and the small band of Scotstoun archers to the front. They stood outside the wall of spears and sent arrows into the air as fast as they were able. Most of these clattered uselessly off helmets and shields, but a few thudded into horses' flanks and caused them to drop out from the charge or to veer into their companions and throw sections of the English line into disarray. The archers ran for the safety of the spears only when the English charge was upon them and every Scotsman braced himself against the crashing weight of English horseflesh, knights and armour. The wall of spears was bent back all along the line and was breached in several places, but it held and brought the English charge to a shuddering halt. Despite the chaos, the thrashing hooves, the flying earth and dust, the screaming horses and the flailing swords, maces and axes of England, the schiltrom stood its ground and men kept their discipline. They stepped sideways to fill the gaps where holes had been torn open and left the invaders faced with an unbroken wall of spears.

The Scots now began the grim work of whittling away at the knights trapped against the spears by the weight of their fellows at their backs. Men with axes and swords ducked out between the spears and furiously chopped and hacked at legs and bellies, before quickly retreating from the threat of weapons wielded from above by the knights still ahorse. Those Scots who were unlucky or too slow of foot had their skulls split open and died in the crush at their comrades' feet. The losses suffered by the Scots, devastating though they were, paled into insignificance when compared to those inflicted upon the English. Nearly a third of their number had fallen during that first charge and the corpses of knights and horses were piled high at the place where the charge had met the schiltrom. The pressure on the spearmen was lifted the moment the English horn was sounded and the knights began to disengage.

John staggered through the line of spears and surveyed the carnage upon the field. The dead and dying men and horses stretched the full length of the Scottish line. He paused to wipe the sweat, dirt and blood from his face and watched the English halt in their flight and begin to form up on the far side of the field.

'Rest your arms!' He shouted at the top of his voice and the air was immediately filled with the clattering of wooden poles being released from aching arms and dropped onto the ground.

Strathbogie came to his side clutching at his left hand. 'Fucking horse!' He cursed. 'The bastard turned around and bit me while I was hacking at his master's leg. Look! He took the best part of two fingers.'

'You can still wield your axe even with those two gone!' John replied with a wry grin.

'I knew that I would get little sympathy from you. Have they had enough, do you think? Or will they come back for more?'

'They'll be back!' John replied with absolute certainty. 'Their commander will be none too keen on returning to his King with only losses to report. He'll need a victory now to sweeten his report. Let the men rest while they can. They will be hard pressed again before the day is too much older.'

'Few of them are resting.' Strathbogie observed. 'They strip the English of their loot or search for nobles not yet dead to please the Earl of Moray.'

John shifted his gaze from the English and watched impassively as the Scots picked over the corpses of the fallen. The sky was already thick with crows eager to swoop down and begin their feast.

'Did I hear my name?' Randolph enquired as he joined them.

'You did, m'Lord.' John replied. 'I was just saying that I was pleased to see that the men are searching for any noble likely to win a ransom for you.'

'Excellent! Will they come again?'

'Aye, m'Lord.' John replied. 'They will come, but I doubt that they will oblige us with another charge. Few men have an appetite for a second course when the first has cost them so dear. They will probe for our weaknesses and attack only those places where they can hurt us with impunity.'

The Earl of Moray nodded his agreement. 'We should form circle then?'

'Aye, m'Lord. And we should do it now. See? They prepare to come at us.'

The English knights rode in more cautiously than before and circled the schiltrom in search of vulnerabilities to exploit. Many a Scots peasant found that his hands trembled as he clutched at his pole and peered out into the rising dust as the heavy horse thundered round and round, the thudding hooves raising enough din to deafen them and crashing down with enough force to shake the very earth. Some brave knights lunged in and drove their horses hard at the Scots at an angle that took them beyond the tips of the spears. The great weight of knight, beast and armour sent men crashing to the ground with enough force to snap their necks. Those left upon their feet were felled by mace and sword and the vicious, kicking hooves of well-drilled horses reduced Scots legs to splinters in an instant. John stood in the schiltrom's centre with the Earl of Moray and sent men to cut down these knights with sword and axe and to fill any gaps that opened in the line. Other men were ordered to stand ready to rush out from the ranks with their poles and unseat knights as they galloped by and then finish them as they lay helpless upon the ground. The struggle continued on until late into the afternoon, the Scotsmen bathed in sweat and choking in the clouds of dust kicked up by the horses' hooves, while the English continued in their attempts to grind away at their enemy. The English grew more frustrated as their casualties mounted without any sign that the schiltrom was about to break. In their anger and desperation at their inability to penetrate the great hedge of spears, they began to throw their battle axes, maces and swords at the Scots. The Scots did what they did best at such times and jeered and goaded the English knights, thanking them for their gifts.

The Earl of Moray came to John's side, his face caked in a layer of dust darkened by the sweat that poured down his face in the summer's heat. 'I would kill for a single mouthful of dirty marsh water.' He gasped. 'How long can they stay at this?'

'Longer than us.' John replied. 'See how they take turns to ride to yonder burn to water their horses and refresh themselves. We marched out with such haste that no one thought to carry water with us.'

Moray grimaced. 'Our men grow tired. If the English can punch a single hole in our line, the rest will charge through it and we shall be slaughtered.'

'Did you hear that?' John demanded with urgency.

'Aye!' Moray replied, cocking his head to one side. 'Twas the horn of Sir James Douglas! He marches to join us!' The Earl's grin was so wide that his teeth shone white against his dirt-encrusted face.

The English were so discomfited by the advancing Douglas spearmen that they broke off from circling the schiltrom and gathered together on the far side of the field.

John turned to Moray and grabbed at his sleeve. 'Look! The English have not yet formed up. If we go at them at the run we will split their force in two.'

'Should we not wait for the Douglas?' Moray asked, his brow wrinkled with indecision.

'No!' John snapped back. 'Let us strike while we can and end it now!'

John did not wait for the Earl's reply. He shouted the command and the schiltrom snapped immediately into a square. Four short horn blasts set the spearmen to running and they filled the air with their war cries as they closed upon the disordered English knights. The cavalry stared in disbelief and seemed rooted to the spot in their astonishment. It was then that they broke. The greater part of the force left under the command of Sir Robert Clifford and Henry Beaumont turned tail and galloped back towards the main body of the English army. The remainder flew north towards Stirling Castle in their eagerness to evade the fast approaching spikes of the Scottish vanguard. The exhausted, dirty and thirsty Scots sent them on their way with a great rattling of their spears and volley after volley of cheers.

The Earl of Moray clapped John hard on the back. 'We have done it! Like the King himself, we have faced the enemy and seen him off. Praise be to God, for he is surely on our side.'

Sir James Douglas now galloped towards them. 'Bravo!' He cried as he approached. 'I saw that they pressed you most vigorously but you withstood the test and sent them away in great disorder. Let the Lord be thanked! I begged King Robert's leave to come to your aid, but, when I saw that they wavered, I thought that I would leave you to finish it and take all the glory for yourselves.'

'Your advance was enough to halt them.' John replied. 'That opening was sufficient to allow us to divide their force in two.'

Sir James acknowledged John's gratitude with a bow of his head. 'Let us ride to the King!' He declared. 'I know that he will want to praise you for this victory.'

John slapped Moray on the shoulder. 'You go, m'Lord. I will stay to see that the men have water and the opportunity to take their reward and loot the dead. I will follow on directly.'

John watched the two nobles ride off and turned to Strathbogie. 'See that the men take the best of the English weapons, especially the shields. We will have need of them if we face the English archers tomorrow. Have anything that is left taken to the sma' folk on Gillies Hill. If we decide to run or suffer defeat, they will need more weapons if they are to defend themselves.'

John scarcely recognised the Robertson when he approached them. The thick coating of dust, blood and sweat covered his face so completely that every hair in his great white beard was concealed from sight. The old man lowered himself stiffly to the ground.

'You are wounded, Laird?' Strathbogie asked with some concern.

The Robertson waved his hand dismissively and grinned up at them. 'It's nothing. The tip of a lance grazed my ribs, nothing more.'

John called for water and crouched down at the Robertson's side. 'You are too old for the fighting, Faither.' He said, his voice filled with tenderness. 'If I had known that you marched with us, I would have sent you back.'

'You might have tried, but I doubt that you would have succeeded.' The old man replied, his eyes sparkling with delight. 'I would not have missed this for anything. I give thanks to God that I lived long enough to see this day. Though I am old and have lost my strength and speed, I stood this day and struck out at those who sent my family to their graves. My axe drips with the blood of ten English knights and now there are ten fewer greedy English bastards to spread their misery across this kingdom. My heart is so filled with joy that I fear it is about to burst open.'

John was greatly cheered to see the Laird so happy. 'Then I am glad that I did not see you in the ranks. It would have been a sin if I had denied you such contentment.'

447

The Robertson reached out and grasped John's hand in his own. 'It near broke my heart when I lay dying on the field at Falkirk. I felt that God had betrayed me by ending my life with such a defeat. I believe that he must have heard my prayers, for now he has made amends by granting me the part I have played in this victory.'

'Come!' John commanded, as he pulled the older man to his feet. 'The Lord is about to reward you further. Now we will march back into the camp and King Robert, all his great nobles and his whole army will applaud us for our victory.'

32

Long years of plotting and scheming to bend the nobles of England to the old King's iron will had left Walter Langton with few friends and many bitter enemies amongst their ranks. In normal circumstances he would have taken the greatest of pleasure in seeing them humiliated, but he now found himself cringing as the young King berated them mercilessly for the day's disasters. He cast his eyes around the King's pavilion and saw that every noble gathered there had his eyes fixed firmly on the floor. Not a single one of them looked up as the youthful Earl of Gloucester's cheeks blushed ever more red and tears of anger and frustration welled up in his eyes.

'I should rest the men, my Lord?' King Edward boomed. 'You who was dumped from his horse by a naked savage would counsel me to hide myself and all the might of England away from that ragged Scots rabble. Hereford here tells me that they have not a single horse worthy of the name. Should it be known that the King of England was too afeart to face peasants armed with poles? If our enemies were to hear of this, they would think us weak and would

449

rush to attack us. The King of England will not cower and hide away from Robert Bruce.'

'I would not dare suggest that you hide, my Lord.' Gloucester stuttered in a voice pitched higher than he would have liked. 'I merely counsel caution and think that it would do no harm to wait until the men are recuperated. If we have learned anything from the day's events, it is that the Scots should not be under-estimated.'

The King's cheeks now burned red with fury. 'If the day's events taught us anything, they revealed to us that my commanders are incompetent! Now you besmirch your honour by laying blame for your failures on fatigue. I do not know how you dare to chide me for under-estimating the Scots. We have four times as many men as them, four thousand more armoured horse and five thousand more archers. If I had ignored my feeble, fainthearted counsellors, we would already have faced our enemy and swept him from the field. Our losses are slight only because of my wisdom in restricting the numbers sent forward under your command. If I had committed the entire army to your strategy, our losses would be much higher.'

'I must protest, my Lord!' Gloucester retorted, though without much force.

'You have no right to protest! If it was not for your high rank I would have you flogged for your treachery and deceit. I can stand your craven lies no longer! Leave my presence at once. Take early to your bed so that you are rested. We will take to the field against the Scots on the morrow, whether you have the courage for it or not.'

Gloucester stamped out of the pavilion with his head held low. The remaining nobles shuffled in uneasy silence as they waited for the King to speak. Langton hoped that one of them would have the courage to counsel him, but not one man there had been spared the sharp edge of King Edward's tongue and none of them seemed willing to risk bringing it down upon themselves a second time. The first words to pass the King's lips caused Langton to wince and groan internally.

'Hugh and I have given considerable thought to our plan of battle. Today's skirmishes were minor and necessitate no alteration to our strategy.'

'The King is correct.' Sir Hugh Despenser interjected. 'We must delay no longer. At dawn we must advance towards the Scots, just as the King originally suggested. There is no good reason why we should procrastinate any further. I do not doubt that they will flee at their first sight of our army. Only a madman would attempt to stand against such superior forcc.'

'You mean to fight the Scots on the field Robert Bruce has chosen, on ground he has had months to prepare?' The Earl of Pembroke asked incredulously. 'Did you not hear my Lord Hereford report that the meadow upon which the Scots are positioned is narrow, hemmed in on two sides by impenetrable forest and has had its width reduced still further by the trenches and ditches the Scots have dug to impede the advance of our heavy horse?'

'I heard the Earl of Hereford's report quite clearly, my Lord. Though it seems that is has not frightened me quite as much as it has alarmed you.' Despenser paused to take in the approving glances of the King and the white-haired Earl of Trasque. 'Did you not hear the King say that the Scots will run at the sight of us?'

'I did hear the King.' Pembroke retorted. 'Though I doubt that any man would run at the sight of you.'

'Come now, gentlemen!' Tarquil de Trasque implored. 'Let us not bicker amongst ourselves. We have our enemy within our sight and must make preparations to bring him to heel.'

'Very well.' Pembroke said in exasperation. 'If the King's mind is set, I will argue no more. What measures do you propose to prevent Robert Bruce from attacking us in the night? He is not above employing such underhand tactics.'

'I have thought of that.' Hugh responded with great satisfaction. 'We will bivouac the cavalry at the foot of the meadow below the Scottish positions. Our heavy horse will then be protected on three sides by the Pelstream and the Bannock Burn. If Robert Bruce attempts to advance down the slope towards us, he will run straight into our knights. Our men can rest without any fear of attack and the rest of the army can cross the Bannock Burn at dawn and muster in good order.'

'How will you get our cavalry across the Bannock Burn?' Pembroke demanded. 'It is deeper than you might think.'

The smile on Despenser's face was as smug and as self-satisfied as any Pembroke had ever seen. 'I have already sent men to the hamlet of Bannock and to Stirling with orders to tear the doors from every last hovel and bring them here to lay across the stream. Do not trouble yourself, my Lord. Everything is in hand.'

Pembroke made his excuses and left the King's pavilion as soon as he was able. The King's Knight hailed him as he approached.

'I am told that we are to deploy on the other side of that stream.'

'We are.' Pembroke replied.

'Do you think that the Scots will fight?' The King's Knight asked. 'Or will they run and hide as they are want do?'

'I hope that they will run.' Pembroke replied wearily. 'I have an uneasy feeling about this whole campaign. The King is too easily influenced by men who understand nothing of battle and even less of the Scots and Robert Bruce.'

'You have beaten him before, my Lord. I do not doubt that you will do so again.'

Pembroke nodded. 'If I were in command I would agree with you. I am unsettled because I must put my trust in others and I fear that such faith might be undeserved.'

John Edward could seldom sleep the night before a battle. His mind raced with a thousand thoughts and his guts churned painfully. The day's events had done little to either cheer him or calm his spirits. Al's death weighed heavily upon him and he found himself constantly turning from the fire to check that his friend's body was still wrapped up in its blankets and was not troubled by dogs or rats. It seemed that sleep also eluded other men, for Malcolm Simpson came out of the darkness and sat down at John's side. He placed a long, thin, cloth-wrapped parcel at his feet and joined his old comrade in staring forlornly into the glowing embers.

'I came to pay my respects to Al.' He stated flatly in explanation of his presence. 'I counted him among my friends and would like to say a prayer over him.'

John nodded and let out a long, heart-felt sigh. 'He was with me from the very beginning. Every loss, every defeat and every triumph was shared with him. I still turn my head expecting him to slip out from the shadows. I know that he has gone, but still I cannot accept it.'

'I would say that it gets better with time, but you would know that I lie. Even after all these years, I still find myself turning at the sound of a galloping horse and half expect to see Wallace charging towards me.'

John smiled but the expression was tired and tinged with sadness. 'I was thinking of Wallace earlier in the day. I was hacking down at an English knight who had broken through into the schiltrom's centre, when my eye fell upon the

Abbey Craig. Do ye mind when we stood there with him the night before the battle at Stirling?'

'Christ John! We were just boys then. What days!'

'And here we are again! Back here after all those years of struggle. Another English army intent on defeating us. It makes me think of what Wallace always said to us. Do ye remember it?'

Malcolm nodded. 'How could I forget it? Fight on! Fight on! It is those words that have kept me from wearying whenever the English have swarmed across our land. Whenever I felt like giving up, I would say those words to myself like a prayer.'

'Me tae!' John replied. 'I swore that I would honour him and I will keep my vow till death.'

'That is why I have come.' Malcolm kicked at the parcel lying at his feet. 'I thought to wield it myself. That is why I have kept it all these years. But now I am thinking that he would have wanted you to have it. He had greater love for you than for any other man.' He then leaned down and untied the strips of leather that bound the cloth together. He then pulled the cloth aside and sat back.

'Christ!' John exclaimed. 'I thought that it was lost.' He reached out tentatively with his fingers and touched the hilt of William Wallace's great broadsword as if it was the most holy of relics. The leather binding still bore the sweat stains from where Sir William had gripped it and, though newly sharpened, the many nicks along the edges of the long blade

455

stood as testament to the great numbers of Englishmen who had fallen under his hand.

Malcolm saw that John was on the brink of tears and he laid his arm across his old friend's shoulders to comfort him. 'There are many of us here who fought at Wallace's side. It will give us great heart to see you carry his sword into battle against the English. It will give men courage to think that he is with us. If you would honour him, then you must do this.'

John nodded his agreement and then sat a while with Malcolm, drinking ale and speculating on what the dawn would bring. When the Borderman had taken his leave, John lay down on his blanket on the hard earth and fidgeted and turned in a bid to make himself comfortable. The day's fighting had strained every muscle and those that were not stiff were tender and sore. With sleep beyond his reach, his thoughts turned to his Lorna and he stroked at the scrap of cloth that hung at his neck. His mind drifted back to happier days and, though they filled him with sorrow, the memories brought a bitter-sweet smile to his face. Exhaustion and ale finally carried him off into a fitful sleep with a picture of Lorna's sweet smile in his mind.

When he jerked awake, he looked around himself in confusion. The meadow was lit up like day, but there was no sun in the sky. A strange and eerie hush hung over the camp and not a murmur of sound came from the thousands of men sleeping upon the ground, the hundreds who still sat around their fires and the hundreds of horses tied up at the forest's edge. The strangeness of the moment made him panic and he felt his heart begin to beat hard in his breast. John was about to call out in fright, but then realised that he was caught in a dream. Relief flowed through him and he turned his head to lose himself in unconsciousness again.

The voice seemed to come from far away, but he recognised it immediately and sat up in fright. He gasped when he saw that three figures dressed in robes of pure, unbesmirched and brilliant white now sat on a rough, rectangular rock a little way down the slope from him. Though they had their backs to him, their forms were so familiar that he identified them immediately. Al sat on the left and gazed down the slope with Wallace and the Robertson at his side. Although he knew that he dreamed, he crossed himself to protect his soul.

Al slowly raised his arm to point down the slope with a short length of stripped willow and spoke again. 'Look!' He said, his voice sounding clearly in John's ear, though the phantom sat at a little distance away.

John followed his gaze to the meadows's far bottom and saw that the English knights had crossed the Bannock Burn and were now bivouacked along its bank. His sight seemed to be magnified, for he could see every detail of the enemy's position, though no man could see for such a distance on even the clearest and sunniest of days. His heart beat still faster, for the great warhorses numbered in their thousands and knights still in their armour and unarmoured grooms lay upon the ground at their hooves for as far as he could see. His eyes travelled across the water and he saw that the whole of the English foot now took their rest on the far side of the burn's depths. Though one man slumbering upon the earth looks much like another, the stacks of spears, the piled armour and the carts of bundled arrows told him where common foot, men-at-arms and archers were now positioned.

The voice came to him like a whisper from the depths of a shadowed cave. 'Do you see it, John Edward? Do you see it?' John shivered, for the voice was that of William Wallace and the words were those he had spoken to him on the eve of the Battle of Stirling Bridge all those years ago.

The Robertson then slowly turned his head around and gazed at John with eyes that burned red like the embers in a fire. He smiled before he spoke, his voice a distant, echoing whisper. 'Make haste, young Edward! Make haste!'

John awakened with a start and found himself staring up at the night sky in befuddlement. He sat up, rubbed at his eyes and gazed around himself in bewilderment. The camp was just as it had been when Malcolm Simpson had left him. The ground was covered with men who slept and snored, those who tossed and turned in frustrated, anxious wakefulness and those who chose to take comfort in drink and whispered conversations with their fellows. It seemed that the dream, despite it being so vivid, had lasted for only a little time. While most dreams faded away before he had even left his bed, John found that this one lingered on and he remembered every detail with absolute clarity. Deciding that sleep was now beyond him, he rose to his feet and made his way down the slope towards the rock. He stopped when he reached it and looked in the direction of the Bannock Burn. Although the night was much lighter than those in the depths of winter, the land was cloaked in darkness and he could make out nothing that lay at the meadow's end. He shook his head in dismissal of the dream and turned his feet back towards the camp. He halted when an object at the base of the rock caught his eye. He crouched down and dug down into the grass with his fingers. The stick was old and weathered, but in every other aspect it matched the one Al had used to point towards the English positions in his dream. It was willow, it had been stripped of its bark and was of roughly the same length. John shivered at its touch before reproaching himself for his superstition. He could not, however, bring himself to toss it aside and he carried it with him when he made his way back to his fire.

He picked his way through his slumbering men and crouched down when he came to the Robertson's side. He told himself that he came only to check on him and would have furiously denied it if any man had suggested that he came to reassure himself that he had not been visited by ghosts in the night. The old man lay on his back with his thin blanket wrapped tightly around him and firmly tucked in under his chin.

It gladdened John's heart to see that the Laird's face still wore the happy smile he had displayed in his delight at defeating the English knights. His heart sank when he reached out to pat the Robertson's bald head in affection and found that his skin was icy cold. He pushed at his chest to rouse him without success. He then pulled the blanket away and saw that his tunic was stained dark with blood.

'His wound must have been worse than he let on.' Eck said sadly from John's rear.

John nodded and tried to blink away the tears that flowed into his eyes 'Christ Eck! How many more corpses must we collect? Our friends fall like flies.'

'Look at his face, John! He now stands before God with that same smile upon his lips. He died happy and will now be reunited with his wife, his sons and his daughters. That is all that he ever wanted. We may mourn his loss, but must comfort ourselves knowing that he died well. He died just as he wanted to.'

John nodded and rubbed the tears from his cheeks. 'You're right. He died with a victory and I am thankful for that. It is no more than he deserved. Now, help me wrap him up. We'll lay him beside Al.'

33

King Robert had ordered his commanders to attend him an hour before the dawn. The council of war was already underway when John arrived and he tried to slip in unnoticed by standing at the back of those already gathered there.

'It is kind of you to join us!' King Robert boomed, as he glared at John in disapproval. 'I hope that we do not keep you from your bed.'

'I apologise, m'Lord.' John said with a bow, though the Bruce's criticism stung him badly. 'Laird Robertson died from the wounds he suffered while fighting your enemies. I had great love for him and paused just long enough to wrap him in his shroud and speak a prayer over his remains.'

The King seemed oblivious to John's barbed response and a look of genuine sadness crossed his face. 'It causes me great sorrow to hear of this. Men always spoke of him with the greatest of affection and respect. When all of this is done, I will see that a Mass is said for him in the Abbey. He deserves no less.'

John was genuinely grateful for and taken aback by the King's gesture. He bowed his head again and thanked him for his kindness.

'To business then.' King Robert declared. 'We have bloodied the nose of the English King and sent his great knights scurrying back to his side. I am told that his nobles bicker amongst themselves and that they have lost heart and are sore discouraged. Their men have lost confidence in the invincibility of their heavy horse and can scarcely believe that the great knight Sir Robert Clifford was driven from the field by a parcel of peasant foot. It is said that they whisper that their war is not righteous and that they have offended God. Now we must decide whether to disperse and preserve our army or risk all and give battle upon this field.' The King paused to look into the eyes of each of his commanders. 'If any man here feels that he has shown mettle enough and wishes to retire, know that I will not hold it against him. We have performed such feats already, it would be no disgrace to withdraw.'

Edward Bruce stepped forward with an expression of grim determination upon his face. 'Have we not suffered enough? We have lived under the threat of the might of England all these long years. Even when no English knight has ridden across the border, the threat has hung over us like a black thundercloud. That threat now sits not a mile from here. Let us fall upon them with all fury and settle this once and for all.'

Sir James Douglas stepped to the Lord of Galloway's side. 'I concur. We must be daring. The men are emboldened by our victories upon the field. If we command them, they will fly at the English. If our enemy is as divided and as dispirited as we believe, they will falter and we will prevail.'

Sir Thomas Randolph, the Earl of Moray, shook his head. 'I would like nothing better than to put the English to flight, but I saw how hard they pressed us yesterday. The discipline of the schiltrom held us together, though I fear that they would have broken us if Sir James had not marched to our aid. We should not forget that we saw only a fraction of their strength. They boast four times our numbers and will decimate our formations should they deploy their archers. Let us not throw away what has already been won.'

John scowled when he saw Sir John Menteith step forward. The urge to slit his throat in revenge for his treachery in handing Sir William Wallace to the English had lost none of its intensity in the years since his execution. King Robert had given the foul traitor his protection and had made the Scotstoun man swear that he would not lay a hand upon him. John had promised that he would do the false Menteith no harm while he had the King's protection. What he did not say aloud was that he would murder him the moment that protection was lifted, either through loss of favour or King Robert's death.

Menteith thought of nothing but his own advantage and John knew that he would argue for the course most likely to bring him the greatest benefit. He was not surprised when he argued for caution rather than for the gamble which might cause him to lose position or fortune. 'The Earl of Moray is both wise and prudent.' He wheedled. 'Why risk all when it is not necessary?'

King Robert seemed bowed under the weight of responsibility pressing down upon his shoulders. His commanders were divided and it seemed that the decision must be his and his alone. 'What of you, John Edward?' He asked, fixing John in his gaze. 'I have never known you to gamble recklessly with the lives of your men. Will you too urge caution and provide a counterweight to the arguments of my headstrong and impetuous brother? If we are defeated here, the kingdom is lost. Should I risk all when sanity screams against it? What say you?'

John held the King's gaze and gritted his teeth. 'I do not urge you to caution, m'Lord. I once told you that a crown must be won and the crown of Scotland will be won or lost upon this very field. If you command it, every last Scot will charge down this hill and at its bottom they will find all the knights of England encamped there. They have advanced across the burn without their archers or their spearmen and they have the depths of the Pelstream and the Bannock Burn at their backs. If we advance quickly, we will trap them there and deny them the chance to charge against us. Without the room to stretch their legs, the heavy horse are of little threat. They are cumbersome and can do little against our spears. If you have courage and make haste, you will have a victory greater than that won by any other Scottish King.'

'What of their archers?' The King snapped, though John could see that his words had swayed him. 'You were at Falkirk. You know better than most how quickly archers can devastate a schiltrom.'

'Their archers have yet to cross the stream. The battle may be lost before they can be deployed.'

King Robert nodded. 'Your scout has seen this? He has crawled close to the English lines and reported the position of their knights to you?'

John smiled at the King. 'Aye, m'Lord. It was Al who told me where they have arrayed themselves.'

'Very well. He served us well in the north and I have never known him to be wrong. It is decided then. We will stand here and leave our fate to God!'

The Earl of Pembroke had not slept a wink and stood with the King as the light of day dawned and he gathered his commanders around him.

'The moment the Scots break, we must pursue them with all urgency. The fewer men Robert Bruce has around him, the quicker we will run him to ground.' The King instructed them as his squires strapped him into his armour.

King Edward had also been too agitated to sleep, but the lack of rest had done nothing to dim his excitement or his energy. His favourites were similarly invigorated and seemed barely able to contain their elation. Hugh Despenser could not keep himself from checking his armour and he chirped and cheeped like a bird attracting mates. Tarquil, Earl of Trasque, could not mask his state of heightened nervousness and nodded so excitedly at the King's every utterance that his armour never ceased to rattle. The same could not be said for the other magnates. The Earl of Hereford and Sir Robert Clifford were much subdued after the defeats they had suffered the previous day. They chose to remain uncharacteristically quiet while the King issued the order of battle and they left the discussion in the inexperienced hands of the King's young favourites. The condition of the Earl of Gloucester was even worse. He had already mounted his horse and muttered darkly to himself with a sullen and surly expression upon his face. Pembroke had tried to cheer him but to no avail.

'Today it will be clear that I am neither a traitor nor a liar.' Gloucester had snapped in response to his greeting, the King's scolding evidently still ringing in his ears.

Though denied any meaningful command for the battle ahead, Pembroke felt compelled to offer his counsel. 'We should order the archers to this side of the stream lest the Scots decide to stand, my Lord. I well remember how those under your father's command tore the heart out of Wallace's army at Falkirk and won him his most famous victory. Perchance they will win you the same this day.'

Hugh Despenser grinned back at Pembroke in amusement at his words. 'Calm yourself,

Pembroke! We will have no need for archers today. Look around you! The Scots peasants will scatter when they see that they face our heavy cavalry.' His eyes flashed with excitement. 'Then we shall have our hunt.'

'Look!' The Earl of Trasque cried as he pointed up at the meadow's top. 'The hedgehogs come!'

Pembroke snapped his head around and gasped at the sight of the Scottish divisions marching out of the morning's light mist in echelon with their great spears pointing towards the sky. The banners of Edward Bruce fluttered at the head of the foremost division on the Scots right. The next division marched a little way behind the first and occupied the centre of the field under Douglas banners. The third formation marched a little behind the second with the pennants of the Earl of Moray fluttering above their heads. Pembroke strained his eyes and saw the spear tips of a fourth division at the rear and the light breeze disturbed the mist enough to give him a brief sight of the bright colours of the banners of Robert Bruce.

'They mean to deny us the opportunity to outflank them.' Pembroke stated with urgency. 'Their spearmen are stretched across the field from forest to marsh. We must bring up the archers.'

'Hush now, my Lord.' Despenser said in soothing mockery. 'They mean only to display their colours before us. Once honour is satisfied, they will melt away into the forest and seek to evade us.'

When the Scots continued to advance in good order, Pembroke grasped at Rank's arm and pulled him close. 'King's Knight, go and order the archers to cross the stream. Tell them that the King has commanded it. There may yet be time to deploy them if you make haste.' Rank nodded his understanding and made for his horse.

King Edward watched on incredulously as the Scots continued to advance across the open ground. 'What?' He declared. 'Will yonder Scots fight?'

Sir Ingram de Umfraville shook his head in disbelief at the King's side. 'Indeed, this is the strangest sight I ever saw for Scotsmen to take on the whole might of England by giving battle on hard ground.'

Even as he spoke, the Scots divisions came to a halt, laid their spears upon the ground and fell to their knees.

'See!' King Edward cried in triumph. 'They kneel for mercy!'

Sir Ingram gestured at his squires to bring his horse. 'For mercy, yes, but they ask it not from you.' He pointed towards a priest who stood before the serried ranks of kneeling Scots. 'They ask God for mercy for their sins before they give battle. These men will surely win or die.'

Pembroke cast his eyes towards the Bannock Burn but saw no sign that the archers were being brought up. Above him on the sloping meadow, the Scots pushed themselves to their feet, lifted their spears up from the ground and resumed their advance in good order. The Earl of Gloucester called for his helmet and his lance.

'Ask the King if he still thinks me a traitor and a liar.' The young Earl snarled petulantly as he dug his spurs into his horse's flanks.

Pembroke realised what he intended, but reached out to seize his reins a mere second too late. The Earl charged across the field, his lance already tilted at the centre of the schiltrom under the banners of Edward Bruce. Pembroke froze at the sight of Gloucester racing to his death on the wall of spears and turned in horror as the air was filled with the thunder of hooves as the knights of the vanguard charged out behind their young commander. The Scots roared their defiance at the disordered English charge, their first rank falling to their knees and bracing their long spears against the earth. Pembroke rode across the line and ordered the main body of English horse to hold. The King stared on in open-mouthed astonishment as his vanguard crashed against the thick hedge of spears and horses and men alike were impaled on the spikes. Though the ground was thick with dying men and horses and a score of riderless mounts now charged around the field, the knights under Gloucester's command continued to press Edward Bruce's division hard. The Scottish centre and left wing had continued their advance and marched past the schiltrom commanded by their King's brother. The men of Douglas now broke formation and charged in at the vanguard and attacked their flank with spears, swords and battle-axes. The English could not stand against such an onslaught and wheeled back towards the main body of cavalry.

'We must advance!' Pembroke shouted at King Edward.

'But the vanguard is in our way.' The King stammered. 'We must allow them to form up and then advance together.

Pembroke pointed towards the fast-approaching Scots. 'They will hem us in against the stream. If we are to have any room in which to deploy, we must advance now!' The King nodded uncertainly and Pembroke immediately commanded that the advance be sounded.

No English horse had moved forward by more than six paces and the great body of English heavy horse had barely formed up when the panicked stampede of the fleeing vanguard and hundreds of riderless beasts crashed into the thick of the still-mustering squadrons. The ensuing crush disrupted the English formations and hindered their advance. All the while, the drums of the schiltroms beat out their relentless tattoo and the Scots screamed taunts and threats at their enemy as they carried their spears onwards. Sir Robert Clifford succeeded in driving his wing forward, but the line was still ragged when it reached the Scots and his men suffered on their spears just as badly as they had the day before. Pembroke steadied his line sufficiently to batter into the Scots, but, with the horses only half-way to the gallop, their momentum was not sufficient to break through the ranks of spears and they were held there while the Scots stabbed at them with their poles and ran out beneath the shafts like vermin, tearing at the horses' bellies and chopping at the legs of men and horses with their axes.

The English fought hard as the sun soared towards its highest point and the heat of the day caused them to stew inside their armour. The King struggled hard at Pembroke's side and more than one Scottish skull was split by his royal sword. The Scots proved to be remarkably disciplined and, in spite of the weight of horseflesh pressed against them, they inched their formations forward yard by hard-won yard. The battle now fell into a slow, horrific rhythm and the air was filled by the grunts and curses of exhausted men as they pushed and struggled against one another in search of an opening that would allow them to strike out at their enemy. Too many men to count were crushed beneath hooves and boots as the press was too dense for any who had fallen to right themselves again. More than one English nobleman was turned into a cripple when a leg was trapped and crushed between their own mount and that of a comrade. The Scots learned quickly that they should aim their spear-points at horses rather than knights, for the horses had no armour and, if fatally injured, the thrashing of their death-throes caused great injury within the English lines.

'We must bring up the archers!' The King gasped, his throat as parched as Pembroke's was.

The Earl pointedly ignored the King as he was annoyed that he had not heeded that very

471

counsel when he had given it at the break of day. He twisted around in his saddle in search of any sign that Rank had heeded his own command. At first, he could see nothing, but he then growled in delight when he caught sight of the King's Knight's familiar frame stealing through the trees on the far side of the field. Satisfied that the day was not yet lost, he pulled hard at his reins so that his horse would rear up and kick out against the wall of poles. He was rewarded by the sound of a wet, bloody crunch and smiled grimly as one long spear wobbled and then disappeared from sight.

John Edward flinched back and let the tip of the knight's blade scythe uselessly through the air a hair's breadth from his face. He reacted immediately and brought his sword down with all of his strength and groaned as the blow landed on armour and jarred his shoulders in their sockets. Though he had drawn no blood, the knight's arm now hung limply at his side and his weapon dropped from his shattered grip. With no threat from above, Strathbogie swung his axe at the horse's foreleg with enough force to reduce it to bloody, splintered ruins. The spearmen around them took a pace backwards and let the beast fall where its flailing hooves would threaten only those on the English side.

John leaned heavily on his sword and tried to catch his breath whilst surveying the field behind him. He reckoned that they had advanced no more than fifty paces since meeting the English charge, but every inch of that ground was now covered with the corpses of men and horses. There were Scotsmen among them but, for every ragged Scot, there were fifty Englishmen in their armour and fine surcoats. He glanced along the line and smiled when he caught sight of the Earl of Moray. Randolph's sword was stained with enough blood to show that he had not kept himself from the fight, but he now busied himself with ransoms and was seeing to it that another noble prisoner was bound tightly enough to ensure that he would not make off when his back was turned. The Earl might have noticed that not a single prisoner was tied up behind John's side of the schiltrom, but he made no comment on it.

John did not know what made him turn to his left, but if he had not done so, the arrow would have torn his throat out and sent him spinning to the ground. The bright afternoon sunshine made it difficult for him to see much beyond the treeline, but when he shaded his eyes and peered hard into the forest, he felt his heart seize in his chest. The archers were close enough to his flank to pour their arrows directly into the schiltrom's side. Men already jumped back as they were struck and their spears fell to the ground. The gap was not yet wide enough to allow knights to ride through, but another few volleys would open it sufficiently to threaten the Scots rear.

'Shields!' He screamed at the top of his voice. 'Shields!'

Those men who had been ordered to duck out beneath the spears and stab at the knights and their horses, now turned at John's urgent command. They followed his gestures and set to running the moment they saw the archers at the forest's edge. John had ensured that the shields taken from the fallen English knights the previous afternoon were piled on the field at the schiltrom's rear. He had never forgotten the scale of the slaughter at Falkirk and his fear of seeing it repeated had guided his actions. The men seized the shields up and ran to form a wall at the Scots army's flank. They rocked back as arrow after arrow thumped into their shields, but the line was protected and the spearmen did what they were trained to do and shuffled along so that all spaces were filled and the line was unbroken. John knew what would come next and ran along the line urgently ordering the men in the second rank to raise their shields so that both the rank in front and that behind would have some protection. Even as he screamed his orders out, shafts rained down from the sky and began to thin the ranks.

'M'Lord!' John cried as he approached the Earl of Moray. 'You must ride to the King. He must send his horse to drive those archers off.'

'King Robert prefers to keep his cavalry in reserve, John. Do we not have shields enough to withstand their assault?'

John shook his head. 'We barely have enough shields to cover a third of our men. See how our ranks already grow thin. If he does not send Sir Robert Keith with his cavalry, he can use them to cover his retreat. If our line breaks, the English will outflank us and assail us from all sides and the day will be lost. If you are hesitant about requesting his help, know that your reticence will end with our slaughter. Battles are lost and won in moments such as this. Go now! Ride to our King and tell him that his crown hangs in the balance.'

Randolph called for his horse and rode hard towards King Robert's banner at the far side of the field.

'My Lord!' He called as he rode in. 'The English have deployed archers on our flank. Their arrows fill the sky and leave us hard pressed.'

King Robert nodded and turned to Sir Robert Keith. 'It seems that the Marischal of Scotland will not be kept from this battle. Take your horse and drive the archers from Lord Moray's flank. It seems that they vex him greatly.'

'They will vex him no more, my Lord.' Keith replied with a bow. 'I will ride around and drive them away and leave the Earl unencumbered to wear away at the English horse.'

'Do they falter?' The King asked without taking his eyes off the struggle taking place at the foot of the slope.

Moray shook his head. 'They are penned in so tightly that only those at the front can fight. Those at the back would be fresh if only they could advance against us.'

'If we continue to press them, those at the rear will be pushed back into the Bannock Burn and will drown in its depths.'

'Aye, my Lord.' Moray replied. 'The question is whether or not our men can continue to advance. They have been fighting hard for hours already and grow weary.'

'Then I will stiffen their sinews. It seems that I must throw everything into the pot.' King Robert now turned to Angus Macdonald. 'Your Islemen have been eager to join the battle and will now have their wish as I find that I must commit my reserve to the fray. My hope is constant in thee. Lead your men in at our centre and push the men of Douglas forward. Have your men scream their battle cries as they go so the English will lose heart at seeing fresh warriors fly at them.'

John Edward cheered as Sir Robert Keith led his light cavalry into the trees and sent the English archers fleeing for their lives. The forest was too dense for the English heavy horse to pass through, but the little Scots ponies were nimble enough and left not a single English archer to threaten their flank. John examined the line and concluded that the Marischal had arrived not a moment too soon. The archers had thinned the ranks considerably, though there were men enough to keep the English back. He turned his head as a great roaring filled the air and his heart filled with pride to see the King's division race down the slope at speed. They lowered their shoulders as they reached the rear ranks under Sir James and pushed them forward. That charge won more yards in an instant than three hours of bitter, brutal, bloody struggle. The right wing under Edward Bruce did not want to be outdone and they too pushed forward with renewed vigour and cries of alarm sounded amongst the English ranks as the seething mass of men and panicking horses was further constricted against the steep bank of the Bannock Burn. The left wing now heaved and heaved and tried to make ground, but their ranks were thinned too much and they could make no progress. John then watched in horror as the line began to bend and bulge backwards under the weight of the English horse and armour that had been shifted to the side by the sudden advance of the centre and the right wing. He turned and ran for Randolph.

'Give me your horse!' He demanded when he reached him. 'Look! Our line is close to breaking! If it gives, those knights will pour through in a torrent and overwhelm us. We must reinforce the line!'

He did not wait for the Earl of Moray's reply, but pulled himself up into the saddle and spurred the horse towards Gillies Hill. He galloped with no regard for his own safety, for he feared that the disaster would unfold long before he reached the hill where the grooms, servants, camp-followers, carters, labourers and those who had arrived too late to be drilled in the schiltroms had been ordered to wait. He could have wept with relief when he saw that they had ignored their King's command and had come down the hill to St Ninians so that they could watch the battle unfold. They stood as he thundered in and halted before them.

John pulled Wallace's sword from where it had been strapped to his back and held it high above his head in the hope that some there would recognise its significance. 'Yesterday I came to you with weapons so that you could defend yourselves if our army was defeated. That army now teeters on the very brink of victory with only one last push required to so secure it. Will you now wield those weapons against those same Englishmen and drive them from our kingdom?'

The sma' folk roared their response and John dismounted and led them on foot as they streamed towards the field of battle at the run.

King Robert now saw that his left wing was being pushed gradually backwards just as the centre advanced and he cursed himself for not sending his reserve there. If the left wing collapsed, all was lost. He could see that the Earl of Moray had gone to Angus Macdonald to ask for men, but knew that those Islemen who now rushed to the wing were too few to make a difference. He called for his horse, intent on riding to Randolph's side so that the men there would be inspired to greater deeds by the sight of their King fighting alongside them. He mounted his horse and called for heralds to go to his brother and Sir James Douglas with orders to send reinforcements to the Earl of Moray. He had scarcely begun to issue his commands when a great howling and roaring sounded across the field. He whipped his head around, fearing that the din came from English knights crying their triumph at breaking through the Scottish line. The sight that greeted him caused his jaw to drop in wonderment.

John Edward was sprinting towards the English line with a great broadsword held high above his head. A rabble followed closely at his heels. Old men, boys, peasants brandishing sticks and hoes and women screaming like banshees tore down the slope as fast as their legs would carry them. He doubted that more than a hundred of them wielded swords worthy of the name and at least that same number were unarmed and seemed intent on assaulting the mass of English knights with only the weight of their own flesh and bones.

'My God!' He exclaimed, as the unruly mob crashed into the schiltrom's rear and tried to heave it forward. 'Those peasants have straightened the line!'

'No, m'Lord!' A smiling herald replied. 'They push them on. Look! The sma' folk are pushing the English back!'

34

The Earl of Pembroke felt it rather than saw it.
Some instinct developed over long years of
soldiering and commanding men against the
Scots enabled him to sense it when those around
him continued to push forward and swing their
swords in complete ignorance of the change.
The screaming charge of the fifth Scots division
had sent a ripple through the English throng. No
man cried out or articulated their dismay at the
arrival of a fresh Scots army upon the field but,
like a sentient entity, the army of England had
shuddered. Even as he looked about him,
Pembroke saw the convulsion grow in strength.
The Welsh and English foot, though they were
safely stationed on the far side of the stream,
were the first to break. Already alarmed by the
sight of the indomitable heavy cavalry being
pushed back by the Scots, the arrival of fresh
reinforcements had convinced them that the day
was already lost. Pembroke pointed across the
stream and screamed for someone to stop them
from deserting. The battle may have gone badly,
but the greater part of the English army had
gone untouched and, if the foot soldiers were to

stand, the day would end with the Scots still outnumbered by more than four to one.

Unable to make himself heard above the din of battle, Pembroke watched on in impotent frustration as the far bank of the stream emptied, with men jostling with one another in their haste to make away. His heart jumped into his throat at the sight of noble English knights struggling with each other as they fought to turn their horses and gallop across the few remaining rickety, makeshift bridges over the stream in order to join the commoners in their flight.

'Cowards!' He roared in contempt, but no words of his could halt the collective failure of the courage of the nobles of England.

These few isolated, noble desertions quickly escalated into a torrent of knights spurring their horses towards the Bannock Burn. Weapons intended for the crushing of Scottish skulls were instead employed in beating and bludgeoning their fellow knights in their panic and desperation to leave the field. Horses teetered on the edge of the burn's high banks and then plunged down into the water's icy depths, sending their riders sinking to the bottom swimming vainly against the great weight of their armour. All the while, the drums of the schiltroms beat on and the Scots pushed their wall of spears forward and forced the English back harder against the stream's bank.

Pembroke forced his horse in alongside that of the King. 'We must flee, my Lord!' He shouted.

King Edward of England stared at Pembroke in disbelief. 'The King must fly?' He demanded. 'From this rabble?'

Pembroke responded by pointing towards the Bannock Burn. The King's eyes opened wide in horror. The ground so recently occupied by over twenty thousand English soldiers was now empty save for those possessions they had hurriedly abandoned in their haste to be away. The slow-moving waters of the stream itself were now white with the foam kicked up by the thrashing hooves of a hundred horses fighting to stay afloat or to claw their way up the steep, muddy banks. Pembroke leaned in and took hold of the King's reins and, with Sir Giles d'Argentan on his other side, began to lead him from the field. Many knights made way for their King, for they knew that it would be a disaster for England if he was captured or killed upon the field. Others had to be moved forcibly, particularly once they drew close to one of the last bridges still standing. The King's bodyguard fought hard for those last few yards and their maces and swords left more than one English noble with a crushed skull or a fatal wound.

When they had clattered across to the far side of the burn, they turned to see a sight that would be burned indelibly into all of their memories. Not one of them could believe the evidence of their eyes as the flower of English chivalry was laid low, some of it nobly and with honour as they were overwhelmed by the advancing Scottish spears and some in ignoble cowardice, as they cut down their comrades so that they could scramble away in panic.

When Pembroke could stomach no more, he turned to the King with tears in his eyes. 'I have escorted you from the field, my Lord. Sir Giles d'Argentan and the King's Knight will see you safely away from here.'

Tears ran down the cheeks of Edward Plantagenet now that the scale of his defeat and his disgrace had dawned upon him. 'You must come with us, Pembroke.'

The Earl of Pembroke shook his head. 'No, my Lord. I brought five hundred men of Wales across the border with me and, if God wills it, I will see them safely home again.'

Pembroke turned his horse and went off in search of his men.

Sir Giles d'Argentan watched him go and shook his head in admiration. 'There goes a man of great honour. He knows well that the Scots will ride him down once our army has broken and yet he still goes to his men. May God go with him!'

'Then may he go with us as well!' Rank replied with urgency. 'We should make for the castle without delay for the Scots advance quickens!'

The sight of the royal standard leaving the field caused the English ranks to falter. To their eternal shame, great magnates such as the Earl of Hereford, the High Constable of England, Sir Ingram de Umfraville, Sir John de Seagrave, the Earl of Angus, Sir Antony de Lucy and Maurice,

Lord of Berkeley fled the field by riding over a causeway across the Bannock Burn formed from the drowned and drowning bodies of their countrymen. Other men conducted themselves more honourably as the defeat unfolded. Sir Pain Tiptoft, having struggled in the melee all through the morning and afternoon, kicked at his horse when he saw a space open between his comrades and the Scottish line. With the room to gain momentum, he kicked his steed on and then turned it sharply into the schiltrom. The angle of his turn took him beyond the tips of the Scots spears and his horse crashed through three full ranks before a Highlander ripped at its belly with his long-handled axe and tore its innards out so that they fell into a steaming pile upon the ground. Sir Pain jumped from his saddle before the screaming beast rolled onto the earth and turned to hack at the Scots who still wielded their spears and pushed his comrades back.

The demonic creature who came at him with a sword in both of his hands was soaked in blood and gore and looked as if he had been fighting since the break of day. He rained blow after blow upon him and Sir Pain was soon breathing hard from the effort of parrying them. He attacked like an animal, relentlessly striking with his right hand and then his left. Sir Pain was forced to give ground and was eventually undone by his own faithful mount. His foot slipped on the slick, steaming and glistening pile of guts and he fell hard onto his knees. The first blow rattled his helmet, the second shattered his left wrist as he held his hand out to halt his attacker and the third knocked his sword from his grip. He pulled at his helmet and removed it so that he could ask for quarter. The first syllable of his plea had barely formed on his tongue when the devil rammed the point of his sword so hard into his throat that it almost severed his spine.

Eck was in act the act of retrieving Sir Pain's purse when the Earl of Moray rode to his side. 'My God, Eck!' He declared. 'You have slain Pagan Tiptoft. He was a knight banneret who fought and won in many a tournament and you have bested him!'

'He did not ask for quarter.' Eck offered truthfully, for he knew of Moray's eagerness to take noble prisoners and earn ransoms for himself.

Moray slapped Eck across the shoulders. 'I would expect no less from him. You have made your name from besting a knight as great as he.'

John was leaning through the wall of spears and stabbing Wallace's great sword at the flanks of a black charger when the English line gave way. The wall of horseflesh seemed to disappear in an instant and through the gap he caught a glimpse of the royal standard of England on the far bank of the burn. But it was not the sight of Edward Plantagenet fleeing for Stirling Castle that caused him to growl like a raging beast. Though it had been just a flash of the shield held by a knight at the King's side, it was enough for him to recognise the insignia of an upright broadsword resting upon three skulls and three sets of crossed bones. The King's Knight, his wife's murderer, was within his grasp. He turned from the schiltrom and called for his brother, cousin and Strathbogie as he went. It took them only moments to find horses, for there were so many abandoned English mounts spread across the field. With the way across the Bannock Burn still blocked by the churning mass of English knights and chargers, they set off overland with the intention of cutting off the English King's retreat and putting the King's Knight within reach of their swords. The thick forest slowed them, but their familiarity with the terrain enabled them to make good progress and they emerged onto the cobbled street at the foot of Castle Hill in time to see the back end of the King's bodyguard trotting up away from them. The Scotstoun men did not hesitate in putting their heels hard into their horses' flanks and galloping after them towards the castle.

Sir Giles d'Argentan turned at the sound of pursuing hooves clattering against the cobbles and echoing from the close-packed houses of the narrow street. 'You four!' He ordered those at the rear of the group. 'Hold them until I deliver the King safely into the castle!'

The four knights immediately turned their horses and began to retrace their steps back down the tight, twisting street. The King's Knight led the way with Sir Edmund Mauley, the steward of the King's household, Sir Roger de Northburgh, Keeper of the King's Privy Seal, and Sir John Osbourne, knight of the King's household, following on behind. The Scotsmen were coming on so hard they were upon the King's men almost before they realised it. Scott and Eck Edward's horses collided with that of Sir Roger de Northburgh so hard that all three men were thrown from their saddles and Sir Roger, despite the finest helmet that money could buy, was knocked unconscious when he fell. Strathbogie near decapitated Sir Edmund Mauley with the first swing of his axe and reduced the shield of Sir John Osbourne to splinters with his second. The King's Knight scarcely had time to realise that his attacker was the same man who had grievously wounded him during the Battle of Methven, before the tip of his great broadsword ripped up through his jaw, tearing teeth from his gums and opening a gash that ran all the way to his scalp. The wound would surely have killed him if it had not been for the carts and hooves that had worn away at the cobblestones in the years since they had been laid. John Edward's horse slipped on the smooth, stone surface, pulling both him and his blade downwards and away from where they could do more harm. Ignoring his pain, Rank swung his great mace as hard as hc was able and arced it upwards at his attacker's face. John's skull would have been crushed like an egg but for his horse's struggle to regain its feet. It lifted him up by just enough to ensure that the mace struck his breastplate instead of his face. The blow landed with enough force to crumple the armour and throw John backwards from his saddle.

Strathbogie, having put an end to Sir John, buried his axe in the skull of Rank's horse. The dazed and dying beast staggered six steps backwards before collapsing onto its rump and sliding slowly onto its side with a disgruntled and unhappy groan. With the wounded Englishman now trapped beneath his horse, Strathbogie turned and went to John's aid. Eck and Scott were already at his side, but seemed frozen with indecision as he gasped for breath and clutched desperately at his sunken chest. Strathbogie drew his dagger and fell at John's side.

'His chest is crushed!' Strathbogie cried. 'Get that fucking armour off him or he's dead.' He cut through the leather straps and threw the buckled plate aside. He then pulled at his maille and tunic and groaned when he saw that John's chest was caved in horribly. He stabbed his blade in under his ribs and attempted to lever them up.

Dazed from his fall and starved of air, John saw the concern on the faces of his brother and cousin, but found that he could not grasp what was troubling them so. He felt only a momentary sensation of panic when Strathbogie flew at him with his dagger and started to stab at him. He opened his mouth to ask what he had done to cause such anger, but was carried away on a woozy wave of fast-encroaching darkness before he could speak.

He felt himself descend into the warm and comforting darkness and the sound of his brother's panic grew muffled and was replaced with perfect silence. He floated in the way that a man does when he is as tired as a dog and has lain down in a meadow to doze on a warm summer's day. It was then that she came to him. He could feel a smile form on his lips even although his physical body was far, far away. It was her sweet scent that first told him that she was near. It was the scent of her hair and the crook of her neck and of those soft areas he nuzzled whenever they were entwined together beneath their blankets. Then came sight of her beautiful face, her eyes shining with life and with love for him. Tears flowed from his eyes, but they were tears of unadulterated joy instead of the agony and misery of his years of hard and grinding grief.

'I have missed you!' He sobbed. 'My heart has broken afresh with each new dawn and I have prayed only to be with you again! The very sight of you fills my heart with joy.'

'I have missed you too, my love.' She replied as she smiled tenderly and reached out to cup his cheek in her warm hand. 'Fear not! It will not be long. The days left to you will pass by so very quickly.'

'I will not leave you again, my love! You cannot ask that of me. God knows how much I have suffered and He would not have me suffer more!'

'You must, John.' She said gently. 'This world is not done with you, though the worst is already behind you. Be strong! Your life will pass in a heartbeat and then we shall be together for all eternity!'

Strathbogie had tossed his dagger aside and now slid the tip of Eck's sword between John's ribs.

'If I cannae lever his ribs up wi' this.' He grunted. 'He's beyond our help.'

'Did I hear him right?' Scott asked. 'I'm sure he just said 'Don't go my love!' He must be delirious.'

'He calls me that all the time.' Strathbogie replied with a wry grin as he strained at the blade. 'Though usually when none of you buggers are close enough to hear.' He pushed down sharply on Eck's blade and grunted in triumph when he was rewarded with a resounding crack and John's ribcage snapped back into place.

John gasped as he was ripped back into consciousness on a stupefying wave of agony. He gulped in great breaths of air like a drowning man who has finally broken the water's surface.

Sir Giles d'Argentan reined his horse in the moment the gates of Stirling Castle came into view.

'Sire!' He called to King Edward. 'Your protection was committed to me, but since you are safely on your way, I will bid you farewell for never yet have I fled from a battle, nor will I now.' With these words, he turned his horse and began to retrace his steps back to the field where the army of England was being slaughtered.

The King found that he was too disconsolate to reply and instead turned to where Sir Philip

Mowbray, the governor of Stirling Castle, stood upon the ramparts.

'Open the gates!' He commanded. 'Give shelter to your King!'

'I cannot, my Lord.' Sir Philip called in regretful reply. 'I gave my word that I would surrender the castle keys to Edward Bruce if you did not march to our relief. With your army routed, I must keep my word and give the castle up to him.'

'What is worth more, sirrah?' The King snapped. 'Your word of honour or a King's command? Admit me now, I am pursued.'

Sir Philip again shook his head. 'I will not break my vow. You must flee, my Lord. It would be folly to entrap yourself behind these walls and make yourself prisoner to Robert Bruce. Ride now and you may stay ahead of your pursuers!'

Hugh Despenser shouted angrily at the castle's governor. 'Bastard traitor! We will not forget this treason! Come, my Lord! Let us be away while the Scots still fight upon the field!'

Sir Giles d'Argentan brought his horse to a halt just as the three men jumped up from tending to their stricken comrade. He saw that the King's Knight had been grievously wounded and now struggled to pull his leg out from under his mount. Sir Edmund Mauley lay on his back a little further down the street in a pool of blood with his head only attached to his body by a few strands of gristle. Sir John Osbourne lay at his side, his helmet and armour so badly battered

491

and dented that he was surely dead. Sir Roger de Northburgh groaned groggily in the dirt and filth of the gutter but made no attempt to regain his feet. Sir Giles saw that the bag containing the King's Privy Seal still hung from Sir Roger's belt and that the King's shield was still strapped to his back. The loss of either of these symbols of English power was unthinkable to Sir Giles, so he dismounted, removed his helmet and drew his sword.

'Can you fight, King's Knight?' He called to Rank without taking his eyes off Eck, Scott and Strathbogie.

'No!' Rank growled wetly from his ruined mouth. 'My leg is snapped.'

'Then take my horse and go to the castle. Tell them that I fight for the King's seal and his shield. I doubt that these peasants will trouble me for long, but it would comfort me to know that men come to retrieve these royal possessions.'

Rank hissed in agony as he wrenched his leg out from underneath his horse's flank. He used his mace to push himself upright and limped to Sir Giles' mount. He groaned in agony as he pulled himself up into the saddle and turned the horse towards the castle.

Sir Giles slashed his sword through the air in front of him and took three paces towards the ragged, dirty, blood-spattered Scots. 'I am Sir Giles d'Argentan, the greatest knight in all of Christendom, unbeaten in the tournaments and the winner of countless purses for my skill at jousting and in the melee. I have fought all over

Europe and have been on crusade with the Knights of Rhodes. Honour demands that I give you the opportunity to withdraw. Turn away now and I will do you no harm. Stay and I will kill you one-by-one. The choice is yours, my friends, but you must make your decision now.'

The Scots gave Sir Giles no reply but stared at him sullenly.

'Very well.' Sir Giles announced with a sigh. 'So be it! My conscience is clear.'

Strathbogie raised his great axe behind his head and launched it at Sir Giles with terrible force. The weapon spun end over end in the air and travelled with such devastating speed that Sir Giles had barely raised his sword when the blade smashed into his skull throwing him to the ground in a spray of blood, brains, bone and hair.

'These English bastards cannae half talk.' Strathbogie drawled, as he went to retrieve his weapon.

The Scotstoun men were still looting the dead when Sir James Douglas came thundering up towards the castle at the head of a body of light cavalry.

'King Robert has given me leave to pursue the English King!' He announced excitedly. 'I thought they were headed for the castle.'

'They went that way!' Scott replied, pointing up the narrow street.

'Jesus Christ!' Sir James declared, his eyes widening in surprise. 'You have killed Sir Giles d'Argentan!'

493

'It was Strathbogie!' Eck responded. 'He finished him with his axe.'

'He was a knight of great renown! My God! What honour you have won this day!'

With that, Sir James could contain himself no longer and set off in pursuit of the day's greatest prize.

35

Strathbogie cut strips of cloth from the surcoats
of Sir Giles d'Argentan and Sir Edmund Mauley
and used them to tightly bind John's bruised and
battered ribs. With help from Eck and Scott, he
hefted John up into his saddle. With the King's
Knight long gone and beyond their reach, they
turned their horses back towards the battlefield
and went in search of the men of Scotstoun.
They found King Robert ahorse at the far end of
the field surveying the carnage with the Earl of
Moray at his side.

'My God, John!' The Earl declared on seeing
John divested of his armour with his torso
wrapped tight in cloth. 'Are you hurt?'

'Aye, m'Lord.' John replied with a wince.
'The King's bodyguard turned on us as we
pursued them towards the castle gates. A knight
unhorsed me with his mace. I live to tell the tale,
but did not escape unscathed.'

'Then we have much to be thankful for!' The
King announced in delight. 'It seems that we
have routed the English with the loss of only
five hundred of our foot. Look about you! The
knights of England and their horses litter the
ground from here to yonder burn, where they lie

so thickly that a man could ride dry-shod from one bank to the other. Never in my most hopeful prayers did I dare ask for a victory such as this! Never in the history of our two countries has our neighbour suffered such humiliation in battle or been found to be so helpless in defeat. Twenty thousand men, spearmen, archers and men-at-arms flew from us in terror before a single blow was landed upon them. The great barons of England and all their noble knights left both honour and courage upon the field and took flight without a moment's thought for those they are supposed to lead. My army, only a quarter of the size of that of Edward Plantagenet, now pursues them as they run for England. Sir James Douglas snaps at the heels of King Edward himself, my brother has gone after his commanders and my spearmen now hunt the fleeing English foot. Praise be to God on high, for he has laid his blessings upon the King and kingdom of Scotland this day!'

Despite his very great discomfort, John could not keep himself from smiling to see King Robert's face so uncharacteristically full of joy. 'Then I am happy to report that he continues to bless us, m'Lord. In the struggle with King Edward's bodyguard, we captured Sir Roger Northburgh.'

'Northburgh?' The King demanded incredulously. 'The Keeper of the King's Privy Seal?'

'Aye, m'Lord.' John replied. 'We left him with your servants at your pavilion.'

'Good God!' Moray exclaimed. 'We have taught you the value of prisoners at last, John Edward! In days past you would have executed him in spite of his rank.'

John nodded but did not mention that he had spared Sir Roger only because Sir James Douglas had seen him alive and in his possession. If Sir James had not ridden up when he did, Sir Roger would be as dead as every other Englishman who had suffered the misfortune of encountering the men of Scotstoun.

'I also left the Privy Seal of England and King Edward's own shield in your servants' hands, m'Lord! I thought it would please you to have them. Now I must go and find my men so that I can join them in the hunt.'

King Robert looked long and hard at John before he finally nodded. 'Thank you, John! Your gifts please me greatly. Go and find your men! Perhaps you can school them in the taking of prisoners.'

John did not reply to the King's words until they were beyond his hearing. 'I think not, m'Lord. I think not.'

The Earl of Pembroke had caught up with his Welshmen on the outskirts of the town of Falkirk. He had quickly formed them up into two columns and set them upon the road at a run. He placed archers at their rear to fend off the Scots horsemen who swarmed all around them like slavering wolves. Any man who faltered was left where he fell, for the Earl knew that speed was their only hope of salvation. The screams of the stragglers as the Scots fell upon them helped their fellows to find new strength and to keep placing one sore and weary foot in front of the other. He lost count of the number of corpses left strewn across the road as the relentless Scots took their revenge on lone fugitives and on larger bands of men who vainly thought to find safety in numbers.

He kept them marching without halt long into the summer night and through the hours of darkness. Their pursuers seemed to fall away in search of easier prey, but the cries and screams of less fortunate men still reached their ears and kept them fearful and anxious. He dared not even allow them to halt to make water and sensible men swallowed their shame and marched on as they soiled themselves. Some men refused to succumb to such indignity and took their lives in their hands by standing or squatting at the roadside while their bladders or bowels emptied onto Scottish earth. Almost half of these men had luck on their side and made it back into the ranks unharmed. The rest were abandoned by fortune and were attacked while they pished and shat.

When the light of day finally dawned on that dark and dreadful night, Pembroke could see no horsemen tracking alongside them and felt certain that they had outrun their pursuers. They still passed the occasional English corpse at the roadside, stripped and with his throat slit, but he was confident that these men had fallen prey to locals who would hesitate to attack such a large body of men. Nevertheless, he kept them marching until long after they had crossed the border.

John, Eck, Scott and Strathbogie had ridden along the Falkirk road for about three miles before they came upon the first of the corpses. The bodies were piled across the track and were scattered across the fields on either side. This was undoubtedly the place where the pursuing Scots had caught up with the rear ranks of the fleeing English foot. Almost every skull was split open, indicating that they had been ridden down by Scots cavalry as they ran for their very lives. The air was filled with crows as far as the eye could see and they hovered there while the human scavengers below kept them from their feast as they stripped the dead of valuables, clothes and boots. Most of the fallen were naked already, their fragile bodies denied any vestige of dignity before the crows descended to peck at their lifeless, unseeing eyes. They covered another five miles of corpse-strewn track before they caught up with the men of Scotstoun and Perth on the far side of Larbert. They found them in a state of near exhaustion after long, hard hours in the crush of the schiltrom followed by a protracted afternoon's hunt under the heat of the summer sun. The band of men-at-arms they had been pursuing had sought to evade them by taking to the forest. They now had them trapped beneath a rocky escarpment, but had neither the energy nor the inclination to risk attacking such well-armed men in dense woodland. John sent men into the village to procure meat and ale for his tired and hungry soldiers while he and his captains decided on the best course of action.

'Now that you have such a fondness for taking prisoners, you could call on them to surrender their arms.' Eck teased.

John shook his head and continued to peer into the forest.

'We could withdraw.' Strathbogie suggested. 'Once they think themselves safe and set their feet upon the road, we could run them down.'

John shook his head once again. 'These are well-trained and well-equipped men-at-arms. They will cut though our men with ease. I will not risk it.'

'You do not think that we should wait them out?' Scott asked, his tone filled with disbelief. 'The men are exhausted and will soon fall asleep. We'll be slaughtered while we slumber.'

John shook his head again. 'I do not think we should wait them out.' He replied. 'I think we should burn them out. They have trapped themselves. Why should we risk our men when the flames will drive them out just as well?'

The Scotstoun men sat down upon the earth and refreshed themselves as the ring of fires set at the forest's edge began to spread. The dried leaves and twigs went up like kindling and the gentle breeze fanned it into an inferno.

'I don't think any o' these buggers will be driven out.' Strathbogie observed, as he gnawed at a mutton bone.

Eck Edward wiped at his lips with his sleeve. 'Nah! Methinks they'll be roasted right through.'

The screaming started before they had eaten their fill. The Englishmen backed away from the flames until they were pressed hard against the escarpment. The inferno closed in on them from all sides with such intensity that their terrible screams were soon drowned out by the roar of the fire itself. The men of Scotstoun drank to a job well done and lay down to rest their weary bodies after a day which had seen a great reduction in the strength and number of their enemies.

The Earl of Moray burst into King Robert's tent and dropped his helmet onto the parchment-strewn table. 'You will not believe me, my Lord!' He declared excitedly. 'Near six thousand English foot who fled the field are now gathered beneath the castle walls. When we approached to assess their numbers, they threw their weapons onto the ground and fell to their knees to beg for mercy. They are our prisoners now!'

'Good God!' King Robert exclaimed. 'They alone would outnumber us if they had the will to stand.'

'We have disarmed them and put them under guard, but the sheer number of them presents a threat to us.'

The King nodded his agreement. 'Set five hundred of them to clearing the dead from the battlefield and to the digging of pits. Set the rest upon the road south. I cannot have them here.'

'They will die if we send them out. The roads away from here are already like some vision of hell with the dead piled so deep a man could walk from here to Falkirk without ever stepping upon the ground. If we send the prisoners south, our own men will fall upon them before they have advanced a single mile.'

'It cannot be helped, Thomas.' Robert Bruce replied, his voice full of sadness and resignation. 'I cannot have them here. Armed or unarmed, if they were to rebel, I scarcely have enough men to contain them. They must take their chances upon the road and hope that fortune favours them as much as it has their King.'

'You have heard from Douglas then?' Moray enquired.

'Aye. King Edward and his escort of five hundred knights ran like frightened girls from the bold Sir James and his sixty men. He harassed them all the way to Dunbar and, such was their panic, they dared not pause to lead their horses through the castle gates. In their terror, they abandoned their mounts and rushed through on foot, screaming for the gates to be closed behind them. The English King was so afeart he took immediately to ship and has already sailed for England. Sir James intends to return to us tomorrow and brings five hundred English destriers with him.'

'My God!' Moray exclaimed. 'The humiliation is absolute! All will know that we put the English King to flight!'

'That is not the best of it.' King Robert replied, his eyes sparkling in spite of his fatigue from a long day in the saddle and a longer evening dealing with the battle's aftermath. 'My brother has sent a messenger from Bothwell. His pursuit has proven to be more fruitful than we could have hoped for.'

'Christ! He has captured an English magnate? Tell me, my Lord, who has he taken?'

King Robert beamed with pleasure as he retrieved the parchment bearing the seal of Edward Bruce. 'It seems that my brother has persuaded the constable of Bothwell Castle to change sides and join with us. He has demonstrated his new-found loyalty by making prisoners of those who fled from the battlefield and sought sanctuary within his walls. When he reaches Stirling tomorrow, my brother will have more than fifty noble, English prisoners. The most prominent of these include the Earl of Hereford, the Earl of Angus, Sir Ingram de Umfraville, the Lord of Berkeley and the Lord of Seagrave.'

Moray threw his head back and roared with laughter. 'Christ! We shall leave the English treasury empty to ransom those five men alone.'

'I know.' The King replied happily. 'We shall not want for coin for years to come. No English King has ever suffered such disaster.'

'And no Scottish King has ever won a victory of such magnitude! We must mark it, my Lord. Celebrate it and strengthen your hold upon the crown!'

The King nodded his agreement. 'You are right, Thomas. Recall our men! Tell them that they must gather beneath the castle walls at dusk tomorrow. We shall feast and celebrate what we together have achieved.'

The Scotstoun men were not left to rest for long after their feast beside the burning forest. The sun had not yet risen in the sky when a Borderman rode into their makeshift camp and cried out in alarm.

'Up! Up! The English come! They are almost upon us!'

John had been in too much pain to sleep and was so stiff that he needed Strathbogie to pull him to his feet and heave him up into his saddle. He then followed the Borderman back along the road to Stirling until they had sight of the advancing English.

'There's enough of them.' Strathbogie announced, before stifling a yawn.

'Four, maybe five thousand.' Eck guessed.

'They are unarmed.' John pointed out to his comrades. 'See? No spears, no shields, no bows and no swords.'

'Armed or not.' Scott Edward exclaimed. 'There are too many of them for us. We could muster two hundred men at most. They would mob us and pull us from our horses.'

'Do we just leave them to wind their weary way back across the border?' Strathbogie asked reluctantly.

John snorted. 'Just to have them arm themselves and march straight back here to spread their misery across the kingdom? No! We do not leave them in peace. Every one we cut down today is one who cannot return tomorrow.'

'There's far too many of them, John.' Strathbogie replied with a shrug.

'There's only too many of them if they stand together. If we scatter them, we can pick them off one-by-one.'

The plan was as simple as it was effective. The Scots ranged themselves on a hillside overlooking the road and let the English see them as they approached. The column slowed uncertainly at the sight of them and then marched on with every set of English eyes turned to keep a wary watch on the scowling, skulking Scots. When half the column had passed them by, every Scot with a bow sent his arrows flying into the English ranks. Though only a handful of men fell down dead or grievously wounded, the arrows caused panic and the column began to run. John chose this moment to order his horsemen to charge at the column's rear. A strong and capable leader would have commanded them to stay together and use the weight of their numbers to repel the attack. For the second time in as many days, the English rank and file found that they lacked such strong leadership and they broke and ran from the Scots in all directions.

John watched on in satisfaction. 'Now they do not have the strength of numbers. We will hunt them until the sun goes down and ensure that they can never again do harm to our countrymen.'

The Scotstoun men hunted on into the late afternoon and left a trail of dead that stretched all the way to Linlithgow. They stopped only when the King's herald caught up with them and ordered them back to Stirling at the King's command. Though reluctant to allow a single Englishman to escape their grasp, they were so hungry, saddle-sore and weary that they could not refuse the King's invitation to feast with him.

36

The ride from Linlithgow to Stirling was an
agony for John Edward as his whole body
protested at every little movement and screamed
whenever it was jolted. However, his suffering
was all but forgotten when he rounded the crag
and saw what awaited him on the plain beneath
the castle heights. Nearly two thirds of that great
expanse was filled with row upon row of
wagons of every imaginable size and type.
Common haywains were lined up in their
hundreds alongside rank after rank of carts,
heavy wagons and carriages of such quality and
scale that they dominated the field. John shook
his head in disbelief at the sight of the English
baggage train captured in its entirety and now
safely guarded and in the possession of King
Robert. His mind fairly reeled at the thought of
what treasures and riches were hidden there. The
next portion of the plain was filled to bursting
with horseflesh. Thousands of the great, English
chargers had survived the slaughter and were
now tied up in rows in the shadow of the castle.
They were joined there by hundreds of small
ponies and a thousand carthorses.

The last part of the plain contained the Scottish army and the area it occupied was dwarfed by that taken up by what the fleeing English had left behind. John found himself laughing to think that such power and wealth and materiel had been defeated by a few thousand Scots peasants with sticks. The whole situation was surreal and he had to shake himself to check that he was awake and not dreaming. He found himself salivating as they approached the chattering and excited gathering and the aroma of roasting meat hit his nostrils.

'I could eat a horse!' Strathbogie growled as he rubbed at his empty belly.

'Well, there's plenty here to choose from!' Scott replied, his eyes wide with excitement as grooms came to take their horses and directed them to enter the great square of flaming torches.

Every table in Stirling had been carried through the town and placed upon the plain. Every empty barrel and every single wooden plank had been seized on royal command to make tables so that every man who had fought for their King could sit and feast with him. As was only right and proper, the nobles were to be seated closest to the castle walls, with commoners and peasants allocated places at the far end of the field.

'Where shall we sit?' Strathbogie asked as he looked about himself. 'You boys should probably sit down the far end, seeing as you're as common as shit. But if you promise to behave yourselves, you can sit up here wi' me.'

John groaned as he lowered himself onto a rickety bench. 'You can sit where you like. I'm no' moving from here.'

King Robert had evidently decided to be most generous with the English supplies, for servants came running with hot meat, fresh bread, and jugs of ale and wine.

'If King Robert means to give a speech.' Strathbogie said though a mouthful of roast pig. 'He had better hurry. If I eat much more and drink even one more goblet of ale, I am so tired I will be asleep before he starts.'

They were not made to wait for long. Strathbogie had only just drained another goblet when the trumpets were blown and a procession of torch-bearers heralded the King's approach. All men there leapt to their feet at the sight of their King and cheered him lustily as he made his way to the centre of the gathering. John thought that he looked most regal. He had thrown off his armour and donned kingly robes. He wore his simple circlet of gold upon his head and walked forward beneath the great banner of Scotland with the Earl of Moray, the Lord of Galloway, Sir James Douglas and Sir Robert Keith following on behind. King Robert smiled and nodded in acknowledgement and waited patiently for men to decide that they had roared for long enough. Just when it seemed that there was no end to the men's appetite for cheering, a hush suddenly fell over the company and died to absolute silence as King Robert surveyed his army with serene confidence.

When he finally broke the silence, his voice was strong and clear and carried through the still evening's air so that all could hear his words. 'No Scotsman in all of history has ever won as great a victory as we have won here!' The men cheered at these words and hammered at their tables with their fists. The King smiled and raised his hands for silence but displayed no impatience when it took moments for the din to subside.

'As we sit here and celebrate our victory, messengers carry news of our deeds south to London, west to Ireland and across the sea to France, Italy and Spain. Soon the whole world will know what we have done. They will know that the greatest army ever mustered in all of Europe marched across our border not ten days past and that it was the courage of the men of Scotland that repulsed it, destroyed it and sent its King running for his ship as though his skirts had been set ablaze.' The King paused again and waited for the racket to quieten.

'No one will ever again doubt our courage or strength. All will know that our borders can no longer be breached with impunity. They will know that Scotland is a kingdom once more. But they will have their eyes upon us at this time of victory. They will look to judge us and determine what kind of men we are. They will judge us by our treatment of our own folk and by the way we treat our enemies in defeat. So, let me start with you, who have been ever loyal to your King. There are men here who fought with me at Methven, who ran with me through the heather and men who struggled at my side when we were hunted in the mountains. All men here stood firm when faced by all the might of England when no one would have blamed you if you had turned and fled for your lives. Such courage and constancy must be rewarded, for I do not want a single one of you to think that your deeds are not valued by your King. The riches of the English baggage will be distributed amongst those commoners who fought beneath my standard. Provision will also be made for the families of those who perished in the struggle.'

The cheering was deafening and lasted for many minutes. When it began to subside, Strathbogie shook his head in wonder. 'I assumed that he would keep the treasure for himself. Christ! He has made poor men rich in the course of a single sentence!'

'I doubt if there will be a family in Scotland that does not benefit from this generosity!' John replied in disbelief as the King prepared to resume his address.

'So, when the world looks at us, they will see that we treat our people well. They will see a good and Godly nation. How then will we treat our enemies? We will not do as the English have done. We will not execute men of noble family or imprison them in cages. We will show the world that we are better than that. We will show them that we are magnanimous in defeat and that we treat our enemies with courtesy and respect. Almost one hundred barons, baronets and knights were captured during the battle and every last one of them will be treated as my guest until their ransoms are arranged. Two of them I will release immediately and without ransom. Ralph de Monthermer, for a kindness he did me in the past, and Sir Marmaduke de Tweng, in tribute to his great courage upon the field of battle. All English knights who fell upon the field will be buried honourably in consecrated ground. The bodies of the great noblemen, Gilbert Clare, Earl of Gloucester and Sir Robert Clifford will be speedily returned to their families at my own expense.' King Robert paused here so that men could applaud, but it was noticeable that they did not cheer as loud or as for long as they had before.

'I give thanks to all men here and would have you know that I value your loyalty and constancy over all else in life. I now wish to recognise and reward those among you who have undertaken great acts of courage in my service.' King Robert then turned and ordered that his sword be brought to him.

The first man to be knighted was Sir James Douglas, who was made a knight banneret. The King then so honoured a multitude of men drawn from Douglas, the Isles, Moray, Carrick, Galloway, Lothian and the Borders. John clapped hard and pushed himself stiffly to his feet when Malcolm Simpson was called forward and fell to his knees before the King. He knew that Wallace would have burst with pride to see his former captain so honoured. He was left reeling when King Robert called out for Alexander Edward to approach him. Eck looked around himself in confusion and shock and only rose to his feet when Edward Bruce came forward and gestured at him to hurry up. The King spoke warmly of Eck's bravery and of how he had slashed his blades at the King's enemies in battles all across the nation and on the other side of the English border. He also praised him for besting the English knight Sir Pain Tiptoft on the banks of the Bannock Burn. John's chest swelled with pride to see his cousin so honoured and he embraced him tightly in congratulation when he returned to their table. King Robert then surprised and delighted the Scotstoun men again by calling for John Strathbogie to step forward and kneel before his King. Strathbogie's face was a picture of astonishment as he rose from his bench and made his way to the centre of the gathering. King Robert spoke briefly of Strathbogie's bravery and made the assembled company laugh by saying that he would never dare put himself at the wrong end of Strathbogie's great axe. He then made them cheer by praising Strathbogie for besting Sir Giles d'Argentan, the greatest knight in all of Christendom, in combat beneath the castle walls. With that, he sent the newly knighted Strathbogie back to his comrades with a grin upon his face and handed his sword back to his attendant.

John forced a smile onto his face and rose to embrace Strathbogie and join with the others in pounding him on the back in congratulation. The joy he felt for his cousin and his friend was genuine, but he could not choke off the feeling of disappointment which now rose in his chest.

He slumped back and grabbed for his goblet, leaving the others to chatter excitedly and to try out Eck and Strathbogie's new-won titles. Though he had never had the slightest desire for status or position, he found himself devastated now that it had been denied to him. He could scarcely believe that Robert Bruce could hold a petty grudge and ignore all that he had done for him and all that he had risked and lost in his name. He felt as if all energy had been drained from his body and he was more weary than he had ever been before. He suddenly wanted to be away from them all, to be on the road back to Scotstoun so he could bury Al and the Robertson and grieve for them.

The King continued to speak and reward those who had supported him as John fought to overcome his disappointment. He had called a woman before him and told the gathering that she had given him shelter when he was lost, alone and hunted through the heather. He told them that he had almost abandoned all hope when she fell to her knees before him, hailed him as King and pledged her three sons to his service. He asked the widow to name her reward for her loyalty and shook his head theatrically when she asked for a small holding by the Cree estuary. To great roars of approval from his army, the King instead granted her a parcel of land three miles wide and five miles long. The King embraced the widow with great affection and then waved the crowd to silence.

'I am indeed blessed to be surrounded by such loyal subjects!' King Robert boomed, his smile lighting his face. 'But not all men here have always given it so unquestioningly. There is one among you who did question my right to rule in Scotland.'

John felt himself tense although he did not really believe that the King would seek to humiliate him here before the whole of Scotland. His heart leapt into his throat when King Robert locked eyes with him and knitted his eyebrows together in a frown.

'This man thought to scold me on the very day of my coronation.' The Bruce paused while the gathered men growled and booed to hear of such impudence. 'Do you remember what you said to me, John Edward?'

The King pointed at the Scotstoun table and every set of eyes turned to look at them. John felt himself reel from suddenly becoming the subject of such intense and hostile scrutiny. He looked to Edward Bruce for support, but the Lord of Galloway would not hold his gaze and instead set his eyes upon the earth.

John rose slowly and reluctantly to his feet. 'I do, m'Lord.'

Robert Bruce nodded. 'You told me that placing a circlet of gold upon my head did not make me King! You told me that I must earn my crown. Well! What think you now, John Edward? Have I done enough to win the right to perch upon my throne?'

'You have, m'Lord.' John replied, his voice wavering under the weight of so many eyes upon him. 'And not solely through force of arms. I have seen you display all the qualities I would wish for in a King. You have put the kingdom before yourself by forgiving those who have sinned against you and your family. Lesser men would have taken their revenge and left the country at war with itself. You have walked among your people and not confined yourself to the company of nobles and all ordinary men will gladly follow a King who has the common touch. I have also seen moments of great wisdom, such as your Christian treatment of our noble prisoners. I stand by the words I spoke within the Abbey of Scone and am glad to say that you have passed all tests of kingship.'

'I asked you then to swear your sword to me and you threw it at my feet. Will you now kneel before me and swear fealty to your King?'

'I will do so gladly, m'Lord.' John replied, before stepping quickly before King Robert and falling upon his knees with his head bowed down.

King Robert gestured to one of his servants and the boy ran forward holding a sword in his hands. The King took the sword by its hilt and bent down so that his lips were close to John's ear. 'Of all of my commanders, you are the most wilful, obstinate and disobedient. You do as I command only when it suits you and ignore my instructions when you do not consider them wise. I do not forget your insubordination or your insults, but neither do I forget your courage, loyalty and skill in battle. I know well that my grip upon my crown would be much less firm without all that you have done for me and for my family. You have the gratitude of your King.'

King Robert stepped back and raised the sword before dubbing the blade on each of John's shoulders in turn. 'Arise, Sir John!' He announced with relish.

The men cheered for John nearly as loudly as they had for Sir James Douglas, for many of them had fought with him over the long years of struggle and all had heard the tales of the daring deeds carried out by the men of Perth.

King Robert held his hand high and called for silence. 'In recognition of Sir John's loyal service, he is hereby granted title in perpetuity to the lands stretching from Scotstoun Loch to that of Marlee.' The King then leaned towards John and offered him the hilt of the sword he had just used to perform the adoubement. 'You recognise the blade, Sir John?' He enquired with a smile.

'It is my father's sword, m'Lord.' He replied. 'I last saw it when I threw it to the floor at Scone.'

'I had always intended to return it to you when the time was right. My brother suggested that I return it in this way.'

'I did indeed!' Edward Bruce declared as he came to embrace John and offer his congratulations. 'Now we must drink, for we have much to celebrate.'

The celebrations went on long into the night, for the English had carried with them supplies enough for twenty-five thousand men to celebrate their anticipated victory. No more than six thousand Scots made merry beneath the walls of Stirling Castle, but it was said that they near finished the wine and ale intended for four times that number of Englishmen. Neither did they go without entertainment, for the English King had brought jugglers, jesters, tumblers and eaters-of-fire across the border to keep him from boredom. King Robert promised these men safe passage to England if their performances were enough to amuse and to thrill his loyal spearmen. Not a single one of them failed to impress, though all agreed that Baston, the Carmelite friar, was the most entertaining of them all. King Edward had employed him to immortalize his inevitable victory in verse and, in keeping with the traditions of his trade, he had penned his epic poem long before the English army marched its way onto Scottish soil. A few threats were sufficient to persuade him to replace the names of the English leaders with those of Scots and his reading of his work was enjoyed so much he was not allowed to leave until he had delivered it twice.

John Edward was aware of little of it, for events had left him in a daze. His joy at being so honoured and rewarded by the King was tempered by alcohol, his injuries, his state of exhaustion and by his grief, both old and new. It was time to return to Scotstoun, to bury his dead, to mourn them, to lick his wounds and to prepare for whatever lay ahead.

Epilogue

John found the Black Dog at dawn and sighed sadly to see him shivering as he lay with his great head upon his paws on the freshly turned earth of Al's lochside grave. He crouched down and gently stroked his muzzle.

'How did you get here, Dugal?' He asked. 'We thought you had crawled away to die in the forest.'

It was a wonder that he had been able to cover all the miles from Stirling to Scotstoun after the English arrow had torn his back open wide enough to expose his spine. The wound was rotten now and pus oozed from it ceaselessly. The dog's breathing was growing shallow and every exhalation was accompanied by a low moan. John's petting and the sound of his voice seemed to comfort him so he sat down at his side, stroked him and spoke to him as soothingly as he was able.

He spoke of how the Black Dog had joined with the Edward lads when they first set off to fight the English. He fondly remembered that many men had tried to make themselves his master and that none had been able to tame him until he had chosen to devote himself to Al. He thanked the ailing beast for his loyalty and for being a constant companion to Al during the long days of loneliness and isolation whilst scouting the land and protecting the patriots from their enemies. He smiled as he reminded the hound of the great battles he had seen and of how he had been fed morsels of meat by the hands of great men like Wallace, John Comyn, Prior Abernethy, Edward Bruce, Bishop Lamberton and the Robertson. He kept on talking and stroking the grey fur that had once been blacker than night long after the dog had stopped breathing and had moaned his last. Then he wept. He wept for the Black Dog and for all that he had lost. In that moment at the lochside, he realised that the joy of winning victories, lands and titles is inconsequential when compared to the pain of having those you love ripped away from you.

When he could weep no more, he wrapped the Black Dog in his cloak and set about burying him in his rightful place beside his master.

When he stood at the graveside with Al's son later that afternoon, the little lad looked up at him with an expression of the utmost solemnity. 'Will Dugal go to heaven, Uncle John?' He asked. 'The priest says that animals don't go to heaven, only people.'

John squeezed the little boy's hand and smiled at him. 'Animals don't go to heaven. It would be too crowded with them all there, wouldn't it? But Dugal always went wherever he wanted to go and he always found your father, no matter how far he had travelled or how wild the forests and mountains were. I doubt that God and all his angels will be able to keep him from your father's side.'

The boy's expression remained very grave, but he nodded enthusiastically in agreement with John's assessment. 'I'm glad he'll be there with Pa.' He exclaimed. 'I wouldn't want him to be all alone.'

'Me neither!' John replied as he affectionately ruffled the boy's hair. 'Just don't tell the priest. He'll be annoyed if he knows Dugal's in heaven when he's not supposed to be.'

Printed in Great Britain
by Amazon

34505308R00312